# THE
# ADVOCATE
# GUIDE
# TO
# GAY
# HEALTH

# THE
# ADVOCATE
# GUIDE
# TO
# GAY
# HEALTH

**R. D. Fenwick**
with a Foreword by
**Richard C. Pillard, M.D.**

E. P. Dutton | New York

For information contact:
E. P. Dutton, 2 Park Avenue,
New York, N.Y. 10016

Library of Congress Cataloging in Publication Data

Fenwick, R D
  The Advocate guide to gay health.

  Bibliography: p.
  Includes index.
    1. Homosexuals—Health and hygiene.    2. Hygiene,
Sexual.    3. Homosexuality—United States—Societies,
etc.—Directories.    I. The Advocate (Los Angeles)
II. Title.    III. Title: Guide to gay health.
RA788.F46 1978    613    78-6577

ISBN: 0-525-05050-7

Published simultaneously in Canada by
Clarke, Irwin & Company Limited, Toronto and Vancouver

Illustrations by Radu Vero

Designed by Joann Robyn Berg

10 9 8 7 6 5 4 3 2 1

First Edition

# Contents

# Acknowledgments

First, my special thanks go to the many gay men and gay women who shared their health concerns during the preparation of this book and buoyed me with their assurances that there was a need for it.

For their technical assistance and uncanny ability to point me in the right direction, I am indebted to Michael Bujazan; Lisa Campbell, R.N.; Lois Dolan; Darryl Inaba, M.D.; Dorr Jones; Lucienne Lanson, M.D.; Philip R. Lee, M.D.; Fred Minnigerode, Ph.D.; John Newmeyer, Ph.D.; S. J. Stegman, M.D.; Boyd G. Stephens, M.D.; and John Walters.

A number of the physicians I interviewed requested that I not acknowledge them by name. They know who they are, and they have my gratitude.

The initial research by Randy Shilts, whose ground breaking health series in *The Advocate* provided the impetus for this book, was of immeasurable help in building a framework within which the topics he reported so ably could be explored in greater depth. I am also grateful to David Goodstein, the publisher of *The Advocate*, and Alan Rinzler, editor of Liberation Books, for their ongoing interest and support.

Richard C. Pillard, M.D., who has written the Foreword, contributed to the scope and authenticity of this guide with his many helpful suggestions and sound overview of the role that stress plays in the health of us all, regardless of sexual preference.

Bill Whitehead, my editor at E. P. Dutton, goaded me on when the going got rough and saved me from polemical excesses, errors in judgment, and lapses in taste.

Finally come two people "without whom this book could not have been written." Those words may ring counterfeit to the reader but not to the writer, who knows how true they are. They apply from the heart to my sister, Molly B. Fenwick, and Frederick C. Ketteman, both of whom provided the cheerful space required for the completion of the manuscript.

R.D.F.

*New York*
*May 27, 1978*

# Foreword

Early in my career as a psychiatrist, a young man whom I'll call Nick was admitted to our ward. Frightened and suspicious, Nick waited many weeks before he was able to confide his story: always different, humiliated at school, rejected by his family, fired from jobs because his behavior was judged inappropriate, picked up for sex by straight-looking men and then abandoned, arrested for drunkenness, arrested for hustling, arrested for "exhibitionism," treated for drug overdose at a general hospital and finally, after a deliberate and nearly fatal automobile crash, sent to the state psychiatric hospital.

Nick was an important patient for me because, incredible as it seems, he was the first openly gay person I had encountered in my six years of medical training. In those days, one's gay feelings were dissociated from the rest of life and to be out indeed seemed crazy. Nick was a patient for whom the procedural side of medicine did not have much to offer—heaven knows he had had enough drugs.

A therapeutic relationship would have to count for everything, yet the only things I knew about an openly gay life-style were negative and frightening. Supportive listening was difficult because it forced me to realize that he and I were not so different. This was an uncomfortable realization for me but I believe it formed the basis of a healing relationship.

The scientific accomplishments of medicine will never make the healing relationship obsolete nor diminish its importance. But to be effective, the doctor must know the life and values of his patient and the way he or she relates to those in the environment. These factors are different enough for gay people to make the perspective of gay medicine an important one.

It will be no surprise to learn that almost no aspect of the gay health movement originated with physicians. Changes originated with gay people whose experience told them that they deserved a quality of care which they were not getting. Often, developments were ordinary and not newsworthy, but some of the developments were dramatic: Many psychiatrists were angry when a gay group interrupted their annual convention in 1970; however, one heterosexual psychiatrist was impressed by the demonstrators and the following year he sponsored a panel at which the needs of gay people were discussed. This panel was big news. A momentum had begun and within two years the "homosexuality" diagnosis was dropped by the American Psychiatric Association.

The Advocate Guide to Gay Health will help you to get care that is oriented to your needs as a gay person. Physicians should endorse the perspective of this book because informed consumers are healthier people and they make our job easier. You will learn how to stay healthy and, if illness comes, you will know where to get help and what to expect. R. D. Fenwick has compiled information on sexually transmitted diseases, drugs, mental health, hepatitis, theraputic and cosmetic surgery, aging, nutrition, and exercise. You will also see that health is a positive quality for which each of us must take a share of responsibility.

RICHARD C. PILLARD, M.D.

# Introduction

Competent physicians, particularly those specializing in psychiatry, know that homosexuality is not a disease. The finest theologians, despite the official mutterings of the institutional Church, do not regard it as a sin. Most simply stated, male homosexuality and lesbianism are variants of human behavior, statistically less frequent than heterosexuality.

The majority of gay men and gay women know these truths as well—if sometimes only intuitively. We know, too, that sex is one of life's greatest joys, and that we have the right to experience it within the context of a life-style characterized by sexual preference for our own kind. But in the midst of the very struggle to endorse and protect that right, we often lose sight of the truth that we *are* different. Ironically, in demanding that we be treated "just like everyone else" in society, we may be risking not only our right to be different, but our health as well.

As its title states, this book is a guide to *gay* health, which differs from general, or straight, health to the extent that our life-styles differ. Like it or not, we belong to a minority group, one that requires special medical monitoring and extraordinary self-care in the management of our health.

Everyone is susceptible to the same diseases and vulnerable to the same problems that affect health. The greatest killers—heart disease, cancer, hypertension, obesity—stalk society at large and are indiscriminate when it comes to sexuality. And as members of a stressful society, one bedeviled by stress-induced diseases, we homosexuals are no different from anyone else. But in practicing our gay life-styles, we often experience additional health-threatening difficulties that straight persons seldom, if ever, encounter.

In this book we'll be discussing these difficulties in detail. Our first task, however, is to acknowledge what may, in the final analysis, be the worst disease of all: our self-image.

A lot of people believe that the problems arising from the gay life-style prove that homosexuality is "wrong." As we shall see, it is statistically true that gay men are far more likely to contract a variety of sexually transmitted diseases than are straight men. But how do the moralists in our midst explain that among gay women, syphilis and gonorrhea are practically unheard of? Would they wish to imply that it's okay to be gay if you're a woman, but not if you're a man?

For that matter, how do they rationalize the growing inclination of gynecologists to consider cancer of the cervix a venereal disease? Although not all of the clinical evidence is in, it is now almost certain that cervical cancer (virtually never found in nuns or gay women) is caused by a virus that is transmitted by having intercourse with one's husband—particularly in the missionary position.

If we choose to pass judgment on a life-style by the particular problems it engenders—the businessman's hypertension, or the housewife's blahs—then *any* life-style can be proved "wrong." And not all of the penalties that some people attach to the gay life-style derive from what we choose to do with our genitals. Like everybody else, we can slip into the twin ruts of poor nutrition and insufficient exercise, and we can experience chronic loneliness and the sudden loss of love, which are contributors to, and often the primary causes of, poor health and premature death.

The negative programming that warps our self-image comes from a variety of sources, including our fellow gays. Some would have us believe, for example, that a stable relationship is not only unrealistic but "wrong" because it apes heterosexual marriage; others preach that the only acceptable arrangement is strict monogamy. For the time being, it can be said that many of us are being programmed from all sides and don't know which way to turn—a stressful situation that can scarcely enhance health.

But the most debilitating programming comes from within ourselves. We may think there is nothing "wrong" with being gay, but let one of us come down with the clap and somewhere, from the hidden recesses of the psyche, comes that still small voice: "See? See what happens when you break the rules?"

The most "liberated" of us can still fall prey to these moments of stress, even to the extent that we confuse that inner voice with conscience and neglect to ask to whose rules it refers. The question is important, because it has to do with who *we* think we are as opposed to what others think. It has to do with the image we carry of ourselves, and the choice is always our own: Are we emotional cripples upon whom life has laid a heavy burden, or are we healthy and whole?

The best way to prevent disease is to be healthy. But health is more than the absence of disease, or even the absence of a negative self-image. In a broader, holistic sense, it is an approach to living that will let us enjoy life. Health means a lively consciousness of the fact that while we are what we eat, drink, breathe, and do with our genitals, we are also what we think, believe, feel, and express about ourselves and others. But most importantly, health means taking full responsibility for the physical and mental stresses that can dull, if not prevent, the pleasures of the gay life-style we celebrate.

The following chapters will examine some of the diseases that these stresses cause—health-threatening problems that we homosexuals can encounter. Any life-style carries risks, and ours is no different in that respect. For gay men and gay women, some problems *are* unavoidable. But for most of them there is a solution—an exciting, healthy alternative to the inappropriate ways we sometimes choose in coping with the stress that afflicts us all.

# 1.
# The Sources
# of Health Care

The three sources generally available to gays in the management of personal health are the private physician, clinics both public and private, and *ourselves*. Although we'll examine each separately, very rarely can one be a strict alternative to the others. Depending on individual circumstances, the health-oriented gay would be well-advised to combine the three.

If you're not taking drugs, and if you're eating nutritionally and exercising regularly, then you're already practicing a high degree of self-care. But remember: *Knowledgeable physicians and public health officials are in adamant agreement that anyone who is even moderately active sexually should have a VD checkup every three months.*

This precaution is the irreducible minimum of gay health care. But even if you adhere to it, you're still subject to occasional bouts of unhappiness, anxiety, depression, anger, worry, and all the other stress factors that weaken resistance to nonvenereal diseases, many of which only a competent physician can manage. Much can be done, however, before a visit to a physician becomes necessary.

## SELF-CARE

Self-care is nothing if not personal responsibility for one's own physical and emotional health. Physically, it entails heeding the messages of the body, recognizing certain symptoms, and sometimes treating yourself—as long as you know what you're doing. Mentally, self-care means choosing the attitudes that facilitate adaptation to a changing, and often dangerous, environment. Self-care is also consulting your own intuition and paying attention to feelings.

One of the more dramatic self-care stories making the rounds is about the chairman of a major California corporation who was recently told that he needed a coronary bypass operation. So ravaged by the pain of angina that he could scarcely walk across the street, the 63-year-old executive turned instead to a natural foods clinic and, through biofeedback and meditation, learned how to express his inner feelings. He now practices meditation regularly, watches his diet, jogs five miles every morning, reports a lower pulse rate, and, *with his physician's approval,* has discontinued almost all medication. "I had thought of myself more as a victim than a contributor to my condition," says the executive. "Now I've taken responsibility for my own predicament—and my own welfare."

Self-care is not, however, an alternative strictly unto itself, nor is it always synonymous with self-treatment. At its best, it is first of all preventive and encompasses, as we'll learn in Chapter Seven, good nutrition, a vigorous program of exercise, and positive attitudes.

An extensive program of self-care was recently undertaken by San Francisco's Haight-Ashbury Free Clinic, which has a large gay clientele. "We want to make our people as free and independent of the health delivery system as possible," reports David E. Smith, M.D., the clinic's founder and director. "But at the same time, we want them to know how to use it intelligently when they have to."

Although several of the clinic's counselors are gay, no attempt is made to match them with gay clients. The first line of defense in the clinic's strategy consists of persuading clients to take more responsibility for themselves. All else flows from that.

Subsequent emphasis falls on nutrition, drugs (including alcohol and tobacco), and a life-style that makes room for exercise. Whenever possible, the client's lover joins in the counseling sessions and is urged to support his or her partner's program of self-care.

The clinic has found that the worst self-abuse, particularly among those heavily into drugs, is a diet consisting primarily of refined sugar and carbohydrates, with little to none of the protein so essential to the repair of drug-ravaged body tissues. Many clients, the clinic finds, are so nutritionally ignorant that they don't know what the sources of protein are. While drug abuse and poor nutrition are frequent companions, you don't have to be a drug abuser to be nutritionally ignorant. Unfortunately, some people do know the sources of protein—and ingest little else.

B. Leslie Huffman, M.D., president of the American Academy of Family Physicians, would like to see the limits of self-care pushed even further; but he also warns that any self-care program should be monitored by each patient's physician. "Much of the published information has been conflicting," complains Dr. Huffman, "particularly in terms of diet and exercise. People come in with one book that tells them to fast and another that says they shouldn't."

Because we gays live in a subculture that places such a high premium on a youthful appearance, we often embark on fad diets or exercise programs that are dangerous without proper medical guidance. A person who has been subsisting on little but protein (perhaps meat, eggs, and cheese) may have pushed his cholesterol level to the limit in a misguided effort to stay slim. If he takes up jogging, he could become a potential cardiovascular accident.

All but the most radical physicians agree that self-care is not for everyone, and particularly those with highly specialized problems. This is not to suggest that homosexuals, because we belong to a minority group with special problems, should forget about self-care. To do so would be an abdication of personal responsibility. If anything, we need to take further responsibility for our health, but only with the cooperation of a competent physician.

## CHOOSING A PHYSICIAN

When you enter into a patient–physician relationship, the fact that you're gay demands complete candor between you and the man or woman you choose—a requirement that can cause great anxiety in the patient, as well as threaten the doctor. The process of choosing a physician with whom you can be candid may be fraught with frustrations at every turn, but if you truly care for yourself, you'll make the effort.

Philip and Michael, both in their late twenties, had been lovers for three years and appeared to have everything going for them. Theirs was the ideal relationship, one of those "marriages made in heaven." Or so everyone thought. But what their friends didn't know—and what Philip found out—was that Michael had become infatuated with a newcomer at the office and was seeing him on the side.

There was a confrontation, replete with the usual, dreary mix of angry accusations, vehement denials, extracted confessions, and ultimatums. Although Michael agreed to stop seeing his new friend, Philip harbored a gnawing feeling in his gut that Michael had every intention of continuing the affair. As Philip grew increasingly watchful and suspicious, the "ideal" relationship was rapidly becoming a fiasco.

Just as Philip was reaching the conclusion that there was no saving the situation, he experienced an episode of rectal bleeding and hurried to his doctor, who was a specialist in internal medicine and himself gay. The doctor asked if Michael had been screwing Philip. "Figuratively, perhaps, but not literally," replied Philip bitterly. They hadn't had sex for two weeks, not since Michael had been "found out." The doctor proceeded with a proctoscopic examination that revealed an acute case of diverticulosis, an intestinal disorder requiring medical and dietary attention.

The doctor said he would prescribe the usual pills and bland diet. But unless Philip managed to work things out with Michael, all the pills and all the diets would be powerless against the anger, resentment, and jealousy that were chewing up his insides.

Philip was fortunate because he had a doctor who understood the principles of holistic medicine. Had he gone to just any physician—straight or gay—he might have been shunted from waiting room to examination room then back to the street with nothing but a prescription to be filled and a mimeographed sheet detailing the dietary dos and don'ts in the management of acute diverticulosis. Philip's physician was competent, however, not because he was gay and therefore understanding, but because he took time to examine the behavioral, sociocultural, and environmental factors that were determinants of his patient's health.

"The competent physician," wrote Cicero, in *De oratore II*, "before he attempts to give medicine to his patient, makes himself acquainted not only with the disease which he wishes to cure, but also with the habits and constitution of the sick man." In other words, it is more important to know what sort of patient has a disease than what sort of disease a patient has. Some gay doctors, even those with an almost exclusively gay clientele, are grossly incompetent because they run what amount to factories and don't take time for the truly important questions: Are you living alone, or are you enjoying a stable, ongoing relationship? Do you cook for yourself and watch your diet, or are you subsisting on junk food eaten on the run? Are you taking vitamins? How much do you drink and smoke? Using any drugs? Are you exercising? Are you spending every possible moment broiling yourself in the summer sun in an effort to look more youthful? Are you "promiscuous"? In short, to what degree *are* you practicing self-care?

If you're shopping for a personal physician and interview one who fails to ask such questions—even if he or she is gay—move on. You'd be better off seeing a competent straight physician, someone nonjudgmental of your sexuality and interested in treating you holistically.

Philip was doubly fortunate because he didn't have to shop for his physician. The man had been recommended by friends who could attest to his competency. There is no pat formula for choosing a physician; still, because they are so readily obtainable, personal recommendations remain the means by which most gay people find the person they need. In the absence of such recommendations, you can telephone one of the gay resources I have provided (see Appendix); but I cannot guarantee their reliability or even their existence by the time this guide reaches your hands.

In a recent experiment, this writer telephoned the San Francisco Medical Society, misrepresented himself to the woman who answered as a man with a gay health problem, and asked to be referred to a physician. The conversation ensued:

"Did you say gay?" she asked.

"Yes," I replied.

"Is that the same as homosexual?"

"Yes."

"Oh . . . just a moment . . . yes, here it is. You're to call the Daughters of Bilitis, they'll help you."

"Thank you, but I believe that's a lesbian organization."

"Oh, of course, I'm sorry. Men are to call the Society for Individual Rights."

Neither of the organizations she'd mentioned was listed in the current telephone directory, and the Society for Individual Rights is now defunct. Had I been a newcomer to San Francisco and in genuine distress, I would have been better off sniffing out the nearest gay bar, swallowing my pride, and buttonholing the patrons for a referral—a haphazard approach, to say the least.

One of the biggest problems gay people face in choosing a physician is deciding whether he or she must be gay. Even when you're candid with a straight physician, he or she may lack the empathy you require as part of the healing process. There are, of course, notable exceptions among straight physicians.

A recent newcomer to Chicago, a young man in quest of "a good gay doctor," bridled when one of his friends recommended a physician who was not only a woman but as straight as they come—as a matter of fact she was a grandmother. But he decided to go anyway and promptly found himself in the competent, caring hands of a person he could trust.

Most gay doctors, however, believe that the physician–patient relationship—an indispensable factor in any therapeutic process—is enhanced when gay patients are matched with gay doctors. "Because I'm gay," a physician told *The Advocate*, "I think my gay patients can come in and feel comfortable discussing certain medical problems openly. If they've been screwed in the bottom and suddenly something happens, going to a straight physician and outlining the details can be absolutely mortifying." How true that can be, particularly if one lives in a small town and goes to the saintly old doctor who brought him—and perhaps his parents—into this world.

A further advantage in seeking out a gay physician has to do with the art and science of referral. Because no one physician can possibly have all the medical answers, the competent gay doctor directs his patients to specialists who he knows are accepting of gay people—and he chooses them on the basis of their expertise, not their sexual preference.

Theoretically, a gay doctor is no more adept at referral than his straight counterparts, but in practice, he enjoys an advantage. With the possible exception of actors and clergymen, doctors talk about each other more than all other professionals. Consequently, a gay doctor almost always knows if the specialist to whom he refers a gay patient is either gay or accepting of gays, whereas a straight doctor often doesn't.

Sam, one of the men we interviewed, reacted to the break-up of his first serious love affair with loss of appetite and nausea. Even when he tried to eat, he couldn't keep anything down. He went to his straight internist, with whom he had never been candid, and submitted to a number of tests. In the absence of any organic findings responsible for Sam's condition, the internist asked if there might not be an underlying emotional problem. Sam admitted that there might be, but he disclosed no details. Unwittingly, the internist referred him to a psychiatrist who believed that homosexuality could be "cured."

After Sam told the shrink what was happening in his life and heard that his problems could be sorted out over the course of the next three to four years—at fifty dollars a session—he asked if there was a quicker and cheaper way to stop throwing up.

"I was referred to a so-called behavioral psychologist," Sam told us, "a creep who told me that the first thing I had to do was cut off all my gay relationships, even if it meant changing my phone number. Then he wanted to wire me up, have me look at male pornography, and give me a jolt of electricity if my responses indicated a turn-on. He told me his method works. I replied that so does torture."

Without realizing it, Sam had fallen into a network of homophobia, which would not and could not have happened had his internist been gay. "The only good thing," says Sam, "was waking up to how I had to take more responsibility for myself. Once I got that, the vomiting stopped."

When the doctor is gay, however, the relationship can sometimes get out of bounds. Some physicians are unprofessional to the point of viewing their patients as potential sex partners, and attempts at seduction are not uncommon. Others are unscrupulous enough to offer drugs in exchange for sexual favors.

If you and your physician find yourselves attracted to each other, tensions can intrude. If you're turned on by a doctor the moment he touches you, your normal physiological responses (a racing pulse, for example) can muddy the accuracy of an examination; if your doctor is turned on by you, he's apt to be nervous—and nervousness can lead to mistakes.

When mutual attraction leads to an affair, don't be surprised if your doctor asks if you'd mind seeing another doctor, perhaps one in his office. Just as the competent straight physician, aware of the importance of objectivity, refuses to treat members of his own family unless there's an emergency, no gay physician we interviewed treats his own lover for much beyond such common maladies as the flu. Some physicians even go to the extreme of declining all social invitations from their patients.

Living in a metropolitan area can facilitate the choice of a physician for the simple reason that there are hundreds, if not several thousands, of candidates. If you find yourself uncomfortable with a doctor, you're always free to move on to another. The only "penalty" you'll pay for being so particular is a small fee for the transfer of your medical records.

If you're the gay resident of a small, one-doctor town, your choice can, of course, be severely limited. That one doctor may be ignorant of gay health problems and concentrate on your morals instead of your health. You need that as much as Evel Knievel needs an orthopedic surgeon who greets him with a harangue about staying off motorcycles.

But regardless of where you live, you're probably within at most several hundred driving miles of a larger city where you might be able to find the person you need. By going to a city with a large gay population, you'll also gain access to the network of support and referral systems that is beginning to emerge between physicians. Gay and straight doctors, in pooling their information, are developing a better grasp of the medical problems that can result from the gay life-style. For example, a straight physician sees a gay patient whose penis is red, raw, and becoming infected. He immediately assumes that the patient is into SM.

"Oh no," replies the patient. "I'm sure it was because I was rubbing against my partner's stomach."

The concerned but suspicious physician treats the patient, then telephones a physician he knows through the grapevine is gay.

"Larry? It's Mike. I've just seen a guy with what looked like first degree burns on his penis, and he told me it was caused by rubbing against his partner. Is that possible?"

"Absolutely, Mike . . . it's called the Princeton rub, or *frottage*. You can get what amounts to a burn, especially if the passive partner has a hairy belly. Tell your patient to use a lubricant."

As more and more physicians become aware of the gay life-style and its special medical requirements, the task of choosing a physician is bound to become easier. In the meantime, don't make the task more difficult than it already is. If you have a chip on your shoulder when you interview a physician—if you're uncomfortable with and judgmental of your own gayness—you can project your feelings onto a physician who is far more accepting of your behavior than you are!

Don't hobble the patient–physician relationship from the outset by assuming that your physician is going to judge what you choose to do sexually as disgusting, morally contemptible, or just plain silly. The question is, how do *you* feel about it?

Should your physician be a general practitioner (GP) or a specialist? As some GPs are fond of remarking about specialists, if the only tool you have is a hammer, you tend to see every problem as a nail! (Nevertheless, a GP will refer you to a specialist if you need one.) If you're a man who is highly susceptible to venereal warts, you might want to go first to a dermatologist; in the absence of specific, recurring problems, you might be better off with an internist or a competent GP. Initially, a woman might consider a gynecologist.

Finally, there's the matter of cost. Private medical care is expensive. At this writing, the average total expense of an initial visit to a physician is over a hundred dollars. Some physicians charge for an exploratory talking interview, others do not. Some, but not all, will answer basic questions about their practice over the telephone. Finding the right physician is a matter of shopping and footwork.

Current trends suggest that the prospects for "gay medicine" as something of a specialty are bright. *Medical World News* estimates that there are at least 13,000 gay physicians in the United States, a figure that is probably ridiculously low. Only a few, however, have come out of the closet, including the late Howard J. Brown, M.D., former chief of New York City's Health Services Administration.

But while most gay doctors are still fearful of announcing their sexual preferences publicly, there are discernible stirrings of activism within the gay medical community. A group calling itself the Gay Medical Students Alliance has been formed in New York, and over 100 gay psychiatrists, at a recent national convention of the

American Psychiatric Association, met in a separate caucus with the stated aim of educating their colleagues about homosexuality through papers and panel discussions. For the gay person in need of ongoing medical attention, then, the situation is improving dramatically.

Equally encouraging is the attention that medical schools throughout America are finally paying to sexuality in general and homosexuality in particular. Until fairly recently, standard medical textbooks, in discussing venereal diseases, often failed to acknowledge the existence of such problems as anal gonorrhea in men; if they did acknowledge them, it was timidly. Today, the textbooks are up front and avoid moralizing. Some medical schools are even renting the better gay skin flicks as classroom teaching aids—a sensible practice in that it relieves some lecturers from talking about things with which they may not have personal experience.

Much of the credit for this opening up must go to physicians with large gay practices. Only a few years ago, for example, it was not known that a number of gastrointestinal ailments were transmitted sexually; but as more and more physicians with gay patients began encountering what seemed to be an epidemic, they pooled their findings and, with the cooperation of the local department of public health, sounded the alarm in *Lancet*, a prestigious, internatonally distributed medical journal. Their article has become a landmark in medical literature, one that medical schools can scarcely ignore.

## PUBLIC AND PRIVATE CLINICS

Before you resort to government agencies for help, you should know that the lack of a coherent national health policy is nowhere more apparent than in the federal government, which presides over a bewildering array of at least twenty departments, or independent agencies, responsible for health programs. But take a look at the U.S. Budget, and you're face to face with the fact that our government is basically confused as to what health is. For example, the many air and water pollution control programs are administered by the Environmental Protection Agency, which is fine; but because they are primarily preventive in nature (as opposed to Medicare and Medicaid, which give little emphasis to preventive medicine) pollution of the environment is not considered a *health* problem by the Office of Management and Budget, or by any other federal agency. If that kind of confusion exists on the federal level, it can't help but filter down to state, county, and city governments.

Although some public resources are excellent, others are poor when it comes to gay health problems. In any case they are often difficult to locate. For example, the current New York City directory is unfortunately typical. There is no listing whatsoever under "venereal." Nearer the front of the "V" section, however, one finds listings for "VD Clinical News," "VD Information," and "VD Information Hot Line." The first is a private publication; the second is a recorded message from the health department extolling the virtues of wearing a rubber; the third, the "Hot Line," doesn't answer.

When one turns to "New York, City Of," "VD Information" (the recording) is listed under "Services And Frequently Called Numbers," as is the Health Department itself. Under "Health Department," one finds a listing for "Venereal Disease Control." With patience—the line is more often than not engaged—one reaches a party who, upon request, will reveal the whereabouts of the various clinics, which are scattered throughout the city, and their hours.

If you have the staying power to wade through all this bureaucratic slush and reach the clinic itself, you'll be asked to provide your name, address, and date of birth. You're then handed a number and asked to have a seat. When your number is finally called, you're taken into a cubicle and asked why you're there. You're also asked to provide the names and addresses of recent sex contacts. From there it's back to the waiting room. When your number comes up again (depending on the case-load, this can take from twenty minutes to an hour or more), you're taken into an examination room to see a physician who asks routine questions, takes cultures, and points you in the direction of the area set aside for blood tests.

If you have syphilis or gonorrhea, you'll receive a notice in the mail or a discreet telephone call, as will anyone you've identified as a recent sex partner. You must then return to the clinic for the appropriate treatment.

The tracing of sex partners is objectionable to most gays, who feel it's an assault on their anonymity and an invasion of privacy. Worse, it adds more names to the files of an already bloated bureaucracy. Worst of all, it's totally unnecessary. If you care for your sex partners, *you* will assume the responsibility of urging them to get help; if you don't know who they are, that's another matter, one that is beyond your, or anyone else's, control.

Nevertheless, you owe it to the gay community to make every effort to trace the person you might have infected. If you remember what he looked like and so much as a first name, keep your eyes peeled and ask around. If you're lucky enough to find him, quietly advise him to visit a clinic as soon as possible. While it is only courteous to notify your contacts, some people simply cannot bring themselves to do it; in such cases, the clinic will do it for them, and they will be utterly discreet. Medical records are considered by law to be the property of the patient, and no one—including other government employees, doctors, insurance companies, and researchers of any kind—may have access to them without the patient's permission. Also, the patient has the legal right to see his own records upon demand.

Public clinics are free. Private physicians are expensive, especially if extensive lab work is indicated. Privately funded, gay-oriented clinics, while few and far between, may ask for a token donation, or a pledge. But the small amount you'll be asked to give is worth the support you'll receive from your fellow gays. Private clinics have an added advantage in that counseling is generally available; and as a client, you'll have access to the clinic's referral system, which is often extensive, if you have a problem they are not equipped to handle. You might also look into the Health Maintenance Organizations (HMOs), which are becoming the models of holistic medical practice. These are large, total-care group practices that usually have a contract with an employer and that the individual employee may choose to join or not. Unfortunately, the only way to discover an HMO's attitude is to *ask* them if they have any openly gay physicians or group therapy programs oriented toward gay people. They probably won't, but your asking can create an awareness of a growing demand that could eventually lead to a supply.

Whether or not you use them yourself, the private, gay-oriented clinics deserve whatever support you can give. They receive no federal funding for their efforts to maintain health and prevent disease and must depend on donations, pledges, benefits, foundation grants, and drives. In some places, they receive small sums from the city and county; but Uncle Sam continues to ignore them—unless their tax-exempt status as nonprofit organizations is involved.

The Internal Revenue Service has consistently hassled gay rights groups and gay clinics, depriving them of postage discounts and discouraging the tax-deductible contributions that other nonprofit groups enjoy. A gay rights group in Colorado, for example, had its tax-exempt status revoked by the IRS for refusing to state that homosexuality is "a sickness, disturbance, or diseased pathology." In Pennsylvania, when a gay community clinic applied for tax-exempt status, their initial request was summarily rejected.

"We appealed the decision," reported clinic officials to the National Gay Task Force, "and were sent a letter with a list of questions to which we were asked to respond. Basically, the questions demanded a renunciation of the position that being gay was healthy and valid as an alternative life-style. We circumvented them as best we could, stating that we would not 'advocate' homosexuality as a valid life-style."

It was not until such a charade was acted out that the tax exemption was granted.

In summary, it is advisable to establish a relationship with a competent physician in whom you can confide, and you should practice as much self-care as your common sense and your physician allow. Beyond that, you may choose, depending on availability and quality, additional sources of health care whether your government approves of them or not.

But whatever you do to patch together a personal health program, don't forget that irreducible minimum of gay health care: *If you're even moderately active sexually, you should have a VD checkup every three months.*

# 2.
# Sexually Transmitted Diseases

Sexually transmitted diseases, or STDs, are not caused by sexual promiscuity. They are caused by "bugs," be they bacteria, viruses, or parasites, which prey on run-down bodies. But given the epidemic proportions of STDs in the gay community, it would be dishonest to pretend that there is no link, even though it is not, strictly speaking, one of cause and effect, between sleeping around and getting sick. Acknowledging the existence of this link is easy, but sorting out the reasons for gay promiscuity is quite another matter. Most sexologists, however, agree that any consideration of promiscuity must begin with the nature of male and female response, regardless of sexual preference.

Aside from our preference for members of our own sex and a growing solidarity in the face of those who would deny our human rights, gay men and gay women have little in common when it comes to life-styles. It may have become fashionable to believe that, in terms of responsiveness, there is no marked difference between

14

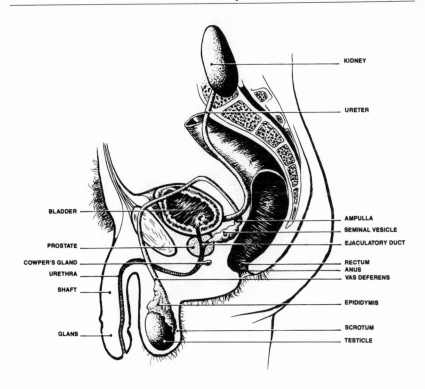

the sexuality of men and women, but sexologists know otherwise.

According to the Kinsey reports and other reliable data, almost a third of the total female population have little to no sexual response at all. Another third are definitely responsive, but more slowly and less intensely than males. Most of the remaining third have a sexual responsiveness equal to males. But that remaining three to four percent have an ability to be aroused that no male can match, as evidenced by their ability to achieve orgasm through fantasy alone. Still, according to C. A. Tripp, Ph.D., in *The Homosexual Matrix*, "not even this extraordinary capacity opens the door to the kinds of promiscuity men display: the ability to respond to entirely anonymous partners, and frequently to prefer them."

Men are more "driven" and more easily aroused by visual stimuli, while women generally require the proper psychological preparation for sex. This is particularly true when the men and women happen to be gay. "In fact," concludes Dr. Tripp, "the most extreme forms of promiscuity, those in which the partner is and remains anonymous, simply do not exist among lesbians."

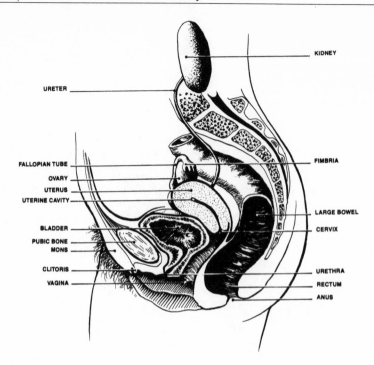

There are, of course, exceptions that would seem to defy such a conclusion. Some gay women (but so few as to be satistically insignificant) *are* promiscuous; conversely, some gay men could never bring themselves to have sex without knowing a great deal about their partners over a substantial period of time. But generally, the conclusion is correct. "I don't know how you can write a book about gay health for men *and* women," most of the gay women interviewed told this writer. "We're different. We're just not, well, we're not promiscuous."

That dreadful word again—one that has so long been bandied about by the moralists that it's difficult to know what, if anything, it truly means. Some gay people define it quite narrowly as having sex with anyone but your lover; most interpret it as bouncing from one sexual partner to another.

If we don blinders and examine promiscuity negatively, we can find ample reason for condemning it as part of anyone's life-style:

It is linked to health-threatening problems.

It can imply a desire for something more than can be obtained from one partner.

It can be a way of avoiding entangling personal commitments.

It can be a way of massaging one's ego.

It can be no more than a cheap escape from a frustrating, deep-seated problem that one lacks the courage to face consciously and is therefore an inappropriate way of dealing with stressful inner conflicts.

But what can be said *for* promiscuity—in light of its promi-nence as an aspect of the gay life-style, especially among men? Even though there is no denying the prevalence of male homosexual pro-miscuity, sexologists have yet to produce a shred of evidence that it is any greater than heterosexual promiscuity would be if straight men were given the same opportunities. On that score, men have a great deal in common regardless of their sexual preferences. They have a natural and, if you will, *normal* predisposition toward pro-miscuity. That's simply the way it is.

Almost any dictionary definition of promiscuity invariably re-sorts to the word "indiscriminate," but few homosexuals, unless they've drugged themselves into a stupor, will have sex with "just anyone." *Homosexual* promiscuity, unlike its heterosexual counter-part, entails remarkable discrimination because consciously or un-consciously, the partners involved are often motivated by a genuine desire to seek out and establish a healthy, ongoing relationship.

For the young homosexual, who often feels alienated from

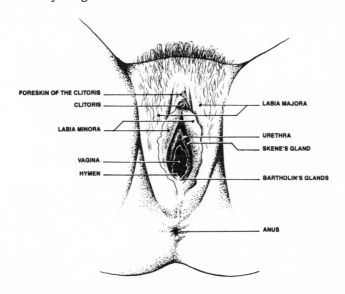

parents, Church, and society, a healthy self-image depends on meeting and getting to know a variety of understanding, accepting individuals. In the gay subculture, then, promiscuity can be an efficient shortcut to membership in a peer group.

Even when one or both partners in an ongoing relationship are occasionally promiscuous, it isn't necessarily unhealthy. Each may require the novelty that "a little fluff on the side" can provide in an otherwise good relationship that both wish to maintain.

When considered both positively and negatively, which is to say morally, promiscuity is a very mixed bag indeed. That the word itself will not submit to a facile definition compels us to consider each case of promiscuity individually, or situationally. Your doctor, if he's savvy, is not being impertinent when he asks if you're "promiscuous," because your answer can reveal a great deal about who *you* think you are and whether *you* think your life-style is healthy.

The competent, holistically oriented physician knows and accepts the truth that males have a natural, almost inexhaustible capacity to respond quickly to new partners. In the final analysis, writes Dr. Tripp, "the relatively high promiscuity of homosexual men is almost entirely attributable to a combination of circumstantial opportunity and the escalating effect of males dealing with males." The physician who understands this will be accepting of not only your life-style, but of you as a whole person. But if your promiscuity is thoughtless, uncaring, and dangerous to you, your partners, and the gay community at large, you can expect some rather stern medical directives about self-care and temporary abstinence. Incredibly, a lot of gay men continue to have sex when they *know* that they have an infectious STD. "If one of my tricks catches something, that's *his* problem," one man told us. "He can go to a clinic just like everyone else."

One of the doctors I interviewed remarked that such a cavalier attitude, while regrettable, no longer surprises him. "VD has become so rampant that too many guys are taking it for granted," he told me. "What they don't seem to understand is that they're hurting themselves just as much as they are the rest of the gay community. I'd guess that the root of this problem isn't promiscuity, but sheer ignorance. Once you know what VD can do to you and your friends, you respect it."

Traditionally, the term "venereal disease," or VD, has encompassed only gonorrhea and syphilis. Today, we know that a broad spectrum of diseases, *some of them unique to gay people,* can be transmitted sexually. While VD can continue to denote gonorrhea and syphilis, it should be subsumed by the umbrella-term, STDs. This needs clearing up, because some so-called VD clinics treat *only* gonorrhea and syphilis; others deal with all the STDs.

Although promiscuity is an undeniable factor in the several epidemics now sweeping the gay community, we should remember that *nobody* is immune to STDs. In some cases, even gay women who confine their activities to one partner can develop them.

That we gays are different is nowhere more apparent than in the statistics. Gay men may not comprise forty percent of the male population, but we account for a whopping forty percent of the reported cases of gonorrhea in the United States alone—which means we're four times as likely to catch gonorrhea as straight men. Better than half of the male syphilis victims in the United States are gay, and in some areas it's even higher. According to a survey conducted by *The Advocate,* public health officials in Hawaii reckon that ninety-five percent of their state's reported cases come from the gay community. Some physicians believe that hepatitis, now reaching epidemic proportions, is the major disease-related cause of death among young gay men.

"If the U.S. Government were to spend just a fraction of what it does on the goddamn defense program, we could wipe out STDs just like *that,*" reports a physician, angrily snapping his fingers. Most of his fellow physicians tend to agree. They agree further that until the government "does something," gay people must assume even greater responsibility for themselves.

It isn't that the government is unaware. According to figures from the Department of Health, Education and Welfare, the government spent $33.1 million during 1976 for VD control and prevention. But of that amount, only $160,000 (one-half of one percent) can be traced as earmarked for projects serving the health of the gay community, despite the government's *own* figures indicating the high incidence of VD among gays.

We know that awareness can increase acceptance. But it can also increase reaction. That *government* awareness may be part of the problem is a political rather than a paranoiac consideration. When the Pill was introduced as a birth control device, much of the opposition came from those who were afraid it might liberate women so much that they would actually enjoy sex. "If they're gonna screw," or so the attitude seemed to be, "let 'em pay for it." Implied in that comment is that an unwanted pregnancy was the price.

The analogy is exact. As long as STDs are regarded by our politicians and their constituents as moral rather than health problems, it is unlikely that much money will be granted to the researchers who are eager to develop effective vaccines. "If they're gonna be perverts, then let 'em pay for it." The price here is our health, even our lives. We are a minority group, and like all minority groups, we are subject to the oppressive tactics of those who would seek our extermination—whether they admit it or not—because we choose to be different.

There may be ample cause for alarm, but we needn't panic. We need to get on with an important part of defending ourselves: awareness of what STDs can do, and the resolve to act on what we learn.

## GONORRHEA

If STDs were contesting for popularity, gonorrhea, now second only to the common cold as the world's most communicable disease, would be the declarable winner, and its biggest boosters are gay men who, as noted, account for forty percent of the cases reported. Moreover, public health officials estimate that for every known case of the clap, there are three to four that go unreported and, presumably, untreated. Gonorrhea is more than just another gay health problem. It is a raging epidemic, one that is increasing at the rate of ten percent per year.

Perhaps more ominous than any statistic is the widespread ignorance about gonorrhea that festers in the gay male community. As everyone knows (or thinks he knows) we're all subject to the clap, which is easier to cure than the common cold. The telltale discharge from the penis and a burning sensation when urinating call for a quick trip to a doctor, who dispatches the problem with a shot of penicillin and a few words about temporary abstinence.

But what many gay men don't know—and what too many public health officials and private physicians of a homophobic persuasion are loath to admit—is that only half of all gay gonorrhea is penile. At least forty percent is anal, while another ten to fourteen percent shows up in the throat, where it is known as pharyngeal gonorrhea. Because sixty-six percent of anal and ninety percent of pharyngeal gonorrhea are asymptomatic, *you can have it and not know it,* a problem compounded by the refusal of some public VD clinics to take anal and pharyngeal cultures for testing.

**How do you catch it?** By having sex with an infected partner. But the *cause,* or actual culprit, is a microscopic, gram-negative bacterium called the gonococcus (*Neisseria gonorrhoeae*), which loves and thrives in the membranes, the warm, moist lining of the mouth, throat, urethra, vagina, and rectum. The common factor in *all* modes of intense sexual contact is that these mucous membranes are brought into contact. Because the gonococcus dies within seconds outside the human body, it is practically impossible to catch it from toilet seats, soiled towels, or dishes used by an infected person.

In penile gonorrhea, or gonococcal urethritis, symptoms generally appear from three to five days after contact with an infected partner, but they can show up as early as one day and as late as a month. So don't consider yourself home free simply because you've been asymptomatic over what may seem a long period of time.

The first signs that you've been unlucky may be a feeling of discomfort inside the penis and the seeping of a thin, clear fluid, which should not be confused with the normal discharge released during sexual excitement. Generally, this fluid becomes profuse, thick, white, creamy, and often yellow or yellow-green. Then there's the painful, burning sensation when urinating—the symptom that led the French to dub gonorrhea *la chaude pisse,* or hot piss. The urine itself is hazy with pus, and blood can be present. If you're uncircumcised, the bacteria can proliferate under the foreskin until the glans, or head of the penis, becomes red and irritated.

It cannot be emphasized too strongly that while symptoms of penile gonorrhea are generally present and markedly so, the unhappy medical fact is that despite infection, they do not always occur. Undetected and unchecked, the disease can go systemic, or spread to other parts of the body, with serious consequences; and the person who has it becomes a chronic, asymptomatic carrier. If that fails to give you pause, remember that when gonorrhea attacks the anus and rectum (gonococcal proctitis) there are no symptoms exhibited by *most* people.

When anal symptoms do occur, they may include soreness,

burning, itching, a feeling of wetness, pain when defecating, and blood or pus in the feces.

A sore throat, sometimes accompanied by a low fever, may indicate pharyngeal gonorrhea, or infection of the throat cavity and tonsils (if you still have them). In nine out of ten cases, however, pharyngeal gonorrhea shows no symptoms; even when it does, physicians may not recognize it unless they test for it specifically and often treat the patient for something else. Pharyngeal gonorrhea generally remains localized, but it *can* spread to other parts of the body, and it can, in rare cases, be spread by kissing and going down on your partner.

Patrick, one of the men I interviewed, reports that when the pressures of his job as an account executive in a large advertising agency become intense, he relaxes by checking into the baths on his lunch break and sucking people off in the steam room. After one such episode of extending his courtesies, Patrick himself concluded that his behavior was an inappropriate way to deal with stress, swore off sex, and promptly opted for the three-martini lunch.

A month later, he and Donald, a married colleague, flew to New York for an important presentation and shared a hotel room, where they got smashed one night. One thing led to another, and Patrick wound up blowing Donald. Five days later, back home, Donald came down with a drip and angrily confronted Patrick.

"Look, Don," protested Patrick, "you've probably got something else. I swear, I went for a month without sex before our trip."

"You swear?" replied Donald.

"I swear. Besides, if you'll recall, you didn't screw me." Under the circumstances, he didn't dare suggest what he thought—that Donald had caught it from his wife.

"You can't get it from what we—from what you did?"

"Of course you can't, Don. Don't be ridiculous."

Skittish about going to his own physician, Donald sought out the public VD clinic, where he was tested and denied having had sex with anyone but his wife. And why shouldn't he, he reasoned? He knew he hadn't screwed Patrick, so why admit to anything else?

Two days later came word from the clinic confirming Donald's worst fears: gonorrhea. The upshot was that his tearful wife, still denying everything, had to be treated.

Meanwhile, Patrick—who didn't know there was such a thing as pharyngeal gonorrhea—decided the only way to clear himself with Donald was to make his first trip to the VD clinic and come back with a clean bill of health. He asked for, and got, "the works"—including, much to his surprise, a throat culture. Then it was his turn to receive a notice in the mail. The story doesn't end there, but for our purposes it can.

**Can gay women catch it?** Gonorrhea is so rare among female gays that to encounter it would suggest that the women concerned had been up to some rather fancy sexual gymnastics indeed, probably of the bisexual variety. It is of course theoretically possible for an infected woman with an extraordinarily heavy discharge to pass the disease to another woman from finger to vagina (or rectum), or from tongue to vagina (or rectum), or from vagina to vagina; but a woman whose sex life is *exclusively* gay can be almost certain of never contracting gonorrhea.

You're not all that exclusive? In the throat and rectum, the symptoms, if they manifest at all, are identical to a man's. The vagina is another matter, however, and in more ways than one. The incubation period for a woman is generally longer than a man's— from one week to a full year—and *if* symptoms occur (seventy to ninety percent of vaginal gonorrhea is asymptomatic), they are often less pronounced than in men. There can be a discharge and a burning sensation when urinating, but these symptoms are often so temporary and mild that many women mistake them for a passing bladder infection and do nothing about them. Undetected, vaginal gonorrhea can easily spread to the rectum.

**What happens if men don't get help?** If treatment of gonococcal urethritis is neglected, the disease can spread up the urethra and infect the deeper penile tissues. Pain when urinating becomes increasingly severe and is felt throughout the penis, not just at the tip. These symptoms, *if* they appear, subside and eventually disappear after two weeks, but you can still infect your partner. Meanwhile, the bacteria invade the prostate gland, where they cause a feeling of heat; there can also be pain or swelling in the lower pelvic regions and around the anus. Severe pain when moving the bowels and a high fever are sometimes present. The infected prostate can press against the bladder, making urination difficult. Thereafter, the untreated disease can continue for a long time with only minor symptoms.

Incredibly, some men, because of ignorance, don't seek treatment when these symptoms occur. They assume they've been felled by "a bug," or "stomach flu."

In other men, the bacteria travel down the vas deferens to the epididymis on the back of the testicles, causing a condition known as gonococcal epididymitis. Symptoms of this complication include pain in the groin and a heavy sensation in the testicles; the scrotal skin can become red, hot, and painful. Gonococcal epididymitis, even when treated, leaves permanent scar tissue that blocks the passage of sperm from the affected testicle and, when untreated, can leave a man sterile if both testicles are involved.

Gonorrhea can also impair vision. This can happen if a person accidentally carries the bacteria to his eyes, as when rubbing them. If you have a discharge, use common sense and wash your hands with soap and hot water immediately after touching your genitals.

Untreated, the bacteria can invade the bloodstream and cause a condition known as gonococcal septicemia (when any kind of bacteria are present in the bloodstream, the infected person is said to have septicemia). Symptoms include fever, chills, loss of appetite, and pain in the knees, wrists, fingers and hands, ankles, and elbows, in that order. When this happens, the person is said to have gonococcal arthritis. Again, these aches and pains, combined with the other symptoms, mimic those of what many persons think is "the flu."

In some fifty percent of such cases, there is an accompanying skin rash, particularly on the arms, hands, legs, or feet, and especially around the joints. This condition is known as gonococcal arthritis-dermatitis.

Interestingly enough, gonococcal arthritis-dermatitis is more often found in men who have had asymptomatic pharyngeal or anal gonorrhea over a long period of time. To avoid permanent damage to the joints, antibiotic treatment must be given as soon as the symptoms appear.

**Can untreated gonorrhea be fatal?**  Yes, but only indirectly. In rare cases, among both men and women, blood-borne gonorrhea bacteria can attack the heart, where it causes lesions, and the central nervous system, where it causes meningitis.

Among women, the infection can spread from the Fallopian

tubes to the ovaries, forming massive abscesses; if one of these abscesses ruptures, flooding the pelvic and abdominal cavity with pus, peritonitis results. When this happens, sometimes only a complete hysterectomy—the removal of uterus, tubes, and ovaries—can save a woman's life.

**How is gonorrhea diagnosed?** Unfortunately, medical science has yet to develop a reliable blood test for gonorrhea; diagnosis must depend on a smear, or culture. The first thing the physician looks for is the characteristic white or yellow discharge. If this isn't noticeable, he will obtain a sample of secretions within the urethra by holding the penis and inserting a cotton-tipped swab. Not a very pleasant experience, but the sting is only momentary.

To be certain that the disease has not spread to the epididymis, the physician will squeeze each testicle very gently and check the lymph glands on each side of the groin for swelling.

You should also request (insist, if necessary) that samples of anal and pharyngeal secretions be taken for testing. These are obtained painlessly with cotton swabs.

Once these cultures reach the lab, there are two basic methods of testing. In the smear method, the cotton swab is streaked across a glass slide stained with dye and examined microscopically. If the gonococcus is present, it will show up as pink, bean-shaped bacteria cuddled up in pairs, usually within a white blood cell. The smear test is not always accurate, however, and can result in a "false negative" report; conversely, because there are other bacteria in the mouth and anus which mimic the gonococcus, there can be a "false positive" report. In women, the smear test is notoriously unreliable.

The far more accurate method—and be sure you know which method is being employed—is the bacteriological culture. When this is used, you'll notice that the physician, after obtaining the sample, will streak the cotton swab across the surface of what looks like brown Jello, which is actually a nutrient. The Jello, in its round glass plate, is put in an incubator where, after twenty-four to forty-eight hours, any gonorrhea bacteria will have multiplied so rapidly that colonies on the surface of the Jello are visible to the naked eye. To be sure, the colonies are stained, smeared, and tested with two chemicals. If both tests are positive, then you definitely are.

**What if you've been exposed and test negative?** You may have been lucky. On the other hand, you should be treated even if you test negative and have no symptoms whatsoever. Remember, the incubation period is highly variable.

**Is there a way to test and treat yourself?** Not unless you are a physician. Even then, it's been said that the physician who treats himself has a fool for a patient. The testing procedures are complicated, require elaborate and expensive equipment, and depend for accuracy on the expertise of trained technicians.

You should never attempt to treat yourself for what you think may be gonorrhea with leftover antibiotics, or with pills borrowed from friends. Only thirty years ago, when penicillin was introduced, an injection of 300,000 units was needed to eradicate the disease, but today it takes 4.8 million units. The development of penicillin-resistant gonorrhea is *directly* attributable to the indiscriminate use of antibiotics, particularly by American servicemen in Vietnam, as well as to the virulence of the various strains that are now spreading so rapidly throughout the world.

If you attempt to treat yourself, you may minimize the infection; you're also running the risk of developing a chronic infection of gonorrhea, one resistant to the now accepted dosages of antibiotics. That is antisocial. Think of your brothers and sisters.

**How does a physician treat gonorrhea?** You'll be asked to grin and bare your butt. Expect two injections, each containing 2.4 million units of procaine penicillin G, given at the same time. To delay excretion of penicillin by the kidneys, some physicians will ask you to swallow one to two grams of Benemid (probenecid) half an hour before the shots. Because both alcohol and sex (including masturbation) irritate the infected urethra, you'll be instructed to abstain from both for two weeks. Penicillin is ninety to ninety-five percent effective in curing gonorrhea; to cover that five to ten percent margin, you'll need a follow-up examination and culture tests to be sure you're rid of the disease.

**What if you're afraid of shots?** A lot of people are, including some of the butchest numbers you've ever seen. If you're apt to go into a faint when you see a needle, say so at the outset. Your doctor will understand. Instead of shots, you'll probably receive ampicillin, a semisynthetic form of penicillin, to be taken orally at prescribed intervals. The one drawback of ampicillin is that while it's an effective treatment for gonorrhea of the penis and rectum, it doesn't work in the throat.

**What if you're allergic to penicillin?**  You'll be put on a course of tetracycline, to be taken by mouth (injection of this drug is excessively painful), over a period of five days. The major problem with tetracycline is that too many people stop taking it the moment the symptoms of penile discharge and painful urination disappear, which they generally do in two or three days. The pills are then loaned to friends, who use them foolishly: The *widespread* habit of popping a pill before a night at the baths is partially responsible for the development of a new strain of gonorrhea that is resistant to tetracycline.

If you're allergic to both penicillin and tetracycline, you're a rare bird indeed. Ask your doctor about erythromycin and spectinomycin, two drugs recently approved for the treatment of gonorrhea.

**Is there a way to prevent gonorrhea?**  The best prophylactics are physical fitness and a positive mental attitude. If you're chronically run-down and not practicing good nutritional habits, if you don't carry an image of yourself as a healthy, whole person, and if you're distressing yourself unnecessarily by worrying about catching an STD, you're increasing your chances considerably. Despite what you may have heard, you will *not* always catch gonorrhea after a single sexual exposure. Statistically, your chance of coming down with it ranges from twenty to fifty percent. Most of the doctors and public health officials I interviewed believe that physical and mental fitness can reduce that chance even further.

Washing your genitals, urinating, douching, and gargling immediately after sex are not reliable preventive measures. The best that can be said about such hygienic orgies is that if you *think* they help, they very well might. The worst that can be said about them is that they detract from the joys of postorgasmic tenderness and cuddling.

You and your partner can both wear condoms, or rubbers—if you enjoy showering while wearing a raincoat. This method works very well indeed, but it's not always effective against syphilis (of which more anon). Many men find rubbers objectionable because donning them interrupts foreplay: Trying to put one on a soft penis is almost as difficult as putting the toothpaste back in the tube.

Finally, always get treatment when you've been exposed to the clap, whether you have the symptoms or not.

## NONSPECIFIC URETHRITIS (NSU)

A discharge accompanied by painful urination could mean NSU rather than the clap. Roughly half of the *suspected* cases of gonorrhea turn out to be NSU. But because NSU does not respond to penicillin, it is essential that you be tested. Without a lab test, it is impossible to distinguish gonorrhea from NSU. Don't *ever* let a physician give you penicillin without one.

**What causes it?** Because NSU is not one disease but several, there are a variety of causes, including unidentified but perfectly normal microorganisms in your partner's rectum or mouth to which *you* may be susceptible while others are not. It is rather common to develop NSU after beginning sex with a brand-new lover, or when resuming a relationship with an old one after a long absence. Even so, it is by no means certain that NSU is always transmitted sexually; for that matter, it's possible for a virgin of either sex to develop it. Nor is NSU necessarily a sign of promiscuity: It can appear in but *one* partner in a strictly monogamous relationship.

The time period between exposure and symptoms in NSU varies considerably, but a number of physicians believe that when the disease is transmitted sexually, the incubation period ranges from one week to a month. The symptoms are almost identical to gonorrhea, except that the discharge is usually thinner. In many cases, NSU disappears within two weeks without treatment; but like gonorrhea, the disease it loves to mimic, it can cause complications.

Untreated NSU can spread to the bladder, causing pain when urinating and some bleeding. It can also move down to the testicles, causing swelling and tenderness, and to the prostate, where it causes pain in the groin.

In *very* rare cases, a man can develop Reiter's syndrome, an aggregate of symptoms including inflamed eyes, arthritis, skin rashes, and ulcers in the mouth and on the penis. The arthritis can be crippling, and the inflammation of the eyes can damage vision.

**How is NSU diagnosed and treated?** Urethral discharges are always tested for gonorrhea. If none is found, the urethritis is said to be nonspecific, or nongonococcal (NGU). Unfortunately, some misinformed physicians assume that *any* penile discharge—particularly when the patient admits recent sexual contact—is gonococcal and proceed with penicillin without a lab test. But *no* form of penicillin is effective against NSU.

NSU must be treated with tetracycline or, when the patient is allergic to it, with alternative antibiotics. When "treated" with penicillin, NSU is difficult to cure and may keep recurring months or even years later, and sometimes with complications. When there's a discharge, *insist* on that lab test. If your doctor rejects the idea, zip up, walk out, and find yourself another doctor!

**Must you abstain?** You must abstain from both booze and sex, including masturbation, for at least two weeks. The urethra has been damaged and needs time to heal. Regular periods of abstinence from sex, be they occasioned by an STD or not, can be a tonic. Some of the men we interviewed report that several weeks of willingly doing without lifts the very real burden of "performing" on cue. When sex is resumed after such periods, it is frequently more pleasant, controlled, and appreciated.

## SYPHILIS

Although not as common as gonorrhea, syphilis is far more sinister. In a third of all untreated cases, it causes paralysis, blindness, insanity, early senility, and premature death. There is no vaccine for it, and until there is, its control must depend on self-care, diagnostic screening, and being scrupulous about informing your known contacts if you are positively diagnosed.

**What causes syphilis?** The spirochete (*Treponema pallidum*) is an organism that burrows its way into the mucosal tissues of the lips, mouth, tongue, tonsils, throat, urethra, vagina, and rectum. It has even been known to make an entry through a finger if there's the slightest scratch. Wearing a condom, then, is not always effective. Several hours later, the bacteria reach the bloodstream and are spread to all parts of the body. Because the bacteria perish very quickly outside the body, it's practically impossible to catch them except sexually.

Invariably, the incubation period ranges from nine days to three months. But on the average, symptoms appear three weeks after infection.

Syphilis develops in stages, and each stage has its own syndrome, or group of symptoms. In the primary stage, a sore, called the chancre, appears where the bacteria entered the body. Although this can be almost anywhere, it is generally in or around the genitals, the rectum, or mouth of both sexes.

When (or *if*) it's first noticed, the chancre is a hard, dull red bump that weeps a colorless fluid. It neither hurts nor bleeds and, without treatment, will disappear in a few weeks. During this stage there may also be some painless swelling of the lymph glands in the groin, but there is no feeling of illness.

Syphilis can always be cured in the primary stage—if you notice a chancre and see a physician immediately. A blood test will not always reveal the presence of syphilis during the primary stage, but a microscopic examination of the fluid from the chancre will. Penicillin, or, if you're allergic, another antibiotic, will eradicate the problem.

However, it's not always that easy. Because the chancre can and does appear deep in the throat or in the rectum (eighty percent of reported cases among gay men result from anal intercourse), it's impossible to notice. The germs are still active in your body, and you can pass them on to others. Some uncircumcised men overlook the chancre because it appears under the foreskin.

Again, if you find what looks like a chancre, see a physician at once. If it's in or around the mouth, *do not* assume it's a cold sore. Regardless of where it is, *do not* try to treat a chancre yourself with creams or ointments, because almost any chemical will kill the syphilis bacteria near the surface and make microscopic examination inaccurate.

Some people are so susceptible to cold sores that they'd spend the rest of their lives in doctors' offices if they thought that every sore meant syphilis. If this applies to you and you're sexually active, ask your doctor for pointers on how to distinguish a cold sore from a chancre. You'll learn that a chancre is utterly painless; cold sores, however, can be exceedingly uncomfortable. Another important difference is that cold sores often come in clusters, whereas a chancre is always solitary and can measure almost half an inch across.

If you're anxious about syphilis, remember that your best insurance against it is a blood test, which you should have every three months.

If syphilis remains untreated, the secondary stage, during which you're just as contagious as you were in the primary stage, manifests itself in symptoms that begin as early as two weeks and as late as six months but averaging six weeks after the chancre disappears. A highly variable skin rash develops, one that may begin with small, almost invisible pink spots on the shoulders, upper arms, chest, back, and abdomen. These spots generally fade to a brownish color within a few days and disappear.

More commonly, the rash consists of raised bumps on the chest, back, arms, legs, face, and even on the palms and soles. If your skin is white, the bumps are pink, then coppery or brown; on black skin, they are gray-blue. In warm, moist parts of the body, particularly around the anus and the skin between the buttocks, the rash may ooze a clear fluid which is swarming with syphilitic bacteria and *extremely* contagious.

You may also experience a sore throat with hoarseness, pains in the bones and joints, loss of appetite, nausea, constipation, and a low fever. There is often a patchy loss of hair. All of these symptoms can be mistaken for something else.

Brian, a 29-year-old air steward and part-time prostitute, made a practice of seducing male passengers on night flights aboard the Tri-Star L1011, an aircraft equipped with elevators to the galleys below the passenger compartment, where, depending on his inclination and the price his customers were willing to pay, he would let them blow or screw him.

One day he developed a skin rash. But because he flew to tropical areas, he decided it was a simple heat rash. Then he came down with what he thought was the flu, which lasted several days. He celebrated his recovery by going to a smart men's "salon," where his hairdresser noticed some patchy hair loss and positioned the mirror so that Brian could see it.

"*Look* at that!" exclaimed the hairdresser. "You've been worrying yourself silly over somebody, haven't you?"

They say that only your hairdresser knows for sure—but not this time, because shortly thereafter Brian decided to have a long-postponed blood test and was positively diagnosed as syphilitic.

Assume nothing about your body. Regard *any* sudden change as potentially dangerous and see a physician. And don't ever allow someone not medically trained to do your diagnosing for you. Brian was lucky. His syphilis was detected and cured before passing into the latent stage, where it could have remained hidden and lethal.

**Is latent syphilis contagious?** No, and it can last for years with no symptoms. (A pregnant woman, however, can infect her unborn child with what is known as congenital syphilis.) In some instances, people with latent syphilis may relapse and manifest symptoms of primary and secondary syphilis, such as the reappearance of the chancre and the rash; but generally, the only way to know if you have syphilis in this stage is through a special blood test known as the FTA.

One out of three people progress from latent syphilis to the late, or what used to be called the tertiary, stage, and develop frightening complications. Cardiovascular late syphilis, for example, can strike the heart and circulatory system from ten to forty years after the original infection and often leads to death. Neurosyphilis, which affects the spinal cord and brain, causes paralysis, insanity, and death, and can develop between ten and twenty years after the original, untreated infection.

**How is syphilis diagnosed?** If a chancre is noticeable, its fluid is examined microscopically for the telltale presence of spirochetes. Again, the standard blood test, or VDRL, will not always reveal syphilis in the primary stage.

The VDRL (Venereal Disease Research Laboratory) reads positive in not more than seventy-six percent of cases of primary syphilis (the remaining twenty-four percent gives a "false negative" result). The VDRL is 100 percent accurate, however, in detecting secondary syphilis.

Another of the difficulties with the VDRL is that it can read positive in people who do not have syphilis but some other condition, such as measles, chicken-pox, mononucleosis, and infectious hepatitis. When a VDRL produces a *suspected* "false positive" report, a more sensitive (and more expensive) test—the FTA (fluorescent treponemal absorption) test is employed. Because the FTA is more accurate than the VDRL in detecting syphilis in the primary stage, it is often preferable to the VDRL. Still, it is accurate in only those patients who have never had syphilis. (The FTA remains positive for life once syphilis has been developed, even after treatment and cure.)

Your physician, in reporting the results of your VDRL, may refer to "titers," which are a measurement of the concentration of antibodies in the blood. Low titers indicate a low concentration, and high titers a higher concentration. When syphilis goes untreated, the titers progress to the maximum level found in the secondary stage of the disease. After secondary syphilis, they usually decrease, even though the disease remains active in the body.

Following treatment, the titers become lower and eventually negative over a period of many months. Patients who have been treated and cured can therefore have elevated titers but are not infectious.

**How is syphilis treated?** In the primary and secondary stages, penicillin by injection is always used unless you're allergic to it, in which case you'll be given tetracycline, or some other antibiotic, over a period of ten days. The usual dosage of penicillin is 2.4 million units. Latent, late, and congenital syphilis are also treated with penicillin, but in larger doses.

Shortly after your injections (one in each buttock), the syphilis organisms suddenly die, break open, and release their contents into the blood. Within twelve hours after treatment you may develop a high fever, and the chancre, if present and noticeable, may become swollen and enlarged. This phenomenon, known as the Herxeimer reaction, is not invariable; if it does occur, it lasts but a few hours and does not mean you're having an allergic reaction to penicillin per se, something your doctor, if he's on his toes, will have taken time to explain.

If you've been treated for primary or secondary syphilis, you must be reexamined a month later and then once every three months for a year. Follow-up examinations after treatment for latent and late syphilis are more extensive and involve spinal taps.

**What about abstinence?** Most physicians, in their understandable zeal to expunge this scourge, recommended a period of abstinence from sexual intercourse, but not from masturbation, for one month after receiving treatment.

**Are gay women immune to syphilis?** As with gonorrhea, you have little to worry about provided that your partners are exclusively gay; if they're not, you're just as subject to syphilis as men.

The symptoms in women are identical to those in men, as is the progression of the disease, its diagnosis, and treatment. The chancre generally appears somewhere in the genital area, including the labia, or outer lips of the vagina, within the vaginal canal, or on the cervix. It can also appear in the mouth or in and around the rectum.

**What can men do to prevent syphilis?** You can minimize your chances of catching it by wearing a rubber and insisting that your partner do the same. (But the spirochete can enter the body in other places.) You can also choose not to have sex with people who appear to have skin rashes. Neither suggestion is practical, of course, if you're a regular at the baths.

Until a vaccine is developed, the most effective way of combating syphilis remains the regular checkup. Because your chances of catching it are directly proportionate to the number of sexual contacts you have, you must, if you're sexually active, have a checkup *every three months*. Write down the dates you are due for the checkups and *go*. And once you're there, request throat and anal cultures as well. Should suspicious symptoms appear, don't wait for the due date. Go to a private physician or a clinic immediately and do whatever you can to trace and warn your sex partners.

You can also help by spreading the word. Public health officials agree that VD (syphilis *and* gonorrhea) is increasing so rampantly because:

There is a lack of funds for VD prevention and control programs on all governmental levels.

In the gay community, there is a casual attitude about the dangers of VD.

Many people have VD without any of the symptoms.

When symptoms appear, they are often mistaken for something else.

People who do recognize symptoms and seek treatment often fail to have *all* their known sex contacts examined and treated.

Syphilis and gonorrhea may be problems that only gay men encounter, but if you're a gay woman you can't afford to be smug. You, too, can help by spreading the word to your brothers—thereby discharging a share of your responsibility to the gay community at large.

Venereal disease is a very heavy subject. Still, in their effort to get the facts out, public health officials are to be commended for their refreshing, and sometimes pointed, directness. The prize here must surely go to the San Francisco City Clinic, which hands out a little pamphlet called *Do You Love Your Fellow Man?* Some excerpts:

> Well, if you want him to continue loving you, take rear-guard action. Don't give him VD.

> Syphilis and gonorrhea are easy to spread (in fact, the more you spread, the more they do) and hard to find, especially in the anal area. Both Siff and Clap have gone underground the last few years—you may never notice any signs or symptoms but you will be spreading it to all comers—so to speak.

## HEPATITIS

> The dark moods didn't make any sense. It was a sunny mid-July. My career and life seemed to be running smoothly. But the blackness persisted, each day a little darker than the day before.

> By the beginning of August, I had grown sullen, listless, even morose. Work became dull, meaningless; friends phony and uncaring. I begged to miss deadlines. Friends, editors, and colleagues pulled me aside to ask what was wrong. I didn't know.

> Mid-August came and my life was a quagmire of apathetic depression. I was a record player from which the plug had been pulled. I kept turning, but with each revolution I went a bit slower and slower. Even eating became a bore and I began to notice dozens of aches and pains.

> None of it made any sense—until I was putting in my contact lenses one morning in August and noticed that my eyes were turning yellow. The pieces then came together. I had fallen victim to the newest venereal disease—hepatitis."

Thus does Randy Shilts, a San Francisco writer, describe his own initial encounter with a disease that is emerging as one of the most dangerous health problems among gay men.

In a frightening study recently published in the prestigious *Annals of Internal Medicine,* researchers tested a sample of 600 gay men and found that fifty-one percent showed either the hepatitis-B virus or its antibody. In other words, more than half of them were either walking around with hepatitis at the time of testing or had a history of the disease in the past—*whether they knew it or not.* Were the general population tested, the figure would be closer to three to five percent.

Hepatitis is an inflammation of the liver, the body's largest and most mysterious organ. While much remains to be learned about the liver, physiologists know that it has at least two basic functions: It synthesizes a number of chemicals necessary to the efficient operation of the entire body, and it cleanses the blood of its toxins and wastes.

When hepatitis strikes, these functions are interrupted and hampered. The liver becomes so deranged that it creates unusual chemicals that sometimes have an unpredictable effect on the brain. Because the liver cells can no longer detoxify the blood properly, the remaining poisons can also affect the brain. The result? The most difficult symptom of all: an altered mental and emotional state that ranges from depression to euphoria.

"Hepatitis is in epidemic proportions in the gay community here," reports the Washington D.C. Gay Men's VD Clinic. The same alarm is sounded from New York by the City Bureau of VD Control, and from Chicago, where one out of sixteen men tested had the hepatitis-related antigen. Another sixty-eight percent of those tested in Chicago had developed antibodies to the B virus. If you have the antibody, you've had hepatitis whether you knew it or not.

In San Francisco, the number of reported hepatitis-A (infectious) cases has doubled in the last two years, and the incidence of type B (serum) has catapulted a dizzying 240 percent since 1974. The Bureau of Disease Control of the San Francisco Department of Public Health reports that between eighty and eighty-five percent of these cases are in men between the ages of twenty and forty.

Speaking for a growing number of physicians practicing in cities with large gay populations, Dan William, M.D., director of research for the New York City Bureau of VD Control and a physician at the Gay Men's Health project, puts it flatly: "In general, when a young male adult comes down with hepatitis, you can assume he's gay."

To date, the government has been lax in dealing openly with the gay aspects of hepatitis. In 1976, for example, John Bryan, M.D., until recently chief of the Hepatitis Branch and deputy director of the Viral Diseases Division, Bureau of Epidemiology, Center for Disease Control (CDC), U.S. Public Health Service, Department of Health, Education and Welfare (and how's *that* for a bureaucratic mouthful?), and another CDC official coauthored what they called a "primer" on hepatitis which ignored the gay community as a high-risk group. The "primer" admits that hepatitis-A is most easily contracted via the fecal–oral route, but the sexual aspects of that transmission are alluded to only parenthetically. Incredibly, the "primer" concludes that hepatitis-B "is usually transmitted percutaneously, especially by inoculation with contaminated needles." In other words, most of the victims of hepatitis-B have been shooting up.

Although hepatitis can kill if it goes undiagnosed and untreated with rest and diet, there is much you can do to prevent it.

**What are the symptoms?** The initial symptoms of infectious and serum hepatitis are fairly nonspecific and can be mistaken for the flu. Victims feel generally worn out and ill, lose their appetites, and may be nauseated. There may also be a sense of pain or fullness in the upper right side of the abdomen. Other "flu" symptoms, such as painful joints, a cough, a sore throat, and a low-grade fever, can be present.

Another indication that you've got hepatitis is jaundicing, or yellowing of the whites of the eyes and the skin, but this symptom appears in only half of all known cases. Jaundicing is "announced" from one to four days before it begins by dark-colored urine and light, ash-colored stools, or "ghost turds."

Hepatitis has been known to break up relationships.

David and Fred were sailing along smoothly when David started complaining about a lack of energy and bizarre, sometimes frightening, dreams. Some mornings he would wake up so depressed that he could scarcely pry himself out of bed, and he'd usually take it out on Fred, who, all of a sudden, could do nothing right.

These black periods would be interrupted by fleeting moments of artificial brightness in which Fred, all of a sudden, could do no wrong and was, in David's eyes, the most beautiful person in the world.

After three months of such ups and downs Fred, unable to take it any longer, decided to split. "I love David," he told their friends, "but with him you don't know where you stand from one minute to the next . . . maybe it's because he's a Gemini."

David had hepatitis and didn't know it. It was finally diagnosed, but the damage to the relationship had been done. Had both of them been aware that wildly fluctuating moods *can* be symptomatic of hepatitis—particularly when accompanied by the so-called flu sumptoms—they could have got help before it was too late.

**How is hepatitis diagnosed?** By special blood tests generally referred to as liver studies, or profiles. The VDRL, which you should have every three months, is used for diagnosing syphilis only and will *not* reveal hepatitis.

**How do you catch it?** Both forms of hepatitis attack the liver, impede its functions, and produce identical symptoms, but they travel by different routes. Because the type A virus likes to hide in fecal matter, it is easily transmitted by oral–anal sex, or rimming.

The type B virus, which causes an illness more severe than type A, can be present in saliva, semen, blood, urine, and vaginal secretions. It is generally agreed that the virus must come in contact with the victim's blood in order to infect—a fairly easy process, given the numerous small cracks in the gums, lips, and anus. The more people with whom you have sex (in all its varieties), the greater your chances of catching not only hepatitis, but any number of diseases.

Even though the B virus can inhabit vaginal secretions, gay women seem removed from the hepatitis problem.

**How is hepatitis treated?** No treatment or cure exists aside from waiting for the virus to go away. This means resting in bed for an average of six weeks. Some victims are out of commission for three to six months, and a feeling of fatigue can linger for as long as a year following recovery. But if diagnosis is early enough and the patient goes to bed at once, he can sometimes be up and about in as little as two to three weeks. Regardless of the amount of time spent in bed, until tests indicate that the liver is functioning normally again, the patient is prohibited from touching alcohol and drugs (some physicians don't object to pot, however).

**What's the death rate?**  For hepatitis-B, between one and two percent (type A is seldom fatal). Compared with diseases like cancer, that may seem quite low, but considering the huge number of gay men who are being felled by the disease, one to two percent is a dangerous level.

In some acute cases, the disease hangs on for months and requires hospitalization. Aside from feeling miserable physically, the victim, because of the effects of toxins and other chemicals created by the deranged liver, becomes disoriented and easily confused. A coma follows, then death.

Even when hepatitis doesn't kill directly, it can cause permanent liver damage. From five to ten percent of B-victims may become chronic carriers for the rest of their lives, and chronic hepatitis can lead to cirrhosis of the liver and early death.

**How can you prevent it?**  If you know you've been exposed, a shot of gamma globulin, if given early in the incubation period, may prevent or lessen type A, but its usefulness in preventing type B has not yet been established. For type A, the incubation period ranges from two weeks to two months; for type B, two to six months. Gamma globulin promotes a temporary passive immunity. But because it is such an expensive substance, it is only given after a known exposure. For hepatitis-B, there is now available a high titer B globulin which should be given to those who have had sexual contact with an active case. It is newly developed, not available everywhere, and very expensive. Researchers are now working on an effective vaccine, but it may take years to develop.

If you already have the hep, you must not prepare other people's food or mix their drinks. Razors, toothbrushes, towels, washclothes, dishes, and utensils should be kept separate.

If you have a known history of hepatitis, don't give blood. Because so many gay men have had relatively mild cases without realizing it, you shouldn't give blood at all without a prior liver profile. Don't use needles. Finally, if you're just turning a trick and don't know your partner, *don't rim*. A number of apparently "healthy" people are walking around with hepatitis without knowing it.

Hepatitis-B is an extraordinarily complicated disease. New information about it is coming out every month. If you're sexually active, you owe it to yourself and other members of the gay community to *keep informed* through an ongoing relationship with a competent physician, either privately or with a qualified clinic.

## AMEBIC DYSENTERY, SALMONELLA, AND SHIGELLOSIS

An "epidemic" means that a disease invades the general population, spreads around, and burns itself out. A disease is said to be "endemic" when it establishes itself in a particular group of people and continues to rise in both incidence and prevalence.

Amebic dysentery, salmonella, and shigellosis—"tropical" diseases traditionally associated with poor hygiene—are now endemic in the gay community, and the problem they pose is more complex than that of VD and the more serious threat of hepatitis.

Unless they are practicing medicine in places like San Francisco or New York, most physicians compound the problem because of their ignorance of the sexual gymnastics involved in transmitting these gastrointestinal maladies. "Been south of the border recently?" That simple diagnostic question is frequently used to rule out the possibility of amebic dysentery, salmonella, and shigellosis, and the physician looks no further. The horror story is that gay patients are frequently carried along for years with treatment for something else.

It is now known that what once were classified as hygienic diseases are sexually transmittable. In New York City, tropical disease clinics report that a significant percentage of patients come from the gay community. And in San Francisco, *reported* cases of shigellosis rose over 300 percent between 1974 and 1976 alone. Public health figures show that men between the ages of twenty and thirty are six times more likely to catch shigellosis than women, while the amebic dysentery rate for the same male group is *forty* times that of their female counterparts.

These diseases are primarily a *gay* problem—except for those who have picked them up in tropical lands, cases are exceedingly rare in the general population.

**How come you've never heard of these diseases?** It may be that you don't live in San Francisco or New York or live in other places that do not have a large gay community. As Dan William, M.D., told *The Advocate*, the diseases appear first in the major port cities because of the large tropical populations common to those areas. Such populations bring the disease into the country and then spread them into the gay communities. From the time they hit these gay meccas, it's only a matter of time before they work their way inland to such places as Chicago and Cleveland. And make no mistake, they're on their way to where you live!

**What causes them?**  In amebic dysentery, the bugs, or pathogens, are parasites; in salmonella and shigellosis, they are bacteria. In all three diseases, which resemble each other and require lab work for specific identification, the bugs go from the mouth to the stomach and then to the intestines. So, once again, rimming can lead to problems! As the bugs multiply, they attach themselves to the intestinal walls, where the damage they inflict depends on the breed to which they belong.

The amebic parasites feed directly on the intestinal walls. The bacteria responsible for salmonella and shigellosis simply grow on the intestinal walls but do a lot of damage through the waste products they excrete. These products are toxic and can destroy the intestinal walls.

**What are the symptoms?**  Some people have no symptoms at all; with others, symptoms can be so subtle that they are dismissed as a passing stomach upset. But when symptoms are severe, they usually begin with throwing up. Because the bugs irritate the gastrointestinal tract, the body reacts by trying to vomit them out, but this rarely does the job. The intestines then react by secreting fluid to wash the pathogens out of the system, resulting in diarrhea— frequently of the explosive variety. Because of the dramatically increased movements of the intestinal walls, another symptom is severe cramping, and victims often experience excessive amounts of gas. All of these symptoms can alternate with bouts of constipation.

When present, diarrhea can lead to dehydration. When the body loses large quantities of water, the electrolyte balance of the blood and the calcium–phosphorus and sodium–potassium ratios are altered. The disturbed blood then goes on to upset the rest of the body.

Meanwhile, the bugs are wreaking havoc on your guts. As the intestinal walls begin to erode, the pathogens enter the blood vessels surrounding the intestines. Blood will appear in the feces, and the bugs, which are now in the bloodstream, will cause the body to react with fever and chills.

Many infected people, though, are not ill in any way. The bugs simply live inside the feces and don't infect the intestinal wall. But such people are *carriers*, and contact with their feces, however slight, can be dangerous.

**How are these diseases diagnosed?** Until just recently, these diseases have been restricted to the so-called underdeveloped countries; consequently, many laboratories and hospitals in the United States and Canada have neither the facilities nor the expertise required to make specific diagnoses. Even when they do, tests are difficult, expensive, and depend on a number of cultures taken directly from your fecal matter, which is sometimes difficult to obtain because of the intermittent constipation and diarrhea these diseases cause. And, as noted, the problem of diagnosis is often compounded by the ignorance of many physicians and by the gay patient's lack of candor about his sexual proclivities.

Once diagnosed, however, treatment involves the administration of antiparasitic drugs or antibiotics. Because the latter kill *all* bacteria in the stomach, you should eat lots of yogurt during the treatment to replace the good bacteria that the medication wipes out.

The two drugs that are used most frequently are Flagyl and Humidin; both are expensive, and the latter is wildly so. Both must be taken over a long period of time. Because the safety of Flagyl is clearly questionable (metroindazole, its operative ingredient, has caused cancer in rats and mice), Humidin is generally the better choice. If your doctor does prescribe Flagyl, don't drink. The combination with alcohol could cause headaches, nausea, and other side effects. Nor should Flagyl be taken by anyone with peptic ulcers, another infection elsewhere in the body, a history of blood disease, or a disease of the central nervous system.

Untreated? The first thing that will happen is serious damage to the intestinal tract. The parasites can also travel to the liver, where they form large abscesses. If these abscesses rupture, serious complications involving the abdominal cavity, the lungs, and other vital organs can result; untreated amebic dysentery can kill via dehydration.

**What can you do to prevent these diseases?** To put it bluntly, little can be done to prevent them short of total abstinence from anal sex, and that means both screwing and rimming. Scrubbing with a germicidal soap may kill *some* of the bugs, but don't forget that it takes very little contact to spread the infection; just washing won't do the job. As Dr. William told *The Advocate,* "the more meticulous the personal hygiene, the less chance of getting them there is. But that's not very good, because if you're going to stick your tongue in somebody's anus, no amount of hygiene will help."

If you're into anal sex, it's a good idea to have a periodic stool check, even though you're free of gastrointestinal symptoms. Ask your doctor to arrange for one when you book your next annual physical.

Finally, if you've been diagnosed as having a "tropical disease," complete the full course of treatment prescribed, even if your symptoms disappear. And because relapses are apt to occur, you'll *really* have to get your shit together! Stools must be reexamined at monthly intervals for several months before a cure is certain.

## VENEREAL WARTS

Only on rare occasions can the virus that causes venereal warts be transmitted without oral–genital or anal intercourse. *Condylomata acuminata,* to give them their official handle, appear one to three months after exposure to an infected partner, but they can also be found in individuals whose sexual partners have no sign of the disorder.

On a straight man, particularly if he's uncircumcised, the warts usually appear toward the tip of the penis, sometimes under the foreskin, and occasionally on the shaft and scrotum. But in gay men, the most commonly afflicted area is the rectum.

In both straight and gay women, particularly if they're sexually active and between the ages of fifteen and thirty, the warts cluster along the labia, inside the vagina, on the cervix, and around the anus. They have even been known to cover the entire vulva and block the vaginal opening, necessitating plastic surgery under general anesthesia.

**How are they diagnosed?** Because diagnosis is obvious on the basis of appearance, laboratory tests are seldom necessary. In moist areas, the warts are usually pink or red with an indented, cauli-flower-like texture. Moist warts often grow together to form a single mass. On dry skin, such as the penile shaft, they are generally smaller, hard, and yellow-gray, resembling ordinary skin warts on other parts of the body.

**Are they dangerous?** They can be deadly to your morale. Physio-logically, they are problematical only when they become infected, which can result from scratching (they itch) or poor vulvar hygiene. Scratching can also make them spread.

Needless to say, they make anal intercourse difficult to impos-sible because of pain and bleeding. And not at all incidentally, don't *ever* assume that rectal bleeding is a sign of warts, because it could mean something else, including rectal cancer.

**How are they treated?** There are three common methods: podo-phyllin, liquid nitrogen, and electrocautery. Different physicians and clinics use these methods in different ways. For small warts, several applications of podophyllin at weekly intervals may do the job. But when warts are large and clustered, treatment by freezing, electric cauterization, or surgical removal may be necessary.

Rectal and anal warts are especially difficult and discouraging. The highly experienced Anal Wart Clinic of San Francisco General Hospital (yes, they have a special clinic), proceeds as follows:

Very large warts on the outside of the anus are treated by freez-ing with liquid nitrogen. This is uncomfortable during the few sec-onds it takes and will cause some swelling and drainage over the next few days as the warts turn loose and drop off.

Smaller warts outside the anus are painted with podophyllin, a dark red resin obtained from the mandrake plant. This burns some-what and will continue to burn through the rest of the day. You'll be asked to wash the area about six hours after treatment. Dis-comfort generally lasts for four to six days, with swelling and drain-age.

Because the time needed to rid the outside of the anus may take weeks to months, the clinic asks that patients come in at least weekly.

The clinic has found that it's impractical to treat external and internal warts simultaneously. There is also the concern that with people not actively engaged in anal intercourse, or in what the clinic delicately calls "instrumentation" (the use of dildos, vibrators, and other toys) examination may carry the virus inside, if it's not already there. Some physicians feel that the area around the anus is suitable "soil" for the warts to grow in, especially if the soil is occasionally "plowed" during anal intercourse or "instrumentation." It is also possible that the virus is present but dormant in the area and causes warts to form only when activated.

Once the external warts are cleared up, the internal warts, if small in number, can be treated with electrocautery without an anesthetic. However, in the majority of cases the internal ones are so extensive when first seen that an anesthetic is required.

The anesthetic, which is necessary not only because of the pain, but to relax the sphincter muscle so that the physician can work inside, is administered by injection, and it's painful. The warts are then burned out with the electrocautery.

This operation is performed in either the outpatient department or in a regular hospital operating room. The anesthetic and the procedure are the same; the only difference is the amount of premedication with relaxing drugs that you'll require in order to tolerate the procedure without excessive pain.

After the operation, you'll have to keep returning to the clinic for cauterization of any new warts until the problem is eradicated. The length of time is variable, but it's usually somewhere between one and six months, and occasionally as long as two years. The longer it takes, the more discouraged you'll become, but try to remember that everyone who has stuck with the treatment has eventually been cured.

**What can you do to prevent them?** Aside from giving up sex, not much; if you get them, you get them. They might even disappear spontaneously, on their own, without treatment of any kind. In the meantime, women can best care for themselves by avoiding moisture-trapping nylon underwear and panty hose; men should abstain from anal intercourse and any other activity that might give them to others (use your imagination, the virus is *highly* contagious).

But if treatment seems indicated, by all means go to a physician or clinic with an established reputation for dealing with the problem. Some physicians have never seen a case of rectal warts and haven't a clue as to how to treat them; others, who know precisely what they are and what causes them, treat them improperly.

Father Malcolm, a young priest serving a small town parish, learned that the hard way. After discovering some warts around his anus and not knowing that they could be sexually transmitted, he visited his physician, who was also a parishioner. If the physician knew that he was face to face with an STD he wasn't about to tell his pastor; nor did he suggest that the warts could also be internal. Alluding vaguely to "a virus," he proceeded with liquid nitrogen. Several days later the warts disappeared.

Not long afterward, the priest spent one of his rare evenings out at the baths, in a nearby city, and was mortified to discover that he'd given his partner a slightly bloody penis. Understandably fearful of confiding in his own physician-parishioner, he asked for the name of "a good gay doctor" at the checkout desk, was provided with one, and made an appointment, via long distance, the following morning.

The place was a factory. The receptionist, after finding out why he'd come ("rectal bleeding"), told him to wait. Half an hour passed before he was finally called. He waited another half an hour in an examining room.

The doctor finally arrived and examined his new patient hurriedly.

"Get fucked a lot?" he asked.

"Uh . . . once in a while," replied the anxious cleric.

"You're loaded with warts, but I can get rid of 'em."

Without further explanation, Father Malcolm was told to kneel on the table, bend over, and keep his cheeks spread with his hands. After daubing his insides with something, the physician announced that the treatment was concluded and began scribbling on a prescription pad.

"This is for the pain. And while you're there, buy yourself some Kotex for the drainage. Don't forget the belt, either. You'll want to shit like hell after you get home, but you've got to hold it for six hours, got that? Six hours. Then let it out and sit in a warm tub for a while. You'll also need some Milk of Mag. Okay, that's it. Check back in a week."

And he was off to see his next patient.

That night was one of the most agonizing the priest had ever spent. Doubled up on his bed, his eyes fixed on the clock, frightened out of his wits that he might be called out on an emergency, he prayed for those six hours to elapse so that he could expel the fiery pain.

A week passed, but Father Malcolm didn't return to that doctor; instead, he took time to shop as quietly and as discreetly as he could for a competent physician, one with whom he could be candid, a need he realized was long overdue.

## GENITAL HERPES

Although genital herpes is increasingly common to both sexes, it is more severe and potentially more dangerous when it strikes women. Usually but not necessarily transmitted sexually, it is caused by a virus known as Herpes simplex type II, which is closely related to Herpes simplex type I, the cause of common cold sores, or fever blisters, which respond to symptomatic treatment with superficial anesthetics such as Blistex. Although a lab test is required to distinguish one variety of herpes from the other, as a general rule type II appears below the waist and type I above; but there is an estimated ten percent crossover, probably resulting from oral–genital sex. There is no known cure for either variety, nor is the incubation period known.

What makes type II so dangerous for women is that gynecologists are increasingly convinced that it is linked to the development of cervical cancer. Although type I is much less serious, the physical symptoms can be just as painful.

**What are the symptoms?** Painful, blisterlike eruptions along the vulva and genital mucous membrane, accompanied by fever, intense itching, swollen and tender lymph nodes, and a feeling of general malaise. Inflammation and swelling around the urethra can make urination exceedingly painful and even impossible, necessitating catheterization. When the culprit is type II, the cervix can redden, ulcerate, and lead to discharge and vaginal spotting.

Because the open sores are vulnerable to bacterial infection, they should be checked by a physician. The sores generally heal on their own anywhere from a week to a month, after which the virus enters a latent stage and is no longer contagious.

**Can herpes come back?** Yes. Once infected, a woman continues to harbor the virus, which can be activated under circumstances that seem related to emotional stress. Although there is no limit to the number of recurrent outbreaks, for most women the first attack is the worst.

**How is it treated?** Because there is no known cure for herpes, treatment consists of easing the symptoms with a local anesthetic ointment such as lidocaine. Another effective technique involves the use of special dyes in conjunction with flourescent lighting, but there is a serious question as to whether the dyes themselves may cause cancer.

Self-care consists of applications of cold milk compresses four to six times a day followed by a local anesthetic, which can be obtained through your physician. When pain during urination is excessive, spraying the vulva with cold water while voiding can be helpful. Some women find that urinating while sitting in a pan of cold water is preferable to spraying.

**What can you do to prevent herpes?** Very little; but if you've had it, the best way to prevent a recurrence is to do everything you can to avoid emotional stress. You can also take the necessary steps to insure that the disease won't lead to something more serious. A microscopic examination of a smear taken from the base of the sore and/or the cervix will generally reveal whether you have type I or II, as will a special blood test for antibodies. If it's type II, you should have a Pap smear once every six months.

**What about men?** It is currently believed that the virus is transmitted by anal or oral–genital intercourse, but there are many cases of herpes in men whose only sexual partner has no evidence of the disease.

The first symptoms are small, painful blisters or bumps on the glans or shaft of the penis. Blisters can also appear around the anus, where they soon rupture and form soft, extremely painful sores. After four to five days, these sores become less painful and begin healing on their own.

The herpes virus can be reactivated in men, just as it can in women, under circumstances including emotional stress, fatigue, colds, and sunburn.

Because herpes is often misdiagnosed visually as syphilis or chancroid, the disease is probably more common than generally suspected. To be certain, a cotton swab is passed gently over the sores and the secretions are examined on a microscopic slide. To be doubly sure, many clinics insist on a VDRL for syphilis at the time of examination and another one a month later.

Treatment consists largely of self-care and includes, in addition to keeping yourself in good physical and emotional shape, rinsing the sores with a mild solution of salt water. Some men report that long, long hours of sleep are helpful.

A final word of caution: If physicians can misdiagnose that sore, so can you. Don't *ever* assume it's "just herpes."


## CHANCROID, LYMPHOGRANULOMA VENEREUM, GRANULOMA INGUINALE

Although exceedingly rare (less than one individual per 100,000 contracts them), these diseases are sexually transmitted and could eventually reach the epidemic proportions that other previously obscure STDs have. Untreated, all three can cause destructive genital lesions. It's best to know about them.


**Chancroid:** Sometimes called "soft chancre" or "soft sore," chancroid is caused by a bacilus, or rod-shaped bacterium. The incubation period is three to five days, and the initial symptoms are an ulcer on the genitals of either sex and painful swollen glands. Either sex can be a carrier with symptoms.

When diagnosis is visual, chancroid is often mistaken for herpes. Definitive diagnosis depends on microscopic identification of the offending bacterium. Treatment is with antibiotics and other drugs.


**Lymphogranuloma venereum:** (LGV): LGV, although usually transmitted sexually, is one of the few STDs that you can also catch from such items as infected bedding and clothing. The incubation period is from five to twenty-one days, after which a genital blister resembling herpes appears. Definitive diagnosis depends on microscopic identification of the bacterium responsible, and treatment is with antibiotics.


**Granuloma inguinale:** This one's fairly easy to identify because after one to three weeks' incubation, it produces bright red genital sores that are painless. Treatment is with antibiotics.

## CRABS, SCABIES

In France, crabs are called *papillons d'amour*, or the butterflies of love. In America, they are known less elegantly as crotch crickets. Their official handle is *Phithirus pubis*, or crab lice.

When examined under a microscope, crabs look very much like, well, crabs. They even have pairs of claws and four pairs of legs. Unlike body and scalp lice, they are most at home in the pubic areas of both sexes, where they love to mate, lay their eggs, and swing from hair to hair like so many tiny Tarzans. They survive by burying their ugly little heads in human skin and sucking blood from the capillaries near the hair follicle.

**What are the symptoms?** Usually, it's an awful itch that seems to worsen in the middle of the night. But not always; some people have no itching at all and can only tell if they have them by looking carefully. They're about the size of a pinhead and yellowish-gray— unless they've just had a meal, in which case they are more easily seen as rust-colored specks near the junction of the pubic hair and skin. Another dead giveaway that you're infested is the visible presence of the eggs, or nits, which are oval and whitish. Because the eggs are quite hard, they are often more easily felt than seen. In some people, the bites cause a mild rash composed of small, sky-blue spots.

**How do you catch them?** Through intimate physical contact with someone who has them. They can also be caught from bedding, sleeping bags, and clothing. Finally, you can even get them from an object that has, since mid-Victorian times, been maligned as caus-ing everything else: a toilet seat.

**What is the treatment?** You can treat yourself successfully with over-the-counter preparations such as A-200 and Cuprex. The most effective medication, called Kwell, requires a prescription and is available as a cream, lotion, or shampoo. The cream or lotion should be massaged into the affected areas and left there for twenty-four hours, after which it should be rinsed off thoroughly.

You don't need to see a physician for crabs, but if you want to use Kwell, you'll have to ask your doctor to telephone a prescription to your nearest pharmacy. A word of caution: Avoid the opening to the penis and the eyes. Crabs are generally confined to the pubic hair, but they've been known to infest eyebrows, eyelashes, armpits, and hairy chests.

You can prevent a recurrence by having all your clothing, bedding, blankets, sleeping bags, mattresses, and anything else you've come in touch with either laundered or dry–cleaned. Such measures are probably unnecessarily heroic, and expensive. The least you can do is make sure your partners treat themselves. And don't forget to give that infamous toilet seat a good scrubbing.

If you're downright paranoiac about crabs, you could move out of the house for two weeks: If deprived of human companionship, adult crabs die within twenty-four hours. The nits, which will hatch up to a week to ten days after your departure, will also die within twenty-four hours if you're not around to feed them.

Unfortunately, such measures may be required after an invasion of scabies, which are far more insidious than crabs. *Sarcoptes scabiei* are microscopic mites that can be transmitted by close physical contact of any kind, and not necessarily sexual. Characteristically, they spread among family members, sexual partners, school children, and in very rare cases from pets to their masters.

**What are the symptoms of scabies?**   The initial infection may produce no symptoms at all. But about a month later, the itching begins and becomes progressively more intense. As with crabs, the itching seems worse at night and is often unbearable. As a result of scratching, even in your sleep (you should be so lucky), the skin develops small groups of open sores.

Scabies are particularly at home just beneath the surface of the skin, especially on the inner thighs, wrists, genitals, and between the fingers.

**How are they diagnosed?**   The characteristic location and appearance of the sores are suggestive of scabies, especially if the people with whom you've had contact have the itch as well. Definitive diagnosis depends on scrapings from the sores and microscopic identification of the mite.

**What is the treatment?**   Lengthy and expensive. Kwell, in cream, lotion, or shampoo form, remains the treatment of first choice. After a hot, soapy shower, it must be applied to the entire body from the neck down and left for twenty-four hours. After five days of this routine, the mites are probably dead, but the itching can take as long as a week to stop.

There is no known way to prevent scabies. To prevent reinfestation, everyone in your household should undergo the treatment whether there are symptoms or not. If you have pets, consult your veterinarian. Ideally, all clothes, bedding, mattresses, sleeping bags, draperies, rugs, and carpeting should be laundered or dry-cleaned. People are known who treated only themselves and weren't reinfested, but if you can afford it and want to be sure, delouse the lot.

## VAGINITIS: TRICHOMONAS, CANDIDIASIS, HEMOPHILUS VAGINALIS

Because the vagina needs moisture and lubrication just as the mouth needs saliva, secretions from the cervix, vaginal walls, and Bartholin's glands are both normal and necessary. In most women, these secretions form a discharge that's milky and rather slippery. After drying it takes on a yellowish tint.

Estrogen level, emotional stress, and sexual excitement can increase the flow. During ovulation (midcycle), the higher estrogen levels increase cervical secretions, as will emotional stress. During sexual arousal, dilation and engorgement of the blood vessels in the vaginal walls result in a copious, clear secretion. An increased flow under these conditions is also normal. Moments of emotional stress are of course to be avoided, but they're often inevitable.

As long as the discharge is not excessive, foul-smelling, or does not cause itching, irritation, swelling, and vulvar burning, there's nothing to worry about. But if these symptoms are present and occasionally accompanied by frequent urination, you've got vaginitis, or a vaginal infection. Specifically, you may have one of three diseases or any combination thereof that can be transmitted sexually: trichomonas (trich or TV), candidiasis (thrush or yeast), and *hemophilus vaginalis* (or HV).

**What are the symptoms of TV?** First, some gynecologists believe that at least fifty percent of all women have the trich organisms, i.e., one-celled parasites, in their vaginas without symptoms, while others state that *Trichomonas vaginalis* is not a normal inhabitant of the vagina or anywhere else in the human body. Be that as it may, if you're a sexually active gay woman, you're vulnerable to TV.

If you've caught it, you'll notice a heavy, watery, smelly, yellowish or greenish-white discharge. When particularly severe, the discharge can cause vulvar irritation and chafing of the upper thighs and rectal area. Accompanying symptoms are itching, tenderness, and inflammation of the vaginal opening. If another infection is present (TV and candidiasis like to go steady), the discharge may be thicker and whiter.

**Is it transmitted sexually?**   It *can* be. Because sixty to eighty percent of the male partners of infected women carry the offending organism in their urinary tracts without knowing it, the vast majority of all TV infections are contracted through penile–vaginal intercourse. But in your case, infection can imply close vulva-to-vulva contact. The organism does not survive in the mouth or rectum of either sex, so oral or anal transmission by any other means is impossible.

Trich can, however, be caught from using someone else's damp washcloths or wet bathing suits. And there's that old standby, the toilet seat.

**How is it diagnosed?**   In addition to the characteristic discharge, definitive diagnosis depends on microscopic identification of the culprit. The presence of asymptomatic TV is also a frequent and incidential finding in routine Pap smears.

Even when you're asymptomatic, most gynecologists believe that preventive treatment is indicated. This usually consists of oral doses of metronidazole (Flagyl), a very expensive drug. To make sure the problem is eradicated, it's best that your sexual partner be treated simultaneously. Otherwise, the infection can ping-pong between the two of you.

**Isn't flagyl supposed to be dangerous?**   According to Ralph Nader's Health Research Group, it is. They point with alarm to various tests in which metronidazole, when administered to rats and mice, has caused gene mutations and birth defects. Be that as it may, don't ever take Flagyl if you have peptic ulcers, another infection elsewhere in the body, a history of blood diseases, or a disease of the central nervous system. If you do take it, avoid alcohol; the combination can cause headache, nausea, and other unpleasantries.

**Is there an alternative treatment?** Local vaginal therapy (medicated creams, suppositories, douches, etc.) can sometimes relieve your symptoms, but they have a poor history of effecting a complete cure. This is important to know, because TV organisms, when treated locally, are apt to escape and remain potential sources of reinfection, especially in the urinary tract.

If you have candidiasis, however, you'll *have* to use creams and suppositories, as no effective pill is available.

**What are the symptoms of candidiasis?** Whether known as moniliasis, thrush, or just plain yeast, few infections are more difficult to treat than those caused by the fungus *Candida albicans*. Your first symptom is apt to be an intolerable itch, and the more you scratch, the more you'll increase the irritation, inflammation, and swelling of the labial structures. Excessive scratching (and you'll scarcely be able to constrain yourself) can also break the skin, inviting a secondary bacterial infection.

The discharge varies from woman to woman, but it's often thick, white, and looks like cottage cheese. It doesn't smell bad, however; in fact, the odor may remind you of baking bread.

**How do you catch it?** *Candida albicans* is a normal vaginal inhabitant in about forty percent of women and can be found in the mouths and fecal matter of both sexes, where it generally causes no problems. It can also be present in urine, semen, and between opposing skin surfaces, particularly between the buttocks. Its "gay" transmission can be vulva-to-vulva, mouth-to-vulva, and rectum-to-finger-to-vulva.

When the fungus is already present in the vagina, or when it is introduced by a sexual partner, nothing will happen as long as conditions for its growth remain unfavorable. Flareups are caused by a variety of factors, some of which remain unknown. What is known is that they include increased blood sugar levels. Antibiotics can sometimes trigger an infection.

**How is candidiasis treated?** After diagnostic inspection or microscopic examination of the vaginal secretions, or following a successful culture, suppositories consisting of some form of nystatin (e.g., Mycostatin) are prescribed for you and your partner, if any—whether she has the symptoms or not. Local therapy is continued for at least two weeks, but in stubborn cases, as long as five weeks.

Some gynecologists will paint the vagina, cervix, and vulva with gentian violet, an extremely messy, staining medication that necessitates the use of a sanitary napkin.

**What can you do to prevent it?** The "pH" of the vagina (which has an internal ecology all its own) is a measure of acidity and alkalinity. A pH of 7.0 is neutral; the stronger the base (alkaline), the higher the pH. *Candida albicans* thrives best in a very mildly acidic environment. The pH in the vagina is normally more acidic than the fungus prefers (4.0 to 5.0) and is even higher during menstruation. Women whose pH is occasionally supportive of *Candida albicans* can douche with two tablespoons of vinegar to one quart of water, or with boric acid suppositories. If the infection is already under way, however, such procedures won't cure it.

The best preventive measure you can take is dietary. Cut down on your carbohydrate and sugar intake, including cocktails and wine. Eating yogurt can also be helpful. Some women even apply it locally (but use plain, rather than flavored, yogurt). Unpasteurized yogurt contains lactobacilli, "good" bacteria normally found in the vagina but often destroyed after a course of antibiotics. The yogurt actually replenishes these bacteria, thereby restoring chemical balance to the vagina.

**What about HV?** In many areas, *Hemophilus vaginalis* is becoming more common than TV and candidiasis. Still, it remains a comparatively mild disease, one that can be cleared easily and quickly if both you and your partner take oral antibiotics for five or six days. Nitrofurazone (Furacin) in a suppository or cream, or sulfa suppositories are also helpful. Symptoms can amount to no more than a slight but foul-smelling, grayish-white discharge. To make sure it's HV and not something else, you'll have to see your physician.

No woman is immune to TV, candidiasis, and HV, but by following some basic rules, you'll significantly reduce your chances of catching them.

Because a generally lowered resistance is a prime factor in preventing all forms of vaginitis, keep yourself fit through exercise, good nutrition, plenty of sleep, and a positive mental attitude.

vulva and bottom regularly. Pat your vulva dry after
and try to keep it dry. Don't use other people's towels,
washclothes. Avoid irritating soaps and sprays—especially
"feminine hygiene sprays," which *no* healthy woman
needs.

Wear clean, cotton underpants. Avoid nylon underwear and
panty hose, since they retain moisture and heat, which help
harmful bacteria to grow faster.

Avoid pants that are tight in the crotch and thighs.

Always wipe your anus from front to back to keep anal bacteria
away from the vagina and urethra.

Make sure your sexual partners are clean.

If lubrication is needed for "instrumentation," make sure it's a
sterile, water-soluble jelly, such as K-Y, and *not* Vaseline.

Avoid any sexual activity that is painful or abrasive to your
vagina.

Cut down on your sugar and refined-carbohydrate intake (diets
high in sugars can radically change the normal pH of the
vagina).

Finally, don't put anything in your vagina you wouldn't put in
your mouth!*

## CYSTITIS

You may be surprised to find cystitis, or bladder infection, included as an STD. After all, this disease is something that almost
every woman, regardless of sexual activity and sexual preference,
can expect at least once in her life. Gay women are theoretically no
more vulnerable to it than straight women. But because certain gay
practices can trigger it, you may find yourself encountering cystitis
more than your straight sisters.

---

* Adapted from Judy Norsigian and Norma Meras Swenson, "Common Medical
and Health Problems—Traditional and Alternative Treatments." In *Our Bodies, Ourselves,* by the Boston Women's Health Book Collective. New York: Simon & Schuster,
1976, p. 137.

**What causes it?** Cystitis usually means that intestinal bacteria, particularly *E. coli*, get into the bladder. TV can also cause the disease. Like vaginitis in all forms, cystitis is more likely to occur when your resistance is low.

In addition to these circumstances, which are common to all women, gay women can contract the disease because of a partner's dirty hands, the use of dildos which, if penetration is from the rear, put excessive pressure on the bladder, and stretching and traumatizing the urethra during sexual play.

**What are the symptoms?** If you suddenly have to urinate every few minutes and nothing comes out, you've probably got it. In some women, there is also a pain just below the pubic bone, and the first urination in the morning can carry a strong odor. Cystitis almost always requires a visit to your physician.

**How is it diagnosed and treated?** You'll have to supply a urine sample, which is analyzed for the offending bacteria. Treatment, which may take as long as two weeks, is usually with Gantrisin, a sulfa drug, or other antibiotics.

Your doctor may ask you to control the pH of your urine by drinking cranberry juice or taking vitamin C. Many women have learned that drinking cranberry juice regularly is an excellent and pleasant preventive to cystitis.

Once you have the disease, you can best care for yourself at home by drinking as much water as you possibly can—enough to produce a good stream of urine every hour. You should avoid such irritants as alcohol, coffee, tea, and spices. Soaking in a hot tub two or three times a day and using a hot-water bottle or heating pad on your abdomen and back can also help relieve the symptoms.

It would be comforting to conclude this chapter by stating that if there are other STDs, they haven't yet raised their ugly heads. Unfortunately, the list seems to be increasing. In the spring of 1977, a 25-year-old man was hospitalized near death in San Francisco. He had typhoid fever, of all things, which he had contracted through rimming.

Whether typhoid is about to take its place as an STD endemic in the gay community remains to be seen. In the meantime, remember that while some of the STDs are almost unavoidable if you're sexually active, *all are curable* provided that you report any bodily changes or unusual symptoms that last more than a day or two to your doctor or clinic and have a regular checkup even when you're free of symptoms.

With the remote exception of death-wishers and other neurotics, nobody goes out looking for an STD. They come looking for us. And if they catch us, the responsibility is ours alone. The best way to thwart them is to take good care of ourselves and choose our sexual activities for the real pleasures they give rather than as potentially dangerous forms of escape from stress.

# 3.
# The Hazards of Sex

We were in the coroner's office in a city with a large gay community. "Flip through these and you'll see what we're up against," said the coroner, dropping a short stack of slick magazines into my lap. They were devoted to the joys of SM, with the emphasis on discipline and bondage. The photography, in living color, was superb. The dungeonlike sets were interestingly lighted. The props included whips, ropes, chains, handcuffs, rubber masks, lighted cigarettes, razor blades, and elaborate harnesses.

Before I had a chance to comment on the heavy theatrics of it all, the coroner handed me a stack of 8 X 10 glossies that were in stark contrast to the pictures I'd been looking at in the magazines: The costumes and props were often identical, but the 8 X 10s were in black and white; ordinarily furnished bedrooms substituted for gimmicky "dungeons," and the young men tied down to a bed or strung up in a harness were suddenly very much alone.

They were also very dead.

"Kids can walk in a sex shop just two blocks from this office," said the coroner softly. "They buy the magazines, they buy the toys. Then they get zonked out on drugs and try to replicate what they've seen in the pictures."

He tapped the stack of photographs. "Some of them wind up like that."

I braced myself for a lecture on the dangers of "pornography," but none was forthcoming. Instead, I heard a reasonable plea for more common sense in the gay community.

"Most of this so-called pornography panders to fantasy in general and to the 'kidnap-rape' theme in particular. There's nothing wrong with that. But if you don't know what you're doing and try acting these fantasies out—when you start suspending people and leaving them in positions that make it difficult to breathe, or put a rubber mask over someone's face, or ram something up someone's ass—you're not using common sense. The people who do these things may have as much common sense as anyone else, but it simply evaporates when they craze themselves on drugs and alcohol. I don't think we've ever seen an injury or death resulting from sexual play in which there wasn't a lot of mixing—pot, booze, amyl, uppers, downers. What chance does common sense have against an armada like that?"

Precious little. So little that drug abuse and sexual injuries and death are often inextricable. We'll be discussing drugs in greater detail later on; in the meantime, suffice it to say that if you're intoxicating your mind and body, you're taking leave of the common sense that can obviate most of the sexual hazards you're apt to encounter, including some you may not be aware of.

## SADOMASOCHISM (SM)

No aspect of the gay life-style is more misunderstood than sadomasochism. Despite the dictionary definitions and the preachments of psychologists, it would be inaccurate to describe SM as a simple sexual arrangement in which one partner, the sadist, inflicts pain while the other, the masochist, enjoys being hurt. It would be inaccurate because SM, as practiced in the gay community, is more often than not a complex arrangement in which the roles of master and slave are interchangeable with the circumstances. Only a hardcore handful go only one way. Nor does gay SM have much, if anything, to do with pain, either given or received. Gay people who are into SM are no more eager to hurt or to be hurt than anyone else.

Essentially, SM is a theatrical, ritualistic game in which the players, with the paraphernalia of the theatre (lights, costumes, and props) at their disposal, act out the roles of dominance and passivity.

It seldom follows that the gay man who plays a dominant role in society likes to be the master in a game of SM. The dominant executive, for example, who is used to giving orders at the office, may mitigate his stress by allowing someone to tie him up and give *him* orders for a change, just as the passive file clerk, perhaps in the same office, may find compensation in the role of master. Paradoxically, the man who allows himself to be tied up is free. He has temporarily abdicated all responsibility for himself and is at the "mercy" of his master, who has, at his fingertips, the instruments (props) of torture and death. The appeal of SM lies in the fact that unlike life in the workaday world, the lines of responsibility are clearly and *dramatically* drawn.

**But isn't SM dangerous?**   Only when the use (and abuse) of drugs blot out common sense to the point that the participants are carried away by the props at their disposal. A good spanking never seriously hurt anybody; but if a whip is applied with sufficient force to raise welts or break the skin, or if restraints inhibit circulation or breathing, you're inviting serious trouble.

Believe it or not, SM can often be healthy because of the role that resistance plays. Resistance, especially among men, is an indispensable component in sexual arousal; it can draw partners closer together when they're apart, and it can keep them slightly apart when they're overly close. You might think about this the next time you're cruising a bar: Is it the pursuit of happiness in which you're indulging yourself, or is it the happiness of pursuit? Many men are puzzled to find that they lose their desire the moment sexual contact becomes assured. In a game of SM, however the tension underlying resistance can be amplified to excruciating heights and then exploded in the most pleasurable, self-liberating ways imaginable.

**Isn't SM an inappropriate way to cope with stress?**   Every sex technique, bar none, is bound to seem ridiculous to those for whom it has no value. SM becomes inappropriate only when it endangers your physical health, or when you force yourself to play the game when you really don't want to, thereby creating a stressful situation.

You are the one to say what's right for you. Some men can find perfect freedom and peace by joining a monastic community and taking the three-fold vow of poverty, chastity, and obedience, but for others, that would be an "inappropriate" way to cope with the stress and crushing responsibility of living in the "real" world.

**Is it true that gay women don't do SM?** Generally, this is true. Men often require a high degree of resistance, whereas most women do not. The escalating effect that two men have on each other facilitates all forms of resistance, which is why SM is much more prevalent in gay male circles than it is among heterosexuals. With very rare exceptions, SM simply has no value for gay women.

## SUFFOCATION

To suffocate is to kill or to die by stopping respiration, as by strangling or asphyxiation. Asphyxiation is a deficiency of oxygen and an excess of carbon dioxide in the blood.

Most of the victims I saw in the coroner's pictures were young men who had suffocated. The continuity might have been as follows: drinking, smoking, and pill-popping followed by some mild SM in which the temporary roles of master and slave are at least tacitly agreed upon; frantic trussing of the willing slave with rope or collar and chains; master passes out and slave, suddenly realizing that the rope or collar is too tight (assuming that he's still capable of realizing anything), struggles and begs the now comatose master to free him, but all he does is tighten the restraining device around his neck; death follows.

Or perhaps a slave has doped up and allowed himself to be strung up by the arms. His masters, just as doped up, retire to another room, where they decide to remain and get even higher until the slave has time to reflect on what a naughty boy he's been; unable to reflect on anything, the sedated slave passes out and, because of the position of his body, asphyxiates before his masters return to continue the game.

One of the photographs I saw in the coroner's office was of a corpse wearing a rubber mask and nothing else. There were small eye holes and a mouth hole that could be zipped open and shut. This one was zipped shut—and had stayed shut too long.

**Then suffocation is isolated to SM?**   No. You may not be into SM yourself, but if you're sexually active you probably drink, do a few drugs, and frequent the baths, where suffocation can occur without a hint of SM.

The owners and managers of baths are understandably reluctant to admit it, but bodies *are* found on their premises. When notes are left, it's often a case of suicide, usually with an overdose. But when no note is found, the official cause of death becomes problematical. Some pathologists are convinced that a few of these deaths are caused by suffocation. Consider the scenario:

It's two o'clock Sunday morning. This is your third bar, and you haven't had so much as a nibble. To hell with all this posturing and playing games. You'll go to the baths.

You're walking down that familiar, darkened corridor when you see an open door. The guy on the bed is asleep, but so what? You start touching him up, his eyes flutter open, he smiles. You close the door, he reaches for your eager cock and starts to suck it. Not very well, of course, because he's out of it. He slows down, then stops, but your cock is still well down his pliant throat. Maybe he wants you to mouth-fuck him. Sure, that's it. And you do. But that's all the action you're getting, because now the guy's passed out. Shit, man, you might as well be copulating with a corpse.

And you might be. The gag response, which is controlled by the uvula (or pendent fleshy lobe in the middle of the posterior border of the soft palate), can be neurologically blocked by drugs. Ever noticed how much easier it is to suck cock upon awakening in the morning? That's because sleep has slowed down your bodily processes, including your gag response. After the gag response "wakes up," you can control it by the simple expedient of taking a deep breath before going down on your partner, thereby raising the uvula. But when you're loaded, your body's short-circuited. Another scenario:

Someone attractive staggers into the orgy room and collapses, spread-eagled, on a pile of pillows. You plop yourself on top of him and start making out. Then it's *your* turn to pass out. An hour or so later you come to, still on top of him. Thinking he might be sobered up enough to come back to your room, you try shaking him awake. But there's no response.

He could be dead. Pathologists know that when a body's short-circuited by booze and drugs and there's sufficient weight to depress the chest, suffocation can result very quickly.

Such deaths are admittedly freakish. But then so is choking to death on a piece of steak, or getting so bombed you strangle on your own vomit. Statistically significant or not, death by suffocation in a gay milieu is a hazard to be reckoned with. If you're out on your own and feel as though you might pass out, go home. The last place you should head for is the baths. And if you're even slightly into SM, don't get so loaded that you'll allow someone to place something around your neck. "Sexual asphyxia," the term applied by pathologists to suffocation resulting from tightening a cord around someone's neck at the point of orgasm, claims a known average of half a dozen deaths yearly in San Francisco alone.

## FISTFUCKING

"It's so relaxing," a young man told *The Advocate*. "Many of us carry a lot of tension in our anus, and to break that up is tremendous. To me, getting fistfucked is like getting a heavy massage in my neck and shoulders. You've got this enormous thing you're contracting against. The relaxation lasts all day."

Be that as it may, all of the many doctors I spoke to in preparation for this book felt that fistfucking is about the most dangerous current sex practice. Most of the large intestine, or colon, is coiled inside the peritoneal cavity, together with other digestive organs. The colon's function is to drain bodily wastes of their water and compact them into fecal matter. To connect with the rectum, itself only the last seven or eight inches of the colon, the large intestine drops from the peritoneal cavity to make an S-shaped curve to the right. The horizontal part of the colon in this curve is called the rectosigmoid, and it's lined with extraordinarily delicate tissue.

The medical problems with fistfucking occur where the rectum ends and makes its turn into the rectosigmoid. If fingers flare open too forcefully, or if a fingernail penetrates the delicate tissue, fecal

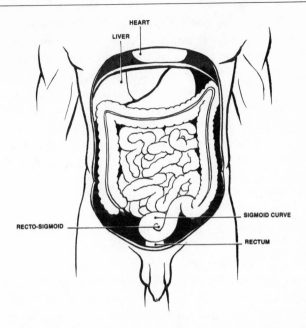

matter can leak out of the colon. Muriel Steele, M.D., a surgeon with years of emergency room experience in San Francisco, describes what happens next:

"Once the stool gets loose in the peritoneal cavity, it infects the peritoneal space, coating all the organs. It's the same as having a perforated appendix, only worse. With a perforated appendix, you've got a tiny pinhole that's leaking slowly in the peritoneal cavity. Here you've got a tear that's two inches long, just spewing stool. The peritonitis from this is much more severe, much more deadly than from a perforated appendix."

Gerald Feigan, M.D., a San Francisco physician certified by the American Board of Proctology, has seen a number of cases in which the colon has been punctured by fistfucking: "The scene starts with a lot of agony—very severe cramps. You're taken to the hospital, subjected to x-rays. Then you have to operate. First you wash everything out. You see, everything that's been in the colon spills out into the cavity. One guy had his whole dinner in there—vegetable fiber, potatoes that hadn't been digested. Then you're going to get a colostomy where you have to wear a bag that your bowels empty into. You'll have that maybe three or four months before you go back to the hospital to get sewed back up. It's a long, expensive, tedious process requiring lots of hospitalization."

The intestines are not equipped with pain receptors. Although nerve endings can report impulses that make a *sober* person aware of a tear, the nervous system malfunctions when it's been numbed by drugs. Virtually all the physicians surveyed by *The Advocate* report that those who sustain serious damage from fistfucking are almost always very drunk or very stoned and usually both.

Intoxication can also cause what can be a fatal delay for treatment. "We tend to see people when they already have peritonitis," Dr. Steele told *The Advocate*. "I think this kind of forceful activity does not take place unless the person is out of it with drugs or alcohol or whatever—or they just wouldn't allow that kind of damage to happen. They don't realize until ten or twelve hours later—when they're in excruciating pain—that something really bad has happened."

Despite the dangers, members of the Fistfuckers of America, or FFA, claim that most men can accommodate a fist without injury provided that they relax completely, and provided further that the person doing the fucking isn't so carried away with his *macho* role that he forgets to be gentle and caring. But even the most ardent advocates of this most exotic of gay sexual techniques admit that drugs can craze both partners to the extent that neither knows what he's doing.

**Fistfucking can kill you:** It can kill you. You may feel no pain, but if you're being fistfucked your partner quite literally has your life in his hand(s). One false move can cause a fatal injury, one you may not notice until it's too late.

**What's the death rate?** In San Francisco, physicians estimate the death rate at close to ten percent—a far cry from fifty percent estimated several years ago, when emergency room physicians didn't recognize the damage for what it was and therefore didn't move quickly enough.

Because of the ignorance of the medical profession outside the cities in which fistfucking is most prevalent—San Francisco, Los Angeles, and New York—the chances of a person dying in a small town are high.

Just recently, a young man living only a hundred miles from San Francisco spent a weekend in the city, got fistfucked at the baths, and drove home early Sunday morning. By mid-afternoon he was so wracked by abdominal pain that he asked a friend to drive him to the local hospital.

Once in the emergency room, the young man blurted out that he'd been "messing around" the night before, that his sexual partner had "stuck his arm up me, all the way to the elbow."

The physician on duty was immediately skeptical. "What kind of drugs were you taking?"

"Just some grass and a little amyl."

"No, you've dropped acid," replied the physician. "You know and I know that it isn't possible to stick your arm up someone's rear end. You're hallucinating."

The young man was heavily sedated with Thorazine, a drug used to minimize the horrors of a bad trip. His friend was instructed to drive him home, put him to bed, and keep an eye on him.

That night the pain become so intense that he had to return to the hospital, where an emergency "appendectomy" revealed extensive peritonitis. The young man died.

**Why do people do it?** Because physically, there's nothing like it. According to those who are into it, it's the ultimate trip, one that creates the most pleasurable sensations imaginable. Psychologically, there's the undeniable thrill of breaking a taboo, of flirting with danger (assuming that both partners are aware of the danger). When treated as dominance and passivity, it takes on even further dimensions.

**Is there a safe way to do it?** No, but certain precautions can minimize the danger. The man on the receiving end should flush all fecal matter from the lower intestines and rectum, which means a thorough enema. Some men even prepare by fasting, and among these some unwisely control the subsequent hunger pangs by taking speed. The rectal muscles must be in a state of total relaxation. While some men can accomplish this by ordinary anal intercourse, most resort to booze, pot, amyl, and muscle relaxants such as Quaaludes.

The person doing the fucking must remove rings, watches, and bracelets, and make sure that his fingernails are not only immaculate but filed quite short. The lubricant, usually the cultic Crisco, must be copious.

Most fistfuckers initiate their partners with one or two fingers, then a third, and finally a fourth. The fingers are withdrawn, the hand and forearm are liberally coated with more Crisco, and the thumb is folded against the palm. Then the hand is inserted up to the wrist, and sometimes further. Some men like to insert their penis as well and masturbate inside their partners.

**Do you have to go all the way?** Of course not. You don't have to do anything you don't want to do. But once fistfucking is under way, some men are so fueled by curiosity and drugs that they find it difficult not to go all the way, which is to say up to the elbow. One man told us he doesn't consider fistfucking successful unless he can feel the pounding of his partner's heart. (And if that partner is on amyl, the pounding is terrific.) A physician we interviewed in New York City, a man who has given illustrated lectures to members of the Fistfuckers of America, believes that the greatest safety factor is mutual fear. Although he can't prove it, he suspects that most men never venture past the rectum—the point at which fistfucking becomes forearm fucking.

But even so there can still be tears and scratches that can become infected to form abscesses or fistulas. As long as such infections remain confined to the lower rectum, where they can be easily checked, they present no major problem; but if they go unnoticed in the upper reaches, they can become serious.

Aside from the estimated ten percent mortality rate for perforations, there are no statistics available on how dangerous fistfucking actually is. Out of the thousands who are fistfucking every weekend, there may be only a dozen perforations. "The extreme hazards aren't that common," concludes Dr. Feigan. "The simple hazards are. The future hazards? No one knows."

## TOYS

Broomsticks, vibrators, dildos, candles, billiard balls, carrots, bananas, cucumbers, flashlights, candy bars, water glasses, screwdrivers, vacuum cleaner attachments, light bulbs, butter knives, spoons, wine bottles. . . .

So runs a *partial* inventory of objects that doctors are regularly extracting from people's behinds. There are no statistics available as to why such an incredible array of "toys" are finding themselves lodged where they do, but the practice is becoming so common that the personnel of various emergency rooms have begun playing a macabre game of "can you top this?"

"What did you guys pull this week?"

"A wristwatch and a couple of cucumbers. How'd you do?"

"Oh, just a Polish sausage."

"You're kidding!"

"No, honest . . . the guy said he froze it first."

The toys that cause the most trouble, be they the most improbable household items imaginable or the professionally manufactured gadgets available in sex boutiques, are anally oriented. Others, such as cock rings and tit clamps, are surprisingly harmless.

**Why do people stick things up their rectum?**   Gay men regard the anus as a highly sensitive sexual organ, one that's loaded with nerve endings which, when stimulated, can flood the body with erotic sensations. Physicians reckon that perhaps half of the items extracted were inserted by the patient himself during solitary masturbation. The young man who came in with the Polish sausage, for example, had just come out. He had never had anal intercourse and wanted it, but he felt he had to practice first. He froze the sausage, lubricated it, sniffed amyl to relax the rectal muscles, and simply got carried away. After the sausage "disappeared" and he was unable to abort it, he panicked and went to the hospital.

Regardless of how or why it got there, anyone with an object stuck in his rectum needs immediate medical attention. Because the rectal membranes are sticky, trying to extract a toy yourself could literally pull the rectum inside out, or cause tears and fissures that can develop into serious infections.

Losing an object in your rectum is no occasion for coyness; nor is it a laughing matter. Still, one physician couldn't help laughing when he told me about a patient he'd seen, a young man who presented himself to the emergency room receptionist as nonchalantly as possible. He refused, however, to reveal what had impelled his visit. Because he appeared to be in no obvious distress, he was told that he'd just have to wait, that there were other cases requiring immediate attention.

Three hours later, when the physician was finally available, the young man was taken to an examination room.

"Now, then. What seems to be the trouble?"

"I'm not sure," said the patient, "but I think there's a sterling silver butter knife inside me. Would you mind looking?"

"No, I wouldn't mind," said the physician, scarcely able to contain himself, "but tell me—what makes you *think* there's a butter knife in there?"

"Well, we've looked everywhere else . . ."

**How do doctors extract lost toys?** "Some of them are real challenges," Dr. Steele told *The Advocate*, "especially if you're dealing with a light bulb, which has gone in socket-end first. All you're faced with is the glass. It's big, and you can't squeeze it because it will break."

Water glasses present an equally formidable challenge, because they're always solid-end first, leaving the surgeon with only the rim. A coke bottle, if inserted neck-end first, can create a vacuum; to reduce dangerous suction, it is sometimes necessary to drill a hole in the bottom before extraction is attempted.

The first step in the surgical procedures required is to relax the sphincter with a spinal anesthetic. Then, according to Dr. Steele, doctors use forceps, suction cups, "and any ingenious thing you can think of to retrieve the object."

Lost dildos have become such a problem that one doctor has suggested only half-jokingly that the Food and Drug Administration license only those with great big graspable balls.

**Are dildos dangerous?** The king-size models can be deadly. Anything over ten inches, and you're asking for a perforated colon that can result in peritonitis. Don't buy one that's made of hard plastic or metal; the material should be soft and pliant. Avoid ones that can be cranked and twisted, as the metal wire in the center of such devices can break through the rubber and tear or perforate the colon.

Some men (and many gay women) use a double dildo that makes it possible for them to enjoy penetration simultaneously with a partner. Because these are almost impossible to lose, they're relatively safe provided that the size isn't excessive and the material is flexible.

Penis-shaped vibrators, or animated dildos, come in all sizes and are especially easy to lose. While almost all are battery-powered, there are a few that plug into the wall. Unless you're in quest of a particularly novel mode of electrocution, you might want to pass on these.

Needless to say, all "instrumentation" requires adequate lubrication. Saliva alone won't do.

**What about jerkoff machines?**   Hand-operated pumps that create a vacuum are effective for masturbation; but don't let false advertising convince you that such devices can increase the size of your cock, because they can't.

You can also purchase, at a rather high price, an electrically operated machine that will suck you off by creating a partial vacuum similar to the kind used in automatic cow milkers. More expensive models can suck off several people at once; the ultimate is a machine that sucks and fucks you simultaneously.

The purveyors of these contraptions (like vacuum cleaner salesmen, they'll often provide a demonstration in the privacy of your home) will tell you that their product is completely safe. But before you sign on the dotted line, consider that *any* mechanical device can malfunction.

There's a new SM device on the market which, for want of a more original tag, is advertised as a male chastity belt. This gadget consists of a padlocked leather belt around the waist and a strap between the legs that's attached to a six-inch dildo, or "butt plug."

The story may be apocryphal, but it's making the rounds in Chicago. An executive was wearing one of these inventions when, at his office, he was suddenly stricken with diarrhea. Unable to locate his "master," who had the key, our hero had to send his secretary to the building maintenance department for a pair of tin-snips.

**What about cock rings?**   They're placed around the balls and over the top of the penis when it's soft. After erection, the ring impedes the flow of blood away from the genitals, thereby keeping the cock hard over a longer period of time. Such a device—which literally cuts off the normal flow of blood—would seem to be dangerous, but physicians report the most serious problem that arises is occasional edema, or swelling. Unless the ring is too tight and worn over an inordinate length of time, any adverse effects are immediately reversible.

Cock rings come in assorted sizes and materials. The best ones are of leather, with several snaps that enable the wearer to adjust the size. Ones made of rubber can cut in too deeply, like a rubber band. Metal ones are okay as long as they're properly fitted, and some men are even buying them in silver and 14-karat gold (a unique investment, to say the least).

A word of caution, however, if you're wearing a metal ring: They can trigger the detectors at airport security stations. At O'Hare International, in Chicago (and this story is *not* apocryphal), a man activated the walk-through detector and was asked to remove all change and other metal objects from his pockets. The detector still registered. He was then examined with a hand-held detector, which went berserk when it got near his crotch. Thoroughly mortified, the supect was taken into that little room set aside for such purposes and asked to drop his drawers.

"My goodness!" exclaimed the young guard. "Now that's what I call first class . . . sterling silver!"

"It's . . . it's a prosthetic device prescribed by my urologist," stammered the passenger.

"Look, buddy, let me give you some brotherly advice. The leather ones are lots better. You can get 'em at the Leather Cell, on North Clark."

**What are tit clamps?** These are metal springs that are applied to a slave's nipples to enhance excitement (usually at the point of orgasm) and boost pain (and pleasure). If you use them, make sure they're equipped with rubber grips; otherwise, they can break the skin and lead to infection.

In a pinch, some men resort to ordinary clothespins.

## RAPE

Rape is legally defined as penetration of a person's body against his or her will. *Anyone* can be a victim of rape: men and women, infants and children, gays and grandmothers, prostitutes, and the mentally or physically handicapped. Aggressors can include family members, family friends, neighbors, group leaders, physicians, clergy, teachers, friends, friends of friends, and occasionally strangers.

Unless it results in pregnancy or VD, rape is seldom the worst thing that can happen to a person physically. The body will heal.

The emotional trauma, however, can engender humility, embarrassment, guilt, disgust, horror, anger, and anxiety—feelings that can scar the victims' personalities for life by making them feel bad about themselves, their relationships, and sexuality in general. When the victim is gay, these feelings can become so intense that crisis counseling is almost always necessary. Some gay victims require ongoing psychotherapy.

Officials estimate that only ten to twenty-five percent of female rapes are reported. Even when a woman summons the courage to report and prosecute, she can't be sure that the police and courts won't humiliate her further by implying that it was somehow her fault to begin with. Was she "provocatively" dressed? Did her failure to resist (in order to avoid being beaten or killed) not imply that she actually consented? It is little wonder, then, that only one in seven rape cases ever ends with conviction.

Once on the witness stand, the woman who has decided to prosecute will often be assumed to be lying; she will have to face the rapist again; and she will have to relive the rape in cruel detail.

Virginia, the 47-year-old principal of a high school in Iowa, was raped in her office one Saturday afternoon by a recently hired janitor and, with the support of her lover, a woman who was a successful lawyer in a nearby town, decided to go to the police and prosecute. When the trial was finally convened, the public defender took a tack implying that Virginia, essentially a sexually frustrated "old maid schoolteacher," had enticed the janitor.

In this case, the trauma of the rape itself was compounded by the intolerable stress of trying to decide whether she should reveal her sexual preference. Had she done so, with the corroborating testimony of her lover, she could have cut through the crap by stating that because she was gay and therefore uninterested in having sex with a man, there could be no question of "enticement." This she was not prepared to do, nor was her lover. They loved their work and preferred to keep their life-style private.

The price? Virginia suffered what some still call a "nervous breakdown." The rapist was acquitted.

Gay or not, men who are raped can become so emotionally crippled that they take their own lives. In December 1977, in southern California, a handsome, 20-year-old six-footer hanged himself in his parents' garage rather than go to jail, where he knew he'd be raped. He was to have appeared in a court the following morning that probably would have sent him back to the jail where he had spent a few days on a drunk driving charge. It was not until after the funeral that the young man's girlfriend told his parents that he had been assaulted by other prisoners during his brief lock-up.

The young man's parents are pressing for a grand jury investigation. Extensive newspaper of the case has at least made more of the public aware that such a thing as male rape exists.

**Isn't male rape confined to prisons?** The media would have us believe that while male rape is prevalent in prisons, it has nothing to do with homosexuality per se: The offenders, who usually have a sexual preference for women, are simply using their weaker fellow prisoners as substitutes.

It may be true that behind-the-bars rape is rampant, just as it's true that many inmates would rather have a woman. But male rape is by no means confined to the slammer. It's just that we seldom hear about it when perpetrated on the outside.

For example, a youngster, just coming out, goes to a gay bar and is picked up by an older, stronger man who has been drinking. (In one study at a treatment center for convicted rapists, thirty-five percent were alcoholic and fifty percent had been drinking just prior to the rape.) Once home, the older man may force his woefully inexperienced partner to submit to anal intercourse so frenzied that it results in tears and fissures requiring medical attention.

Were such a youngster to go to the police and report that he'd been raped he'd be laughed out of the station house. After all, he was in a gay bar and went home with someone, didn't he? What did he expect? His only recourse is to an understanding private physician (assuming he knows how to find one) or to a sexual trauma center (assuming his city has one), where he can receive both medical attention and counseling.

Judd, a recent victim of rape in San Francisco, was nothing if not experienced. It was a sunny Sunday afternoon, one that invited foraging at Land's End, a heavily wooded outdoor cruising area near the Golden Gate Bridge. What he hadn't counted on, however, was a roaming gang of teenage toughs who, in the name of God and Country, were bent on a little queer-bashing.

The scene requires little elaboration. Dennis was told that unless he blew these pimply ruffians they'd make mush of him with their makeshift clubs. He complied, but that wasn't enough. To show him how a "real man" does it, they then gang-banged him without benefit of lubrication.

Judd's rectal damage was so severe that he required minor surgery and a night in the hospital. The sum and substance of the attending physician's advice? "I hope this has taught you a lesson."

His body healed quickly enough; but three months later, after unremitting nightmares and anxiety attacks precipitated by the mere mention of sex, his spirit was still so shattered that he had to have psychotherapy.

**Should rape be reported to the police?**   Theoretically, yes. If your city has a rape crisis center, they can advise and counsel you. But the adult gay man who reports to the police hasn't the chance of a snowball in hell when it comes to getting action. His energies would be better devoted to obtaining prompt medical attention and the understanding ear of someone who can ease his trauma.

The adult gay woman victimized by rape is free to report to the police if she wishes, but she runs the same risks as straight women do if she prosecutes; she also assumes an additional burden if she prefers to keep her sexual preference private. Like her male counterparts, her first priority should be medical attention and the loving support of someone who cares.

**What about pregnancy and VD?**   A sexually assaulted woman should receive antibiotic treatment for venereal disease as soon as possible; this consists of an injection of 2.4 million units of penicillin G, which is usully sufficient to protect her against the development of syphilis and gonorrhea.

As a precaution against pregnancy, most physicians recommend the use of the synthetic estrogen diethylstilbestrol (25 mg twice daily for five days). If therapy is begun within seventy-two hours after the rape, the estrogen makes the lining of the uterus unreceptive to the implantation of a fertilized egg. Should a period fail to come within three to four weeks following such treatment, most physicians recommend a dilatation and curettage (D&C) of the uterine cavity. When a pregnancy develops despite these precautions, most doctors advise therapeutic abortion.

## WATER SPORTS, SCAT

Being shit on or pissed on, let alone eating feces and drinking other people's urine and sometimes your own, may strike you as aesthetically and hygienically reprehensible. Whether it has anything to do with homosexuality is arguable. Even so, some gay men are into it, and if you're making the scene you're apt to encounter it. If you meet someone who suggests water sports, it's a good idea to find out what kind—the term can also refer to the giving and receiving of enemas.

**Are water sports dangerous?**   Depending on what kind you're talking about, yes and no. When a master "forces" his slave to submit to a high colonic enema with a garden hose turned full blast, the results can be fatal. When partners of a gentler persuasion get off on giving each other conventional enemas, the risks are minimal provided that they avoid swallowing so much as a drop of the effluence.

Generally, the kind of water sports that involve urinating on your partner ("golden showers") or drinking his urine can be surprisingly harmless. According to the physicians surveyed by *The Advocate,* there is no serious hazard involved with drinking a *healthy* person's urine. But because so many gay men are carrying hepatitis, which can be transmitted in the urine, you'd better make sure that your partner is clean.

Men who are heavily into piss will sometimes dope up for a protracted session of recycling, a game consisting of drinking large quantities of beer and pissing in each other's mouths. Again, this is a practice that's repugnant to the majority of gay men, one that's talked about more than practiced. But if you're looking for it, you'll be able to find it.

A far more common water sport is urinating on your partner while he squats or stands in the bathtub and masturbates. Some men find this such a kick that they're able to come the moment the urine spatters their bodies. The tamest water sport involves two men urinating on each other while horsing around in the shower, a throwback, perhaps, to those idyllic days at summer camp.

**What about drinking your own urine?**   Just recently, several popular magazines, including *Time* (October 24, 1977), carried the titilating, rather tongue-in-cheek account of Indian Prime Minister Morarji Desai's practice of drinking his own urine as a daily health ritual, one he refers to as "drinking from your own cistern, the cistern of life." Apparently, a number of his fellow Indians swear by it as an aid to longevity.

There is no evidence whatsoever to substantiate such a claim. There is, however, considerable medical evidence that drinking your own urine (which slaves are sometimes "forced" to do in a game of SM) can be dangerous if you have a kidney problem. Because the function of the kidneys is to flush toxins from the blood, drinking your own urine results in the reabsorption of those toxins; consequently, the consumption of even a small amount of one's own urine by a person with marginally functional kidneys could lead to uremic poisoning by progressively elevating the blood concentrations of toxic substances.

**What does "scat" actually mean?** The coinage derives from *scatology*, or the study of excrement. In gay circles (where it is more talked about than performed), it refers specifically to two men getting off on smearing their bodies with feces, a master shitting on a slave, or a master forcing a slave to eat it as an act of ultimate humiliation.

Scat is exceedingly dangerous. Of all the body's secretions, there is no larger a concentration of viruses and flora than in a stool. Scat can lead to hepatitis, amebic dysentery, shigellosis, salmonella, pinworms, and a host of other intestinal diseases caused by parasites. Because the gut maintains a delicate, internally ecological balance between bacteria and yeast, even a healthy person's fecal matter can be toxic to someone else: One man's normal flora can be another man's poison.

## PIERCINGS, SCRATCHES, BITES

Piercing the ears, always popular with women, is increasing among gay and straight men alike and presents no hazards provided that it is done with sterilized equipment. Even department stores, in their drive to peddle more earrings, maintain a trained staff who can pierce your ears for you with no risks whatsoever.

Similarly, the SM fad of piercing male nipples presents no hazards (but you won't find the service available at Macy's). Common sense should tell you, however, that if the weights attached to the rings through the nipples are excessive, the result can be tearing, infection, and scars.

One form of piercing, largely restricted to SM circles, can be quite dangerous: punching a hole in the fold of skin under the head of the penis and putting a ring and sometimes a padlock through it. Physicians warn that metal worn in this area can erode into the urethra, leading to severe infection.

The light stroking of a partner's body with your fingernails can be a marvelous turn-on, but don't dig in to the extent that you break the skin or nick delicate vaginal and rectal tissues. Women are particularly vulnerable to sharp fingernails, which can cut the urethra. Most gay women keep their fingernails short and well-manicured, a sensible practice that has led to the sexist canard that you can always spot a dyke by looking at her hands. Forget it, she could be a concert pianist, or even a typist.

When it comes to bites, physicians warn that the flora in a human's mouth are much more pathogenic than those in other animals' mouths. If you're bitten in the throes of passion, particularly on the penis or scrotum, you may require prompt medical attention to avoid a raging infection. If you know you've been bitten or inadvertently nicked—perhaps by some ragged dental work—apply an antiseptic ointment or diluted hydrogen peroxide. Even when infection doesn't set in, broken skin on the genitals demands subsequent abstinence until the wound is healed. (Abrasions on the genitals and inner thighs caused by wiry chin-stubble can be treated with a medicated hand lotion and temporary abstinence.)

A lot of "bites" aren't bites at all. Consider the gay man who wears tight trousers and no underwear. If he goes to a bar and gets smashed, he can catch his penis in his zipper after urinating and, feeling no pain, doesn't even notice that he's broken the skin. An hour later he scores, goes home and has sex, and develops an infection that is indistinguishable from one caused by a bite. If you've been cut by your zipper and know it, use a rubber.

## ANAL INTERCOURSE

Contrary to old wives' tales and other horror stories, some of them promulgated by the medical community itself, anal intercourse is a perfectly safe and beautifully expressive way for two men to have sex. Physiologically, its intense pleasure, which can be enhanced by knowledgeable techniques, derives from the penis entering the rectum through the anal canal and massaging the prostate gland, where nerves associated with orgasmic contractions lie. Most of the pleasure, however, comes from the complex network of nerves in the lower rectum which exist to help defecation; their abundance helps create the erotic sensitivity of the anal area.

Psychologically, the benefits of anal intercourse such as intimacy, acceptance, and fulfillment can be unbounded.

**Then why all the fuss?**   Because too many of us have been taught since infancy that the anus is an object of dirt, guilt, and shame, a necessary evil designed for things to come out of, and not into. Anal intercourse *can* cause medical problems, but only when the "passive" partner (who's often more active than the person doing the fucking!) fails to relax his sphincter muscles; when the "active" partner is too rough; and when lubrication is insufficient. Any one or a combination of these conditions can lead to pain and rectal tears.

A man who *wants* to be fucked will have no trouble relaxing; alcohol, amyl, pot, and downers can do the job artificially, but he doesn't need them.

**What's the best lubricant?**   "Who needs a lubricant?" asked one of the men I interviewed. "When I see something I like, those natural oils just start flowing."

While the rectum may have natural secretions in response to sexual excitement, they are for more people insufficient to allow anal intercourse without artificial lubrication. Nor will saliva alone always do the job. The rectum, unlike the vagina, is not equipped with natural lubrication. Saliva alone is generally insufficient. Vaseline Petroleum Jelly works efficiently because it's thick and greasy, but many men find it too messy. At the other end of the spectrum, water solubles such as K-Y dry up too quickly and are unlikely to keep the parts well-oiled for the duration.

Although it's not our purpose here to endorse products, there's one so superior that to fail mentioning it would be irresponsible: Albolene. A close runner-up is Vaseline Intensive Care lotion.

**What about douching?**   If you've had a complete bowel movement prior to anal intercourse, you're ready to go. Some men consider it only polite to prepare further by douching with a bulb-shaped device available in any drugstore (ask for the adult size). Rinsing the rectum *after* a bowel movement (and not before, to induce one) provides the additional assurance that you're rid of fecal matter that your partner might find offensive.

**Can anal intercourse cause incontinence?** That's another old wives' tale, on a par with the horror story that masturbation can lead to blindness or the growth of hair on the palms. According to New York's Dan William, M.D., the notion that anal intercourse causes incontinence is so much rubbish.

"Nobody's ever shown me that there's a problem with incontinence from anal sex," he says. "That's one of the biases in medical literature. Some doctors think that because men have been penetrated a lot, they've lost their tone. What they're seeing are men who are able to loosen up their sphincters easily. That has nothing to do with tone. It's just that gay men have better control over their muscles down there."

Another physician, one with a large gay practice in San Francisco, weighs in with the conclusion that he's "never seen anybody hurt by a good piece of meat under normal circumstances."

**Are there abnormal circumstances?** There can be. Anal intercourse should be avoided if you're being treated for prostatitis, if you have hemorrhoids that protrude beyond the anal opening, if you have warts or are being treated for them, and if you're being treated for any fissures or fistulas.

If bleeding occurs without prior symptoms, you should see a doctor at once. "A cardinal rule in medicine is that any rectal bleeding is potentially serious," says Dr. William. "It should never be taken lightly. Ninety-five, even ninety-nine percent of all rectal bleeding is from things like warts, fissures, fistulas, or hemorrhoids. Maybe one percent is something serious, like rectal cancer. If you find this early, it's curable. If you find it late, it's not."

**Can anal intercourse cause cancer?** There is not an iota of evidence that the incidence of rectal cancer is higher among gay men than straights. Should anyone try to convince you otherwise, simply ask to see the evidence. None will be forthcoming.

**What about prostatitis?** Prostatitis, or inflammation of the prostate gland, is sometimes caused by bacteria that enter the urethra during anal sex. It can also be a side effect of penile gonorrhea. Another common cause is lots of sexual activity followed by periods of sudden abstinence, which is why prostatitis is sometimes known as "the priest's disease."

Symptoms can include burning during urination, painful ejaculation, and, if the gland is swollen, dribbling after urination has stopped. The most frightening symptom, however, is bloody semen.

Simon, one of the men we interviewed, was recently called home to the small town in which he grew up because of his father's terminal illness. The deathwatch lasted an exhausting ten days. The night before the funeral, Simon decided to relieve his tension by masturbating, and was terrified when he spurted blood. Was it a venereal disease or cancer? he asked himself. Under the circumstances, he felt reluctant to contact the only doctor available, the aging general practitioner who had delivered him.

Simon was so distraught and preoccupied during the funeral that he succeeded in laying a guilt trip of monumental proportions on himself: Here he was, burying his father, and all he could think of was that bloody semen. He reports that he became so irrational that, at graveside, he struck a bargain with God to the effect that if this *wasn't* cancer, he'd go straight.

He compounded the stress and guilt by leaving his mother and family earlier than was deemed seemly so that he could fly to his doctor in New York, whom he telephoned the moment he landed.

"Nothing to worry about," said the doctor. "It sounds like prostatitis, and it'll clear up in no time with antibiotics. But no screwing until it does. I'll see you tomorrow morning."

**What about hemorrhoids?** Hemorrhoids, or piles, result from the enlargement of veins in the wall of the rectum or in the anus and can be caused by acute constipation and straining during defecation. There is no evidence that they're caused by anal intercourse; although no research exists to support the claim, many gay men report that anal intercourse can actually cure them. Nevertheless, if you have them and they're painful during intercourse, or if there's bleeding, see your doctor.

# 4.
# Sexual Dysfunction

Rick and Dennis had locked eyes in a bar only hours before. Now, in a state of sweet exhaustion, they were lying naked on the floor, in front of a dancing fire.

"I know it sounds hokey, but that was the best sex I've ever had."

"Me too," sighed Dennis, looking at the incredible body stretched out next to him. "Think we could ever improve on it?"

"I doubt it," said Rick, "but I wouldn't mind trying."

There was no trying involved. The second time was as natural and flowing as the first. Their third time round, upon awakening in each other's arms, was even better.

Over the course of the next several weeks, Rick and Dennis became infatuated with each other. Dennis liked to tell friends that the mere smell of Rick was sufficient to give him an erection; Dennis claimed that all it took for him was a fleeting glance at Rick's muscular, hairy, beautifully sculpted legs. The two men were more than compatible—sexually, they seemed designed for each other.

The decision to take an apartment together was inevitable. After lugging furniture and heavy boxes all day, they celebrated in front of the hearth with a take-out dinner and a bottle of fine champagne. Then it was off to their brand-new bed for the usual marvelous sex, replete with multiple orgasms. But Rick was unable to get an erection.

"Jesus, Rickie, I hope you didn't wreck your back lifting that couch."

"I don't think so. I think I'm just worn out."

"Not to mention all that champagne!"

"Sure that's it . . . it's a combination. Guess I'm not the marathon man you thought I was."

The following morning wasn't any better. Although Rick woke with his usual erection, it disappeared after he urinated, and there was no retrieving it. When they tried again that night, Dennis was finally able to coax some life into Rick's cock, but that's as far as it went—even after trying everything in their not so slim volume of tricks, Rick couldn't come.

As the situation failed to improve, Rick's anxiety mounted to such a degree that he was unable to sleep. To combat the insomnia, which was crippling him at the office, he would sit up until the small hours with a bottle of wine, and sometimes two, until he passed out.

Dennis found it quite easy to convince himself that Rick didn't love him anymore. He began drinking heavily himself and became so chronically depressed that he'd experience a nightly crying jag. Rick tried to assume all the blame, but Dennis was having none of it. No, the truth had to be that Rick no longer loved him, and the sooner he admitted it the better off they'd be.

Rick's cock had become his enemy, one he was determined to conquer. He tried solitary masturbation, always fantasizing a hot scene with the estranged Dennis. But his arm would wear out before he could approach a climax. When he tried doing without the wine, the anxiety would become unbearable. Drinking, he rationalized, was preferable to popping pills.

Unable to take the crying jags and recriminations any longer, Rick began doing his drinking in a nearby gay bar, one equipped with a "back room." Awash in drunken curiosity one night, he decided to have a look, walked in, and was promptly groped.

Despite his alcoholic intake, Rick's erection was instantaneous and rock hard. Before he realized what was happening, an anonymous somebody was giving him head. Less than a minute later, Rick came like he'd never come before.

Alice and Pat, like many gay women, did not put as much emphasis on sex as most gay men do. For them, the security and warmth of a comfortable home, happily alive with romping dogs, was an ongoing high that meant more than what they could find between the sheets.

They did sleep together, and when they felt like it, which was once a week or so, they would make love. Pat always had an orgasm, and sometimes two or three. Alice, try as she might, and although she would come close, just couldn't get off. But nothing to worry about, they assured themselves. As every woman knows, that sort of thing isn't all that important. On occasion, they'd joke about getting a vibrator, but nothing ever came of it.

Alice's forte was cooking. Whenever she felt irritable or down, she could always elevate her mood by plunging into the kitchen and whipping up a chocolate mousse, which she herself would consume in one sitting.

On New Year's Eve, her birthdays, and the morning after each big holiday, Alice would resolve to do something about her increasing weight. It was a task that always failed. Pat, who might have helped, chose not to; she liked Alice just as she was and would pull the old "there's more of you to love" routine. Moreover, Pat would remind Alice that fat people are sweet in temper and warm of heart.

But Alice was becoming anything but. The joys of homemaking, including looking after a growing family of dogs and making love with Pat, were becoming a burden. Ill at ease more often than not, she began requiring more and more caloric overdoses to keep cheerful. She also began experiencing backaches, vague abdominal discomfort, and a sense of pelvic fullness, all of which she attributed to being overweight.

Joe had never had a lover and, at the age of twenty-two, had no intention of trying to find one. Within weeks after moving to San Francisco, where he had always dreamed of living, he had managed to compartmentalize his life quite neatly and felt no need to share it with anyone. A job as a computer programmer working the night shift left him free to spend his mornings shopping, sightseeing, and cruising. Afternoons were for sleeping, early evenings for television and an occasional movie.

Although he disdained tearooms, baths, and bars, he had become addicted to cruising Buena Vista Park, which was near his utilitarian but comfortable little flat. As often as three mornings a week he would stop there before going home, pick up a stranger, take him home, have sex, give him a cup of coffee, and say goodbye. There were never repeat performances.

As the pattern continued, Joe was spending less and less time with his tricks. Sometimes, he'd get so excited upon entering the flat that he'd come with one or two self-administered strokes of the hand while watching his trick undress.

Eventually, he dispensed with the flat altogether and confined his sex to the bushes, where his mute encounters lasted as little as two minutes. One foggy morning, however, saw a departure from the usual wordless scenes: Joe was arrested by a vice squad officer and charged with importuning.

What Rick, Alice, and Joe have in common is that all are gay, and all are experiencing some form of sexual dysfunction, be it "impotence," "retarded ejaculation," "orgasmic incompetence," or "premature ejaculation." But the key common denominator is that all are suffering the stress of anxiety, of which their various sexual concerns are symptoms. Rick, Alice, and Joe actually exist, and all three were cured once they recognized what was truly causing their distress.

Rick's experience in the bar jolted him into an awareness that there was certainly nothing physically wrong with him. But if he could get it up for a shadowy figure in a back room, why not for Dennis? Why had everything gone so wrong so suddenly? Just as he was considering psychotherapy, Rick found the courage to confide in a friend, who was able to help unearth the root of the problem: The act of setting up housekeeping with Dennis was unconsciously symbolic of commitment, and his impotence was his body's way of saying "I'm not so sure about this move, so until I am, I'll just bring everything to a screeching halt." It didn't happen overnight, but once Rick realized that he did love Dennis, as a whole person and not just as a body, he was able to make a conscious commitment, one that freed his body to say "yes."

Alice was also fortunate enough to solve her problem without costly psychotherapy. Her physiological symptoms—the backaches, abdominal discomfort, and a sense of pelvic fullness—finally drove her to a gynecologist, who was herself a gay woman. Alice learned that the weekly sexual stimulation she was "enjoying" with Pat, because it always stopped short of orgasm, was causing pelvic congestion and affecting her general well-being. The gynecologist, while not a psychiatrist, was savvy enough to point out that Alice was so anxious to please Pat that she was squelching her own needs. A vicious circle had developed in which Alice thought that one way to please *Pat*, ironically enough, was to have an orgasm. Her anxiety was so stressful that all she was accomplishing was proving the axiom that when it comes to sex, the best way to make something *not* happen is to work at it. The compulsive eating, she learned, was an inappropriate and dangerous way of trying to please herself. The gynecologist asked that Pat and Alice come in for a conference, one aimed at providing a framework within which the two lovers could articulate their needs and feelings. As a result, Alice is learning that it's okay to enjoy herself in bed. And with Pat's help, she is also eating properly, thereby dropping the pounds that were bound to shorten her life.

After Joe was arrested in Buena Vista Park, he contacted an attorney who, for a fee of two thousand dollars, was able to have the charge of making improper advances dismissed. The shame of being arrested, however, not to mention the financially crippling legal fee, created such stress that he consulted a psychiatrist, who was humane enough to defer all charges until Joe had paid off the attorney.

In Joe's case, psychotherapy was probably necessary. It took almost three years to ferret out the lifelong problems and patterns that had led to the traumatic payoff of being arrested for his sexual behavior, but Joe now regards the course of treatment as the best investment he ever made.

Raised in rural southern Illinois by Calvinistic parents, Joe was taught that sex was a dirty if necessary evil, one that must be confined to marriage for the sole purpose of making babies. Under no circumstances (including masturbation) was it ever to be enjoyed, and to indulge in it outside of marriage would court disease, unwanted pregnancies, and eternal damnation.

He was spied on constantly, as were his two older sisters, whose menstrual periods were duly noted by a watchful, calendar-wielding Mom. Shortly after reaching puberty, he recalls, he was sitting crosslegged on his bed, repairing a model airplane, and spilled some glue on the sheets. When Mom discovered the stains, which she took for semen, he was reported to Dad, who took him to the basement and thrashed him with a paddle fashioned from the slat of an orange-crate.

There was only one bathroom in the house and it could not be locked. Still, it was the safest place he could masturbate when at home. Whenever he was relatively certain of not being disturbed, he would rush in, accomplish the urgent deed, and be out within minutes.

As his psychiatrist led him to discover, Joe had been forced to compartmentalize sex, confining it to certain periods of the day and getting it over with as soon as possible. Joe also learned that his hang-up wasn't homosexuality per se, but sexuality period. And what did he fantasize during his brief encounters in the little flat, and later in the park? An incredible montage consisting of bottles of Elmer's Glue-All, sticky sheets, orange-crate slats, doors without locks, and the railings of a preacher in a church that stank of stale varnish. The only way to dispel these threatening images was to come as quickly as possible and not get caught. When he did get caught that foggy morning by an authority figure to end all authority figures, it was as though Mom and Dad had suddenly materialized, right there in the bushes. "You're under arrest!" became "See? We told you so!"

Now two years out of therapy, Joe is learning to integrate sex rather than confine it. As a result, he is enjoying encounters that consist of more than a premature ejaculation triggered by anxiety. He's even thinking of trying to find Mr. Right and settle down.

Rick, Alice, and Joe were once seriously ill. Their unresolved anxieties had begun assuming some amazingly convoluted and health-threatening forms that were leading to a multiplicity of behavioral problems. But because a degree of anxiety is a normal part of the human condition, *occasional* dysfunction, be it temporary impotence in men or a lack of sexual response in women, is nothing to fret over. Statistically, dysfunction affects almost fifty percent of gays and straights alike at any given time.

Dysfunction can be considered normal when it results from sexual incompatibility. Because sex is learned behavior, some men are unable to get it up when confronted with a practice that either holds no value for them or simply turns them off. A man, for example, may go limp if his partner tries to rim him but will respond eagerly to fellatio. Certain women, unable to enjoy vigorous vulva-to-vulva contact, may not be able to respond fully without mutual masturbation. In short, different strokes (!) for different folks. When partners are incompatible, their bodies will tell them so through sexual dysfunction. And unless they want to create a stressful situation, the body's messages will be heeded.

**When can dysfunction be considered abnormal?** When it is prolonged, and therefore health-threatening. For many gay and straight people, it can become both psychologically and physiologically devastating, leading to ulcers, migraines, insomnia, and even suicide.

When dysfunction is chronic, it is almost always the result of the anxiety generated by negative programming. Men and women may be eager to please their partners, but because of a low self-esteem, they feel they are failing. The resulting tension can cause erectile difficulties, in both penis and clitoris, and the inability to achieve an orgasm.

Another cause is fear or hatred of one's own homosexuality. When self-alienation, guilt, and repulsion are deeply rooted, they can make it impossible to derive or give pleasure from sex.

Negative programming is also responsible for the prevalent notion that sex must be a performance rather than a source of mutual pleasure. "Performance anxiety," as sex therapists call it, can result from the tremendous pressure in the gay community, particularly among men, to "do it" at the drop of a hat. A typical courtship, for example, lasts twenty minutes in a dark bar and moves on to an immediate physical encounter in an environment that is strange to at least one of the partners. According to Rodney Karr, Ph.D., of the University of California Human Sexuality Program, "it's absolutely amazing that there aren't more problems among gay men considering the lousy way people have sex—the fact that it works at all is a testimony to the human spirit."

Again, the pressure to score can often lead to isolated episodes of dysfunction that amount to no more than normal reactions to abnormal situations, namely, going home with someone when you really don't want to. If your mouth won't say no, the rest of your body will. Dysfunction in these circumstances can lead the "victim" to believe that there's something dreadfully wrong with him, and the resulting anxiety, if brooded over, can escalate to the point that serious problems develop.

One of the men I interviewed told me that after several episodes of "impotence" with a new trick he panicked, went to his doctor, and asked for help. Rightly understanding that practically all erectile difficulties are caused by anxiety, the doctor prescribed tranquilizers, which reduced not only the patient's anxiety, but his body's ability to be stimulated. "It took me three months to wake up to what my doctor was doing to me," he reports. "And then I woke up to what I'd been doing to myself."

**What else can cause dysfunction?**   Second to anxiety as an inhibitor to full sexual response is depression. If you've just lost your job, for example, you may be so bummed out that sex is the last thing you'd think about, let alone try performing.

Anger can dampen sexual enthusiasm. If you fight with your lover and storm out into the night to exact revenge, going to the baths could be disastrous. Peter and Tom, one of the couples I interviewed, can laugh about it now, but at the time it wasn't so funny. Following a verbal brawl, Peter took off, only to return several hours later screaming, "I hope you're satisfied . . . I went to the baths and couldn't even do anything!"

An adverse environment can affect response. If you find yourself at a truck stop in the dead of a bitter winter and climb in the back of the cab with a driver, you may be impotent because you're shivering. The body has strict priorities, and warmth comes before sex.

Psychological distractions can contribute to temporary dysfunction. Getting up in the middle of a hot scene to answer a telephone, for example, can break the spell for two gays just as surely as the pitter-patter of little feet and the plaintive cry, "Mommy, I wanna drink of water," can spoil the fun and games of a heterosexual couple.

Fatigue can render sex impossible. If you're physically exhausted, your body will say "no" for the simple reason that it wants to rest, not indulge in activities that will consume more energy. Don't force it to do what it plainly tells you it doesn't want to do.

A variety of physical conditions can affect sexual response. Following a prolonged, debilitating illness of any sort, the body needs a great deal of rest before resuming sex. If you'll listen to it, it will tell you when it's ready. A substantial period of recovery can also be required following the trauma of a serious accident or surgery. Operations for cancer of the prostate and colon are markedly clear causes of temporary impotence in men. In women, a hysterectomy can affect sexual response. Diabetes, damage to the spinal cord, untreated genital diseases (including gonorrhea and syphilis) and simply growing old can be inhibiting.

**Can smoking cause problems?**  It took years to establish the links between smoking, lung cancer, heart disease, bronchitis, and emphysema, and it may take a lot more years before you read the following warning on your pack of cigarettes: "The Surgeon General Has Determined That Cigarette Smoking Is Dangerous to Your Health—Including Your Sex Life."

The clinical evidence that smoking inhibits sexual response is as yet insubstantial, but it is beginning to come in. It is already known that cigarettes can impair sexual performance in three ways. First, nicotine constricts the blood vessels, the expansion of which is essential to sexual excitement and the subsequent erection of both penis and clitoris. Second, the intake of carbon monoxide that accompanies smoking reduces the level of oxygen in the blood and plays havoc with hormone production. Third, because heavy smoking reduces lung capacity, stamina is diminished. We sometimes forget that among other things, sex is vigorous exercise.

Joel Fort, M.D., director of San Francisco's Center for Solving Special Social and Health Problems, has been urging smokers who come in complaining of impotence and poor response to enroll in the Center's stop-smoking program. Almost all of those who kick the habit find that their sex lives improve considerably.

In France a recently published study of the effects of age and tobacco on the libido gives further credence to the idea that smoking is a turn-off. Seventy men, ranging in age from forty-five to ninety, were divided into two groups—thirty-one who smoked one or more packs a day, and thirty-nine who were either nonsmokers or consumers of less than five cigarettes a day. All of the men studied had experienced a decline in sexual response between the ages of twenty-five and forty, which can be considered normal. But there was a significant difference between the smokers and the nonsmokers in that sexual activity between twenty-five and forty, the so-called prime of life, decreased more rapidly in the first group than in the second.

**What about drugs and alcohol?** We'll be discussing them in greater detail in the following chapter. In the meantime, suffice it to say that alcohol, while it can temporarily mask fatigue and relax psychological inhibitions, is a depressant when consumed in large quantities and can drown sexual response in both men and women. Certain drugs, particularly downers, have the same effect. Stimulants, or uppers, can heighten an anxiety that is already present. When drugs and alcohol are mixed, the body becomes so confused that it will often opt out and become incapable of even the minimum response.

**What is the sexual response cycle in men?** Masters and Johnson, in *Human Sexual Response*, have described the *maximum* sexual response of both men and women as a *completion* of a cycle consisting of four consecutive, and admittedly rather arbitrary, phases: excitement, plateau, orgasm, and resolution. No bells ring when we move from one phase to the other; and although excitement and resolution generally last the longest, there are no "normal" time spans for the duration of any one phase. Erection, for example (the beginning of the excitement phase in men), can occur gradually or in as little as three seconds, and it can be lost rapidly or slowly.

Physiologically, male erection depends on small valves in the arteries and veins that regulate the penis's blood supply. Known by urologists as "pillars," they generally remain closed in the arteries that feed the penis and open in the veins that channel blood away from it. During excitement, the pillars in the arteries open more to permit a greater supply of blood to flow into the penis's spongy tissue, while the pillars in the veins close and don't permit the blood to leave. As a result, the penis becomes bloated, hard, and erect. When this process doesn't work, there's an erectile difficulty, one usually triggered by anxiety.

But when it does work, some sort of pressure on the erect penis is required to produce orgasm. One of the men we interviewed was able to experience an orgasm without friction or pressure of any kind, but it was during an LSD trip, while listening to Wagner's *Tristan und Isolde;* under normal conditions, spontaneous orgasm in men is exceedingly rare.

During the excitement phase, the heart rate quickens, the skin of the scrotum thickens, and muscular contractions pull the testes closer to the body. This first phase can be maintained for long periods, or it can be lost and retrieved, without orgasm, many times. With the onset of the plateau phase, the heart rate levels off, and the testicles are drawn still closer to the body. As orgasm approaches, the penis increases slightly in diameter near the tip, and the tip itself may change color, to a reddish-purple. In some men, there is a flushing of skin color around the chest, neck, and forehead. There can also be swelling and erection of the nipples and sweating from the soles, palms, and head. Ejaculation is preceded by fluid from the Cowper's gland, about one or two drops of clear, colorless liquid that neutralizes any acidity in the urethra left by urine; next comes the thin, milky fluid from the prostate; then the sticky, often yellowish fluid from the seminal vesicles.

Upon orgasm, there are muscular spasms in the face, chest, abdomen, and rectum (if you're in a position to see, watch how your partner's face changes); blood pressure, rate of breathing, and heartbeat rise to about two and a half times the normal level. The muscles around the urethra go into involuntary contractions, forcing the semen out of the penis under high pressure. Usually, there are three to four major bursts followed by weaker, more irregular contractions. After prolonged abstinence, semen can shoot three feet or more, assuming there's nothing in the way; but the average distance is seven to ten inches.

Most men ejaculate about 3.5 ml of semen, or what amounts to a teaspoon. After prolonged abstinence, it can be as high as 13 ml, or more than a tablespoon.

As a man enters the resolution phase, the flush disappears, and there is a rapid reduction in penis size. Because your partner's sphincter can act as a literal cock ring, impeding the flow of blood away from the penis, a partial erection can be maintained if you don't withdraw after ejaculating in anal intercourse. If your partner hasn't come yet, his pleasure can be heightened if you masturbate him (or blow him, if you're fucking face to face—and if you're supple enough!) while your semi-hard penis is still well up his rectum.

**Is it safe to swallow come?** The semen of a *healthy* man is perfectly fit for consumption by his partner. Sixty percent of the average ejaculation consists of fluid from the seminal vesicles, while another thirty-eight percent, from the prostate, gives come the characteristic aroma that many men liken to freshly cut grass. The remaining two percent includes other fluids and the sperm themselves; all of it is over ninety percent water.

**Does the size of your penis affect response?**  No. If you're relatively free of anxiety, you'll be able to function nicely whether you're hung like a stud horse or merely average. The idea that the more you've got, the more you enjoy it, does not apply to sexual satisfaction.

However, men who have become self-conscious about their size can experience less than satisfactory sex because they are anxious about being "too small." Just for the record, the longest erect penis for which there is reasonable scientific evidence measured an even foot. But if you're average, your erect penis will be about six and a quarter inches long; almost ninety percent of all men are between five and seven inches when hard. In its flaccid, or unexcited, state, the penis averages about three and three-quarters inches, with most men falling between three and a quarter to four and a quarter inches. Penises that look big when flaccid tend to gain less when erect, while a comparatively short one can grow by as much as three and three-quarters inches.

In some quarters, gay folk wisdom has it that longer penises are easier to take up the ass than smaller ones, which tend to keep coming out; but if you're on the receiving end, length is unimportant as long as you're relaxed. And if your partner knows what he's doing, there shouldn't be any problems with fallout.

There is nothing you can do, including plastic surgery, to increase the size of your cock. Again, vacuum devices, regardless of advertised claims, will *not* do the job.

**What is the sexual response cycle in women?**  The four phases are more clearly defined than in men, for whom the excitement phase is often very short; women, however, get aroused much more slowly.

The first sign of excitement is lubrication of the vagina, which begins to swell until the inner two-thirds doubles in diameter. The inner lips swell and darken, the clitoris becomes erect and wildly sensitive to touch, the breasts enlarge, and the nipples become hard. The uterus enlarges and elevates within the pubic cavity, heart and breathing rates increase, and a flush, or even what looks like a rash, may appear on the skin.

The beginning of the plateau period is generally marked by the narrowing of the outer third of the vagina. In heterosexual women, this allows the vagina to grip the penis during intercourse; in gay women, it permits a great deal of pleasure, because as the outer third of the vagina contracts, it becomes quite sensitive to pressure.

As arousal continues, the entire genital area continues to swell, as do the breasts. The uterus elevates fully. Breathing is rapid, more like panting. During this phase the clitoris retracts under its hood. Stimulation of the inner lips from a partner's hand or tongue, or the pressure of vulva-to-vulva contact, moves the hood back and forth over the glans.

Once a man is on the threshold of orgasm, there is little that can hold him back; if a woman is to achieve orgasm, however, the stimulation of the clitoris—the epicenter of female orgasm—must not be interrupted. When orgasm finally comes, it is supported and intensified by three to fifteen rhythmic contractions of the outer third of the vagina. The uterus and rectum also contract, releasing the blood trapped in pelvic veins, thereby relieving the congestion that can result from long periods of abstinence, or from being stimulated just to the point of orgasm, but not beyond it.

If a woman is effectively stimulated, she can have limitless orgasms, a phenomenon that led Masters and Johnson to speak of the female's "superior physiological capacity for sexual response."

Nancy Press Hawley, Elizabeth A. McGee, and Wendy Coppedge Sanford, in their chapter on sexuality in *Our Bodies, Ourselves*, a book by and for women, have approached the phenomenon with more common sense than anyone else, and their advice is applicable to straight and gay women alike:

> The knowledge that we are physiologically capable of having many orgasms has led many of us to feel that not only must we reach orgasm, but we must have several orgasms. If the old trap was low expectations, the new problem . . . is excessive expectations. We don't know finally what full human functioning is, so in the meantime try to enjoy what feels good to you.

**What problems can women experience?** Sexual dysfunctions in women can take many forms, depending on individual circumstances; but generally they can be summarized under three headings: difficulties having orgasms; no interest in sex at all, which is sometimes called sexual aversion; and physical pain during sex.

Women who have trouble reaching orgasms—either alone or with a lover—are suffering a variety of problems, which Hawley, McGee, and Stanford summarize as follows:

> We don't notice or else we misunderstand what's happening in our bodies as we get aroused. We're too busy thinking about abstractions—how to do it right, why it doesn't go well for us, what our lover thinks of us, whether our lover is impatient . . . when we might better be concentrating on sensations, not thoughts.
>
> We feel ourselves becoming aroused, but we are afraid we won't have an orgasm, and we don't want to get into the hassle of trying, so we just repress sexual response.
>
> We hold our breath the more excited we get and cut off the feeling of our own orgasms.
>
> We can't tolerate too much pleasure and our orgasms—if we have them—are less satisfying and intense than they could be.
>
> We are afraid of asking too much and seeming too demanding.
>
> We are trying to have a simultaneous orgasm—which seldom occurs for most of us. It can be just as pleasurable if we come separately.
>
> We are deeply conflicted about, and often angry at, the person we are sleeping with. Unconsciously we withhold orgasm as a way of withholding ourselves.
>
> We feel guilty . . . and so cannot let ourselves really enjoy it.*

Although directed toward women, these impediments to full sexual response are equally applicable to men, regardless of sexual preference.

Sexual aversion in women, which used to be known as "frigidity," can occur when there is basic disagreement between a woman

---

*Excerpted from Nancy Press Hawley, Elizabeth A. McGee, and Wendy Coppedge Sanford. "Sexuality," in *Our Bodies, Ourselves,* the Boston Women's Health Book Collective. New York: Simon & Schuster, 1976, p. 57.

and her lover about who is going to take the active role. "If you have to argue about who's going to do what to whom," says one woman, "then I feel like, who needs it?"

Sexual aversion can also occur because a woman is absorbed in some personal problem, or because she's fatigued or angry. Women (and men, too) can block their sexual feelings with anxiety and fear. Sometimes there are conflicts about sexuality that run so deep that an interest in sex is all but impossible. Some women even report an extreme, unpleasant sensitivity to touch, or may feel so tickled that they can't relax.

On the positive side, an *occasional* episode of sexual aversion is normal and healthy. Regardless of gender, our bodies react the way they do for a reason, and a respite from sex now and again gives us a chance to figure out what's bothering us, provided that we take the opportunity to learn from it.

**What can a woman do to solve these problems?** The cornerstone of all sexual therapy, for men and women, is masturbation—a delightful, healthy practice that gives us the time and space to explore and experiment with our own bodies. Masturbation, says Betty Dodson, author of *Liberating Masturbation: A Meditation On Self Love*, "is our sexual base. Everything we do beyond that is simply how we choose to socialize our sex life."

From the moment of birth, all of us began learning that we could make ourselves feel good by exploring our bodies with our hands, whether those explorations were explicitly sexual or not. Later, many of us were taught by parents, teachers, and churches that playing with ourselves was taboo, consequently, by the time we were teenagers, we thought masturbation was bad. If we did it, we felt guilty; if we didn't, it was because we were afraid of our sexual feelings and tried to push them away.

For many adults, guilt and repression—reactions that we first learned to associate with masturbation—are now mixed up with sexuality in general. Masturbation can open us up again to healthy sex, because it puts us back in touch with our bodies, and with the origins of our negative attitudes.

Make a date with yourself, at a quiet time when you can be alone. A long, relaxing bath, followed by rubbing yourself all over with a cream or lotion, is an excellent way to begin. Some women

I've talked to like to lower the lights, put on a favorite record, have a glass of wine, smoke a joint, or anything else that will help them mellow out. Fantasies begin when you let your body relax and your mind flow freely to those women and situations that you find sexually arousing.

There are many techniques available to women, so don't be afraid to experiment. Some women like to masturbate by moistening the fingers with saliva, vaginal secretions, or creams and rubbing the clitoris. Still others cross their legs and exert a steady, rhythmic pressure on the genital area. Vibrators are also helpful. But remember that enjoying yourself doesn't just mean the clitoris, vagina, and breasts. By letting go in masturbation, you can learn to enjoy all parts of your body.

Making up sexual fantasies during masturbation is not only exciting, but healthy. The important thing is to let go to the extent that you can begin enjoying your sensations. "Masturbation opens me to what is happening in my body and makes me feel good about myself," says a woman. "I like following the impulse of the moment. Sometimes I have many orgasms, sometimes I don't have any. The greatest source of pleasure is to be able to do whatever feels good to me at that particular time. I rarely have such complete freedom in other aspects of my life."

Once you've learned what really turns you on, don't be afraid to articulate your needs to a partner. Nor should you be afraid to use nonverbal communication, sometimes of a highly directive nature: Take your partner's hand and put it where you want it, or make the noises that will let her know that what she's doing pleases you.

**What about pain during sex?**  Remember, pain is the body's way of saying that something is wrong. If you experience it during sex, it could be for a number of reasons, including endometriosis (see Chapter Six). Vaginal infections, which are sometimes unnoticed, can be exacerbated by the friction of instrumentation, resulting in stinging and itching. You and your partner should see a doctor about medication that will clear the infection. Local irritation of the vagina and inner lips can result from the so-called feminine hygiene sprays. If you've been using one of these and experience itching, don't just switch brands, stop using any of them. They are totally unnecessary. Bodily secretions and smells are natural. As long as you're healthy, and if you wash regularly, you'll smell and taste good to your partner.

Pain can also result from insufficient lubrication during instrumentation. Be sure to give the vagina plenty of time to become moist. If you still feel dry, you can use K-Y or Albolene cream, but not Vaseline, which is too greasy. After menopause, a lack of estrogen can result in the production of less vaginal liquid. Lubricants help, but you may wish to talk to your doctor about a course of hormone therapy.

The clitoris itself, because of its incredible sensitivity, can hurt if fingered or tongued directly. Genital secretions can collect under the hood, so when you wash, always pull it back and gently clean it.

Finally, don't forget the importance of a yearly gynecological examination to make sure that there are no physical difficulties that can threaten your health, including sexual functioning.

**Can you have sex while menstruating?**   Yes, but this is a matter of personal preference. If you're suffering from menstrual cramps, they can sometimes be relieved through orgasm, either by having sex with your partner or by solitary masturbation.

**Are there drugs that solve sex problems?**   If you and your physician conclude that you're one of the *very* rare individuals whose dysfunction is not being caused by anxiety or any of the other psychological culprits (such as depression, anger, or a poor self-image), you might consider some form of drug therapy. Drugs and hormones don't help except for those who are dysfunctional for physiological reasons. If this is your case, your physician will refer you to an endocrinologist.

**What are the most common problems in men?**   Sex therapists surveyed by *The Advocate* report that at least half of their gay clients come in with erectile difficulties. Another thirty percent complain of retarded ejaculations, while the remaining twenty percent comsists of premature ejaculators, an interesting reversal from the heterosexual dysfunction figures, in which PEs, as they are known, far outnumber REs.

It is also interesting to note how sex therapists shy away from "impotence," a word that puts heavy pressure on someone, according to Jose Guitierrez, a clinical psychologist in the University of California Human Sexuality Program. "It means powerlessness," he says, "as if all power were wrapped up in the ability to get an erection."

But regardless of the semantics, when a gay man approaches a therapist for help with his dysfunction, the therapist can be certain that the client has a serious problem. Unlike most gay women, who tend to share their sexual concerns with peers, gay men are generally threatened by dysfunction and will discuss it only when the anxiety becomes unbearable.

When there are no underlying physiological problems, which only a physician can determine, treatment can consist of self-care at home. Sometimes the cure is disarmingly simple. One of Dr. Karr's clients at the UC Human Sexuality Program, for example, always had sex in the dark, until he developed the inability to get it up. Dr. Karr directed him to try having sex in a variety of settings, including one with the lights on. Once out of the darkness, the client was able to get an erection immediately. "He discovered it was a turn-on to see his partner," Dr. Karr told *The Advocate*. "It brought a whole new sense modality."

However, the first step in sex therapy, whether it is directed or at home on your own, is generally a moratorium on sex, including masturbation. "You can usually hear a sigh of relief go up when you tell them that," says Guitierrez.

Charles Silverstein, Ph.D., director of New York's Institute of Human Identity and co-author of *The Joy of Gay Sex*, believes that the no-sex rule, which should last two to three weeks, frees a man with erectile difficulties from the responsibility and pressure to *perform*. At the end of the moratorium, Dr. Silverstein suggests the giving and receiving of massage. After two or three sessions, one can go on to genital massage, but if an erection develops, he should stop immediately and let it go down.

"This is called the 'stop-start' technique," says Dr. Silverstein. "Its purpose is to show you that though this may be your first hard-on in quite a while it will not be your last."

Your partner should then retrieve your erection with either hand or mouth, let it subside, give you a chance to relax, and repeat the exercise three to four times. Finally, he should stimulate you to orgasm. "Normal" sex can follow on a regular basis provided that you don't place yourself in a situation where everything depends on your ability to get it up immediately, as in tearoom quickies, for an extreme example.

Contrary to popular belief, most gay men truly appreciate "failure" in their partners from time to time because it relieves *them* of the responsibility of performing at peak capacity. The next time you're with a trick who suddenly goes limp you might reflect on this. If you do, the next time *you* go limp on a trick and he tells you that it's okay, you're apt to find yourself believing and trusting him.

**What's the treatment for ejaculatory problems?** Jack Morin, a San Francisco sex therapist, believes that PEs begin the arousal cycle with a high degree of tension. Rather than permitting orgasm to evolve from a gradual build-up, the PE triggers the orgasmic reflex almost immediately after sexual contact is made.

Retarded ejaculation stems from anxieties that are manifested in the opposite way, whereas PEs have too little awareness of their bodies, REs have too much. Characteristically, the RE *works* at having an orgasm. The ejaculatory reflex, however, while involuntary, can be blocked by conscious attempts to activate it. As with most sexual dysfunction, the more you work at solving the problem, the more anxieties build, and the worse the problem becomes.

The mode of treatment for PE and RE is also based on the masturbatory stop-start technique. If you're a PE, you should ask your lover or an understanding friend to jerk you off just to the point of coming. As he does so, it's important to be alert to any signals of impending ejaculation. When you "hear" these signals, stop. Repeat the exercise several times, then go ahead and come. Subsequent sessions should consist of sucking and fucking, in that order, using the stop-start technique. The important thing is to go slowly and pause frequently so that you can monitor your body's messages.

Another approach to PE is the "squeeze technique" developed by Masters and Johnson. Ask your friend to sit on the bed with his back against the headboard, then sit between his legs with your back to him while he masturbates you. When you're so close to coming that you can't stop yourself, warn him. He will then press the tip of your penis quite firmly between his thumb and first two fingers for three to four seconds (it doesn't hurt), and you will lose the urge to come. This exercise should be repeated four to five times a session. You can then go ahead and have "normal" sex. The squeeze technique is generally used for six months to a year, and always before at least one session of anal or oral intercourse a week. Who says that therapy can't be fun?

PEs can sometimes be cured with a counseling session or two. It may be that you've been using sex to explode tensions caused by problems at work. You may feel that if you can come as quickly as possible, you'll be able to relax and so you come on like gangbusters. Although sex can explode tensions, its primary purpose is the giving and receiving of pleasure, which involves the expression of affection. By sorting out your problems at work with a counselor or a friend, you may come to the realization that you've been using sex inappropriately.

Retarded Ejaculators can also be helped through counseling sessions in which they are directed to ask themselves some key questions: Have your bouts of retarded ejaculation occurred when you were nursing a resentment against your partner? Were you coming down with a cold at the time? Had you been drinking quite a bit? Were you doing any drugs? Are you able to reach an easy climax when you're masturbating by yourself? An affirmative answer to any of these can indicate an acceptable reason for a retarded ejaculation, one that suggests that the problem is not serious and need not be brooded over.

When retarded ejaculation lasts longer than several months, however, some form of treatment is in order. Dr. Silverstein recommends what he calls a "desensitization" exercise, a gradual conditioning process that sounds silly when described, but one that often works:

Begin by asking your lover or an understanding sex partner to sit in the next room while you masturbate (his physical presence could increase your self-consciousness—and anxiety). The following night, try calling him into the room just as you're about to come, but with the prior understanding that he not look at you directly. The next time, begin masturbating when he's in the room with you—at first with his back to you, then facing you as you approach orgasm. Eventually, let him sit next to you while you jerkoff and finish the job for you just as you're about to come. Finally, try fucking him after you've reached the plateau phase.

The most difficult aspect of treatment for dysfunction is finding that understanding partner. If you're having a problem with your lover, you can always go out and have sex with someone else, as can he, if he's lost patience with you. And how many people do you know who would be willing to help you, assuming that you find them attractive enough and assuming further that you have the guts to ask them?

As a last resort for clients who can't find their own partners, San Francisco's Jack Morin recommends the services of a sex surrogate, an attractive young man known as James Garver. When interviewed by *The Advocate*, Garver insisted that he's simply a professional doing his job. The 23-year-old man was trained in sex education at the San Francisco Sex Information Council and dutifully chronicles his surrogate experiences, which go toward credit for his college degree.

"By the time people are to the point of seeing a sex surrogate," says Garver, "they have very serious concerns about the way they're relating to other people. My job is to give the client a safe environment in which to find what turns him on."

That environment is Garver's home, where he teaches everything from massage techniques to comfortable sexual positions. Sometimes, he reports, his role demands that he delve into such abstract areas as his client's most secret sexual fantasies; at other times, he concerns himself with such banal topics as what brands of lubricants to use. Treatment usually runs no longer than ten sessions and is generally successful, he claims.

Garver is emphatic that his job does not exist to serve the client's sexual needs, but merely as a "catalyst" for getting in sexual touch. Similarly, he seeks to fulfill no needs of his own, sexual or otherwise, as he feels that to do so would be unprofessional. When asked if there isn't a fine line between prostitution and the work of a sex surrogate, he replied:

"I think prostitution is a wonderful profession, but it's not what I do. If someone were paying me just to get his rocks off, I probably wouldn't be very good for him. I'd want to be giving him lessons and exercises for improvement, which might not go over very well."

**How do you find a sex therapist?** If you're looking for a professional one, you might have some luck if you live in San Francisco or New York, where therapists with a broader understanding of gay sexual concerns are concentrated. Ask for a referral from a gay-oriented clinic; the therapist, if he feels it's necessary, can then refer you to a surrogate. But if you live outside San Francisco or New York, you'll find slim pickings. For that matter, you might have trouble in New York, although San Francisco is a city ten times smaller, that's where most of the therapists with a knowledge of gay problems and their employed surrogates can be found.

The few good straight therapists are often of little help to gay people. Some of them even refuse gay clients outright. If they do accept gay clients, ignorance about gay sexual techniques prevents them from knowing where to begin treatment. "In a word," says Dr. Silverstein, "the situation for gay people is awful."

But the outlook is slowly improving. More and more medical schools are requiring courses in sex instruction. In New York, Dr. Silverstein plans to start a one-year training program for gay sex therapists and surrogates at the Institute for Human Identity; and in San Francisco, the University of California Medical Center's Human Sexuality Program is sponsoring symposia on gay sexuality designed to sensitize the helping professions to gay problems.

Despite the often notable success of sex therapy, a lot of people, gays and professionals alike, feel that it's so much bullshit. Richard Pillard, M.D., associate professor of medicine at Boston University and the medical advisor to Boston's Homophile Community Health Services, told *The Advocate* that he is skeptical about sex therapy altogether.

"There's certainly a demand for it," he says, "but these fads come and go. Everybody who's read Masters and Johnson calls himself a sex therapist now. Because the field is new, it's without licensing or registration requirements."

The therapists surveyed by *The Advocate*, however, argue that the behavioral approach is a move in the right direction and far more effective than its predecessors. Most physicians, as previously noted, treat sexual problems with tranquilizers, which relieve anxiety but diminish the body's sexual response. Nor does psychotherapy have a good track record with sexual problems. "In sex therapy," says Dr. Silverstein, "at least you talk about sex—not how you related to your mother."

Therapists such as Morin carry the optimism a step further by claiming that a recovered victim of sexual woes is actually better off than when he was during the period prior to their onset. "The point of all this," he told *The Advocate*, "is not to make people normal. In this society, to be sexually 'normal' is to be crippled. The goal is to get people to discover the full potential of their sexuality. They come out of the experience better than normal."

**Can you discover sexual potential without therapy?** If you free yourself up to the point that you give your fantasies full rein, and if you're able to articulate your needs and anxieties with your partner, you can. Don't be afraid to experiment. If you find your partner's feet attractive and fantasize about "shrimping" (sucking his or her toes, which can be a marvelous turn-on for both of you), then do it. If you're anxious about your partner thinking that you're a "foot fetishist," you can dissolve that anxiety by simply articulating it. Heterosexual men who are turned on by a provocative bustline aren't often called breast fetishists, nor are people who enjoy holding and kissing hands pointed out as hand fetishists. Break out of negative programming by reminding yourself that in sex, no part of the body is taboo.

Don't ever be hesitant about talking during sex; if it turns you and your partner on, as well it might, use language that would shame an Albanian stevedore.

An amazing number of gay people, both men and women, are deluded by the notion that sexual potential with a partner is realized only when orgasms are simultaneous; consequently, they work so hard at achieving what someone has programmed them to believe is the ultimate trip that they block their potential. The most sophisticated partners know that the joy of simultaneous orgasm is a myth. They know that it's often more exciting to watch a male partner squirting a stream of hot spunk, or listen to a woman's moans of orgasmic pleasure, before coming themselves. When simultaneous orgasms do occur, they can be just as exciting because they are spontaneous, not worked at.

Remember, relationships and the sex that helps sustain them tend to break down not because the sex goes stale, but because communication falters with yourself, and with your partner.

When all else fails, one of the best ways to break through to your full sexual potential is to sit down with a list of the possible reasons for your unhappiness. If you think them through, you'll probably be able to identify the cause of your dysfunction, or the lack of what *you* feel full sexual response should be. Hawley,

McGee, and Sanford have worked out such a list, and it is an excellent guide for men and women alike:

We are so concerned with sexual images and goals we cannot think of sex outside the context of success/failure.

We grew up feeling that sex was bad and dirty and deep down we still feel that way.

We are afraid to follow our own feelings—we may not even be sure what they are.

We are ignorant of sexual facts that would help us.

We are too shy and embarrassed to ask for the sort of sexual stimulation we would like.

We fear if we ask for something different we will embarrass or threaten our lover, and our lover might leave.

We sleep with someone we are attracted to but cannot feel comfortable with.

We always have sex at the end of the day when we are tired.

We make love with someone with whom we are angry.

We have been with one partner for many years and are stuck in patterns that no longer excite us.

We expect to be instantly free and at ease with people we do not know well or feel very close to.

We do not have any friends with whom we can talk about our experiences, feelings, and concerns.

We don't have anyone we want to sleep with.*

**What about aphrodisiacs?** Chemically, you can forget them. Alcohol and drugs, as we'll learn in the following chapter, can at best lower inhibitions. There is, however, a highly potent mental aphrodisiac. When Henry Kissinger quipped that the ultimate aphrodisiac is power, he was right on. He might just as well have equated

---

*Hawley, McGee, and Sanford, *loc. cit.*

power with a healthy self-image, which is always hallmarked by self-control, as opposed to control by anxieties, anger, fears, worries, negative attitudes, and other tensions. If you feel good about yourself, your body will act those feelings out.

Physically, the best aphrodisiac is a good level of oxygen in the blood, which can heighten awareness. James F. Fixx, author of *The Complete Book of Running*, writes that "good physical condition involves not just muscles, the heart and the lungs but all the senses as well. Runners are more aware of themselves and of others and are able to participate more fully in all aspects of life, including the sexual." If your libido is sluggish, a sensible program of vigorous exercise, be it running, tennis, swimming, or a regimen of brisk walking in the open air, can perk it up almost at once.

If you believe the claim that it affects the libido, check your diet for deficiencies in vitamin E, which can be found in such foods as wheat germ, green peas, and green, leafy vegetables. If you *believe* that oysters on the half-shell and ginseng tea are aphrodisiacs, then they are, for you. With the exception of drugs, alcohol, and tobacco, this applies to practically anything you ingest. One of the men we interviewed knew perfectly well that raisins are not intrinsic aphrodisiacs, but he arbitrarily adopted them, psyched himself up to believe that they would make him horny, and they worked like an Oriental charm. Nominating some food or harmless substance as an aphrodisiac is a surprisingly effective game we can play with ourselves, one that can demonstrate the power of thought. Our raisin freak could have chosen peanut butter and achieved the same results.

To bring the matter full circle, a healthy self-image is the best agent of all in breaking through to a joyful, liberating realization of the sexual potential that is ours by birthright. But without healthy living habits, which include good nutrition, exercise, and not getting snagged on drugs, alcohol, and tobacco, a healthy self-image—and a satisfactory sex life—will remain a will-o'-the-wisp, always beyond our grasp.

# 5.
# Alcohol and
# Other Drugs

By definition, a drug is any chemical compound that affects the functioning of the human body. The most popular drugs, beginning with alcohol, are psychoactive, that is, they cause changes in behavior and induce relaxation, euphoria, and hallucinations.

An understanding of how drugs work begins with a look at the nervous system. Each nerve consists of a chain of cells, called neurons, and between each cell there is a gap. When a message travels along the nerve, a chemical agent carries the impulse across the gap. Some neurons try to stop the message, while others attempt to pass it on. An impulse is transmitted only when the neurons that promote the message outnumber those that inhibit it.

When a drug slows this system down, it "depresses" the nervous system by reducing the effect of the chemical agent on the next neuron in the chain. Other drugs have the opposite effect in that they increase, or "stimulate," nervous activity. Depressants include alcohol, barbiturates, and opiates (opium, codein, morphine, heroin). In small doses, they are effective sedatives, and larger doses can induce sleep. Overdoses can kill. Tranquilizers fall into a special category of depressants, or "downers."

Stimulants, or "uppers," include caffeine, nicotine, the amphetamines, and cocaine. Because they increase nervous activity, they detract from the desire for sleep.

Hallucinogens, including mescaline, psilocybin, and LSD (lysergic acid diethylamide), because they affect the interpretation of incoming stimuli, produce bizarre hallucinations, delusions, and often dangerous reactions to normal situations.

Marijuana, although closely related to the hallucinogens, is in a category by itself, as is amyl nitrite.

## ALCOHOL

Lest you doubt that the downer known as alcohol is the industrialized world's most dangerous drug, read some of the grisly statistics:

Alcohol may be a factor in almost half of all drownings.

Forty to sixty percent of all bone fractures involve alcohol.

A third of all the general aviation pilots killed each year in plane crashes have a measurable blood-alcohol concentration in their bodies.

Annually, drinking drivers cause more than 800,000 car crashes in the United States alone and kill 25,000 people.

Half of all homicides and as high as sixty percent of all suicides are alcohol-related.

At any given time, thirteen to twenty-nine percent of the patients in *general* hospitals are alcoholics.

A third of the unexpected deaths among young adults can be attributed to alcoholism.

The average life expectancy of an alcoholic is 52 years.

If you don't drink at all, or if you drink only "socially," you may not think these statistics are personally meaningful. You may even be aware of the fact that moderate drinkers live longer than total abstainers.

But think again. Almost all of the gay men and gay women interviewed for this book asked if I had discovered any statistics proving the rumor that homosexuals don't live as long as straight people. No such statistics exist. *The Advocate,* however, has learned of an explosive study on alcoholism that concludes that *one in three members of the gay community is either an alcoholic or well on the way to becoming one.* Without help, that one in three—who could be your friend or lover—can expect to live approximately twenty years less than the average American. And because you may be unaware of the difference between drinking "socially" and drinking sensibly, that one in three could be *you.*

Randy Shilts, who analyzed the study for *The Advocate* and interviewed a number of professionals involved with gay alcoholism, agrees with its conclusion that the gay life-style is a highly dangerous breeding ground for alcoholism. "The parameters of the problem," he writes, "which one expert called 'astronomical,' far exceed those of the heterosexual world."

The pioneering study, financed by grants from Los Angeles County, was conducted by Lillene Fifield, M.S.W., for the Los Angeles Gay Community Services Center and was based on 200 regular gay bar-users. One in ten gay people in the Los Angeles area, she found, is in the "crisis or danger stages" of alcoholism and in need of professional services—a figure that agrees with the National Council on Alcoholism's estimate that one in ten of *all* Americans is alcoholic.

But Fifield also points to a "secondary target group," which numbers twenty-two percent of the Los Angeles gay population. This group is considered "high risk" and will eventually require treatment for alcoholism.

The one in three figure results when the high risk group of twenty-two percent is added to the ten percent who are in the crisis stage. *And it includes both men and women.* Although the lesbian subculture is not notably bar-oriented, Brenda Weathers, of the Los Angeles Alcoholism Project for Women says, "If you added other forms of drug abuse with alcoholism among lesbians, the figure would be even higher. It would be between thirty and forty percent."

With but one exception, the experts in gay alcoholism told *The*

*Advocate* that one in three was not an exaggeration; some even complained that it was too conservative. The expert who demurred pointed out that in the absence of any previous studies of gay alcoholism, it is difficult to judge the study's accuracy or applicability to other areas in the country. That Fifield limited her research exclusively to gay bar-users in one city raises a number of thorny questions: What percentage of gay persons are "bar-users?" Is it a higher or lower percentage than other minority groups? Than the heterosexual population? Would the same percentage prevail among "bar-users" in the swinging singles bars and discos?

The lone critic pointed out that studying "only gay bar-users is much like studying only gay people in psychiatric treatment and concluding that all gay people are sick."

Fifield's work will remain open to question until further studies might substantiate or modify it. In the meantime, a fair conclusion might be that where there's smoke, there's fire. We don't need statistics to tell us what we already know—that alcohol is a prominent aspect of our gay life-style, one that causes lots of problems. If the statistics have a final purpose, it is to make us aware of just how health-threatening and widespread these problems are. In the end, precise figures are probably unimportant. Problem drinking is common to all segments of our society, especially in the bar culture, and it is increasingly serious and harder to stop the longer it goes unchecked.

Because drinking is socially acceptable and legal, we often forget that alcohol is a dangerous drug. Some scientists assert that it is even more dangerous than heroin. We can also forget that the people who abuse it aren't just "problem drinkers." They may be drug addicts. As with any drug popular in the gay subculture, we need to know as much about alcohol as possible.

**How does alcohol differ from other drugs?**   Chemically, ethyl alcohol, the drug present in "alcoholic beverages," is the by-product of the yeast enzyme's interaction with the simple sugars present in the starches of such plants as barley, hops, corn, rice, potatoes, cane, and grapes. The interaction is known as "fermentation." Beers and wines are produced by fermentation alone, but such "spirits" as whiskey, gin, vodka, rum, and liqueurs require "distillation" to achieve a high content of alcohol.

Like all downers, ethyl alcohol depresses the central nervous system—the brain and the spinal cord. (It is not to be confused with methyl alcohol, or "wood alcohol," which causes blindness and death when swallowed.) Essentially, the drug is a consciousness-altering agent, one that can lead to "alcoholic thinking." Although this thinking can be colored by the individual problems that exist prior to drinking, experts agree that most of its characteristics are constant: depression, suspicion, brooding, paranoia, doubt, and vehement denial that there's a drinking problem. As one expert in gay alcoholism told *The Advocate*, "There are no new alcoholism stories . . . just 150 variations on the same theme."

The psychological problems, however, are only part of the damage. Unlike most drugs, alcohol is water soluble, which means it enters every organ and every cell of the body. A brief scan can provide a glimpse of what too much alcohol can do to you physically.

As soon as it hits the stomach, twenty percent of the alcohol spurns the regular channels and is absorbed directly into the bloodstream through the lining of the stomach. If you've diluted your spirits with water or, even worse, a carbonated beverage, thus causing the alcohol to go into solution, it will be absorbed that much faster. Unless there's food in the stomach, which slows the rate of absorption, you'll feel instantly high, warm, and lightheaded. The heart circulates the blood, now laced with the drug, through the vascular system at the rate of three to four liters per minute. When the absorption of the rest of the alcohol from the gastrointestinal tract is complete, the concentration of alcohol throughout the body will be approximately equal. As long as there is any alcohol present anywhere in the body, it will be present everywhere in the body that contains water, and two-thirds of the body is water.

Frequent consumption of too much alcohol can lead to the hardening of the heart muscle itself, which is known as alcoholic cardiomyopathy.

Because alcohol inflames the lining of the stomach and intestinal walls, it makes it difficult for the body to absorb vitamins and nutrients, a situation that can lead to a plethora of diseases related to vitamin deficiency, as well as to malnutrition. Not all of these problems are confined to the GI tract, however, so a short digression is in order.

If you've heard that drinking too much can make you fat,

you've heard correctly. Alcoholic beverages, particularly beer and wine, are nutritious to some degree; but the drug they contain, which measures over 200 calories per pure ounce, is devoid of fat, protein, carbohydrates, or vitamins. Alcohol itself has no nutritional value whatsoever. Aside from adding fat, all those empty calories do is give you a temporary boost in energy, which is artificially enhanced by the drug's ability to depress the nervous system, thereby masking fatigue.

Consumption of too much alcohol over a long period of time can cause a vitamin $B_1$ deficiency, which can lead to polyneuritis, a neurological disorder, and beriberi, a cardiac disease. Alcohol has been shown to deplete the liver of its entire supply of vitamin A, which can result in "night blindness" in some cases. Drinking can decrease vitamin C, which is necessary in raising the general resistance of the body against countless infections. Unfortunately, vitamin deficiencies are not easily corrected in the person who continues to drink, because the alcohol can impede the body's ability to absorb even large doses of vitamin supplements.

Many juicers consider themselves sexier while under the influence, but what appears to be increased libido is only a decrease of inhibitions. Though impotence sometimes comes only in the final stages of alcoholism, *any* amount of alcohol in the body will reduce sexual efficiency. Because alcohol is an anesthetic to nerves all over the body, it dulls your erogenous zones.

To present a complete picture of what too much alcohol can do to you physically would require a separate volume. Suffice it to say that it can also permanently damage the nervous system, the liver, the pancreas, and the prostate.

**How much is too much alcohol?** Scientists who do alcohol research disagree sharply. Some insist that *any* amount of alcohol can be damaging, which most people would agree is extreme. In sensible quantities, alcohol can perk up the appetite, ease tensions, and serve as a useful social lubricant. But anything over two to three ounces of the drug *at any one time,* and you're running the risk of hurting yourself. Roughly, this is equivalent to three cocktails; *or* about two-thirds of a quart of unfortified wine.

If you enjoy two or three martinis before dinner, fine. But if you drink several glasses of wine with your meal and top it off with brandy, or a liqueur, you're over the sensible limit. That doesn't mean you'll feel drunk or appear to be drunk; it does mean that you're giving your body a greater metabolic job than it can comfortably handle, which is another way of saying that you're abusing yourself. And if you abuse yourself day in and day out, you can precipitate diseases and become addicted.

Because of psychological or physiological conditions (the experts themselves aren't sure), tolerance—which is a polite word for need—can vary tremendously. Some people can become alcoholics on two or three drinks a day. According to Rusty Smith, director of the Whitman-Radclyffe Foundation's Alcoholic Services for the Homosexual Community in San Francisco, "Alcoholism is addiction to a drug, and it's evidenced when a person's quality of life is going downhill because of the drug. The addiction can be both physical and psychological."

If you drink to get rid of depression, anxiety, boredom, or because your problems seem monumental, you could find yourself hitting the bottle again and again. Even when you develop a pattern of daily drinking for no reason that you're aware of, you can still become addicted. An occasional drink to ease stressful situations, even ones so banal as loosening up at a party, is acceptable. But if you're drinking in *every* stressful situation, you're scurrying over that fine line between sensible drinking and alcoholism. If you find that you've begun using alcohol like a medicine, it's time to see someone who knows something about alcoholism. It cannot be overemphasized that alcoholism is drug addiction, and the most important symptom of that addiction is the inability to control drinking; being gay has nothing to do with it.

**Then why are so many gays alcoholics?** Generally, there are no simple answers to complex questions, but this one is often treated as an exception. A lot of people believe that alcoholism exists in the gay community to the extent that it does because of gay bars. As one alcoholism counselor told *The Advocate*, "The gay bar has a social role that doesn't exist in the straight world. For gay people, it's the only place they can go to be themselves."

According to the Fifield study, two out of three regular bar-users surveyed go out in hopes of meeting new friends, not for the express purpose of drinking. Socialization is so important that they spend most of their free time in gay bars or at gay parties, where alcohol is available. And where alcohol is on the scene, it is consumed.

The average gay bar-user, Fifield found, has six drinks each of the nineteen nights a month in which he or she goes out. And yet an overwhelming majority of bar-users say the absence of alcohol would have no effect on their attendance at a gay function.

The owners of the bars, whose livelihood depends on pushing as much booze as possible, use every gimmick in the book to insure that you'll keep coming back for more. On one level, gay people are indebted to the owners of gay bars, many of whom have contributed more than anyone else in the movement to insure human rights regardless of sexual preference. Buying lots of drinks is a way we can thank them for that, isn't it? And boozing it up insures that the bars will remain open as arenas in which we can make new friends. In a sense, then, we have no choice.

Bullshit! It may be true that most of the alcoholism in the gay community is a *result* of gay bars, but the blame rests with the individual drinker. We are perfectly free to choose nonalcoholic beverages; we can even alternate them with alcoholic drinks, thereby cutting our intake to an acceptable level. In most bars, a plain soda with lime or a glass of fruit juice costs as much as a "real" drink anyway, and the bar's profit is higher than it is on the hard stuff. But according to experienced bartenders, only five percent of gay bar patrons order nonalcoholic beverages.

The gay bar, however, does not stand alone as a contributor to alcoholism. Without realizing it, you yourself could be a contributor, even if you drink sensibly or not at all. You could be what alcoholism experts call a "co-alcoholic."

Alcoholics need someone to drive them home. They need someone to pay the bills. And the co-alcoholic, sometimes a lover, sometimes a friend, sometimes a family member, is always there to bail them out. Some alcoholics become so manipulative that they manage to develop a veritable network of co-alcoholic support.

According to Rusty Smith, "The co-alcoholic has a personality that gets off on helping people. He *needs* someone, usually because of his low self-esteem. As the alcoholic's disease gets worse and worse, the co-alcoholic feels better and better, often unconsciously. He has a definite interest in the alcoholic staying sick."

The relationship of alcoholic and co-alcoholic is mutually self-destructive. The alcoholic often takes the co-alcoholic down with him, and vice versa. The phenomenon is so widespread that Alcoholics Anonymous has a separate organization known as Al-Anon, which is designed for the friends, lovers, and family members of alcoholics, and gay Al-Anon groups are springing up throughout the country.

For one member of a Gay Al-Anon group in San Francisco, dealing with his own co-alcoholic tendencies has meant surrendering a degree of control over the life of his lover, now a cured alcoholic. "You have to let go," he told *The Advocate*. "The foremost thing to remember is that I'm powerless over whether my lover drinks. I have no power to keep him drinking or to keep him from drinking. Most of the people who live with an alcoholic get on a guilt trip, like they're causing the person to drink. An alcoholic drinks because he's an alcoholic. There's really nothing someone else can do about it."

Rusty Smith believes that the road to recovery for the co-alcoholic is often as difficult as that of his heavily drinking friend or lover: "When the alcoholic recovers, co-alcoholics have to go back to facing that they consider themselves worthless human beings. It's hard for them."

Until he or she gets help, most co-alcoholics are simply unaware that they have a problem. Many alcoholic and co-alcoholic relationships break up when the drinker recovers, leaving the co-alcoholic out in the cold and looking for another dependent lover.

"Nine times out of ten," a member of Gay Al-Anon told *The Advocate*, "the co-alcoholic just finds another alcoholic to live with. I know one guy who is on his third alcoholic right now, and he's not even aware of the fact that he's into a pattern."

Breaking out of that pattern can be facilitated by Al-Anon, or by consciousness-raising groups. Sometimes, the list of the dos and don'ts provided by the National Council on Alcoholism is sufficient to jar people into an awareness that they have cast themselves in the role of co-alcoholic:

## DO

Talk to someone who understands alcoholism.

Learn the facts about alcoholism.

Develop an attitude to match the facts.

Go to Al-Anon and/or seek professional help.

Learn about yourself, your needs, your desires, your reactions, and your behavior patterns.

As much as possible, maintain a healthy and consistent atmosphere in your home.

Take care of your own needs, and let the alcoholic take care of his.

Be committed to your own growth, your own health, your own goals—be constructively selfish.

## DON'T

Preach and lecture to the alcoholic.

Make excuses for the alcoholic.

Rescue—let the alcoholic clear up his own mistakes and assume the responsibility for the consequences of his drinking behavior.

Make threats you won't carry out.

Believe that you are the cause of the other person's alcoholism.

Suffer for the alcoholic.

Protect the alcoholic from alcohol or drinking situations—whether he is still drinking or in a recovery program.

Make an issue over the alcoholic's choice of treatment—like you, he has the right to choose what he wants.*

**Is that all you can do?** If you do no more than this, you'll be helping yourself and the alcoholic tremendously, although it may not seem like it at the time. If you've taken the trouble to learn what alcoholism is, you'll know that the alcoholic *needs* alcohol. And if you care for the alcoholic, you can become addicted yourself, to him or her. The result is that the alcoholic thinks about drinking or not drinking, and you spend most of your time thinking about the alco-

---

* Adapted from "For the Families and Friends of Alcoholics," a pamphlet distributed by the Whitman-Radclyffe Foundation's Individual & Group Counselling Program. San Francisco, 1977.

holic. Both of you are losing a sense of self by making alcohol, and, in your case, another person, more important than yourselves.

Pouring the liquor down the drain, nagging, threatening and not following through, crying, pleading, the silent treatment, and all the other acts you dream up won't work. They will only temporarily relieve your feelings.

Try to develop a more positive attitude toward the alcoholic. He may never be the person you dreamed of, but as long as you go on trying to make him into the kind of person you want him to be or think he ought to be, he will probably go on drinking. Let him make his *own* decisions, and ask for his help whenever possible. The alcoholic feels a great sense of inadequacy and lacks confidence in himself. By beginning to show him that you need him, you can help him reestablish a positive self-image. At the same time, don't delude yourself—you *do* need him. If you didn't, you would have split a long time ago.

There are some practical steps that you can take of an obviously "protective" nature, but because they can save your friend or lover's life, common sense dictates them. If he or she passes out, make sure that the sleeping position is with the head to one side, and not on the back. Recheck the position periodically, for the next few hours. Like other downers, alcohol can cause vomiting in the sleep. The involuntary inhalation of vomit is a common cause of alcohol-related death. Keep other drugs, particularly other downers, out of the house as combining them with alcohol can be fatal.

Finally, if the alcoholic begins expressing an interest in treatment but is slow about putting it into action, don't make a big deal over it. Again, he needs to make his *own* decisions; he needs to feel that he has freedom of choice, just like any adult. Don't push, nag, or urge. At the same time, let him know that you *believe* he is going to do something about taking the initiative and the responsibility for getting help.

**Where can gays get treatment?** The major hurdle to treating alcoholism is denial of the problem. Alcoholics deny it, and so do their friends, lovers, employees, and bartenders. Most of the otherwise responsible spokespersons in the gay community, understandably eager to propagate the notion that we are no different from anyone else, deny that alcoholism is one of our most menacing problems.

But once that hurdle is cleared, there are more problems. They arise, according to Randy Shilts, "from a double lie which this society has perpetrated on gay people and on itself. While drinking generally has been considered social and, to some extent, healthy, homosexuality has long been viewed as an illness. Thus the gay alcoholic is often treated for a sham disease—his or her gayness—while in alcoholism recovery, and the true problem, alcoholism, continues."

Even in San Francisco, a gay mecca and one of the most liberal cities in America, an independent consulting firm commissioned by the city's Bureau of Alcoholism found that local treatment centers were inadequate for gay people. One of the conclusions: "Gay individuals are confronted with alcoholism service and treatment professionals who lose sight of the fact that the primary problem is alcoholism. Instead, these professionals attempt to treat what they define as the problem, namely the homosexual orientation."

Brenda Weathers told *The Advocate* that in the past, the chance that gay women would get services from straight agencies if it were known that they were lesbians was slim. "I know of countless stories of gay women who were turned away from agencies when they were in dire circumstances—only later to puke their way to death or insanity."

The situation is improving. But even in programs that encourage candor about sexuality, gay people can meet with hostility from their fellow alcoholics. "These gay alcoholics," says Lillene Fifield, "are in programs where they can't be comfortably open about their gayness. If they can't be open about this integral part of their life, they can't be open about their whole being. When the gay person gets messages that gay is not okay, it adds to the strain and conflict. In this sense, the agencies are contributing to the conflicts that may be making the gay alcoholic drink."

While other minority groups face alienation and oppression, gay people face them without many of the support structures available to the heterosexual of either sex or any race. The straight alcoholic can often return to some form of family structure after recovery, but that sort of support system is seldom available to the gay alcoholic.

Although unique counseling is necessary for gay drinkers, most of the agencies are doing little to nothing about it. Fifield surveyed forty-six mainstream alcoholism agencies in the Los Angeles area and found these conditions:

Of the forty-six, forty-three said they dealt with gay alcoholics. But only three of these have therapy groups for gay people.

Of the thirty-five agencies with couple counseling, only three advise couples of the same sex.

Only four of the forty-six agencies had workshops to sensitize their staff to the problems of gay people. Of these four, only one holds such workshops on a regular basis.

The agencies that were able to estimate the percentage of their gay clients came up with the startling head count of one percent.

The agencies estimated that only one and one-half percent of their staff were gay. Only nine of the forty-six said they could identify their gay staff members.

On the basis of these data, the Fifield report makes the following conclusion about the ability of mainstream alcoholism agencies to deal with gay alcoholics:

Most of the agencies sampled agreed that gay alcoholics have specific service needs, yet they have not attempted to identify their gay clients in order to meet those unique needs; nor have they developed staff where gays are represented and could create an open atmosphere by their own example. Since it is statistically absurd to accept that only 1.5% of all staff is gay, or that only 1% of all clients are gay, and since 80% of the example could not even estimate the percentage of gay clients, it is apparent that most gay people who work for or receive services from these agencies are not made to feel comfortable in revealing sexual orientation; i.e., *these agencies do not meet the primary need expressed by the sample of . . . recovered gay alcoholics to have a supportive atmosphere and peer contact in the recovery process.*\*

The study goes on to fill four pages with recommendations, including more funding for gay-staffed alcoholism programs for gay

---

\* Randy Shilts, "Alcoholism: A Look in Depth at How a National Menace Is Affecting the Gay Community." *The Advocate*, No. 184, February 25, 1976.

people. If implemented, the recommendations would cost a bundle, and the L. A. Gay Community Services Center couldn't even come up with enough to print a short condensation of the Fifield study for distribution in the gay community!

For the gay person suffering from alcoholism, finding the right source of treatment can be as difficult as choosing a competent physician. There is no pat formula. You can begin by telephoning some of the resources listed in the Appendix. If you're given a referral, ask if the program is gay-oriented or at least accepting of gay people. If your physician is gay, perhaps he or she will know how to direct you. But if you find yourself in a program that is hostile because of your sexuality, keep looking. Don't compound your stress to the point that you fall off the wagon.

## BARBITURATES

Barbiturates, long prescribed for the relief of anxiety and tension and to induce sleep, come in a variety of popular forms. In combination with alcohol, they can be deadly—as proved by Judy Garland, Dorothy Kilgallen, Brian Jones of the Rolling Stones, and Janis Joplin, to name but a few. All true barbiturates are made from barbituric acid. Other sedatives, such as Quaaludes, while not technically barbiturates, can be just as dangerous.

The most familiar barbiturates—and the ones you hear most about "on the street"—are Amobarbital ("blues"), Pentobarbital ("yellows"), and Secobarbital ("reds"). There are many more, under a variety of names, including Tuinal ("double trouble," "rainbows"), Doriden ("goofers"), and Chloral Hydrate ("coral"). All have the same effect.

**What do they do to you?** First, all of them depress the central nervous system, consequently, they have often been prescribed for sedition, the relief of high blood pressure, and epilepsy. But with greater realization of their dangers, medical prescriptions are becoming less common. The psychological effects, which is why they are so popular, are the reduction of anxiety and the onset of euphoria.

People on downers may show signs of drowsiness, restlessness, irritability, hostility, confusion, poor coordination and reflexes, staggering, and slurring of speech.

After the euphoria wears off, which usually takes about three hours, there is a feeling of depression. Chronic use leads to increased tolerance (need), and psychological and physical addiction. Withdrawal symptoms, which can include convulsions, abdominal cramps, and psychotic behavior, are actually worse than those of alcohol and heroin. When someone overdoses on barbiturates, the depressive effect on the nervous system induces unconsciousness and, in extreme cases, death by respiratory failure.

**What happens if you take downers with alcohol?** A lot of people reason that you can have a couple of drinks, not get drunk, take a "normal" dose of barbiturates and, at worst, get stoned. It is, they believe, sort of a one plus one arrangement. But depending on the individual's biochemistry, which is always unique, the combination can kill you. *Never* mix!

**What about tranquilizers?** They differ from barbiturates in that while they depress the central nervous system, thereby relieving anxiety and tension, they do so without anesthetic effects. They are seldom fatal *except* when combined with alcohol. The lethal dose, when consumed on their own, has not yet been determined. The most popular tranquilizer is Valium, which comes in 2, 5, and 10 mg tablets. Valium can be particularly dangerous when mixed with alcohol, as many people unwisely do, because the combination can easily lead to psychological dependence.

Several of the physicians I interviewed are concerned about the habit-forming properties of diazepam, the chemical used in Valium. As one of them told me, "I've seen patients on Valium who eventually need more and more to get the same effect. When the drug is denied, they undergo withdrawal symptoms—anxiety, insomnia, tremors."

In the United States, Valium is now on the dangerous drugs list maintained by the Federal Food and Drug Administration. Nevertheless, some patients have shopping lists of doctors and go from one to another picking up supplies. I've seen some patients," another physician told me, "who become aggressive and paranoid on Valium. Although it's a relatively safe tranquilizer when used in *recommended* doses for a reasonable period of time, it should never be supplied by a doctor *ad infinitum*."

Pharmacologists themselves are confused as to how to classify such tranquilizers as Valium and Librium. They are sometimes called "anti-anxiety" agents, "sedative-hypnotics," and "minor tranquilizers." Regardless of the terminology, they share the ability to produce a general, *reversible* depression of the central nervous system.

Methaqualone, however, is a tranquilizing drug that is almost always classified as a sedative-hypnotic. More popularly known by the brand-name "Quaalude," it has become one of the most popular drugs in the gay subculture, as well as one of the most dangerous.

**Why are Quaaludes dangerous?**   Because intoxication with Quaaludes ("Vitamin Q") is similar to intoxication with barbiturates and alcohol. It subjects the person who takes them to death by overdose, accidents due to confusion and impaired coordination, and increasing tolerance to the point of addiction. In individuals with a low tolerance to the drug, death has occurred with the ingestion of as little as eight grams.

In the 1960s the drug was available without prescription in Japan, where it was marketed as "Hyminal." Between 1963 and 1966, a survey of the drug addicts in Japanese mental hospitals found that 42.8 percent were hooked on Hyminal. Almost all of them had been admitted to the hospitals for violent behavior.

Nevertheless, in 1965, methaqualone was introduced into the American market, under the name of "Quaalude," and became something of a fad. It is highly popular with gay men, who find that its muscle-relaxing effects facilitate anal intercourse and fistfucking. Some even tout Quaalude as the first true aphrodisiac and the "heroin for lovers." Only a few years back, the drug rated the cover of *Rolling Stone* magazine.

Quaaludes are often used in combination with wine, a practice known as "luding out." This is especially dangerous because the drug has a compounding effect when taken with alcohol and can result in an overdose with coma, muscle spasms, convulsions, and hemorrhaging (due to methaqualone's ability to interfere with the normal coagulation of blood).

Methaqualone also comes under the brand names Optimil, Parest, Somnafac, and Sopor; in some European countries, it is marketed as Melsedin and Mandrax, or "mandies."

Because of its now recognized danger and abuse, methaqualone in any form is almost impossible to come by legally. It is available on the street—but as with any street drug, especially the so-called hard stuff, you never know what you're getting. Don't be misled by the authentic appearance of a pill, because embossed trademarks and packaging are easily counterfeited.

**What is meant by "hard stuff"?** Codeine, morphine, and heroin, the drugs derived from the opium plant, and therefore known as opiates, are the hard stuff. All depress the nervous system and cause initial excitement as inhibitions melt away. In large doses, they affect the pleasure centers of the brain, resulting in feeling of peace, safety, contentment, and a general sense of well-being, which wear off in a matter of hours. All are addicting.

The least effective opiate is codeine, which is generally found in cough medicines and headache remedies. Unless you're using the pure stuff, which is white and crystalline in form, you won't get into much trouble with codeine because of the large amounts of cough syrups and headache pills you'd have to consume to achieve a real high. The resulting constipation is another deterrent to abuse.

Morphine is used medically for the relief of pain. But even then, it has to be carefully controlled to avoid addiction. Known as "white stuff" or simply "M" on the street, it is swallowed or injected to produce euphoria.

Heroin, which is three times stronger than morphine, is no longer used medically and can be had only illegally. Known on the street as "H," "horse," "scat," "shit," "junk," "juice," "smack," "scag," "stuff," and "hairy," it comes in a powder that can be sniffed. Addicts normally inject it, however, first into a muscle, and later, as tolerance escalates, into a major vein. Addiction is rapid. Although the use of heroin and other opiates can cause temporary impotence, the long-term effects of addiction are surprisingly minimal provided that the victim is stabilized on methadone maintenance and receives the support of halfway houses and other professional agencies.

## SMOKING

Nicotine, found in cigarettes, is readily available as a stimulant, but it can become both psychologically and physically addicting. It can also kill you. In its pure state, nicotine is so poisonous that an injection of 70 mg is sufficient to kill outright (depending on the brand you smoke, your cigarette contains from 0.5 to 2.0 mg).

**Do gays smoke more than straights?**   There is no statistical evidence. But when you consider that most people smoke to ease stress, it would be fair guess that we smoke at least as much as straights, if not more.

Even if we don't smoke, we can still be exposed to the same health risks as smokers, though in a reduced way, if we are, in fact, spending a lot of time in smoke-filled bars.

**What's the best way to stop?**   If you choose to stop, you will, and not until. All the scare techniques, expensive clinics, over-the-counter pills, and gimmicks you've heard about may help, but the key factor in kicking addiction to nicotine is a simple decision.

A number of people who have given up smoking report that they were able to make the decision with ease the moment they began a program of vigorous exercise, because they were able to *feel* what smoking was doing to their bodies. Still others have been helped along by using a special filter, available under a variety of brand-names in any pharmacy, that cuts down on the tar in cigarettes. They were able to *see* what they'd been inhaling into their systems, and the sight alone made them stop on the spot.

Withdrawal symptoms may include craving, depression, anxiety, and difficulty in concentrating. However, most people who decide to quit discover that the worst part of withdrawal is its anticipation.

**If you stop, how can you avoid gaining weight?**   At first, many people can't. But you can achieve your ideal weight, if, upon quitting, you become more conscious of what you're putting in your mouth (for nutritional purposes) and choose to begin that program of exercise you've been promising your body. The worst way to keep your weight down is to start taking amphetamines, or speed.

## UPPERS

**What's wrong with speed?**   It is a cop-out, and a potentially dangerous one, because you're substituting a chemical agent for the fresh air, good nutrition, exercise, and proper rest patterns that can keep you energetic, healthy, and slim.

Amphetamines, of course, do more than suppress the appetite. Most people enjoy the other effects, which can include alertness, an elevation of mood, increased initiative, confidence, ability to concentrate, and a general sense of well-being. In addition to Preludin, which diet doctors sometimes prescribe, amphetamines come in the form of benzedrine, dexadrine, and dexamyl. Regardless of form, speed raises the blood pressure and increases heart output.

Overdosing on speed produces a wide range of symptoms, including restlessness, dizziness, the shakes, irritability, weakness, insomnia, flushing, chills, hypertension. Serious side effects are rare in doses of less than 15 mg; the lethal dose is probably ten times that. When death comes, it is usually preceded by convulsions and coma.

The chronic use of speed can throw the individual into a cycle of going without sleep for several days, and then into an exhaustion so great that sleep is unavoidable. Upon awakening, the speed freak feels hungry and depressed, so he takes more speed. The use of large doses over a long period of time can alter personality and behavior considerably.

If you're buying your speed on the street, perhaps the worst thing about it is that it may not be speed at all. Strychnine, which is used commercially as a rat poison, is a common adulterant because it acts as a central nervous system stimulant and is, therefore, similar to speed in effect.

*Analysis surveys from a variety of nations indicate that over half of street drugs are not what they are alleged to be. They may contain PCP, as well as other cutting agents, which could spell disaster when mixed with alcohol.*

Nobody can prevent your using drugs if you want to. But if you do, be careful about your supplier—unless he or she is a physician, a pharmacist, or a graduate chemist, you have every right to be suspicious. There is no Food and Drug Administration or department of quality control for street drugs. Much of what passes for cocaine, for example, is not cocaine at all, but a substitute or mixture of various drugs, including PCP and heroin.

**Is coke dangerous?** As long as it's coke and not something else, it is, as uppers go, relatively harmless. It is not physically addicting, but if used in large quantities over a long period of time it can cause problems. Repeated inhalation can eventually lead to deterioration of the nasal linings and the nasal septum separating the nostrils. Prolonged use can also produce insomnia, paranoia, and "coke bugs"—the maddening sensation that there's something alive crawling all over your body.

Because the "champagne of drugs" is so outrageously expensive, it has become a status symbol in the gay subculture. Users quickly become bored with it, however, because it is so short-acting. To maintain the high, it must be snorted repeatedly.

Another drug that is frequently adulterated is the very popular MDA, a close chemical relative of both the amphetamines and mescaline. MDA is known to stand for "mellow drug of America"; but technically, it denotes the compound 3,4-methylinedioxyamphetamine. A number of its devotees claim that it surpasses the hallucinogens, including mescaline and LSD, in its ability to heighten self-awareness.

**Is MDA safe?** In 1970, MDA joined a long list of other drugs (including LSD, mescaline, and heroin) under Schedule I of the Federal Controlled Substances Act. Penalties for the manufacture, possession, or sale of any substance under this category (for which there is "no medically recognized use") are severe and consist of imprisonment, heavy fines, or both. In that sense, then, it is anything but safe.

Because of the adulterants, it can also be dangerous chemically. There are several published reports in the U.S. and Canada of near-fatal and fatal reactions to MDA. Several of the victims experienced major epileptic seizures. Death appears to have been caused by hemorrhaging and/or cardiac arrest. In all these cases, there was an excessive quantity of MDA (documented to be 500 mg in at least three instances); in other cases, there was an excessive quantity of the drug as well as the presence of such adulterants as strychnine and PCP.

The conventional "street dose" of MDA ranges from 120 to 150 mg, with the threshold dose (the minimum required to elicit noticeable effects) somewhere in the neighborhood of 80 mg. But when you're buying MDA or any other drug on the street, there is no way to know just how much you're getting. The drug may be in powder form (white or tan), or it may come in the form of an amber liquid. When in powder, it is either contained in gelatin capsules or pressed into tablets and cut with anything from cocaine and LSD (which themselves are cut) to rat poison and PCP.

Generally, MDA is swallowed; it can also be snorted or mainlined into a vein. Effects begin within an hour after taking it, and the pleasant sense of serenity for which the drug is noted last approximately eight hours.

Some gay men believe that the effects are even better if a large dose is inserted in the rectum. This was the method of administration preferred by one of the expensive and hopelessly narcissistic male prostitutes we interviewed, who told us that if it weren't for MDA, he wouldn't be able to make it with the elderly men who pay for his charms. Because he also works as an "actor" in hardcore films, he reports that he finds the drug indispensable to performing on camera as well.

## HALLUCINOGENS

Also known as "psychedelics," the hallucinogens, which come in both natural and chemically synthesized forms, are commonly defined as drugs that affect sensation, thinking, and self-awareness. They also alter time/space perceptions and produce hallucinations.

Prior to 1943, when a Swiss chemist took the world's first acid trip, the only notable users of hallucinogens were Indians native to the southwestern United States and Latin America. The Indians are still tripping out, but today, they have lots of worldwide company in persons with access to an array of mind-altering drugs that include psilocybin, mescaline, and LSD.

It all began in 1928, when Albert Hofmann, Ph.D., a research chemist with the Sandoz company, a prominent pharmaceutical firm in Basel, Switzerland, isolated the chemical molecule called lysergic acid diethylamide. In an effort to understand their valuable medical properties, Dr. Hofmann had been studying a class of chemicals derived from ergot, a fungus that grows on rye grass. More specifically, he was trying to synthesize properties like caffeine when, on the twenty-fifth try, he came up with LSD.

Because the compound seemed of no interest to pharmacologists, it sat on the shelves of Sandoz for five years. Then, when Dr. Hofmann prepared a fresh batch one April day, he accidentally touched a moistened finger to his tongue. At a recent seminar on pharmacology at the University of California's San Francisco Medical Center, he described what happened next: "I was forced to stop work and go home because I was seized by a peculiar restlessness. I sank into a kind of drunkenness which was accompanied by an uninterrupted storm of fantastic images—a kaleidoscopic display of colors."

Incredulous that he could have taken enough of the stuff to precipitate such reactions, he decided to experiment three days later by ingesting a quarter of a milligram. Four hours later, he was experiencing visual disturbances and laughing uncontrollably. After bicycling home, he babbled incoherently, saw vividly colored images translated from the sounds of passing cars, felt alternately restless and paralyzed, and finally fell asleep—only to wake six hours later feeling fine.

Subsequently, more carefully controlled experiments on himself and volunteers revealed that the drug was much more potent than mescaline, the chemical derived from the Mexican peyote cactus. Since then, Sandoz has made and sold small quantities of LSD for the purposes of research only. But in the 1960s, people with sufficient chemical knowledge to decode the molecule began manufacturing acid and flooded the underground market with it. Today, LSD is available legally only to a few medical researchers, who are using it to open new insights into the chemistry of the brain and mental illness. Despite the moderate to stiff penalties for its manufacture, sale, or possession, some psychiatrists with access to the drug employ it for therapeutic purposes.

Acid is not addicting, and its potential for psychological dependence is minimal. Nevertheless, be wary of street acid, which is more often than not something else—including PCP, or "angel dust." Even when you're sure of purity, never drop the drug in a strange environment, or with people you don't know well enough to trust.

**Mescaline and psilocybin:** Depending on dosage, the effects of psilocybin and mescaline can be identical to LSD. Psilocybin is produced from the Teonancatl, the sacred Mexican mushroom used for centuries for religious purposes, primarily by the Aztecs. Mescaline is produced from the peyote cactus of Mexico and the southwestern United States.

In 1956, French scientists who were interested in the chemical exploration of psilocybin brought a number of dried mushrooms to Dr. Hofmann, who again experimented on himself by eating thirty-two of them.

"Thirty minutes later," he told the seminar in San Francisco, "the exterior world began to undergo a strange transformation. Everything assumed a Mexican character. The physician who was observing me was transformed into an Aztec priest, and I wouldn't have been surprised if he had drawn an obsidian knife. I feared I would be drawn unwillingly into a whirlpool of color. Yet six hours later I experienced a happy return from that strange, fantastic, unreal world."

Eventually Dr. Hofmann was able to synthesize psilocybin in his laboratory and, in 1962, took his pills to a woman shaman in an Indian village near Oaxaca. She took one and gave what he describes as a "gala performance." She also told him that there was no difference between her mushrooms and the pills. "And that," he said, with a twinkle in his eye, "was the final proof of the correctness of my synthesis."

Dr. Hofmann has discovered that the molecules of LSD, psilocybin, amd mescaline are similar to those of chemicals found naturally at the junctions of brain cells where impulses move from cell to cell. Mescaline, for example, is structurally similar to the neurotransmitters called norepinepherine and epinepherine; LSD and psilocybin are closely related to the brain chemical called serotonin. As tools in psychiatric research, and as models for studying the action of the central nervous system, these hallucinogens can be of great scientific value—in competent and cautious hands.*

But again, you are not apt to find any of these drugs on the street. Even when you do, they are almost never pure. What passes for mescaline and psilocybin, for example, is usually LSD mixed with angel dust. Were you to combine such junk with alcohol, you could die.

**Angel dust (PCP):** Also known as "hog" and "the peace pill," PCP (Pheny-cyclohexyl-piperidine) is an extremely potent animal tranquilizer and anesthetic no longer legal for even veterinary purposes. It's greatest threat lies in the prevalence with which it is used to cut practically every drug imaginable, and it is almost always sold as THC and MDA. (Virtually every sample of THC sold on the streets in the last five years has contained *only* PCP.)

---

*David Perlman, "The Father of LSD Describes His 'Trips.' " San Francisco *Chronicle*, October 12, 1977.

Although it can keep you "up," in large doses, it is a heavy psychomotor depressant that becomes so active when mixed with other depressants, especially alcohol, that it can lead to convulsions, coma, respiratory arrest, and death. In spite of its dangers, many people, especially teenagers, dote on it because of its ability to produce delusional behavior and bizarre hallucinations. Just how bizarre can be seen in an experiment that was conducted with the drug before its dangers were recognized. According to Matthew Lampe, writing in *Drugs: Information for Crisis Treatment*, PCP was used as an aid to anesthesia in human childbirth, and roughly one out of ten mothers disclaimed their babies after delivery.

PCP, which comes in tablets, capsules, and powder, is cheap and easy to manufacture. Again, if the drugs you're using aren't supplied by a physician or a pharmacist, your chance of ingesting a lethal dose of the stuff is excellent.

**DOM and DMT:** DOM, sometimes known as STP (for "serenity, tranquility, and peace"), is available in both liquid form and tablets. Depending on dosage, its effects can be even stronger than those of LSD and mescaline, and they can last as long, but doses large enough to produce hallucinations can produce severe physical reactions respiratory paralysis. Contrary to the popular street myth, the effects of DOM do *not* persist for three or four days.

DMT, also known as "the businessman's special," comes in liquid form only and is smoked with tobacco or pot. The duration of action is comparatively short, ranging from half an hour to four hours. During this time, however, the effects resemble those of LSD, to which DMT is chemically related.

There are many other alphabet soup psychedelics, most of which are so rare you probably won't encounter them. They include, for examples, DET and DPT, which resemble DMT.

**Marijuana:** While the active ingredient in pot (THC) produces effects that are sometimes psychedelic in character, marijuana is more properly classified as an intoxicant. Generally, the effects resemble those of alcohol more than any other drug. The physical signs of smoking dope are reddening of the eyes and an increase in heart rate. The primary psychological effects are relaxation, relief of anxiety, the lessening of inhibitions, alterations in visual perception, and drowsiness.

Few drugs have been subjected to more scrutiny than marijuana. It does no known damage to the body, it is not physically addicting, and it becomes dangerous only when the user drives a car or operates machinery. Chronic users, however, can become psychologically dependent and suffer a loss of motivation.

In a Gallup poll conducted in April 1977 twenty-four percent of the Americans over eighteen surveyed report they have tried marijuana at least once, a figure double what it was in a similar Gallup poll in 1973. Of the men polled, thirty-one percent said they had smoked grass, while seventeen percent of the women had partaken at least once.

The drug is approaching social acceptability and may soon become legal. In November 1977, the American Medical Association and the equally conservative American Bar Association issued a rare joint appeal to Congress to repeal criminal penalties for the use of grass. The appeal went on to urge that state legislatures across the nation move to eliminate criminal penalties as well. So far, nine states have enacted such laws, while several others have killed the bills when they were introduced.

The AMA-ABA appeal does not condone the use of marijuana; but neither does it say that the weed is a hazard to health. If there were substantial evidence that marijuana is dangerous, the AMA and the ABA would be the last organizations to call for its decriminalization.

In rare cases, there can be acute reactions to pot, but seldom are they pharmacologic. The most common is panic, or the reaction of the tripper to his reaction to the drug. Even rarer is the reaction known as toxic psychosis, which includes confusion, delirium, and other toxic symptoms. This can happen when large quantities of marijuana or hashish (the most potent form of pot) are ingested. Symptoms may persist for twelve to fourteen hours, and the resulting hangover, which can last up to forty-eight hours, is incredibly severe.

**THC:** Chemically synthetic grass (tetrahydrocannabinol) is being used in research in various parts of the country, but it is *never* available on the street. According to Matthew M. Lampe, the co-founder of Drug Help and the Free People's Clinic in Ann Arbor, Michigan, THC has to be the classic hoax of all time as far as street drugs go. The synthesis of THC is by far the most difficult and complex of all the psychedelics. In addition, THC is a very unstable compound, requiring meticulous care in storage and shipment. For optimum stability, the drug has to be kept at −19° C under nitrogen, or in a vacuum. The most frequent substitution for THC is PCP, all by itself.

None of the sources I consulted disagree. Even if THC were available, the effects would probably be identical to those experienced after eating a sizable chunk of hashish.

## AMYL NITRITE

That "amyl" and its chemical imitators is widespread in the gay community, especially among men, isn't news. Even gays who have no use for the drug have learned to recognize its characteristic "dirty sox" odor, because despite heroic attempts at ventilation and fumigation, many gay bars, baths, discos, and even cinemas reek of it.

What may come as news is the fact that a great deal remains to be learned about amyl, particularly in terms of how it exerts the aphrodisiac effects so consistently claimed by those who use it. Nor is much known about its side effects and the potential dangers, if any, from long-term use in large amounts.

That there are no publicized reports of serious adverse effects among amyl users *may* be a reflection of the fact that most who indulge are young and healthy. With two exceptions, all the physicians I queried agreed that amyl is a fairly safe and innocuous drug, provided there are no underlying cardiovascular problems.

"I don't agree at all," one doctor told me. "The healthy human body is incredibly resilient and can take almost anything—but not heavy doses of amyl over a long period of time. I can't prove it, but from what I know about the heart and the properties of the drug, I'm sure it's caused a lot of deaths that were chalked up to something else because the pathologist didn't know his subject had been into the stuff. That there are no studies to prove me wrong couldn't impress me less. There have been no studies *period*."

This doctor's minority view might be dismissed were he not a cardiovascular surgeon of such national prominence that he has been called in as a consulting physician to two U.S. Presidents. The second dissenting physician, who has a large gay practice, posits the novel theory that amyl exacerbates, and may even cause, emphysema.

"No, there's no proof," he told me. "It's just a hunch. Heavy use can't help but affect the lung membranes. One of my patients, a man in his early fifties, has emphysema that worsens markedly when he uses amyl, which is frequently, but he just won't listen to me."

The controversy surrounding amyl is sociocultural as well as medical. Most homosexuals call it "the gay man's drug." Heterosexual devotees, however, are sure that it's the other way around. Some gays and straights alike see amyl's popularity stemming from the war in Vietnam, when the government shipped tons of Burroughs-Wellcome "poppers" to the battlefield for use as an antidote to the cyanide poisoning that can result from prolonged exposure to gun fumes.

The drug's origins as a medicine are clearer. In 1867, Thomas Lauder Brunton, a young Scottish medical student, synthesized amyl nitrite and noticed that the fumes caused flushing of the face due to the widening of capillaries. Correctly assuming that such a property might ease the pain of angina pectoris, a condition characterized by an insufficient supply of oxygen-carrying blood to the heart muscles, he experimented on some patients and got excellent results.

The primary effect of all nitrite drugs, including nitroglycerin, is the relaxation of the body's smooth muscles. Because blood vessels are comprised of such muscles, amyl causes them to dilate. When the drug is sniffed, the vapors dissolve in the nostrils and open up all the vessels in the body within seconds; the heart pounds wildly, and blood "rushes" to the head. But it also rushes out again, as it does from the extremities, causing a precipitous drop in blood pressure. Some physicians argue that the high is somehow a result of the drug itself. Others claim it comes from the rush of oxygenated blood to the head. Still others think that the subsequent *decrease* in blood to the brain is responsible.

A final theory holds that because a lot of men lose their erections on amyl (the drug is sometimes used medically in adult circumcision to deflate an erection that might be dangerous and painful to a freshly stitched penis), the effect is purely psychological. At the other extreme, the mere aroma of amyl in a room is sufficient to give other men who have been conditioned to associate the drug with sex an erection.

Psychological effects can be spectacular. Some people become so ravenous on amyl that they momentarily lose all sense of self-identity and find themselves doing things they didn't think were possible for them. The drug also has a way of blotting out the identity of your partner, making him just another body. Other adverse effects are throbbing headaches and fainting. Unless you enjoy swooning, it's best not to join the current fad of using it while dancing in discos. In the absence of a heart problem, some physicians theorize that the greatest potential danger is if someone has a weak spot in the blood vessels of the head. The amyl could make it blow out, causing a small cerebral hemorrhage. All of the physicians I interviewed insisted that if people are going to use amyl, they should watch the amount. As one doctor told me, "For Christ's sake, tell 'em to come up for air once in a while!"

Amyl nitrite can no longer be obtained legally without a prescription, but butyl nitrite, which has a similar if weaker effect, can be purchased in both liquid and ampule form in adult bookstores, sex boutiques, and on the street. In December 1977, California's state health director filed a lawsuit against the makers of "Rush," charging that it was being sold as an aphrodisiac drug without state and federal approval. (Why the state didn't file suits against the makers of "Locker Room," "Silver Bullet," "Heart On," "Jac-Aroma," and "Aroma of Men," to mention but a few, remains a mystery.) The state charged further that because the major ingredient in Rush is butyl nitrite, the product "causes blood pressure to drop dramatically and can cause death when used as advertised."

The makers of Rush are countering with the assertion that their product is not a drug, is not sold as an aphrodisiac, and has caused no deaths or injuries. "If it's dangerous," said a spokesman for Rush, "the state should produce evidence and quit pestering private enterprise." He knew, of course, that the state has no evidence.

Nor is it true, the spokesman went on, that Rush is advertised as an aphrodisiac. Although the product's slogan is "Purity, Power, & Potency," the last word was not intended to have sexual connotations but was selected because promoters of the "liquid incense" were looking for a third word that started with "P."

Finally, it was emphatically denied that Rush contains butyl nitrite. A pharmacologist, Norman D. Kramer, with the cooperation of a research chemist, had one sample each of two common nitrite products spectroscopically analyzed and told *The Advocate* that one consisted of isobutyl nitrite, which is more potent and volatile on a weight basis than amyl nitrite; the other sample appeared to be isoamyl nitrite. Both contained impurities.

If the state succeeds in forcing the manufacturers of "aromas" out of business, it will be but a matter of time before the underground market is flooded with a variety of nitrites, which are easy and cheap to make; and it is inevitable that other substances will be passed off as nitrites.

**Methyl alcohol:** Methyl alcohol, a hydrocarbon vapor found mainly in paint, aerosols, glue, and petroleum products, is growing in popularity as an inhalant, particularly in discos, where you're apt to see it being passed around on a rag. Its greatest danger lies in its ability to sensitize the heart muscles to adrenaline. It can also injure the kidneys, lungs, brains, and eyes. When booze and vapors are mixed, the two drugs have a cross-tolerance similar to that of barbiturates and alcohol. *Stay away from it!*

# 6.
# Perspectives
# on Aging

Both statistics and suppositions suggest that the greatest problems threatening the health of the gay community are sexually transmitted diseases and alcoholism. But an overriding danger can lie in the inappropriate ways we sometimes choose in coping with a natural process that involves a complex interplay of physical and psychological factors—growing older. Whether we're male or female, gay or straight, and regardless of how we define aging or cosmetize our way around it, none of us is immune to it.

Growing older can precipitate problems unique to gay people, and the sooner we begin dealing with them from a position of strength, the less traumatic our later lives will be. All of them are health-related:

> We often lack strong family ties, children, and the traditional support systems usually associated with assisting the older person.

> We are confronted with a lack of consciousness on the part of local, state, and federal agencies about our emotional, physical, and social needs which, as members of a definable minority group, are different.

> We can lack legal protection in terms of our wills, community property, insurance, taxes, and the eventual death of a lover.

> Finally, because of the physical changes in our bodies, we can become "old" at forty and find ourselves excluded from the sexual marketplace.

Even if you're only twenty-five, you're growing older with each tick of the clock; if you're already close to middle age, you're hard on the heels of a rock-bottom two million members of the gay community who are defined by the government as senior citizens, or sixty-five and older. (Even the most conservative estimates put the national homosexual population at one person in ten.) According to Newt Dieter, a Los Angeles counselor with a predominantly gay clientele, an inordinately high percentage of the patients in "convalescent hospitals" and "skilled nursing facilities" (euphemisms for old age homes) are gay.

That's part of the bad news about being old and gay. The good news is that being gay and older can sometimes be one of the most fulfilling periods of life. Martin S. Weinberg and Colin J. Williams, in their exhaustively researched *Male Homosexuals: Their Problems and Adaptations*, find no age-related differences in self-acceptance, anxiety, depression, or loneliness. "In fact," they write, "our data suggest that in some respects our older homosexuals have a greater well-being than our younger homosexuals." They go on:

> Why these discrepancies between the folk view and the data? The following explanation, based on our field work and questionnaire data, is proposed. The homosexual world places a premium on youth. This means that as far as certain forms of social interaction and sexual gains are concerned, the older homosexual is less valued. Thus, as one gets older there is a decreased participation in certain public institutions of the subculture, such as homosexual bars. There is also a greater problem in obtaining sexual partners.

> The younger homosexual correctly observes this sociosexual situation, that is, that the older homosexual is isolated from certain public facets of the homosexual scene and that his sexual frequency is lower. On the

basis of these facts, the younger person views the older homosexual's situation as unenviable. The same limited perspective appears among journalists and social scientists. From their position (for example, as a married person with a family), the social situation of the older homosexual seems miserable. What heterosexuals and younger homosexuals do not know, our data suggest, is that the older homosexual can often adapt to his social situation.

Weinberg and Williams conclude that the folk beliefs about the older homosexual erroneously attribute to the older homosexual "the perspectives and expectations of younger homosexuals and heterosexuals who hold these beliefs."*

Fred Minnigerode, Ph.D., of the University of San Francisco's department of psychology, has prepared a paper to introduce a major research project to be funded by the National Institute of Mental Health. Now under way at the Center for Homosexual Education, Evaluation and Research (C.H.E.E.R.) in San Francisco, the project is studying the adaptation and problems of gay men and women sixty years of age and older. Although Dr. Minnigerode told me that the paper describes a "small" pilot study, some of the quotes make for interesting reading.

He and his colleagues interviewed six older gay men and five older gay women. Each interview lasted four to five hours. The sample of gay men ranged in age from sixty-one to seventy-seven, while the women ranged from sixty to sixty-nine. Five of the six men lived alone; one lived with an ex-lover with whom he had been living for fifteen years. Four of the five women lived alone; one had been living with her lover for twenty-seven years.

"While the pilot nature of the study did not demand exact matching procedures," writes Dr. Minnigerode, "heterosexual and homosexual respondents were matched on age and on living status (i.e., whether they lived alone or with someone)." His sample of straight men ranged in age from sixty-one to seventy, while the straight women ranged from sixty-one to sixty-six. Five of the six straight men lived alone; one lived with his wife. Four of the five straight women lived alone; one lived with her husband.

Dr. Minnigerode reports that respondents were largely from middle and upper-middle class backgrounds. The gay respondents tended to be more highly educated than the straight respondents.

---

*Martin S. Weinberg and Colin J. Williams, *Male Homosexuals: Their Problems and Adaptations*, New York: Oxford University Press (A Penguin Book), 1975, p. 310ff.

While most respondents were retired from full-time employment, more women were employed than men. All respondents were obtained through "friendship networks" and from gay organizations such as G40+, a social organization for San Francisco gays who are forty years of age or older.

**Adaptations to physical changes:**  Dr. Minnigerode and his colleagues asked: "How would you describe the state of your physical health?" and "Would you consider your own health to be excellent, good, fair, or poor?" Regardless of sexual orientation, respondents generally reported that they were in "good" or "excellent" health.

Respondents were also asked how they perceived the changes in physical appearance that accompany aging. Gay men more frequently perceived these changes negatively than any other group. One man said: "I wish I were young—that is, I wish I had a different body. I'd like to be slender and attractive—more than I am now."

Another man commented: "When you're young, you don't appreciate how great it is to be young and attractive."

Dr. Minnigerode found that compared with gay men, gay women and both groups of heterosexuals showed less concern than homosexual men with changes in physical appearance and the loss of youth.

**Psychological adaptations:**  Two major aspects of psychological adaptation were examined: (1) self-concept; and (2) loneliness and morale. The dimensions of self-concept were age identification, homosexuality, self-esteem, and self-acceptance.

"We examined age identification because age-status labels have been shown to correlate with other measures of physical and psychological well-being," reports Dr. Minnigerode. He and his colleagues asked: "Do you consider yourself to be young, middle-aged, or old?" Gay men, straight men, and both groups of women generally viewed themselves as middle-aged. Gay women showed less agreement, however. One 69-year-old gay woman considered herself "old," but then she had never considered herself "middle-aged." When asked about when she "first considered herself middle-aged," she replied, "I didn't . . . I was an adolescent until I got old . . . five years ago," when she had experienced serious health problems. Another gay woman, at sixty, considered herself "young." She added: "Once I caught myself acting old. I was so surprised. But I won't be old til after I die."

Gay respondents were asked: "Has your homosexuality become *more* or *less* important over the past few decades?" Dr. Minnigerode found that whether being gay became more or less important did not differ between the sexes. "Differences did emerge, however, in terms of what being homosexual meant to them," he reports. Interestingly, gay men frequently viewed their homosexuality in terms of sexual activity. For example, a gay man said:

"Not more important . . . it was always important. I would say probably now less because I'm not as active. When I was young, I was extremely potent and I would have to have sex almost every day."

Gay women, however, frequently viewed their homosexuality in terms of interpersonal relationships. As one gay woman put it:

"Well, actually it's become more important because I was able to leave my marriage without ever looking back and being free to be myself. I really feel more like a woman. I know that I'm at the right place in my life and that I can be myself with some people."

Almost all of the gay respondents indicated that gaining self-acceptance and self-esteem have been long, sometimes lifelong struggles.

**Psychological problems:** In order to identify possible psychological problems, Dr. Minnigerode examined reported morale and feelings of loneliness. He asked such questions as: "Do things keep getting worse as you get older?" "Are you as happy now as when you were younger?" "As you get older, would you say things are better, worse, or the same as you thought they would be?" He found no major difference in morale scores as a function of either sexual orientation or the sex of the respondents.

Then the respondents were asked: "How often do you feel lonely (very often, seldom, never)?" Gay men and gay women reported that they were "often" or "very often" lonely more frequently than straight respondents. "While not an uncommon problem in old age," concludes Dr. Minnigerode, "loneliness might occur more frequently among older homosexual people than among heterosexuals."

**Sexual adaptations:** While all respondents reported that sexual activity had decreased over their lives, *gay men generally reported* *greater current sexual activity than any other group.* As one gay man said: "Well, it's important. I like sex. Naturally, as you grow older, the fires become a little banked, but they're still burning. I just don't go after it hammer and tong the way I used to, but I still seek it out."

Frequency of sexual activity varied in the other three groups with a few of the respondents in each group reporting themselves to be celibate. But none of the gay men called himself celibate. Dr. Minnigerode also examined the relative priority given to sexual activity and concludes that men, regardless of sexual orientation, give sex a higher priority than women.

**Personal perspectives on life:** Turning points, or milestones, in the respondents' lives were examined. Gay men and gay women resembled straight men in that their milestones frequently pertained to employment, education, and retirement. Straight women differed from the other three groups in that their milestones were more often family-related in terms of marriage, having children, and children leaving home.

Respondents were also asked to indicate which aspects of their lives have been *most* and *least* satisfying. Gay respondents frequently reported that work-related accomplishments were most satisfying and that difficulties related to personal growth (partially achieving self-worth) were least satisfying.

Gay respondents were asked how their homosexuality influenced their lives. Responses varied considerably. One gay man said:

"This is like asking what would it be like . . . would your life have been any different if your eyesight was slightly defective, or if you had one lame leg. The answer is that it's in the background of everything you do . . . I feel that homosexuality has created a narrower horizon than life would otherwise have had for me. I feel also that because of it, I have used in my life less initiative than I would otherwise have. I have been, in a sense, not crippled, but cramped because of it."

But a 69-year-old gay woman saw homosexuality as enriching rather than "cramping":

"I lived in a little suburb for a while outside of Buffalo. It was kind of a snobbish little place where people played bridge and golf and got married in their twenties. I might even have gotten married and had a family, when I think of it now. And in a way, I'm glad I didn't get stuck in that little conventional community and turn into a bridge person, playing golf, or going to the country club and those things. I am glad in a way. If I had been a 'normal' . . . am I saying 'normal'? . . . heterosexual in those days, I might have fallen into that scheme of life, and not known any of the diversity that I have had."

Although Dr. Minnigerode's pilot study is scarcely conclusive, it does suggest the many positive aspects of being old and gay. While we can do nothing to keep our bodies from aging, we can remain mentally young and physically active if we stay open to new ideas and experiences. And we can choose to develop and project certain attitudes in our youth that will insure the respect, affection, and support so often denied to the older members of our community.

> FOR THE DISCRIMINATING MALE WHO PREFERS TO MAINTAIN A VIRILE AND YOUTHFUL BODY APPEARANCE—NO OLD GRAY BODY HAIRS, WE COVER ALL!
>
> Look youthfully fit, whether lounging at the poolside or beach. We will color those ugly gray chest and body hairs away. Restore youthful color to those body hairs before your next date or outing now!

So runs a prominent display ad in a gay publication. When I clipped it and showed it to a man in his fifties, his first reaction was to state that the worst bigots when it comes to age are gay people themselves.

"A lot of these young hunks don't realize that being gay and older can be one of the most fulfilling experiences in life," he told me. "Frankly, I feel sorry for them. If they maintain the attitude reflected in this silly ad, they're going to spend the rest of their lives in a futile race with time. They're going to be the victims of the dual pressures of aging and anti-gayness exerted from both inside and outside the gay community, and chances are they'll try coping with the resulting depression by hitting the bottle—or worse."

Historically, men are twice as likely to kill themselves as women. Most of the men I interviewed stated that they knew gay people who had threatened or attempted suicide, whereas most of the women did not. After a lifetime of being programmed by straight society to think of themselves as sex objects, gay women, for the most part, appear to resist applying those repressive values to others. For that reason, aging is simply not the crucial concern for most gay women that it is for their male counterparts, a significant number of whom see suicide as a way out.

Many of the "young hunks" I interviewed in bars stated that they do not socialize with gay people over the age of thirty-five or so and expressed attitudes about the older male homosexual that are summarized in the following caricature:

> He no longer goes to bars, having lost his physical attractiveness, and his sexual appeal to the young men he craves. He is oversexed, but his sex life is very unsatisfactory.
>
> He has been unable to form a lasting relationship with a sexual partner, and he is seldom active sexually anymore. When he does have sex, it is usually in a tearoom or a bath frequented by the Geritol set.
>
> He has disengaged from the gay world and his acquaintances in it. He is retreating further and further into the "closet"—fearful of disclosure and his "perversion."
>
> Most of his associations are now increasingly with heterosexuals. In a bizarre and deviant world centered around age, he is labeled "an old queen" as he becomes quite effeminate.

Jim Kelley, Ph.D., a social worker in gerontology, devised this caricature as a tool in his 1974 doctoral dissertation entitled *Brothers and Brothers: The Gay Man's Adaptation to Aging*. It was the first piece of research on the subject to be completed in this country at such a comprehensive level and revealed that despite the prevailing attitudes of both straights and younger gays, which are based on the obvious exceptions, *homosexual men are more easily adaptable to aging than their straight counterparts.*

After analyzing a total of 193 questionnaires and 43 taped interviews, Dr. Kelly was able to construct what he calls a "composite man" that is at odds with the popular caricature. First and foremost, eighty-three percent of the men he studied over the age of sixty-five reported being sexually satisfied—a much higher rate than for straight men in a comparable group. His composite of the aging gay man:

> He does not frequent tearooms but occasionally goes out to bars, particularly those that serve his own peer group.

The extent of his participation in the gay world is low to moderate and based largely on his individual desires. He says his concern about disclosure of sexual orientation is related to his many years of working in a profession where known gays are not tolerated.

He has many gay friends and fewer heterosexual friends. His sex life is quite satisfactory and he desires sexual contact with adult men, especially those near his own age—but he is not currently involved in a gay liaison.

He does not consider himself effeminate, nor does he define himself in terms of gay age labels; but he remembers the terms that were commonly applied to older gays when he was younger.

The exceptions to Dr. Kelly's "composite man," because they are so conspicuous in bars, baths, and restaurants, are often taken as the rule by younger gays, who tend to dismiss them as "dirty old men" with a taste for chicken—unless they happen to have money and social prestige, in which case they are referred to as "older gentlemen."

Gentlemen or not, most of them find adaptation to aging difficult because of their ongoing pursuit of men who are young enough to be their grandchildren. Invariably, the younger man falls short of the mark when it comes to providing the depth of companionship and common interests required. Aside from preferring younger men sexually, "older gentlemen" have something else in common: an overriding fear of death. But in the final analysis, the fear is not so much of death itself as it is of not having lived.

Perry, a rich and socially prominent man now close to seventy-five spends about half his time looking for "the perfect lover"—always someone at least fifty years his junior—and the other half running to doctors with the slightest complaints imaginable. "I still believe it's possible for someone my age to find a younger man who's capable of bridging the age-gap," he told me, "and I intend to keep on looking for him until they pat me in the face with a spade."

Perry's innumerable attempts at a permanent liaison have averaged, by his own frank reckoning, three or four months. The first step is to attract the young man's attention. If he's a waiter in a gay restaurant, for example, the most common ploy is to leave an enormous tip. Once contact is established, Perry takes him on a shopping spree at the finest clothing stores. Next comes a carefully planned trip, one that always includes selected visits with his similarly rich and prominent gay friends around the country. "Showing off my conquests gives me pleasure," he says. "God knows my friends have done it to me often enough."

If the young man passes social muster ("I don't want a parlor oaf," says Perry), he is pressured to move in. To cloak him with respectability, Perry enrolls him in a nearby school, thereby conferring the title of "student." If he flunks out, which is often the case, Perry tells his friends that the young man stays at home all the time because he has taken up creative writing.

At the end of three or four months, however, the relationship sours for one of two reasons: The young man complains about Perry's possessiveness and is summarily dismissed from hearth and home as an ingrate; or he is caught tricking with someone his own age.

"I'm philosophical about it," says Perry. "I certainly don't pout. In fact, I don't waste any time at all finding someone else."

When I interviewed him, Perry had just acquired an extraordinarily attractive, and expensive, prostitute. "With that sort of background," he says, "he's easier to control. And because he's been with all the best people, he comes across as exceedingly well-bred, which is important to me."

But Perry and his ilk are the exceptions rather than the rule. Contrary to popular belief, few aging homosexuals use prostitutes, even of the live-in variety.

## OUR BODIES

Physical aging begins in the middle to late twenties and continues to death. We can prolong life through self-care and competent medical management, but there is *no* way to prolong physical youth.

Why we age is still a subject of debate among gerontologists. But most of them believe that the primary cause is the mutation of cells. Our bodies are constantly re-creating themselves by replacing cells that have died. They do this by a process known as "somatic division," or dividing into two, thereby preserving the precise characteristics of the original cell. It is possible, however, for cellular mutations, or chromosomal damage, to occur as a result of any number of factors, including prolonged exposure to the sun, disease, and nuclear radiation. Because mutations are irreversible, the distortion is passed on whenever the original cell reproduces.

A secondary cause of aging is the loss of some cells. From the mid-twenties on, there is a continuous reduction of neurons in the brain and spinal cord. Once gone, they can never be replaced, and the process can be accelerated by arteriosclerosis.

Although the reduction and loss of hormones is an important factor in aging, it cannot be considered a cause. During menopause, ovaries stop producing estrogen in women; and as men grow older, the secretion of testosterone by the testicles declines. It is true that injections of these sex hormones after middle age can reduce some of the symptoms of aging, such as wrinkled skin and a dry vagina, but they cannot stop the process of aging from continuing.

We know that stress can cause diseases and lead to premature death. It is not yet known how, but it can also accelerate the mutation and loss of cells. We may not be able to stop the basic process of growing old, but by modifying or eliminating the stress factors in our lives we can do much to slow it. By getting off a relationship that clearly won't work, for example, we can literally begin a "new lease on life."

As our bodies change and grow older, their susceptibility to diseases can increase because of the impairment of natural defense mechanisms. Respiratory and cardiovascular diseases can be more frequent and severe; scratches are more liable to infection; broken bones heal more slowly. Some of the disorders associated with growing older, while not exclusive to gay people, are of particular concern because of our life-style.

**Prostatic disorders:** The prostate gland, which surrounds the juncture of the bladder and urethra, supplies a fluid during ejaculation without which sperm is sterile. In men, it functions as an "erogenous zone," one that makes anal intercourse that much more pleasurable. Normally, it measures about one and three-quarters inches by an inch and a half; but it can become dangerously enlarged as we grow older, and it is the site of one of the most common forms of cancer in men. (As discussed in Chapter Two, prostatitis, or inflammation of the gland, can be relieved with antibiotics.) Symptoms of an enlarged prostate include slow and sometimes painful urination, lack of a good, forceful stream, lots of pauses, and dribbling. Sometimes urination is blocked altogether.

If the gland is seriously enlarged, or cancerous, it must sometimes be surgically removed. The operation does not render a man impotent (unless he chooses to let it), but the absence of the gland diminishes the delights of anal intercourse and results in the ejaculation of semen backwards into the bladder, rather than externally. If your doctor wants to remove your prostate, you should get at least two additional opinions.

Almost 60,000 American men will develop cancer of the prostate this year, and 20,000 will die. In its earliest stages, however, the disease can be cured by surgery or radiation, or both. Some cancer of the prostate responds to hormonal therapy.

Unfortunately, ninety percent of the prostatic cancers now discovered are diagnosed only after the malignancy has spread beyond the gland. Until recently, diagnosis depended on rectal examination by the physician's finger and the detection of a marked rise in the bloodstream of an enzyme known as acid phosphatase. In January 1978, researchers from the Southern California Permanente Medical Group and UCLA announced the development of new blood tests that can detect the enzyme during the earliest stages of the disease. Ask your doctor about this new test when you go in for your regular physical, which should always include a proctological examination if you're over forty.

**Circumcision:** The tip of an uncircumcised penis is hooded by the prepuce, or foreskin. If your Jewish or Islamic, you were ritually circumcised shortly after birth; in many parts of the world, hospitals circumcise routinely regardless of the baby's religious background.

There is considerable debate (but no hard evidence) that the presence or absence of a foreskin makes a whit of difference in sexual pleasure or the time needed to reach a climax. The best argument for the operation remains a hygienic one. In uncircumcised men, a white secretion known as smegma (or "crotch cheese") can accumulate under the foreskin and, unless washed away, can become smelly, dirty, and cause inflammation. There is a link between smegma and cancer of the penis, as well as growing evidence that it causes cervical cancer in women. (There is no evidence, however, that it can lead to rectal cancer as a result of anal intercourse.) But as long as a man is scrupulous about rolling back his foreskin and washing thoroughly, he has nothing to worry about. In rare cases, however, the foreskin can become so uncomfortably tight in the middle years that the only remedy is circumcision.

Some physicians believe that circumcised men are less prone to attacks of genital herpes. Paul, at thirty, had been experiencing major flareups under the foreskin and decided to do whatever was necessary to rid himself of the nuisance. He reports as follows:

My foreskin was fairly tight, but in my opinion, not to the point of causing any real problems. When I consulted my internist, he diagnosed the herpes syndrome and referred me to a dermatologist, who confirmed the internist's diagnosis and treated me with a special dye and exposure to neon light. It's difficult to say whether the treatment was helpful or not, as the length of time I was afflicted seemed to be about the same as it was when there was no treatment at all for previous bouts. Having read that herpes can be exacerbated by stress, I tried taking Valium during subsequent flareups and found that the tranquilizer seemed to decrease severity and length of recovery time. I also found that long hours of sleep were helpful.

After another major bout with herpes my internist referred me to a urological surgeon with the suggestion that I be circumcised. The surgeon agreed.

Just prior to the surgery my lower abdominal and pubic areas were shaved, and I was given a pre-op tranquilizer by injection. Next came a local anesthetic, an injection at the base of the penis.

My surgeon chose to pull the skin over the head of the penis and lop it if. (Another method, one I saw used when I was a medic in the Navy, consists of clamping the tissue with hemostats before cutting.) My surgeon used a number of individual sutures and tied each one separately. He used gut sutures, he told me, for simpler removal and to reduce scarring. For the most part, this appears to have been successful.

As for recovery, the first few days to a week presented the biggest problem. Swelling began about the second day after surgery. There was some slight bleeding, and my wound had to be wrapped with soft gauze twice a day. Ice packs helped reduce the swelling and, to some degree, the pain. They also helped prevent erections.

My first "permissible" erection came about four weeks after the operation, but just to play it safe, I waited another two weeks before having sex.

Five years have passed, and I haven't had any more trouble

with herpes. However, in retrospect, I don't find the connection to surgery as being logical. Herpes on the lips can occur with or without sex and the sores are open to the air, kept clean, and so forth. Why a circumcision should be a remedy for genital herpes I don't know. Besides, circumcised individuals suffer from herpes as well. Perhaps it's psychological.

While I was self-conscious as a kid about not being circumcised, I now wish I could reverse the operation. I miss that part of me that I had for thirty years! Sex is definitely different now, and it took some getting used to. I won't say it's better or worse, just different.

A person considering circumcision should definitely discuss it with his lover or sex partner to see how *he* feels about it. In my case, I didn't bother. As a result, my lover is *still* having problems adjusting to the change and resents the internist who recommended it.

Medically, if it has to be done it has to be done; otherwise, my advice to your readers is *don't.* Obviously, mine is an individual case. To be fair, I should mention that while a medic in the Navy I assisted in a number of circumcisions and heard several of the patients say how much better they enjoyed sex after recovery, so the issue is certainly a matter of opinion.

Because their concerns are aesthetic as well as medical, most gay men require some counseling before and after circumcision. A competent, caring physician can provide this, as can the surgeon to whom he refers you. One of the physicians I interviewed recalls a gay man who, upon being told that he needed circumcision, replied: "Well, just go ahead and chop away . . . I don't care what it looks like as long as you get the job done." The patient had to be reminded that it was *okay* to be concerned about how his penis would look. "After we talked about it for a while," said the physician, "it became apparent that he was more anxious about that than anything else and had been trying to hide his feelings."

**Breast cancer:** Breast cancer is not only the leading cause of death from cancer among women, but also the most common cause of death among American women between the ages of forty and fifty. Within the next twelve months, more than 30,000 American women will die of breast cancer, and 90,000 new cases will be diagnosed. Ultimately, one out of every fifteen women in the country between the ages of twenty-five and seventy-five will develop the disease. And although *no* woman is immune, your chance of getting it *could* be greater if you're gay.

According to Lucienne Lanson, M.D., the noted gynecologist, columnist, and author of *Woman to Woman*, the most likely candidate for breast cancer is Caucasian, between thirty-five and sixty-five, *with few or no children*, or has postponed pregnancy until the age of twenty-eight. Additional factors include the beginning of menstruation at a relatively early age, a previous breast problem such as fibrocystic disease, and a family history that includes a mother or sister with breast cancer. The hereditary factor alone can increase the risk two or three times over that observed in the general female population. Dr. Lanson emphasizes, however, that such a "profile" is at best a general guide. Many women who match it exactly remain free of the disease.

No woman should rely entirely on periodic examinations by her physician. Self-examination at home, on your own, should be monthly, preferably during the week following your period, if you're still menstruating. It is fair to say that given the enormous amount of publicity about breast cancer within the past five years (thanks in large measure to Betty Ford and Happy Rockefeller), almost all literate women know how to examine themselves. Life-threatening problems arise, however, when the examinations are less frequent than monthly, and when diagnosis and treatment are delayed out of fear. Most lumps in the breast are *not* cancerous, but only your doctor, who is equipped with the latest diagnostic devices and techniques, can tell for sure.

Emily L. Sisley, Ph.D., and Bertha Harris, the authors of *The Joy of Lesbian Sex*, emphasize the profound psychological and physical implications of breast removal:

> Should you or your lover be faced with the necessity for mastectomy, it is essential that you discuss openly your feelings, your fears, your fantasies about how it may affect each of you and your relationship. Most lesbians are fully in touch with how much pleasure they derive from breast-play in lovemaking, both as recipients and givers, so there is no use in denying that something will be missing. The loss needs to be felt and grieved.

They go on to provide some sound advice on further adaptation to an impending mastectomy:

Don't be too quick to protest that it won't matter. Chances are that, eventually, given a mature and loving relationship, it won't. But don't rush to give assurances too prematurely. They won't be believed, and you'll end up doubting how much you meant it.

Demand as much information as you can get about the extent of the operation, how the area will look afterwards (try to get a drawing or, better yet, some photographs of women who have had the same procedure), etc. Discuss all this with your lover. Cooperate in preparing each other.

Try to make contact with other women who have had mastectomies (most major hospitals can be of help here) and especially with lesbians. People who have been in the same boat are usually quite adept at throwing lifelines. Again, share these experiences with your lover.

Since sheer sex is not at the very heart of most lesbian relationships, it is good to spend some time focusing on the things other than sex that you both treasure in your relationship. But don't pretend for a moment that a quick burst of positive thinking will eliminate your anxieties. It just doesn't work like that, but with patience and caring you both will most likely adapt successfully.

Ironically, an unattached gay woman can find a mastectomy easier to cope with than the woman who has a lover and, presumably, a great deal of loving support. "Many relationships are damaged when one of the partners changes," believe Sisley and Harris, "but once a woman is breastless a new lover is likely to accept her state from the outset. It is perhaps a poor consolation, but it does mean that her life can continue much as before."*

**Endometriosis:** A woman who ovulates regularly and who does not become pregnant over a period of several years is a likely candidate for endometriosis, a pelvic disease that affects between five and ten percent of all women, especially between the ages of

---

*Dr. Emily L. Sisley and Bertha Harris, *The Joy of Lesbian Sex*. New York, Crown, 1977, p. 155.

twenty-five and forty-five. Unchecked, it can be responsible for menstrual misery and severe pain during certain forms of lesbian sex-play.

Endometriosis is a condition where fragments of tissue from the uterine lining are deposited, become embedded, and grow outside the confines of the uterine cavity. The exact cause of the disease is unknown. For most women, the onset is marked by increasingly painful periods and a nagging soreness in the lower abdomen preceding menstruation by two and even three weeks. Because the disease often involves the uterine ligaments, which are highly sensitive, the slightest pressure against them can cause a sharp, shooting pain. The thrust of a dildo against the upper vagina or cervix can therefore be unbearably painful, just as is deep penile penetration for a straight woman with the disease.

The best way to avoid endometriosis is to become pregnant, an option not generally open to gay women. Sometimes the long-term use of birth control pills with suppression of ovulation for extended periods can prevent the disease from developing in susceptible women. When a gay woman is stricken, her gynecologist is apt to create a state of pseudopregnancy by means of hormone therapy administered by mouth or injections at regular intervals over a period of several months. In the majority of the cases so treated, the implants dissolve, pelvic pain disappears, and sex can again be enjoyed.

In rare cases, extensive endometriosis can be dealt with only by removing the uterus and at times even the ovaries. "As radical as this procedure may seem," asks Dr. Lanson, "would it be less radical to allow such a woman to remain a pelvic cripple, as well as unable to tolerate sexual intercourse?"

**Pelvic cancer:** The most common forms of pelvic cancer involves the cervix and the uterus, but because cancer of the cervix is almost certainly caused by a sexually transmitted virus during heterosexual intercourse, the disease is virtually never seen in nuns and gay women.

Cancer of the uterus, or endometrial cancer, is most frequently found in women over fifty who have had previously irregular periods and sporadic ovulation. The most common symptom is spotting or bleeding after menopause.

Cancer of the ovaries, while far less prevalent than either cervical or endometrial cancer, is responsible for more deaths than any other pelvic malignancy and currently ranks fourth, behind cancer of the breast, colon, and lung, as the most common cause of *cancer* deaths among American women. Although more frequent in post-menopausal women, it can strike at any age and shows no predilection for any particular group. Early symptoms may include persistent indigestion and a sense of pelvic fullness or lower abdominal discomfort.

Other pelvic malignancies involving the reproductive tract (cancer of the vulva, vagina, and Fallopian tubes) are rare and occur primarily in postmenopausal women.

At present, pelvic cancers account for approximately 24,000 deaths in America each year. Dr. Lanson confirms the estimate that if every woman had an annual pelvic exam, a Pap smear at least every two years, and if she promptly reported any unusual bleeding during her menopause and postmenopausal years, almost 100,000 lives could be saved within the next five years.

Treatment for pelvic malignancies almost always involves some form of hysterectomy and/or oophorectomy. Generally, a hysterectomy means the surgical removal of the uterus; a "complete" hysterectomy removes the cervix as well. An oophorectomy refers to the removal of one or both ovaries, while a salpingo-oophorectomy includes the removal of the Fallopian tubes.

But cancer is not the only pelvic disease treated surgically. A hysterectomy is performed to cure a condition known as adenomyosis, which most commonly afflicts women between the age of thirty-five and fifty and is marked by prolonged, heavy periods. Uterine fibroids, which approximately twenty to twenty-five percent of all women over thirty have, are also treated surgically; more hysterectomies are performed because of fibroid tumors than for any other female pelvic problem.

Regardless of the reason for a hysterectomy and/or an oophorectomy, the gay woman should remember that her womanliness does not depend on her ability to bear children. Nor does her ability to respond sexually depend on the presence of the uterus, ovaries, and Fallopian tubes, which have no bearing whatsoever on lovemaking. "If your lover should need such surgery," write Sisley and Harris, "patiently help her to understand that you love *her*—not her ovaries or her uterus, or her appendix or nasal septum."

**Sexual response:** That the natural physical degeneration of aging slows down the sexual process in men cannot be denied: The production of semen, getting it up, and climax all take more time and stimulation, and the need for orgasm begins to diminish shortly after puberty. From the age of twenty on, the decline in the production of testosterone is steady, but after age sixty, the rate of decline actually eases off. In the absence of adverse psychological, physical (disease), and nutritional factors, the amount of testosterone produced is usually sufficient for sexual activity right to the end of life.

Contrary to old wives' tales, menopause does not diminish sexuality but can increase it. Even though the ovaries stop producing estrogen altogether, women in their fifties, sixties, seventies, and even eighties can and do enjoy a richly rewarding sex-life with each other. In straight women, menopause can lead to psychological blocks and a loss of self-esteem; but because the ability to bear children has not played a dominant role in the lives of most gay women, "the change of life" is seldom traumatic. Many of the women I interviewed stated that they are actually looking forward to the more settled time when they are no longer bothered by monthly periods.

**Skin cancers:** "Too much of a good thing can be wonderful," purred the incomparable Miss West. But she didn't mean the sun. In sensible doses, sunshine can be a source of vitamin D. It can also help clear pimply complexions and take the edges off the heartbreak of psoriasis. Prolonged exposure to ultraviolet rays, however, can cause skin cancers and premature aging of the skin.

There is no evidence that gay people, especially men, are more likely to develop skin cancer than anyone else. But the gay lifestyle, which places such a high premium on a youthful appearance, often includes an inordinate amount of time in the broiling sun. Psychologists are in a quandary when it comes to explaining why people associate a tan with robust good health and youth. Not too long ago, among Caucasians, an alabaster complexion was the ideal. But today, the beach looms large as a social fixture of the gay scene and is seriously rivaled by only the baths and the bars.

Dermatologists agree that the only known way to prevent skin cancer is the avoidance of exposure to strong sunlight year in and year out. People with blue eyes and fair skin are particularly susceptible, whereas those with brown eyes and a naturally darker complexion, because of the higher degree of melanin in their skin, don't have as much to worry about.

When they appear, skin cancers are raised growths, generally on the face, that don't heal. They can be brown, white, red, and scaly. Only a physician, however, is equipped to make a positive diagnosis and proceed with the appropriate treatment, which can consist of freezing, burning, or excision. According to S. J. Stegman, M.D., the noted San Francisco dermatologist, ninety-five percent of basal cell carcinoma, the most common kind of skin cancer, can be cured with one office visit provided that treatment is not delayed. When squamous cell carcinoma—the less common variety that most frequently appears on the lips—goes untreated, it can spread beneath the skin and metastasize to other parts of the body.

Sunlamps are even more dangerous than the sun. They, too, emit ultraviolet rays that can cause cancer and premature aging, and if you fall asleep under one you could wind up in the hospital with severe burns and eye damage, which is what happens to 12,000 people a year. Besides, sunlamps won't truly tan you. At best, they impart a pinkish glow. Use them only when prescribed by your physician for a skin condition, and make sure the kind you buy has an automatic timer and shut-off device.

A light tan, when "worn" with attention to the color and cut of your clothes, can be just as sexy as a deep one, and it can be safely acquired if you use a lotion with a sunscreen and gradually build up the melanin in your skin. Some people have discovered that lightening their hair just a shade can also create the illusion of a darker tan.

**Physical appearance:**   As we age, our skin becomes dryer, loses its elasticity, and wrinkles. As noted, the process can be rapidly accelerated by too much exposure to the sun. As pigment ceases to be produced, hair turns gray and becomes thinner—often to the point of baldness, especially in men. The gradual atrophy of facial bones, recession of the gums, and the loss of teeth are also factors that conspire to make us look "old."

Few things suggest age more than dingy, yellowish teeth. Coffee, tea, and tobacco can stain otherwise healthy teeth and should be kept to a minimum or eliminated entirely. A trip to the dentist every six months for a checkup and a thorough cleaning is a good medical and cosmetic investment (some of the gay men I interviewed have their teeth professionally cleaned every three months).

Unless you're suffering from untreated tooth decay, a gum disease, a gastrointestinal upset, or some other underlying cause that requires medical attention, the best way to eliminate bad breath is to floss between your teeth after meals. And when you brush your teeth, brush your tongue as well. All a mouthwash can do is temporarily mask odors that are already there.

But the two factors that most older people overlook in caring for themselves are nutrition and exercise. The essential difference between the nutritional needs of older and younger people is quantity. As physical activity decreases and the metabolic rate falls, the older person needs less caloric intake. If we eat as much at fifty as we did at twenty-five, it's bound to show, especially if we're not exercising sufficiently.

As we age, our muscles weaken naturally; unless we keep them toned through regular exercise, they can affect posture. A person can undergo a complete face-lift and hair transplants, but if he's stooped and has lost the spring in his step, all the plastic surgery in the world won't keep him from "looking his age." It might be added that while a plastic surgeon can erase most of the wrinkles, he can do nothing about the listless, sometimes bloodshot eyes that betray too much drinking and suggest old age.

**Plastic surgery:** Most of the men I interviewed expressed a keen interest in plastic surgery. Some of them are even building special savings accounts to pay for it when they feel the time is ripe. With the exception of two who were concerned about sagging breasts, the gay women to whom I spoke did not see plastic surgery as much of a solution to looking old.

The men who are actively considering going under the knife believe that plastic surgery is a logical extension of trying to look good. As one man put it, "We diet, we pump iron, and we spend lots on hairstyling and clothes, so why not tighten up the skin when the time comes? If it's just hanging there loose, we don't need it."

Although it can vary, the best time for a man to have his face lifted is in his early forties. If he waits much longer, he runs the risk of looking radically altered rather than more youthful. But the face-lift, and the eye-lift that usually accompanies it, is but one of several surgical procedures that can counterfeit youth and health.

Acne scars, if the result of teenage problems, can be corrected to a limited degree, but if you're suffering from *adult* acne, as a surprising number of men are—and well into their fifties—you may need a dermatologist rather than a plastic surgeon. The procedures for smoothing pitted skin vary (chemical peeling, sanding), and can be combined with face-lifts.

We know that male baldness can be inherited, but we sometimes forget that it can be acquired through accidents or a temporary illness. In either event, the patient who wants to regain his lost hair with transplants needs five to ten "sittings" with a plastic surgeon, and he had best prepare himself for the disconcerting fact that the results are generally limited.

Unfortunately, "chinless" has come to connote "spineless." A relatively simple procedure, one requiring a chin implant, can supply the "character" the patient seeks; but if the condition is extreme, as it is in generations of Hapsburgs, be warned that bone surgery may be necessary.

Some men find a "pectus excavatus" (or fist-sized indentation at the top of the breastbone) sexy, but not everybody. It can usually be filled out with silicone. The so-called pigeon chest, or bowing, is much more difficult to cope with surgically and requires more radical procedures.

Plastic surgeons have learned that when it comes to penises, size is in the eyes of the beholder. The man who has convinced himself that he's too small is almost always suffering from a psychological hang-up, not a physiological anomaly. Although penile implants can provide a permanent erection, there is no way to enlarge the penis.

A lot of gay men are concerned about their penises "looking pretty" in addition to functioning properly. What a plastic surgeon *can* do is correct scarring caused by a sloppy circumcision, or an infection. Certain erection problems, particularly those caused by accidents, operations, or illness, can also be corrected. And believe it or not, the "angle of the dangle" can be altered, thus eliminating lateral aim.

Crash dieting, almost always dangerous, can lead to cosmetic problems that only a qualified plastic surgeon can correct. The older man who loses weight too rapidly can develop what look like female breasts, loose folds of skin around the abdomen, and "bat-wings" under the arms.

The lifting of buttocks is a radical procedure, one that can result in extensive scarring and vein-drainage problems. A much more sensible solution to a sagging ass is a regimen of exercise designed to keep your buns toned and riding high.

Unfortunately, exercise won't help sagging female breasts. But a relatively simple procedure, one that requires no more than two nights in the hospital, can. One of the women I interviewed told me that her pendulous breasts had become such a problem in terms of self-esteem that she was unable to respond sexually. "I finally decided to see a plastic surgeon," she told me, "a marvelous woman who understood exactly how I felt. I went into the hospital on Sunday night, was operated on Monday morning, and went home Tuesday afternoon. It was almost completely painless—unless you count the $2,500 the whole thing cost me. But that was the best investment I ever made. I feel like a new woman."

The cost of plastic surgery can vary widely, but most procedures, including hospitalization, run between $1,500 and $5,000. Unless your surgeon can prove that the operation has medically therapeutic as well as cosmetic benefits, your insurance won't cover it. As a general rule of thumb, you might remember that cheap plastic surgery is not reliable, and reliable plastic surgery is not cheap. It is *major* surgery, with all the attendant risks, and it requires a surgeon who is not only an expensively trained scientist, but an elegant artisan.

If you're looking for a good plastic surgeon, the best place to begin is with your personal physician, who can recommend someone who is board-certified. He will also be able to tell you at which hospitals the surgeon enjoys staff privileges. If you don't have a personal physician, *do not* depend on the Yellow Pages or advertisements. Telephone the local medical society for a list of reputable surgeons in your area.

You wouldn't dream of traveling south of the border, or to Japan, to have your gall bladder removed. But when it comes to plastic surgery, it's amazing how many people see their travel agents first. There are some excellent surgeons in other countries, but you should know that one of the most important aspects of successful plastic surgery is follow-up. Unless you have unlimited time and money, it's generally better to stick close to home.

Finally, don't be surprised if your request for surgery is turned down. If in interviewing you the competent plastic surgeon concludes that your concerns grow from psychological rather than genuinely physical problems, he or she might recommend psychiatry instead of the knife. Unfortunately, you'll eventually be able to find someone who, for a fat fee, will do almost anything you ask, and the results can be disastrous. When only thirty, one of the men I interviewed wanted to have his face lifted but was told by a succession of surgeons that he was letting his mirror lie to him. He finally went to a Mexican border town, underwent a "quickie," and had to spend thousands more several months later to have the botched job mended.

## OUR ESTATES

To digress somewhat, the lack of legal protection when it comes to our wills, community property, insurance, taxes, the eventual death of a lover, and even the custody of children brings the interplay of the physical and psychological factors that affect the aging process into sharp and painful focus. The stress, poor health, and broken relationships that can result from legal misunderstandings with your lover can be avoided through a clear understanding at the outset and the guidance of a competent attorney.

If your lawyer *isn't* gay, it is imperative that he or she be sympathetic to your life-style. This is of particular importance during divorce proceedings, when child-custody squabbles arise; and it is just as important when you and your lover are investing in mutual property, taking out insurance, and drawing up wills.

As a general rule, it is best that real estate be held in joint tenancy; if for some advantageous reason your lawyer recommends otherwise, it is essential that you and your lover have a private, written agreement providing for the disposition of property in the event of a split-up or death. Such an agreement must always insist on airtight wills. If everything is in your lover's name and he or she dies intestate, the law isn't about to recognize you as the surviving spouse with right of inheritance; his or her family can swoop down within hours after the funeral (if not before), evict you from your home, and *legally* expropriate its contents. This happens with amazing frequency—nor is it limited to situations in which the departed lover's family was actively opposed to the relationship.

During the seventeen years they were together, Rob and Allan built up a lucrative antique dealership in Los Angeles that was tragically terminated when Rob, at only thirty-nine, dropped dead from a heart attack. Allan lost everything, including his home, and has no legal recourse.

"Rob and I had agreed that because I had no business sense," he told me, "it would be simpler to keep everything in his name. My forte was waiting on customers and advising them on decorating. Technically, I was Rob's employee. Sure, we'd talked about drawing up a partnership agreement and wills, but that's the sort of thing you tend to postpone when you're still in your thirties. Besides, as Rob always said, his family loved me like a son and would never be a problem. Famous last words."

In the absence of a written agreement and a will, Rob's family displayed their true colors. They had never approved of the relationship and had tolerated it only to keep peace in the family. They were also greedy. Rob's lawyer, who had limited his advice to tax matters, knew Allan only as Rob's employee and could do nothing to help.

"When I went to see him," said Allan, "I told him that Rob and I were lovers. He was straight, but he told me that had he known about us before Rob's death he would have advised him to protect me. But Rob was so uptight about letting people know . . . he used to say that it was 'unprofessional' to reveal your private life when dealing with lawyers and other business types."

Gay couples who espouse the notion that "reducing" a relationship to legal documents is cheapening in that it apes heterosexual unions are headed for certain trouble. Like it or not, we are creatures of a culture that has conditioned us to tie emotions to money. The resulting stress can be damaging to our health, but it can be mitigated by the guidance of a competent lawyer who understands our legal needs as gay people. Choosing the right lawyer can be as difficult as finding a physician, and legal fees can be expensive. But by using reliable personal recommendations or the references provided in the Appendix, you'll eventually find someone who can assist you without charging an arm and a leg.

Finally, when you and your lawyer do draw up your will, consider bequests to gay-oriented clinics and other organizations that are concerned with gay rights and services. The few people I was able to find who have already done this report that it gave them a tremendous psychological boost and a sense of pride.

Newt Dieter believes that regardless of age, everyone has something to communicate and a need to communicate it.

"Far more frequently than I would like to admit," he says, "I see men and women in their forties, fifties, and sixties extending themselves to younger people. What I see them getting back for their efforts, unless they are people of prominence, wealth, or social position, is rejection and an attitude that immediately places attempts at human contact in the realm of sexual overtures."

Like many who are familiar with the problems of the aging homosexual, Deiter points to the dramatic importance of providing ourselves with a network of support that is not delimited by age. Without it, he believes, we can jeopardize our adaptation to aging and the inevitable approach to death:

"As we mature as a community, it is my hope that we will devote some of our efforts to taking care of aging persons by providing them with the emotional support that they so desperately need in the later years of their lives. If we who have the youth and vigor to do this now will take the time, then when *we* have a need for this support group and this care, it will be there."

# 7.
# Holistic Health
# and Preventive
# Medicine

A vast amount of our ill health is caused by the way we live, by the environment we've created and by the life-style we've adopted.

—Jimmy Carter

An advanced industrial society is sick-making because it disables people from coping with their environment and, when they break down, substitutes a 'clinical' or therapeutic prosthesis for the broken *relationships*. People would rebel against such an environment if medicine did not explain their biological disorientation as a defect in their health, rather than as a defect in the way of life which is imposed on them or which they impose on themselves.

—Ivan Illich

The greatest discovery of my generation is that human beings can alter their lives by altering their attitudes.

—William James

Although it is beginning to change, the attitude of most Americans toward health still reflects a curious *dislike* for the human body.

We have come to perceive it as basically flawed, about to disintegrate at any moment, and always verging on some dread disease that can strike us down.

Whether Madison Avenue helped create this attitude or is merely responding to it is arguable. There can be no question, however, that a substantial percentage of the advertising industry's revenues derive from TV commercials dealing with the management of biological symptoms, and the same bias is evident in the health columns of daily newspapers. The message these days is clear: *Instead of concentrating on health and how to maintain it, most of us are obsessed with illness and how to cure it.*

Straight or gay, most of us are still subscribing to a health care system that overlooks the proverbial ounce of prevention in favor of pounds of expensive treatment. Total health expenditure in the U.S. now amounts to twenty percent of our gross national product, and the cost of health care goods and services is bound to double within the next five years.

We spend about $11 billion for nonprescription items, including 20,000 tons of aspirin. The physicians to whom we flock may be experts on illness, but they are largely untrained in prevention. The hospitals and clinics that treat us are "complaint-centered," or disease-oriented—as are most of the philanthropies to which we're asked to contribute. Disease-oriented medicine may play a vital role in research, but it detracts from the holistic concept that life and health depend upon factors that *we* can control.

There are hopeful signs that the holistic concept is finally beginning to seep into the American consciousness. For example, figures recently released by the National Institute of Health show that the death rate from our greatest killer, heart disease, has been dropping because of changes in life-style. Americans are exercising more, there is a twenty-five percent decline in adult smoking, people are consuming less cholesterol, and more attention is being paid to keeping blood pressure under control.

As a result, the rate of heart attacks and other cardiovascular diseases is falling, and the total number of deaths from them is at the lowest point since 1963, when 993,969 people died from heart-related ailments in the United States. Total heart deaths kept rising through 1973, when they hit 1,062,160, but fell to a total of 994,513 in 1975. That's a drop from a high of fifty-five percent of all deaths during 1958–1967 to 52.2 percent in 1976. The peak came in 1962, when fifty-five percent of all deaths in the United States were due to cardiovascular disease.

As encouraging as such signs are, most of us remain saddled with an attitude that emphasizes the curing of disease as against the maintenance of health. But we homosexuals may have a greater opportunity than anyone else when it comes to modifying that attitude and the disease-producing living patterns which it supports. Perhaps more than anyone else, we are free to choose health.

A greater freedom of choice does not imply that we are in any way elite. Nor does it mean that because we often have fewer "responsibilities" than our straight brothers and sisters, many of whom are preoccupied with raising families, we have more time to practice self-care. Our responsibilities, while different, are just as real, just as great, and just as time-consuming.

We may have a greater freedom of choice because most of us are able to state the problem that impels us to choose dangerous ways of coping with stress. And if a problem can be stated, it can usually be solved.

Although he was not limiting his observation to homosexuals, Boris Pasternak defines our problem as neatly as anyone when he writes in *Doctor Zhivago* that ". . . the great majority of us are required to live a life of constant, systematic duplicity. Your health is bound to be affected if, day after day, you say the opposite of what you feel, if you grovel before what you dislike and rejoice at what brings you nothing but misfortune."

The solution is not always as simple as coming out of the closet. A public announcement of one's sexual preference can dissolve the duplicity, but in certain circumstances, which we need not elaborate, it can create a different set of stressful problems. Whatever your decision on that issue, the solution lies in the conscious nurturing of a positive self-image, one that can free us to enjoy a healthy life-style not dictated by what everyone else around us is doing.

*Nothing*, including poor nutrition and a lack of exercise, destroys health faster than constant fears, anxieties, worries, tensions, depression, hate, jealousy, unhappiness, the sudden loss of love, and loneliness. Such *dis-eases* can lead virtually to every pathology in the book, including arthritis, ulcers, asthma, strokes, constipation, diabetes, high or low blood pressure, angina, glandular disturbances, sexual dysfunction, heart disease, venereal disease, hypoglycemia, and even cancer.

To plunge into exercise and nutrition before considering the vital role that our minds play in maintaining health and curing disease would be putting cart before horse. Because they are "practical" steps, exercise and nutrition are generally considered first in a program of self-care. But unless they are combined with a positive, happy, peaceful state of mind, their effectiveness can be diminished.

As a minority group, we gays are unique in that we are not confined to a particular racial, religious, or socioeconomic tribe. We are different only in the sexual preference that leads us to adopt a different life-style. We are free to enhance that life-style with good health. But gay health means more than freedom from STDs, the anxieties of sexual dysfunction, or growing old. In a broader, holistic sense, it entails the conscious acknowledgment that we are responsible for what happens to us.

Holistic health perceives the human being as an equilateral triangle. Health is achieved when the structural, chemical, and emotional sides of the triangle are harmoniously balanced. If the structure of the body is altered, chemical and emotional disturbances can result. If certain chemicals are absent from the diet, the emotional and structural aspects of the equilateral triangle are affected. Finally, emotions affect both structural and chemical aspects.

The Menninger Foundation's Elmer E. Green, Ph.D., one of the pioneers in the exciting new science known as biofeedback, has enunciated what he calls the "psychophysiological principle," which lies at the heart of any definition of holistic health:

> Every change in the physiological state is accompanied by an appropriate change in the mental-emotional state, conscious or unconscious; and, conversely, every change in the mental-emotional state, conscious or unconscious, is accompanied by an appropriate change in the physiological state.

As Dr. Green has proved in his biofeedback experiments at the Menninger Foundation, the psychophysiological principle is not mere hypothesizing, but scientific fact. He draws an arresting conclusion from his work, one based on the idea that a change in attitude can alter living-patterns in the direction of better health:

If every young student *knew* by the time he finished his first biology class, in grade school, that the body responds to self-generated psychological inputs, that blood flow and heart behavior, as well as a host of other body processes, can be influenced at will, it would change prevailing ideas about both physical and mental health. It would then be quite clear and understandable that we are individually responsible to a large extent for our state of health or disease. Perhaps then people would begin to realize that it is not life that kills us, but rather it is our reaction to it, and this reaction can be to a significant extent self-chosen.*

Holistic health is a *total* approach to living, one in which we are, to a large extent, our own physicians, even though we may seek the aid and advice of others along the way. If you're fortunate enough to have found a personal physician who is holistically oriented, you've learned that you're free to participate in your own therapy. But if you've submitted the management of your health to an "orthodox" physician, the results of whatever treatment he or she prescribes will often be limited.

Pasteur taught that disease is caused by bacteria or viruses that attack individuals who have no responsibility for the fact that they get sick. Orthodox medicine, based as it is on the Pasteurian concept, believes that the job of the physician is to kill germs, or drive them out, with the magic of medicine. If the treatment works, fine; if it doesn't, more heroic measures are employed.

Paavo O. Airola, N.D., Ph.D., the internationally recognized nutritionist, naturopath, and a leading exponent of holistic health, takes exception to the Pasteurian concept of disease and the symptomatic drug-therapy approach to healing:

> The *biological* concept of medicine is based on the irrefutable physiological fact that the primary cause of disease is not the bacteria or virus, but *weakened resistance* brought about by one's own health-destroying living habits and physical and mental stresses. Thus, you and I must accept full responsibility for our own health.†

His view is shared by a growing number of physicians who no longer believe that diseases are "things" that "happen" to us but

---

*Elmer Green, Alyce Green, and E. Dale Walters. "Biofeedback for Mind-Body Regulation: Healing and Creativity." Topeka, Kansas, Research Department, The Menninger Foundation, October 30, 1971.
†Paavo O. Airola, "Nutrition in Holistic Health." *New Realities*, Vol. 1, No. 4, 1977.

are, rather, manifestations of the destructive reactions of individuals to their social and physical environment.

With the possible exception of money, more feelings are attached to sexuality than to any other aspect of our lives. If we feel good about what we do with our genitals, if we visualize ourselves as happy, whole, and generally realizing our potential as human beings, and if we don't succumb to the negative forces within our society that would have us believe that being gay is wrong, our bodies will be healthier. But if we've allowed ourselves to become guilt-ridden, or if we force ourselves to do things we really don't want to do just to be part of the gay community, we're apt to get sick.

A number of the men I interviewed reported that while they were "promiscuous" by anyone's standards, they had never contracted an STD. Most of them wrote it off to luck, or to being unconsciously choosy. But without exception, they were also comfortable with their gayness, saw its frequent physical expression as one of life's greatest pleasures, and felt no need to fuel their natural sexual drive with booze and dope. A positive self-image is not, of course, a foolproof prophylactic against STDs or any other disease. But it can and does go a long, long way.

George, now forty, provided me with the most dramatic anecdotal evidence yet of the apparent link between a low self-esteem and frequent illness. I met him ten years prior to the preparation of this book and have been close to him through his mercurial ups and downs (mostly downs) ever since. Of George it could be said that he has everything going for him: a brilliant mind, honed by the finest education that money can buy; a winning personality, when he chooses to turn it on; and physical beauty so overwhelming that several people have been reduced to describing him as "the best-looking hunk in San Francisco."

But scratch this seemingly perfect exterior, and you find a tense, driving, fearful hypochondriac who, despite the appearance of glowing health, is more often than not running to doctors, gulping pills, and worrying about his latest bout with an STD. Since I've known him he's had syphilis three times, more cases of the clap than even he can count, recurring herpes, and amebic dysentery. When he read in *The Advocate* that hepatitis can be sexually transmitted, especially among gay men, he told me he couldn't understand why he hadn't come down with it. I replied that with his attitudes, he probably wouldn't have too much longer to wait.

George is one of the most promiscuous gay men I've ever encountered. The irony is that he hates being gay and has never accepted the fact that he is. When he finally landed the job he had dreamed about, the first props he used to decorate his office were photographs of his brother's children, who bear an obvious family resemblance. Unless he is pressed, he manages to imply that they are his own. After he caught syphilis for the third time he telephoned me from a pay-phone ("I don't trust the phones here at the office") and asked in all seriousness if I knew of a surgeon who would agree to castrate him. "That's the root of all my problems, you know—a misguided cock." When I told him that he needed a shrink, not a scalpel, he said he was sick and tired of my amateur psychologizing and hung up.

Several days later, at dawn, he telephoned me in great anguish to mutter that he'd just spilled some boiling oatmeal on his genitals.

"You *what?*" I yelled.

"I couldn't help it . . . I was late and running around without any clothes on and knocked it off the stove. What should I do?"

I told him to get into a cold shower immediately, then see a doctor. Later, when he was recovering from the second-degree burns, I gingerly suggested the possibility that some accidents aren't all that accidental. He told me that I had my head up my ass and "changed the subject" by trying to convince me that when it's all said and done, "Anita Bryant is right."

My response was that he was turning into such a transparent case of someone who loathes his own sexuality that I was going to use him as an example in *The Advocate Guide to Gay Health*, which was then in the planning stage.

"Be my guest," he told me, "but your readers will think you're as full of shit as I do."

I also found anecdotal evidence that while the mind can treat the body badly, it can just as easily treat it well. Two of the men with whom I spoke were able to cure their anal warts on their own, without recourse to a physician. Interestingly enough, both were graduates of a popular consciousness-raising course whose trainees come away imbued with the belief that all of life, including health, is a matter of personal choice.

"I knew I had warts when I signed up," one of them told me, "and I'd planned to see a doctor the first chance I had. But by the end of the seminar, the warts were sloughing off. The only explanation I can come up with is that the kind of person I chose to become during the training doesn't have such nasty things. It wasn't a *conscious* effort on my part."

The other man developed warts *after* the same course. "My efforts *were* conscious," he told me. "I personified them, called them vile names, told them to get the fuck out of my body and leave me alone. Twice a day, morning and night, I'd order them out and visualize myself free of them. They disappeared, without medical help, and I've had no recurrences."

Even more intriguing is the truly occult way that the body communicates its distress before we're consciously aware of the problem. Because our ordinary, waking state can inhibit the flow of information we receive from the body, we can often find ourselves receiving important messages only when we're in an altered state of consciousness.

One of the men I interviewed told me that he had a recurring nightmare, which he finally came to realize was his body's way of telling him something:

"It was always the same. I'd be tarting myself up, looking forward to a night out at the bars. But as soon as I'd leave the apartment and hit the street, everything would go black. I was blind. I'd have to grope and crawl my way back to the lobby, where I could see.

"One day I was browsing in a bookshop and found myself flipping through a paperback on vitamins. I read that vitamin A helps the eyes adjust to changes from bright to dim light—in other words, it prevents night blindness, which is what I'd been dreaming about. It was just a hunch, but I decided to start doing something about my diet to see what would happen. I began eating lots of liver, fresh carrots, parsley, squash, and apricots, all good vitamin A sources, the book said. The nightmares stopped. It may be my imagination, but I'm sure I see lots better at night now."

There is no room here for an excursion into the fascinating world of dream interpretation; but if your dreams seem to be calling your attention to a physical problem, do something about it whether you have waking symptoms or not. These early warning signals are often accurate.

A positive, personal belief in your body's innate ability to communicate and heal itself can help keep you in peak condition and speed the effectiveness of conventional medical treatment if you do become ill. If you believe that strongly enough, even a treatment based on an absurd theory can be beneficial; conversely, even the most rational, scientifically proved medication can fail if you don't think it will work.

The following holistic approaches are no more applicable to gays than they are to straights. We include them here to underscore the role that our minds play in maintaining health and curing disease, and to suggest that for the person who loves, trusts, and believes in his or her own body, there are alternatives to orthodox medicine that can work wonders.

## HOME REMEDIES

Many of them have little to no scientific basis, and most of them sound downright ridiculous. But as long as they are intrinsically harmless and don't prevent you from seeking competent medical care if the problem is serious, they can, like aphrodisiacs, be of value to the true believer.

Leslie, a gay woman in her thirties, had always suffered from periodic colds so severe that she'd have to take to her bed for up to a week at a time. Then along came the vitamin C craze, and her friends urged her to try it.

"I did," she told me, "but I really didn't think it would work. And it didn't. The colds were just as bad, just as frequent. Then I met Sue, my lover, and I was on top of the world. Still am. Anyway, I warned her that I was a sickly-type lady and highly susceptible to colds. She said not to worry, she'd handle that. We moved in together, and the first time I started feeling all stuffy and achy she made me swallow four enormous garlic cloves, with water, just like pills. She absolutely guaranteed it would work, and it did. I've been doing it ever since, and I haven't had a cold in seven years!"

When we're depressed, our resistance to colds is lower. Could Leslie have been chronically depressed until she met Sue? Perhaps. But an additional explanation for the garlic's effectiveness is that it was prescribed by someone in whom Leslie believed.

Since his late teens, Max had suffered from athlete's foot and, under the supervision of a fine dermatologist, had tried everything—the gamut of antifungal creams, powders, and, finally, a course of expensive pills. The problem would clear up, only to return within several weeks after he ceased treatment.

"It was really getting to me," he told us. "I became so self-conscious about it that when I did have sex, I'd leave my socks on, which ruled out the baths, of course. Well, one night I met this guy in a bar, went home with him, and started getting it on. When he complained about my leaving my socks on I was afraid he was into feet and didn't know what to say. But I didn't have to say anything, because he'd already guessed. He told me he used to have the same problem and had cured it with a simple home remedy consisting of washing the feet with old-fashioned laundry soap twice a day and rubbing them with lots of garlic salt. I tried it, and I haven't been bothered since. My dermatologist said he'd never heard of such a thing but told me that if it worked, why not?"

Dermatologists who are familiar with gay sex practices know that rimming can cause warts to sprout on the face, especially around the lips, even when the passive partner has no warts himself. They can be just as discouraging to treat as anal warts, sometimes requiring weeks of expensive office visits. Jason, another of my interviewees, became so paranoid and depressed about his facial warts that he used them as an excuse for quitting his job.

"I'd get up in the morning, look in the mirror, and shudder," he told me. "For one thing, I couldn't shave properly. Makeup didn't help. So I just threw in the towel, locked myself up, and hit the wine bottle."

Then he heard about a preposterous home remedy that he was told would work, if only he'd try. It consisted of rubbing the warts with a small piece of fresh beefsteak and burying it in the garden during the full moon.

"At that point, I would have tried anything," said Jason. "I checked the newspaper for the next full moon, which was only a few days off, psyched myself up for it, and did it. The warts shriveled up and were gone within five days. And they didn't come back. When I told my dermatologist about it, he mumbled something about witchcraft."

An apple a day *can* keep the doctor away. But only if you believe it.

## EXERCISE

When I feel the urge to exercise coming over me, I generally lie down until it passes away.

—(The Late) Robert Maynard Hutchins

Even though positive mental attitudes are a crucial factor in determining good health, they can stand us in less than good stead if we're not in physical motion. As Dr. Airola points out, the most important "nutrient" our bodies require is not protein, vitamins, enzymes, fats, or minerals, but oxygen. And the *only* way to get enough of it is to exercise regularly and vigorously, preferably in the open air.

Hypoxia, or a deficiency of oxygen in the cells, contributes to disease and premature aging. Oxygen is so important that even the most ardent nutritionists agree that it is better to eat junk foods and exercise a lot than to eat health foods and not exercise at all.

Thanks to the automobile and other modes of transportation, we are, as a species, evolving toward a unique status on this planet—the only mammal that can propel itself without the use of its body. The *British Medical Journal*, with tongue only slightly in cheek, has suggested a new name for this species: *Homo vehiculo constrictus*—a being so constricted by its use of vehicles that it is losing not only freedom of movement, but even vital feelings.

The price we pay for such "progress" is physical and mental breakdown. Our bodies are designed to function efficiently only when moving. Without motion, and plenty of it, we *cannot* attain good health.

**What kind of exercise is best?** Vigorous, exhausting, sweat-producing, physical exertion, such as jogging, running, tennis, basketball, swimming, or even weeding the garden—activities that will raise your heartbeat to 120–140 per minute, as opposed to the normal, sedentary rate of only 78–85 per minute. Such exercises are known as circulorespiratory, or "aerobic," in that they place great demands on the circulation and respiration to supply oxygen to the muscles involved.

Obviously, you can't go out and run five miles without prior conditioning; nor should you embark on a vigorous program of exercise without a physical examination. But if your physician gives you the green light, begin by walking at least two miles a day, and walk briskly, with the arms swinging free. You can then build your endurance gradually by jogging, running, swimming hard (as opposed to paddling), or playing a vigorous sport.

For the best preventive results, your mode of exercise should consume an absolute minimum of three hours a week. Studies have shown that a lesser amount has no measurable benefit in terms of reducing heart attacks. People who play "light" sports, such as bowling, baseball, and golf, are no better off in this respect than those who never exercise at all.

**But aren't running and tennis merely fads?**   If they are, they're the healthiest fads yet. Those who run regularly and play tennis lose unwanted weight, quit smoking, enhance sexual performance, lower cholesterol levels, think more clearly, slow their heart rates, breathe deeper, and find it easier to overcome alcoholism.

Research has shown that running also instills a feeling of well-being and enhances creativity. A recent conference of the New York Academy of Sciences concludes that long-distance runners tend to be more independent, emotionally stable, and less prone to anxiety.

If you dislike being told to do something because it's good for you, then consider doing it because it feels good—the "runner's high" beats anything you'll find in a bottle or a pill. Run for thirty minutes, and you'll experience a euphoria comparable to that obtained from several tokes on a joint. After forty minutes, you'll find creative ideas starting to float into your consciousness. If you keep on going for an hour, you'll achieve an altered state of awareness in which visual perceptions change and colors meld. This can also be a problem-solving state, in which answers to previously puzzling questions suddenly become apparent. Beyond an hour, you'll probably experience a feeling of mystical union with the environment.

**How does running get you high?**   Scientists believe that the increase flow of oxygen to the brain and the general stimulation of the circulatory system is responsible. It is also known that it is practically impossible to run and worry at the same time. Although much research remains to be done, some scientists think that epinephrine, a hormone associated with happiness (among other things), actually doubles in the brain after only *ten minutes* of sustained exercise, be it running or a comparable activity. And the happiness continues long after you've stopped.

**Can prolonged exercise be dangerous?**   Only if you have a dangerous heart condition, or haven't built your endurance gradually. If you've been running for a long time, however, and go in for an annual physical, don't be surprised if your physician points with alarm to certain "abnormal" symptoms, such as a high level of protein and red blood cells in the urine. Because most doctors are used to treating people who have been sitting on their asses, many of them have come to accept "healthy" physical states that are, when compared to full human potential, not only inadequate but downright sick.

If your urine does show protein and red blood cells in "abnormal" quantities, it doesn't necessarily mean that you have nephritis, a potentially serious kidney disease. You may have a benign condition known as "jogger's kidney," or pseudonephritis—it usually clears up within forty-eight hours.

Studies to determine whether jogger's kidney can lead to permanent kidney damage are now under way. But until the results are in, physicians who appreciate the benefits of strenuous exercise are advising their patients to keep at it. The known benefits far outweigh any known or suspected danger.

Aside from hostile canines and human hecklers, about the worst that prolonged running can do is give you "jogger's tits," a painful irritation caused by the rubbing of a shirt against your skin. The most common victims are braless women. Both men and women can avoid this unhappy condition by coating their nipples with Vaseline or covering them with Band-Aids.

Circulorespiratory exercises and sports can be combined with a thrice-weekly session at your favorite gym, where you can build and define muscles by lifting weights. Pumping iron on its own, however, does not provide the same benefits that running, tennis, and the other strenuous activities do.

**What's the best way to lift weights?** According to Ellington Darden, Ph.D., director of Atlanta's Athletic Center, your program should be "high-intensity," which means the repetitive performance of resistance movement carried to the point of momentary muscular failure. Generally, this means that one set of each exercise is performed for ten repetitions. At least eight repetitions should be performed, but not more than twelve. If you can't do eight, there's too much resistance and you should decrease the weight; if you can do more than twelve, add weight.

Dr. Darden believes that in order to be effective, weight lifting should be "full-range," which means that resistance must be provided in the starting position, throughout the midrange of the exercise, and through to the finishing position. Simple barbells and most other gym equipment can provide resistance in either the starting position or in the finishing position, but never in both. "Nautilus" equipment, however, is full-range. Before you invest three or four hundred dollars in a year's membership at a gym, ask what kind of equipment is available.

Use weights every other day, and use them for no more than forty minutes, at the most.

**Can't pumping iron make women look unfeminine?** A woman can profit just as much as a man can from lifting weights, because it tones and conditions her muscles and keeps fat and skin from sagging. Ninety-nine percent of women couldn't develop bulging muscles if their lives depended on it. There is little difference between the muscular size and strength of boys and girls. But with the onset of puberty, testosterone from the testes and estrogen from the ovaries enter the bloodstream and produce the appropriate sexual characteristics. It takes a certain amount of testosterone to influence the muscular growth characteristic of well-developed men. Most women just haven't got it. The exceptions are the very few who have an abnormal amount of testosterone in their systems, or who have inherited larger than average muscles.

**What about spot-reducing?** Forget it. Sit-ups, leg-raises, and other calisthenics will develop abdominal muscles, but they do little or nothing to reduce a spare tire. If you're in quest of a hard, flat belly, your daily caloric intake must be kept below the so-called maintenance level. Consuming 1,000 less calories a day than the maintenance level will require your body to burn several pounds of fat a week as a source of energy. But even then, the fat will come off all over your body, not just one spot.

Spot-reducing gadgets do *not* work. Vibrating belts, for example, may make you feel better by relaxing you (they even make some people giggle), but they can't remove fat. There are also those rubber clothes, which range from belts, shorts, and shirts to head-to-toe wraps. Although they are supposed to sweat the fat off, all they sweat off is water, and fat contains a very small percentage of $H_2O$.

**Doesn't exercise make you hungry?** It makes you *less* hungry, which is why it helps control weight. The most common characteristic of the evolving *Homo vehiculo constrictus* is ugly fat, if not dangerous obesity. When exercise ceases, the brain's automatic appetite regulators go bonkers. The less you exercise, the *more* you want to eat. For the appetite regulators to function properly, you must walk a minimum of two miles daily.

The ideal way to control weight is to eat moderately, nutritionally, *and* exercise regularly.

## NUTRITION

Over the course of five years, Marshall and Stewart had built their picture-framing shop into one of the most prosperous in Chicago and were talking about a long postponed vacation when both noticed that their gums had begun to bleed. Their dentist, suspecting the worst, insisted that they see their physician for tests. The doctor told them that they had scurvy.

"I thought he was putting us on," Marshall told us. "Scurvy is what the British sailors used to get if they didn't eat their limes."

But it *was* scurvy, a disease caused by a lack of sufficient vitamin C, which is found naturally in citrus fruits and green, leafy vegetables. The doctor asked them about their dietary patterns.

"We'd never thought much about it," recalls Stewart, "but for the past five years we'd been sending out for a Danish and coffee around ten in the morning and a hamburger and fries later in the day. If we were working late, which was almost always the case, we'd send out for a pizza. Then there was the vodka. We'd sort of nip and sip all day—about a quart between us."

Thanks to the prescription of supplemental vitamin C and a radical change in diet, with the emphasis on fresh fruits and vegetables, both men recovered nicely. They have become nutritionally conscious and are even taking time out to go to a nearby YMCA for vigorous workouts in the swimming pool. And their vodka is now carefully limited.

Although there are no statistical studies, an educated guess would be that gay people are more subject to malnutrition than are our straight counterparts. We often live alone and eat junk food on the run. Because of our emphasis on a trim, sexy figure, we also periodically subject ourselves to nutritionally unsound and dangerous fad diets. The major nutritional problem in America today is obesity, and to avoid it, a lot of us go too far in the opposite direction by practically starving ourselves to death. Good nutritional habits need not be complicated if we'll remember the three main food elements that our bodies need: carbohydrates, fat, and protein. Although our bodies also need vitamins and minerals, most of them are present in a well-balanced diet and, unless we're being treated for a specific condition, need not be supplemented. The only non-nutrients we require are roughage and lots of water.

**What makes a diet well-balanced?** The well-balanced diet is based on four food groups: dairy products; fruits and vegetables; meat (including poultry and fish); bread and cereals. If each meal consisted of a moderate selection from each of these groups, most of us would be getting all the nutrients we need. The problem, of course, is knowing what foods to select.

In 1977, Senator George McGovern's Select Committee on Nutrition and Human Needs issued a report entitled *Dietary Goals for the United States.* It calls for a reduction of cholesterol, fat, sugar, and salt in the average diet, and a substantial increase in the consumption of fruits and vegetables containing fiber. The report contains sound nutritional advice. You should still select from the four food groups, but with certain modifications. First of all, your body has *no need whatsoever* for sucrose, or refined sugar, be it white, brown, or raw. There is substantial evidence that links sugar to diabetes, heart disease, colitis, some forms of cancer, premature senility, and even schizophrenia. And there is no question that it is the leading cause of tooth decay.

Unfortunately, sugar has got into practically everything we eat, including cereals and breads, peanut butter, "juice drinks," most yogurt, mayonnaise, ketchup, etc. Develop the habit of reading labels and avoid processed foods that list ingredients ending with *ose* (such as dextrose, maltose, lactose). If you're at the baths and feel dehydrated after a long session in the steam room, drink water instead of a can of sugar-laced pop from the vending machine. And stay away from the candy bars. Some of the gay men with whom I spoke admitted that they subsist on little else over weekends. If your favorite bath has a suggestion box, as many of them do, use it to let the manager know that you'd like to see fresh fruit in the vending machines.

Next to sugar, the most pervasive item in the American diet is salt. We need a certain amount of it to maintain chemical balance, but too much can enhance the onset of high blood pressure. Salt is present in cold cuts and cured meats, "snacks," and *all* soft drinks. Again, read your labels and avoid "nitrites."

To cut down on fat, eat fewer eggs, less ice cream (also loaded with sugar), chips and crackers, and most cheeses. One of the most common sources of fat in the American diet is beef. Pork is also high.

If you don't like to cook or your cooking facilities are limited, invest in a small slow-cooker, most of which come with simple recipe books. You can fill it with fresh vegetables and meat, preferably poultry, in the morning and have a tasty dish waiting for you when you come home at night. Combine it with a fresh salad. Breakfast at home can consist of fresh fruit and a small bowl of *unsweetend* bran with skim milk. Lunches out are a matter of personal taste provided that they are moderate in size and devoid of junk.

**What's wrong with beef?** In moderate quantities, it's an excellent source of protein, which contains the amino acids essential to building tissues and manufacturing enzymes and hormones. But beef also contains a great deal of saturated fat. Cholesterol, a particular kind of fat, is a major constituent of the atherosclerotic deposits that clog arteries and cause heart attacks. One can lower blood cholesterol levels by eating the polyunsaturated fats found in fish and vegetable oils and avoiding the saturates. The Japanese, who eat foods low in saturated fat and high in polyunsaturates, have lower cholesterol levels than Americans and fewer heart attacks.

There is still much debate about the role of cholesterol in coronary disease. Some scientists question whether any true conclusions can yet be drawn. But as long as cholesterol is so highly suspect, it's a good idea to watch your consumption.

There is less debate about the implication of fats in cancer of the colon. Nations with the highest rate of this disease—the U.S., Canada, Scotland, and Denmark—are all big consumers of beef. It is now believed that bile acids are secreted in the intestine in higher quantities in response to fat, and they have been shown to promote cancer in animals. If your lust for beef is so great that you don't think you could live without it, increase your intake of roughage, which speeds bowel transport.

**What's the best way to diet?** Continue selecting your food from the four major groups but cut down on quantity and maintain a regular program of exercise. It is always unwise to undertake any other kind of diet without medical supervision.

The "crash" diets, on which people drop as much as twenty-five pounds a month, can be dangerous. There are any number of these, including "Dr. Atkin's Diet Revolution" and the "Drinking Man's Diet." All of them call for a drastic reduction in carbohydrates and an unlimited amount of meats and other foods high in protein. Inevitably, that means an increase of fat and cholesterol. Such diets certainly "work" in that you'll lose weight rapidly; but they can also cause nausea, fatigue, low blood pressure, and overworked kidneys. Another unhappy side effect can be bad breath.

The most dangerous diet of all is liquid protein—six to eight ounces per day of an expensive, foul-tasting, often contaminated gunk derived from slaughterhouse horns, hoofs, and hides. Although a conclusive link has not yet been established, the Federal Food and Drug Administration believes at the time of this writing that it has caused the deaths of at least thirty-six dieters.

**What about vitamin B-15?** Most scientists think it's a medical variation on the tale of the emperor's new clothes—which didn't exist. Marketed under Aangamik 15 and other brand names, B-15 is not a true vitamin at all, but a food additive derived from apricot stones. You'll find it in a tablet that looks like aspirin and tastes like chalk. The health food stores that peddle B-15 (at up to ten bucks for a hundred tablets) will tell you that it is reputed to combat alcoholism, hepatitis, heart trouble, allergies, high blood pressure, and the relentless advance of age itself.

According to the Food and Drug Administration, you'd have to choke down twenty-one pounds of the stuff in one sitting to actually kill yourself; so if you *think* it can help you, have at it—provided that you don't substitute this so-called therapy for proper medical care.

**What about the other vitamins and minerals?** The training of most physicians rarely includes nutrition, including the role of supplementary vitamins and minerals. Consequently, you can probably learn more about "vites" from the clerk at your local health food store, or on your own, than you can by visiting your doctor.

With the possible exception of vitamin C, most people don't need supplements if they are eating well-balanced meals consisting of fresh, unprocessed foods. A few people, however, have specific problems that can be corrected with vitamin and mineral formulas. If you have poor skin, bad night vision, and dry, brittle hair, you may need more vitamin A in your system, but too much of it can cause liver failure. Vitamin D, which helps the body absorb calcium and retain it, can also be toxic in large doses in that it may raise the bood levels of calcium enough to cause cardiac arrest. Unless directed by a physician, don't take more than 10,000 units of vitamin A or 4,000 units of vitamin D a day.

The other vitamins and minerals are thought to be safe, even in megadoses. Its proponents claim that vitamin E slows the aging process, stops and reverses the graying of hair, and boosts the libido. A number of the older men I interviewed swore by it and feel that if they don't take at least 800 units daily they have trouble getting it up.

The B vitamins, which you can buy in a complex form or take in powdered nutritional yeast (which has calcium and magnesium added), promote steady nerves, good digestion, energy production, alertness, and healthy skin. If you're feeling depressed, moody, fatigued, and have trouble concentrating, they might help. But a word of caution—if you're taking them in the form of powdered yeast, begin with only half a teaspoon a day before working up to as much as four tablespoons over the course of three weeks. Too much too soon, before your digestive system can become accustomed to it, can blow you up like a balloon and cause uncontrollable farting.

Finally, don't forget the best regimen of all: sound nutrition *and* vigorous exercise. Again, it's better to eat junk food and exercise than it is to cram yourself with good food, vitamins, and minerals and not exercise at all. Nor should you forget "Vitamin X," the most important vitamin of all—a positive mental attitude.

**What else can you do?** Throughout this guide, we have purposefully tried to avoid a bias toward ongoing relationships as against a succession of brief, sexual encounters. To have come down hard on "promiscuity" would have struck some readers as prudish and most as unrealistic. Lifelong relationships are simply not characteristic of our life-style, especially among men. Whether they become so in the future depends on factors that lie beyond the scope of this book.

It would be dishonest, however, to conclude without citing the disturbing evidence that in almost every case, for both men and women, single people have significantly higher death rates than those who are married. The average U.S. death rates according to marital status per 100,000 population between the ages of fifteen and sixty-four, during the period 1959–1961, show that in the end, human companionship surpasses even exercise and diet in the prevention of disease.

"Life and dialogue are one and the same," writes James Lynch, in *The Broken Heart: The Medical Consequences of Loneliness*. Without companionship and the dialogue that sustains it, our chances of being caught by disease and dying prematurely are increased markedly.

The forms of companionship are many, and the choice is always our own. We can choose to have a lover. We can remain "single" while becoming part of a loving, supportive network of friends. But as gay men and gay women who are first of all human beings, good health and the potential that awaits us all may never be ours if we choose to be alone.

# Appendix:
# Gay Community
# Services

The following resources, arranged geographically, report their availability for inquiries and referrals. Although every effort has been made to provide a directory that is up-to-date, we cannot guarantee the reliability of the organizations listed. Readers residing in states and provinces which are unlisted should write or telephone the resource nearest them. Where no telephone number is shown, none is presently available. Check local directory assistance.

ALASKA

ANCHORAGE

Metropolitan Community Church
Box 3-091
Log Cabin Church
602 W. 10th Ave.
99501
(907) 272-1715

Alaska Women's Resource
Box 188
99501

FAIRBANKS

Gay Co-Op
Box 81265
99701
(907) 456-6517

ARIZONA

COOLIDGE

Gay Episcopalian Caucus
Box 1631
85228

FLORENCE

Caucus on Concerns in Human
  Sexuality
Box 906
85232

PHOENIX

Metropolitan Community Church
Box 83036
1426 E. Maricopa Freeway
85036
(602) 271-0125

Gay People's Alliance
Box 21461
83036
(602) 252-2135

TEMPE

Founders
Box 117
85281

Gay Liberation Arizona Desert
  (GLAD)
Box 117
85281
(602) 252-0713

TUCSON

Metropolitan Community Church
Box 50412
4831 E. 22nd Ave.
85703
(602) 622-0330

Gay Law Collective
Box 3065
85702

Tucson Center for Women
646 S. 6th Ave.
85701
(602) 792-1929

CALIFORNIA

ANAHEIM

Gay Community Center of Orange
  County
(714) 534-3280

ATASCADERO

Atascadero Gay Encounter
Drawer A
93411

CLAREMONT

Gay Student Union of the
  Claremont Colleges
% Counseling Center
735 Dartmouth Ave.
91711
(714) 626-8511, X-3038

COSTA MESA

Christ Chapel Metropolitan
  Community Church
964 Noria St.
Laguna Beach 92651
(714) 497-2142, 752-1220

COTATI

Gay Students Union
Sonoma State College
94928
(707) 795-9950

DAVIS

Gay Students at U.C. Davis
Student Activities Office
Memorial Union
95616
(916) 952-3495

FRESNO

Lesbian Task Force
420 N. Van Ness
93721

FULLERTON

Gay Students Educational Union
CSU, Student Activities
92634
(714) 497-1687

GARDEN GROVE

Gay Community Center of Orange
    County
12732 Garden Grove Blvd., Suite H
92643
(714) 534-5820

HAYWARD

Advocates for Women
1303 A St.
94542

Gay People's Union of Alameda
    County
Box 3935
94540

South County Women's Center
25036 Hillary
94542

LAGUNA BEACH

Concerned Citizens Group
% By the Sea Motel
475 N. Coast Hwy.
92651
(714) 494-1608

LONG BEACH

Metropolitan Community Church
785 Junipero Ave.
90804
(213) 434-1944

Gay Service League
Box 5014
90805
(213) 591-7611

Gay Student Union
California State University
1250 Bellflower Blvd.
90840

LOS ANGELES

Gay Community Services Center
1213 N. Highland Ave.
90038
(213) 464-7485

Beth Chayim Chadashim (Jewish)
1945 Westwood Blvd.
90025
(213) 552-2485

Dignity/L.A. (Roman Catholic)
Box 6161
90055
(213) 664-2872

Integrity/Los Angeles (Episcopal)
4767 Hillsdale Dr.
90032
(213) 225-7471

Lutherans Concerned for Gay
    People
Box 19114A
90019
(213) 663-7816

Metropolitan Community Church
11717 Victory Blvd.
North Hollywood 91606
(213) 762-1133

Dignity/San Fernando Valley
    (Roman Catholic)
Box 911
Van Nuys 91408
(213) 894-7982

Gay Students Union
UCLA
Kerkhoff Hall No. 411
308 Westwood Plaza
90024
(213) 825-8053

Los Angeles Guidance Counseling
    Service
924 Westwood Blvd., Suite 535
90024
(213) 413-2996

Gay Rights Project
American Civil Liberties Union
633 S. Shatto Pl.
90005
(213) 487-1720

Gay Rights Law Panel
6430 Sunset Blvd., No. 1500

90028
(213) 466-6739

Gay Liberation Front
East L.A. College
5357 E. Brooklyn Ave.
90022

Gay Persons Alliance
3701 Wilshire Blvd., 7th Floor
90010
(213) 386-7855

Gay Sisterhood, UCLA
Women's Resource Center
90 Powell Library
405 Highland Ave.
90024
(213) 825-3945

One, Inc.
2256 Venice Blvd.
90006
(213) 735-5252

Whitman-Radclyffe Foundation
9171 Wilshire Blvd., Suite 310-88
90210

MONTEREY

Metropolitan Community Church
1154 2nd St.
93940
(408) 375-2338

NEWPORT BEACH

U.C. Irvine Gay Students Center
% A.S.U.C.I.
Irvine 92717
(714) 833-7229

OAKLAND-BERKELEY

East Bay Metropolitan Community
   Church
2624 West St.
Oakland, 94612
(415) 763-1592

Gay Seminarians
2441 Leconte
Berkeley 92709

The Pacific Center for Human
   Growth
Box 908
Berkeley 94701
(415) 841-6224

Student Health Service
U.C. Berkeley
Berkeley 94720
(415) 642-5012

East Bay Men's Center
2700 Bancroft Way
Berkeley 94704
(415) 854-4823

Berkeley Gay Men's Rap
2339 Durant Ave.
Berkeley 94704
(415) 548-4495, 655-0221

Gay People's Union
Room 320, Eshleman Hall
U.C. Berkeley
Berkeley 94720
(415) 848-7142, X-37

OCEANSIDE

Palomar Metropolitan Community
   Church
Box 228
Escondido 92025
(714) 746-5660

PASADENA

Gay Discussion Group
Cal. Inst. of Technology
Winnett Center
91109

POMONA

Metropolitan Community Church
Box 1082
Upland 91786
(714) 982-7642

REDDING

Metropolitan Community Church
Box 1228
96001
(916) 246-9982

Human Awareness
Box 566
96001
(916) 246-9686

REDLANDS

Lesbian Rap Group
YWCA
16 E. Olive Ave.
92373

RIVERSIDE

Trinity Metropolitan Community
   Church
Box 2451
92506
(714) 682-7445

ROHNERT PARK

Gay Students Union
Student Resources Center
California State College
Sonoma 94928
(707) 795-2391

SACRAMENTO

Dignity/Sacramento, Inc. (Roman
   Catholic)
Box 9643
95823
(916) 422-6305

Metropolitan Community Church
Box 5282
2741 34th St.
95817
(916) 451-5552

California Committee for Sexual
   Law Reform
4949 13th Ave.
95820

Gay Students Union
Sacramento City College
3835 Freeport Blvd.
95822
(916) 422-9313

Gay Youth Encounter Group
Box 15765
95813
(916) 444-0805

Lesbian Feminist Alliance
% ASSC
Cal. State University
95810

Sacramento Gay People's Union
% Programs Advising
Cal. State University
6000 J St.
95819
(916) 454-6595

SAN DIEGO

Dignity (Roman Catholic)
Box 19071
92119
(714) 448-8384

Integrity (Episcopal)
4645 W. Talmadge Dr.
92116

Metropolitan Community Church
Box 3391
1355 Fern Street
92103
(714) 239-3723

Gay Center for Social Services
2550 B St.
92120
(714) 232-7528

SAN FRANCISCO

Achavah: Jewish Gay Union
Box 5528
94101
(415) 451-8743

Committee of Concern (Quaker)
% Friends Meetinghouse
2160 Lake St.
94121
(415) 431-3344

Council on Religion and the
    Homosexual
83 Sixth St.
94103
(415) 781-1570

Dignity/Bay Area (Roman Catholic)
Box 5127
94101
(415) 863-4940

Integrity/San Francisco (Episcopal)
Box 6444
San Jose 95150
(415) 621-0182

Lutherans Concerned for Gay
    People
566 Vallejo St., #25
94133
(415) 397-5666

Metropolitan Community Church
1076 Guerrero
94110
(415) 285-0392

Gay Referral Switchboard
Box 6046
94101
(415) 431-3995

Golden Gate Liberation House
758 Haight St.
94117
(415) 431-7688

Helping Hands Services
Box 1528
94101
(415) 771-3366

Operation Concern
% Pacific Medical Center
2323 Sacramento St.
94115
(415) 563-0202

Women's Switchboard
63 Brady St.
94103
(415) 431-1414

Haight-Ashbury Free Clinic
529 Clayton St.
94117
(415) 431-1714

San Francisco City Clinic
250 4th St.
94103
(415) 558-3804

Bay Area Gay Liberation
1800 Market St.
94102
(415) 431-1522

Gay Students at Hastings College of
    Law
% Associated Students
198 McAllister
94102

Gay Students Coalition
% Student Activities
S.F. City College
94123
(415) 661-9561

Pride Foundation
Box 1983
94101
(415) 864-9476

San Francisco Gay Action
627 Ellis St.
94109

Gay People's Union at Stanford
Box 8265
Palo Alto 94305
(415) 497-1488

Sexual Trauma Center
135 Polk Street
94102
(415) 558-3814

Whitman-Radclyffe Foundation
2131 Union St.
94123
(415) 346-7929

SAN JOSE

Metropolitan Community Church
Box 24126
300 S. 10th St.
95154
(408) 267-3211

Gay Student Union
% Student Activities Office
San Jose State University
95192

Lesbian-Feminist Alliance
Box 783
Campbell 95008
(408) 378-7665

SAN LUIS OBISPO

Metropolitan Community Church
Box 1706
93401
(805) 722-8496

SAN RAFAEL

The Other Side (Mormon)
Box 132
94902

SANTA ANA

Interfaith Community Church
2103 W. Greenleaf
92707

The Other Side (Mormon)
Box 1643
92702

SANTA BARBARA

Gay People's Union
Box 15048
U.C. Santa Barbara
93107
(805) 962-7373

SANTA CRUZ

Lesbian and Gay Men's Union
Box 5188
95063
(408) 426-LIFE

SANTA MONICA

West Bay Metropolitan Community
   Church
1100 Granville Ave., #8
90049
(213) 398-8220

Lesbian Activists
% Women's Center
237 Hill St.
90405

SANTA ROSA

Metropolitan Community Church
1607 Howard St., #4
San Francisco 94103
(415) 864-0543

STOCKTON

Metropolitan Community Church
2606 Wilson Way
95205
(209) 463-0478

San Joaquin County Gays
Anderson Y Center
University of the Pacific
95211
(209) 466-1496

VENTURA

Metropolitan Community Church
362 N. Ventura Ave.
93001
(805) 648-7060

Ventura County Gay Alliance
362 N. Ventura Ave.
93001

# COLORADO

ASPEN

Aspen Gay Coalition
Box 3143
81661

BOULDER

Boulder Gay Coalition
Box 1402
80302
(303) 492-8567

COLORADO SPRINGS

Colorado Springs Gay Relief Fund
% Hide & Seek
512 W. Colorado Ave.
80905

DENVER

Dignity Denver/Boulder (Roman
  Catholic)
Box 2943
80201
(303) 377-8691

Integrity (Episcopal)
1734 Washington
80203

Lutheran Gays
% Joel Schmidt
2225 Bucktell, #509
80210

Metropolitan Community Church
Box 9536
1400 Lafayette
80209
(303) 832-2586

Gay Coalition of Denver
Box 18501
80218
(303) 831-8838

Gay Legal Workers
412 Majestic Blvd.
80202

Gay Students Association
Metropolitan State College
250 W. 14th Ave.
80204
(303) 892-6111

Gay Youth
815 E. 18th, #9
80203

Lesbian-Feminist Workers
% Woman to Woman Bookstore
2023 Colfax
80206

Lesbian Task Force of NOW
1400 Lafayette
80218
(303) 831-7707

FORT COLLINS

Fort Collins Gay Alliance
Student Center
Colorado State University
80521

Sisters of Sappho
% Fort Collins Gay Alliance
Student Center
Colorado State University
80521


CONNECTICUT

BRIDGEPORT

Gay Academic Union
Bernhard Humanities Center
University of Bridgeport
06602
(203) 576-4425

HARTFORD

Integrity/Hartford (Episcopal)
Christ Church Cathedral
45 Church St.
06103
(203) 522-2646

Metropolitan Community Church
Box 514
11 Amity St.
06103
(203) 522-8651, 522-5575

George W. Henry Foundation
45 Church St.
06103
(203) 522-2646

Kalos Society/GLF, Inc.
Box 403
06101
(203) 568-2656

NORWICH

E. Conn. G.A.
37 Otrobando Ave., #2
06360
(203) 889-7530

STORRS

UConn Gay Alliance
U-8 Univ. of Connecticut
06268
(203) 429-1448

DELAWARE

GREENVILLE

Delaware Separatist Dyke Group
Box 3526
19807
(302) 478-1246

DISTRICT OF COLUMBIA

Gay Al-Anon
St. James Episcopal Church
222 8th St. NE
20002
(202) 966-1779

Dignity/Washington (Roman
  Catholic)
1616 4th St. NW
20007
(202) 474-0566

Integrity/Washington (Episcopal)
11917 PH1 Winterhur Lane
Reston, VA 22091

Jewish Gays of Balti-
  more/Washington
Box 34038
20034
(202) 547-4562, 544-1615

Metropolitan Community Church
945 G St. NW
20001
(202) 232-6333

Unitarian Gay Community
All Souls Unitarian Church
16 & Harvard NW
20009
(202) 722-0439

Gay Switchboard
1724 20th St. NW
20009
(202) 387-3777

The Gay Connection
Box 622
Riverdale, MD 20840
(202) 277-9183

Gay Men's VD Clinic
1556 Wisconsin Ave. NW
20007
(202) 965-5476

Gay Activists Alliance
Box 2554
20013
(202) 331-1418

Gay Youth
1724 20th St. NW
20009
(202) 387-3777

Mattachine Society of Washington
Box 1032
20013
(202) 363-3881

Men's Awareness Network
807 A St. NE, #5
20002

Washington Area Women's Center
1424 16th St. NW, #105
20036

FLORIDA

BOCA RATON

Gay Academic Union
Florida Atlantic University
Student Activities Office
33432
(305) 395-5100

Southern Gay Liberator
Box 2118
33434
(305) 391-8693

CLEARWATER

Suncoast Gay Alliance
Box 2423
33517

FORT LAUDERDALE

Dignity/Fort Lauderdale (Roman
  Catholic)
Box 8503
33310
(305) 491-1114

Metropolitan Community Church
1127 SW 2nd Court
33312
(305) 462-2004

Universal New Age Church
1426 Lauderdale Villa Dr.
33311
(305) 763-5775

FORT MYERS

Metropolitan Community Church
Box 32
4427 Palm Beach Blvd.
33905
(813) 694-253

GAINESVILLE

Gay Community Service Center
Room 300
J. Wayne Reitz Union
University of Florida
32612
(904) 377-2306, 373-6212

Gay Community Services Center
Box 103

107 NW 15th Terrace
32602
(904) 377-2081

HOLLYWOOD

Stonewall Committee
Box 2084
33020

JACKSONVILLE

Dignity (Roman Catholic)
Box 5012
32207

Integrity (Episcopal)
Box 5524
32207

Gay Alliance for Political Action
Box 52043
32201
(904) 354-4640

Humanity
2954-B Park St.
32205

MIAMI

Dignity (Roman Catholic)
Box 381736
33138
(305) 932-7407

Fellowship Chapel (Evangelical)
Box 331299
33133
(305) 446-6090

Center for Dialog & Lutherans
  Concerned
2175 NW 26th St.
33142
(305) 638-4085

Metropolitan Community Church
Box 370963
33137
(305) 633-5733, 758-7190

Metropolitan Community
  Synagogue

Box 330132
33133
(305) 758-7190

Alliance for Individual Rights, Inc
Box 330414
33133

Dade County NOW Lesbian Task
  Force
Box 330265
33133
(305) 672-5133

Gay Community Services of So.
  Florida
Box 721
Coconut Grove Station
33133
(305) 445-3511

ORLANDO

Florida Coalition of Gay
  Organizations
Box 26274
32816

Gay Students Assn.
Florida Technical University
Box 26274
32816
(305) 821-6049

PENSACOLA

Lambda Society
Box 4479
32507
(904) 456-9034

ST. PETERSBURG

Metropolitan Community Church
1050 Parkview Lane
Largo 33504

Lesbian Task Force of Pinellas
  County NOW
210 5th Ave. South
33701

TALLAHASSEE

FSU Women's Center
FSU Box 6826

32306
(904) 644-4007

TAMPA

Dignity/Sun Coast (Roman Catholic)
Box 3306
33601

Metropolitan Community Church
2904 Concordia Ave.
33609
(813) 839-5939

Feminist Women's Health Center
1200 W. Platt St.
33606
(813) 251-4089

University of Florida Gay Coalition
Box CTR 2466 USF
33602
(813) 974-2749

GEORGIA

ATHENS

Committee on Gay Education
Box 2467 Univ. Station
30602
(404) 599-4015

ATLANTA

Dignity (Roman Catholic)
Box 77013
30357
(404) 335-1416

Integrity (Episcopal)
% Dr. Ara Dostourian
Dept. of History
West Georgia College
Carrollton 30117

Metropolitan Community Church
800 N. Highland Ave. NE
30306
(404) 872-2246

Alternative Therapy Center
20 4th St. NW
30308
(404) 873-2000

Gay Help Line
Box 7974
30309
(404) 892-5855

Atlanta Lesbian Feminist Alliance
Box 5502
1326 McLendon St. NE
30307
(404) 523-7786

## HAWAII

HONOLULU

Metropolitan Community Church
Box 15825
2500 Pali Hwy.
96815
(808) 922-3029

Love and Peace Together
Sexual Identity Center
Box 3224
2457 Kanealii Ave.
96801
(808) 538-7940

WAHIAWA

Gay Liberation Hawaii
95-065 Waikalani Dr. F205
96786
(808) 623-4334

## IDAHO

MOSCOW

North West Gay People's Alliance
Box 8758
83843

Women's Center
Univ. of Idaho
Administration Center Bldg., #109
83843

## ILLINOIS

CHAMPAIGN-URBANA

Metropolitan Community Church
Box 5015 Station A
Champaign 61820

Gay Switchboard
(217) 384-8040

Gay Illinois
284 Illinois Union
Urbana 61801
(217) 384-8040

CHICAGO

Alcoholics Anonymous
Good Shepherd Parish
615 W. Wellington
(312) 922-5822

Gay Alcoholics Anonymous
Augustana Hospital
411 W. Dickens
(312) 346-1475

Congregation Or Chadash (Jewish)
% Second Unitarian Church
656 W. Barry
60614
(312) 929-9180

Dignity (Roman Catholic)
Box 11261
60611
(312) 281-8094

Integrity (Episcopal)
Box 2516
60690
(312) 386-1470

Lutherans Concerned for Gay
   People
% R. Anderson
655 Buckingham Pl.
60657

Metropolitan Community Church
Box 2392
343 S. Dearborn St., 1704
60690
(312) 922-5822

Counseling Resource Center for
   Lesbians
3523 N. Halsted
60657
(312) 973-4769

Gay People's Counseling
2745 N. Clark St., 213
60614
(312) 929-9181

Gay Self Help
% Mary Houlihan
1221 W. Sherwin Ave.
60626
(312) 262-9609

Institute for Human Relations
561 W. Diversey Parkway
60614
(312) 248-8588

Mattachine Midwest
Box 924
60690
(312) 337-2424

Community Mental Health Center
Ravenswood Hospital
1920 Sunnyside Ave.
60640
(312) 769-6200

Rogers Park Gay Center
7109 Glenwood
60626
(312) 262-0587

Chicago Women's Liberation Union
3411 W. Diversey Parkway
60647
(312) 772-2655

Emma Goldman's Women's Clinic
1317 W. Loyola
60626
(312) 262-8870

Howard Brown Memorial Clinic
Box 1319
La Plaza Medical Center
1250 W. Belden
60690
(312) 871-5777

Gay People's Legal Committee
413 W. Fullerton
60614
(312) 248-1508

Midwest Women's Legal Group
% R. Hanover
54 W. Randolph St.
60601
(312) 641-1905

Circle Campus Gay Liberation
University of Illinois
750 S. Halsted St.
518 Circle Center
60607
(312) 996-4843

Lavender Elephants (Weight
  Control)
% Lambda Associates
2745 N. Clark St., 210
60614
(312) 281-0686

DE KALB

Gay Liberation Front
Northern Illinois University
Box 74, Student Activities
60115
(815) 753-0518

EVANSTON

Northwestern Gay Union
Northwestern University
Box 60, Norris Center
1999 Sheridan Rd.
60201
(312) 492-3227

LA GRANGE

Holy Covenant Community Church
Box 9134
Chicago, Il. 60690 (mailing address)
900 S. La Grange Rd.
60525
(312) 274-5582, 274-5586

MACOMB

Friends
Box 296
Western Illinois University
61455

NORMAL

Gay People's Alliance
255 N. University, 2-C
61761
(309) 438-3411

STREAMWOOD

Fox Valley Gay Association
Box 186
60130
(312) 697-0623, 892-5278

## INDIANA

FORT WAYNE

Metropolitan Community Church
Box 5443
46805
(219) 744-3898

INDIANAPOLIS

Club Baths of Indianapolis (VD
  Clinic)
341 N. Capitol
46204
(317) 635-5796

Dignity (Roman Catholic)
Box 831
46206

Metropolitan Community Church
1940 N. Delaware
46202
(317) 283-3340

NOTRE DAME

Earlham Gay People's Union
Earlham College
46556

WEST LAFAYETTE

Purdue Gay Alliance
Box 510
47907

## IOWA

AMES

Open Line
2502 Knapp St.
50010

CEDAR RAPIDS

Pride of Lambda
Box 265
52406
(319) 362-2629

DES MOINES

Metropolitan Community Church
Box 4546
50306
(515) 244-4342

Gay Community Services Center
3905 Crocker
50312

GRINNELL

Grinnell College Gay Community
Student Affairs Office
50112

IOWA CITY

Gay Liberation Front
University of Iowa
Student Activities Center
52240
(319) 353-7162

Iowa City Lesbian Alliance
3 E. Market St.
52240
(319) 353-6265

## KANSAS

EMPORIA

Gay People of Emporia
Gay Student Organizations Office
Memorial Union
Kansas State College
66801
(316) 342-0641

LAWRENCE

Gay Services of Kansas
Box O, Kansas Union
University of Kansas
66045
(913) 842-7505

MANHATTAN

Gay Counseling Service
% UFM
615 Fairchild Terr.
66502
(913) 539-2311

WICHITA

Metropolitan Community Church
Box 2639
67201
(316) 681-1573

Wichita Gay Community
  Association
Box 13013
67231
(316) 681-1573

KENTUCKY

LEXINGTON

Lexington Gay Services
  Organization
Box 1677
40501
(606) 269-5192

LOUISVILLE

Gay Liberation
416 Belgravia Ct.
40208
(502) 635-5841

LOUISIANA

NEW ORLEANS

Dignity (Roman Catholic)
Box 50723
70150

Metropolitan Community Church
1934 Burgundy
70117
(504) 945-5976

Tulane University Gay Students
  Union
% Associated Student Body
University Center
70118
(504) 865-6208, 865-4735

MAINE

AUGUSTA

Central Maine Gay Alliance
Box 2242
04330

BATH

Women's Counseling Service
72 Front St., 23
04530
(207) 443-9531

BELFAST

Maine Lesbian Feminists
Box 125
04915

LEWISTON

Gay Rights Organization
Box 1163
04240

ORONO

Wilde-Stein Club
% Memorial Union
University of Maine
04473
(207) 581-2571

PLEASANT POINT

Maine Gay Indians
% D. Francis
Passamaquoddy Library
04667

PORTLAND

Gay People's Alliance
92 Beford St.
04013
(207) 773-2891, X-535

Maine Gay Task Force
Box 4542
192 Middle St.
04112
(207) 773-5530

Southern Maine Lesbian Caucus
% Johnson/Breeding
205 Spring St., 5
04102

# MARYLAND

BALTIMORE

Dignity (Roman Catholic)
761 W. Hamburg St.
21230
(301) 235-0333

Metropolitan Community Church
Box 1145
4201 York Rd.
21203
(301) 435-3443

The Women's Growth Center
1110 St. Paul St.
21202
(301) 539-3588

Lesbian Community Center
3028 Greenmount Ave.
21218
(301) 235-8593

Baltimore Gay Alliance
Box 13438
21203
(301) 235-HELP

Baltimore Women's Center
101 E. 25th St., B-2
21218

Women's Union of Baltimore
906 Gorsuch Ave.
21218

COLLEGE PARK

Gay Students Alliance
Student Union Bldg.
University of Maryland
20742
(301) 454-4855

LARGO

Gay People's Group
Prince George's Community College
Student Activities Office
301 Largo Rd.
20870

SIMPSONVILLE

Peer
Box 27
21150

# MASSACHUSETTS

AMHERST

Everywoman's Center
Goodell Hall
University of Massachusetts
01002
(413) 545-0883

Lesbian Union
University of Massachusetts
920 Campus Center
01002
(413) 545-3438

People's Gay Alliance
RSO 368
Lincoln Campus Center
University of Massachusetts
01002
(413) 545-0154

Southwest Women's Center
McKinnie House
University of Massachusetts
01002
(413) 545-0626

ANDOVER

Dignity (Roman Catholic)
Box 348
Lowell 01853

BOSTON

B'nai Hashkalah (Jewish)
131 Cambridge St.
02114
(617) 265-6409

Dignity (Roman Catholic)
1105 Boylston St.
02215

Integrity (Episcopal)
Box 2582
02208
(617) 846-6580

Metropolitan Community Church
131 Cambridge St.
02114
(617) 523-7664

Counseling Alternatives
419 Boylston St.
02116
(617) 536-1381

Women's Counseling
186 Hampshire St.
Cambridge 02139
(617) 876-4488

Gay Hotline
(617) 426-9371

Project Place
32 Rutland St.
02118
(617) 267-9150

Women's Educational Center
46 Pleasant St.
Cambridge 02139
(617) 354-8807

Gay Academic Union
Box 212
02101
(617) 266-2069

Gay Men's Center
36 Bromfield St., 310
02108
(617) 338-7967

Fenway Community Health Center
16 Haviland St.
02115
(617) 267-7573

Homophile Community Health
    Service
80 Boylston St., 885
02116
(617) 542-5188, 426-9371

Women's Community Health
137 Hampshire St.
Cambridge 02139
(617) 547-2302

Black Gay Men's Caucus
% GCN
Box 9600
22 Bromfield St.
02108

Boston University Gays
31 Program Resources Office
Student Union
775 Commonwealth Ave.
02215
(617) 353-2000

Charles Street Meetinghouse
70 Charles St.
02114
(617) 523-0368

Emerson Homophile Society
Box 1253
Emerson College Union
96 Beacon St.
02108
(617) 262-2010

Gay Alert
(617) 523-0368, 267-0764

Gay People's Group
University of Massachusetts
% Center for Alternatives, 620
Columbia Point 02125
(617) 287-1900, X-2396

Harvard-Radcliffe Gay Students
  Association
198 Memorial Hall
Harvard University
Cambridge 02138
(617) 495-1927

MIT Student Homophile League
142 Memorial Dr., 50-306
Cambridge 02139
(617) 235-5440

NOW
45 Newbury St.
02116
(617) 267-6160

Northeastern Gay Students
  Organization
Student Activities Office
155 Ell Center
360 Huntington Ave.
Medford 02115
(617) 253-5440

Tufts Gay Community
Student Activities Office
Medford 02115
(617) 776-0921

CHARLEMONT

Pioneer Valley Gay Union
% Windy Hill Grace Church
01370

FITCHBURG

Homophile Union of Montachusett
Box 262
01420

HAVERHILL

Gay People's Center
Campus Center
100 Elliot St.
01830
(617) 327-0929

NEW BEDFORD

New Bedford Women's Health
  Center

15 Chestnut St.
02740
(617) 999-1070

NORTHAMPTON

Valley Women's Union
200 Main St.
01060
(413) 586-2011

PROVINCETOWN

Homophile Assistance League
Box 674
02657
(617) 487-9633

Lower Cape Women's Center
Box 675
02657
(617) 487-3075

Provincetown Drop-In Center
Box 391
02657
(617) 487-0387

Gay Activists Alliance
% General Delivery
02657
(617) 487-3393

Gay Community Services
Box 815
02657

Everywoman's Center
Box 949
02657
(617) 487-3075, 487-3344, 487-3455

SPRINGFIELD

Dignity (Roman Catholic)
Box 488
Forest Park Sta.
01108

Springfield Gay Alliance
Box 752
01101
(413) 583-3904

Sexual Identity Awareness
  Organization
% Sue Elmasion
Scanton Hall
Westfield State College
01085

WORCESTER

Metropolitan Community Church
2 Wellington St.
01601
(413) 756-0730

Clark and Holy Cross Gay People's
  Alliance
Box A-70
Clark University
01610

MICHIGAN

ANN ARBOR

Gay Community Center
% Guild House
802 Monroe
48104

Ann Arbor Lesbian Band
% Susan
533 N. Main
48104

Gay Advocates Office
3405 Michigan Union
48104
(313) 763-4186

Gay Hotline
(313) 761-2044

Gay Liberation Front
325 Michigan Union
48104
(313) 763-4186, 761-2044

Gay Women's Advocates Office
326 Michigan Union
48104
(313) 763-4186

Male Liberation Collective
Box 1025
48106

DETROIT

Dignity (Roman Catholic)
2846 17th St.
48216
(313) 894-1064

Metropolitan Community Church
13100 Woodward Ave.
Highland Park 48203
(313) 868-2122

East Side Ministry of Social Services
9162 Crane
48213

Feminist Women's Health Center
2445 W. 8 Mile
48203
(313) 892-7790

Association of Suburban People
  (ASP)
Box 568
Plymouth 48170
(313) 349-4487

Gay Liberation Front
Wayne State University
701 W. Warren
Room 208
48202
(313) 577-3450

One in Detroit
724 W. McNichols
48203
(313) 341-1980

EAST LANSING

Gay Liberation Movement
309 Students Services Bldg.
Michigan State University
48823
(517) 353-9797

Lambda, Inc.
Box 416
48823

FLINT

Dignity (Roman Catholic)
Box 281
48501

GRAND RAPIDS

Western Michigan Gay Alliance
240 Charles St.
49503
(616) 456-7129

MOUNT CLEMENS

Equadare Society
36 Ahrens St.
48043
(313) 463-9138

MOUNT PLEASANT

Central Michigan Gay Liberation,
Inc.
Box 34
Warriner Hall
Central Michigan University
48859
(517) 774-3822

OKEMOS

Lutherans Concerned for Gay
People
% Cathy Spooner
1577 Cranwood
48864
(517) 349-1843

ROCHESTER

Gay Liberation Front Oakland
% Community House
Oakland Center
Oakland University
48063

SOUTHFIELD

Circle Club
Box 1003 Northland Sta.

48075
(313) 835-3450


MINNESOTA

DULUTH

Arrowhead Gay Resource Center
Box 538 Civic Center Sta.
55802

Duluth Gay Group
Route 6
Box 382
55804

MINNEAPOLIS

Lavender AA for Gays
Pharm House
1911 Pleasant Ave. S
55403

Maverick AA for Gays
1430 W. 28th St.
55408

Dignity/Twin Cities (Roman
  Catholic)
Box 3565
55403

Gay United Methodists
923 Fuller St. SE
54414

Invisible Group
% First Unitarian Society
900 Mt. Curve Ave.
55403
(612) 377-6608

Integrity/Twin Cities (Episcopal)
Box 3565
55403

Lutherans Concerned for Gay
  People
Box 3590 Upper Nicollet Sta.
55403
(612) 871-1190

Metropolitan Community Church
Box 8402
55408
(612) 338-2773

Gay Community Services
Box 3589 Upper Nicollet Sta.
55403
(612) 871-3111

Gay House, Inc.
4419A Nicollet
55409
(617) 822-3322, 824-4449

Neighborhood Counseling Center
1801 Nicollet
55403
(617) 874-5369

Lesbian Resources Center
2104 Stevens Ave. S.
55404
(617) 871-2601

Metro Gay Students Union
Metropolitan State Union College
50 Willow St.
55403

Minnesota Committee for Gay
  Rights
Box 4226 St. Anthony Falls Sta.
55414
(617) 871-3111

Minnesota Women's Alliance
Box 14362
55414

NORTHFIELD

Carleton College Gay Friends
Carleton College
55057

ORTONVILLE

Shalom
Box 523
56278

ROCHESTER

Lambda Friends

P. O. Box 454
55901

MISSISSIPPI

JACKSON

Mississippi Gay Alliance
Box 8342
39204
(601) 372-3449

Mississippi Lesbians
Box 8342
39204
1003 Walnut
(601) 355-6935

Gay Counseling
% Mississippi Gay Alliance
Box 4470
Mississippi State University
39762

MISSOURI

COLUMBIA

Gay Liberation Executive Board
Ecumenical Center
813 Maryland Ave.
65201

Gay Liberation Front
University of Missouri
% Lawrence Eggleston
1723 W. Worley Rd., Apt. 6A
65201

Missouri Alliance for Gay Rights
Box 1672
65201

JOPLIN

Metropolitan Community Church
207 W. 4th St.
64800
(410) 321-3200, 781-9494

Pride Community Center
207 W. 4th St.

64800
(410) 781-9494

Committee for Gay Justice
% Pride Community Center
207 W. 4th St.
64800

KANSAS CITY

Dignity (Roman Catholic)
Box 10075
64111

Metropolitan Community Church
Box 5206
4000 Harrison
64112
(816) 921-5754

Gay Community Services, Inc.
Box 703
64141
(816) 921-4419

Mid-America Gay Ecumenical
    Foundation, Inc.
2 Janssen Place
64104
(816) 753-4419

ST. LOUIS

Dignity (Roman Catholic)
Box 23093
63159

Metropolitan Community Church
Box 3147
5108 Waterman Ave.
(314) 361-7284

St. Louis Women's Counseling
    Center
6808 Washington Ave.
63130
(314) 725-9158

Metropolitan Life Services Center
4746-A McPherson Ave.
63108
(314) 367-0084

Gay People's Alliance
Box 1068

Washington University
63130

SPRINGFIELD

L.I.F.E
Box 161
65801

## MONTANA

MISSOULA

Lambda
770 Eddy, Room 4
59801
(406) 728-0419

## NEBRASKA

LINCOLN

Univ. of Nebraska Gay Action
333 N. 14th St.
65808
(402) 475-5710

OMAHA

First Metropolitan Community
    Church
803 N. 20th St.
68102
(402) 345-2563

## NEW HAMPSHIRE

PORTSMOUTH

Seacoast Gay Alliance
Box 1424
03801
(603) 436-7196

## NEW JERSEY

ASBURY PARK

Metropolitan Community Church
Box 1051
07712
(201) 988-4343

GARWOOD

United Sisters
Box 41
07027
(201) 233-3848

GLASSBORO

Together, Inc.
7 State St.
08028
(609) 881-4040

HACKENSACK

Gay Activists Alliance of New
  Jersey
Box 1734
South Hackensack 07606
(201) 343-6402

Gay Teachers Caucus
32 Bridge St.
07601
(201) 489-2458

JERSEY CITY

United Faith Church
132 Bergen
07305
(201) 659-3840

Gay Rights of People Everywhere
  (GROPE)
Jersey City State College
% SGAC
2039 Kennedy Blvd.
07305
(201) 432-8815

MAHWAH

Alternative Sexual Lifestyles
  Association
Ramapo College
07043
(201) 825-2800, X-463

MONTCLAIR

Drop-In Center
Montclair State College

Upper Montclair 07043
(201) 893-5271

MORRISTOWN

Gay Activist Alliance
Box 137 Convent Station
07961
(201) 347-6234, 347-3959, 884-0653

NEW BRUNSWICK

Rutgers University Coalition of Les-
  bian-Feminists
% Women's Center
Tillett Hall
Livingston College
08903
(201) 932-4678

Rutgers University Homophile
  League
RPO 2901
Rutgers University
08903
(201) 932-7886

Task Force on Gay Liberation
Box 416
08903

NEWARK

Dignity (Roman Catholic)
Box 337
Irvington, NJ 07111

ORANGE

Organization for Gay Awareness
Box 41
07050

PRINCETON

Gay Alliance of Princeton
306 Green Annex
Princeton University
08540
(609) 452-5338

Gay People, Princeton
Box 2303
08540
(609) 921-2565

Princeton Women's Center
210 Green Annex
Princeton University
08540

PRINCETON JUNCTION

New Jersey Gay Switchboard &
    Info. Center
Box 323
08550
(609) 921-2565

TRENTON

Gay Student Organization
Mercer C.C.C.
Box B
08690

WAYNE

Gay Activists Alliance
William Paterson College
% Student Center
300 Pompton Rd.
07470
(201) 881-2157

NEW MEXICO

ALBUQUERQUE

Metropolitan Community Church
Box 26554
87125
(505) 299-0512

New Mexico Gay People's Union
3214 Silver SE
87106

NEW YORK

ALBANY

Dignity (Roman Catholic)
95 Chestnut St.
12210
(518) 462-1469

Gay Community House
332 Hudson Ave.
12210
(518) 462-6138

Capital District Gay Community
    Council
Box 131
12201
(518) 462-6138

ANNANDALE-ON-HUDSON

Gay Liberation Front
Bard College
Box 87
12504

AURORA

Gay Students Organization
Wells College
13026

BINGHAMTON

Binghamton Gay Liberation
Box 2000 Harpur College
State Univ. of New York
13901
(607) 798-4470

BUFFALO

Gay AA
(716) 883-7400, 883-8244, 886-8380

Gay Community Services Center
1350 Main St.
14209
(716) 881-5335

Gay Liberation Front
Gollege F (Tolstoy) House
Winspear Ave.
14212
(716) 831-5386

Mattachine Society
Box 975 Ellicott Sta.
14205

Sisters of Sappho
Box 975 Ellicott Sta.
14205

Student Alliance for Gay Equality
(SAGE)
1300 Elmwood Ave.
14222

FREDONIA

Homophile Education
State University College
Student Center
SGA Office
14063
(716) 672-4128

GENESEO

Gay Freedom Coalition
Box 38 College Union
State University College
313 College Union
14454
(716) 245-5891

ITHACA

Ithaca Gay People's Center
306 E. State St.
14850
(607) 277-0306

JAMESTOWN

Lambda
Box 273
14 E. 2nd St.
14701
(716) 487-1876

LIVINGSTON MANOR

Sullivan County Gay Liberation
Box 191
12758

MECHANICVILLE

N.Y. Coalition of Gay
Organizations
% Rev. Kennedy
Rd. #1 Malta Gardens, Apt. 10
11218

NEW YORK CITY & LONG ISLAND

Metropolitan Community Church of
Brooklyn
50 Monroe Pl.
Brooklyn Heights 11201

Congregation Beth Simchat Torah
Box 1270
10001
(212) 255-2599

Dignity (Roman Catholic)
Box 1554, FDR Sta.
10002
(212) 832-7756, X-29; 624-4429

Evangelicals Concerned
% Dr. Ralph Blair
30 E. 60th St.
10022
(212) 688-0628

Integrity (Episcopal)
31 Stuyvesant St.
10003
(212) 982-3559

Lutherans Concerned
% John Eggleston
111 Third Ave., 8-K
10003
(212) 260-1971

Metropolitan Community Church
Box 1757
210 W. 13th St.
10001
(212) 691-7428

Metropolitan Community Church
Hispana
Box 110
10009
(212) 478-3298

United Church of Christ Gay
Caucus
% Milton Lounsberry
421 E. 78th St., 2-D
10021
(212) 628-2038

Dignity/Long Island (Roman
  Catholic)
Box 341
Centerport 11721
(516) 691-3328

Community Sex Information
888 Seventh Ave.
10019
(212) 586-6666

Counseling Women
655 Madison Ave.
(212) 720-8510

Downtown Welfare Advocacy
  Center (Lesbian Mothers)
134 W. 4th St.
10012
(212) 674-7744

East Village Counseling Service
319 E. 9th St.
10003
(212) 228-5153

Gay Canarsie
(212) 267-5097

Gay Counseling
61 Gramercy Park No.
10010
(212) 475-0390

Gay Switchboard
(212) 924-4036

Homosexual Community
  Counseling Center
30 E. 60th St.
10022
(212) 688-0628

Identity House
544 Sixth Ave.
10011
(212) 243-8181

Institute for Human Identity
490 West End Ave.
10024
(212) 799-9432

Lesbian Switchboard
(212) 741-2610

Lesbians' and Gay Men's
  Counseling at NYU
566 La Guardia Pl., Rm. 608
10003
(212) 598-3806

Ninth Street Center
319 E. 9th St.
10003
(212) 228-5153

Middle Earth Switchboard
485 Fulton Ave.
Hempstead 11550
(516) 292-0100

Gayphone
(516) 751-6380

Gay Men's Health Project
74 Grove St., Rm. 2RW
10014
(212) 691-6969

St. Mark's Free Clinic
44 St. Mark's Place
10003
(212) 533-9500

Women's Health Alliance
% Peggy Farber
68 Perry St.
10014
(212) 989-2751

Women's Health Forum
175 Fifth Ave.
10010
(212) 674-3660

ACLU Sexual Privacy Project
22 E. 40th St.
10016
(212) 725-1222

Lambda Legal Defense & Education
  Fund
Box 5448, Grand Central Sta.
10017
(212) 758-1905

Gay Integrated Group
Bronx Community College
181st St. & University Ave.
10468

Gay People at Lehman
Herbert Lehman College
Bedford Park Blvd.
10468

Gay City Workers
916 Union St.
Brooklyn 11215
(212) 857-6549

Gay Liberation Front
Long Island University
% Student Activities
365 Flatbush Ave. Extension
Brooklyn 12201

Gay People at Brooklyn College
% Student Activities
LaGuardia Hall
Bedford Ave. & Ave. H
Brooklyn 11210
(212) 449-8432

Gay Students League of NYC
  Community College
Student Activities
300 Jay St.
Brooklyn 11201
(212) 824-6334

Gay Teachers Association
204 Lincoln Pl.
Brooklyn 11217
(212) 789-8176

Hispanic United Gays-Liberado
% 5619 14th Ave., Apt. 1-C
Brooklyn 11219
(212) 851-1612

Mongoose Community Center Gay
  Group
782 Union St.
Brooklyn 11215
(212) 783-8819

New York Lesbian Feminist
  Conference

229 Dean St.
Brooklyn 11217
(212) 624-3536

Pratt Gay Union
Student Affairs
Pratt Institute
Brooklyn 11205
(212) 636-3505

Gayteens Encounter (age 19 or
  younger)
Box 145
Hempstead 11551

Hofstra United Gays
Box 67
Student Center
Hofstra University
Hempstead 11550

Long Island Gay Alliance
% Gay Activists Alliance
Box 2, Village Sta.
New York 10014

Stony Brook Gay Student Union
Stony Brook 11794
(516) 246-7943

Women's Liberation Center of
  Nassau County
14 W. Columbia St.
Hempstead 11550
(516) 292-8106

Eulenspiegel Society (SM)
Box 2783 Grand Central Sta.
10017
(212) 254-2144

Gay Academic Union
Box 480, Lennox Hill Sta.
10021

Gay People at City College
Findlay Student Center, CCNY
Convent Ave. & W. 135th St.
10031
(212) 690-4191

Gay People at Columbia
304 Earl Hall
Broadway & 116th St.

10027
(212) 280-3574

Hunter College Gay Men's Alliance
695 Park Ave., Rm. 124
10017
(212) 360-2123

Lesbian Activists at Barnard College
McIntosh Center, Rm. 106
10027

Lesbian Feminist Liberation
Women's Center
243 W. 20th St.
10011
(212) 691-5460

Lesbians Rising Collective
Hunter College Women's Center
47 E. 65th St.
10021
(212) 360-5162

National Gay Task Force
80 Fifth Ave.
10011
(212) 741-1010

Third World Gay Women
% Washington Square Church
133 W. 4th St.
10012

Gay Community at Queens College
Student Activities
Queens 11367

Gay Human Rights League of
   Queens County
Box 1224
Flushing 11352

Gay Liberation of Staten Island
   Community College
Student Activities
715 Ocean Terrace
Staten Island 10301

Gay Men's Collective
Richmond College
% Student Government
130 Stuyvesant Pl., Rm. 542
Staten Island 10301

Lesbians United
Richmond College
% Student Government
130 Stuyvesant Pl., Rm. 542
Staten Island 10301

Dignity Overeaters Anonymous
% West Side Discussion Group
37 Ninth Ave.
10011
(212) 675-0143

Lesbian Overeaters Anonymous
Women's Center
243 W. 20th St.
10011
(212) 255-9802

West Side Gay Overeaters
   Anonymous
% West Side Discussion Group
37 Ninth Ave.
10011
(212) 675-0143

ONEONTA

Gay Rights Organization of
   Oneonta (GRO)
Box 541
13820

PLATTSBURGH

Plattsburgh Gay Students
   Liberation
College Center
State Univ. College
12901
(518) 564-2165

The Gays of Clinton County
% TGOCC
Box G
109 Margaret St.
12901
(518) 561-6863

POTSDAM

Potsdam-Canton Gay Community
College Union
State Univ. College
13676

POUGHKEEPSIE

Vassar Gay People's Alliance
Box 1921
12601

ROCHESTER

Dignity (Roman Catholic)
Box 8295
14617
(716) 458-8628

Gay Brotherhood of Rochester
713 Monroe Ave.
14607
(716) 244-8640

Lesbian Resource Center
713 Monroe Ave.
14607
(716) 244-9030

Rochester Gay Task Force
2 Fuller Pl.
14680
(716) 235-4961

SARATOGA SPRINGS

Skidmore Sapphic Society
% Casey Crabill
Skidmore College
11866
(518) 584-5000

SYRACUSE

Gay Community Ministries
Box 57 Elmwood Sta.
13207
(315) 478-5225

Unitarian Universalist Gay Caucus
May Memorial Unitarian Society
3800 E. Genessee St.
13214
(315) 478-1288

Lambda Center
503 S. Geddes St.
13204
(315) 472-3917

Gayphone
(315) 423-3599

Gay Citizens Alliance of Syracuse
Box 57 Elmwood Sta.
13207

Gay Political Caucus
Box 399 Colvin Sta.
13205
(315) 476-5157

Lesbian Feminists of Syracuse
Syracuse University Women's
  Center
Ostrom Ave.
13210
(315) 472-3917

Syracuse University Gay Students
  Association
103 College Place
13210
(315) 423-2081, 423-3599

UTICA

Hamilton-Kirkand Gay Alliance
Hamilton College
Clinton 13323

WHITE PLAINS

Westchester Gay Men's Association
% WESPAC
100 Mamaroneck Ave.
10601

NORTH CAROLINA

CHAPEL HILL

Carolina Gay Association
Box 39 Carolina Union
27514
(919) 942-2039

DURHAM

Duke Gay Alliance
6298 College Sta.
27708

Triangle Area Lesbian Feminists
Box 2272
27702

GREENSBORO

Gay People's Alternative
Box 6806
27405

GREENVILLE

Eastern Gay Alliance
Box 1126
27834
(919) 752-4043

RALEIGH

Metropolitan Community Church
900 W. Morgan St., Apt. BA
27603
(919) 832-1582

## NORTH DAKOTA

LEONARD

Aware
% Lynn Runck
Box 177
58052

## OHIO

AKRON

Dignity (Roman Catholic)
143 S. Union St.
44304

Metropolitan Community Church
Box 563
44309
(216) 253-8388

ATHENS

GAA
% United Campus Ministry
18 N. College St.
45701

Lesbian Collective
% Women's Center
Baker Center
Ohio University
45701

BOWLING GREEN

Bowling Green Gay Union
Box 9, U Hall
Bowling Green State University
43403
(419) 352-8712

CINCINNATI

Dignity (Roman Catholic)
Box 983
45201
(513) 621-4811

Metropolitan Community Church
Box 39235
45239
(513) 591-0303

Gay Line Cincinnati
65 E. Hollister
45219
(513) 241-0001

Cincinnati Free Clinic
2444 Vine St.
45219
(513) 621-5700

University of Cincinnati Gay
  Society
% Student Affairs Office
420 Tangeman Univ. Center
45221
(513) 475-6876

CLEVELAND

Gay Alcoholics Anonymous
(216) 687-0416

Community of Celebration
  (Interfaith)
Box 18226
44118

Dignity (Roman Catholic)
Box 18479
44118
(216) 791-0942

Cleveland Free Clinic
12201 Euclid
94196
(216) 696-5330

Gay Switchboard/Hotline
(216) 696-5330

Cleveland Area Lesbian Feminist
  Alliance
Box 18458
Cleveland Heights 44118
(216) 932-2669

Gay Education & Awareness
  Resources
Box 6177
44101
(216) 696-5330

COLUMBUS

Dignity (Roman Catholic)
Box 4826
43202

Columbus Gay Women's Peer
  Counseling
Box 3321 University Sta.
43210
(614) 263-0229

Columbus Gay Activists Alliance
232 Ohio Union
1739 N. High St.
43210
(614) 422-9212

DAYTON

Dignity (Roman Catholic)
Box 153
45402
(513) 426-1836

Lutherans Concerned
Box 134
45401

Dayton Gay Center
665 Salem Ave.
45406
(513) 278-3963

Dayton Lesbian Feminist League
1938 Rugby Rd.
45406
(513) 275-3606

KENT

Kent Gay Liberation Front
233 Student Center
Kent State University
44242
(216) 672-2068

TOLEDO

Metropolitan Community Church
Box 1052
43697
(419) 241-9092

Pro/Toledo
Box 4642, Old West End Sta.
43620
(419) 243-9351

WOOSTER

Gay Caucus
Box 3166 Lowry Center
44691

YELLOW SPRINGS

Antioch Gay Liberation
Antioch College Student Union
45387
(513) 767-7331 X-217

YOUNGSTOWN

Dignity (Roman Catholic)
Box 4204
Austintown 44515
(216) 482-2481

Gay Rights Organization
% Youngstown State University
44503

## OKLAHOMA

### OKLAHOMA CITY

Christ the King Metropolitan
  Community Church
401 SE 22nd St.
73129

Libertarians for Gay Rights
1206 NW 40th St.
73118

### TULSA

Metropolitan Community Church
Box 4187
74104
(918) 939-0417

Tulsa Gay Community Caucus
Box 2792
74101

## OREGON

### EUGENE

Metropolitan Community Church
Box 3076
97403
(503) 746-7427

Gay People's Alliance
University of Oregon
EMU Suite 1
97403
(503) 686-3327

Lesbian Rap Group
% Women's Center
2nd & Washington
97401

One Step Beyond
323 E. 12th
97401

### KLAMATH FALLS

Klamath Gay Union
The Church
428 S. 9th St.
97601

### PORTLAND

Metropolitan Community Church
Box 8348
97207

Counseling Center for Sexual
  Minorities
Box 8773
320 SW Stark St., #303
97208
(503) 228-6785, 227-2765

Gay Liberation Front
Portland State College
% Steve Fulmer
1232 SW Jefferson, #403
97201

Gay Student Affairs Board
Rm. 438, Smith Center
Portland State University
97201
(503) 229-4458

Gay Teens
% Moon Brothers Collective
729 SE 33rd Ave.
97214
(503) 238-0146

Lambda House
1867 SW 14th Ave.
97201

### SALEM

Salem Group
% Portland Town Council
320 SW Stark St., #303
Portland 97204

## PENNSYLVANIA

### BETHLEHEM

Lehigh Valley Homophile
  Organization
Box 1003 Moravian Sta.
18018

### BRYN MAWR

Bryn Mawr-Haverford Gay People's
Alliance
College Inn, Rm. 24
19191

### HARRISBURG

Dignity (Roman Catholic)
Box 297 Federal Square Sta.
17108

Integrity (Episcopal)
Box 3809
17108

Metropolitan Community Church
1001 W. Spring St., #1-2
Middletown 17057

Gay Community Services
Box 297 Federal Square Sta.
17108
(717) 232-2027

Gay Switchboard
(717) 234-0328

### INDIANA

The Open Door
948 Wayne Ave.
15701

Homophiles of Indiana Univ. of
Pennsylvania
Box 1588
Indiana University
15701

### LANCASTER

Gays United Lancaster
3002 Marietta Ave.
17601
(717) 898-2876

Women Oriented Women
Lancaster Women's Center
230 Chestnut St.
17600
(717) 299-5381

### LEBANON

Gay League of Lebanon
Box 431
17042

### NORTHUMBERLAND

Susquehanna Valley Gays United
Box 182
17857
(717) 473-9923

### PHILADELPHIA

Gay Alcoholics Anonymous
(215) L07-0100, KL6-1270

Beth Ahavah (Jewish)
(215) BA2-2647

Beth Ishih (Feminist Synagogue)
643 Ritner St.
19148

Dignity (Roman Catholic)
250 S. 12th St.
19107
(215) 425-4440

Integrity (Episcopal)
% Rev. John Lenhardt
St. Mary's Episcopal Church
3601 Locust Walk
Hamilton Village 19104
(215) 726-1089

Metropolitan Community Church
Box 8174
19101
(215) 732-8298

Gay Switchboard
(215) 929-1919

Lesbian Hotline
(215) SA9-2001

Women in Transition
3700 Chestnut St.
19104
(215) 383-7016

Women's Switchboard
Pennwalt Bldg.

3 Parkway
19103
LO3-8599

Gay Community Center of
  Philadelphia
Box 15748
326 Kater St.
19103
(215) 923-3792

Gay Nurses Alliance (Men &
  Women)
Box 5687
19129
(215) VI9-1171

Gay Students at Temple
Student Activities Center, Rm. 205
13th & Montgomery Sts.
19122
(215) 787-7902

Gays at Drexel
% Educational Activities Center
33rd & Chestnut
Drexel University
19104

Gays at Penn
% Christian Association
3601 Locust Walk
Hamilton Village 19104
(215) 243-3888

SM Society of Philadelphia
Box 15786
19103

PITTSBURGH

Pittsburgh Alcoholics Together
Box 9045
15224
(412) 683-2459

Dignity (Roman Catholic)
Box 991
15230
(412) 682-0165

Metropolitan Community Church
Box 9045

15224
(412) 683-2459

Persad Center
5100 Centre Ave.
15232
(412) 681-5330

Gay Alternatives
Box 10236
15232
(412) 363-0594

Gay Students at Pitt
Box 819 Schenley
University of Pittsburgh
15260
(412) 624-5944

READING

Gay Coordinating Society
Box 3131
19603
(215) 373-5123

SHAVERTOWN

Northeast Pennsylvania Gay
  Alliance
Box 1710
18708

SHIPPENSBURG

Shippensburg Students for Gay
  Rights
% CUB
Shippensburg State College
17257

STATE COLLEGE & UNIVERSITY PARK

Homophiles of Penn State
Box 218
State College 16801
(814) 863-0588

SWATHMORE

Swathmore Gay Liberation
Swathmore College
19081
(215) KI4-7900 X-296; LO6-9467

WEST CHESTER

Gays of West Chester
Box 2302
West Chester State College
19380

## PUERTO RICO

SAN JUAN

Dignity (Roman Catholic)
Box 22000 U.P.R. Sta.
00901

Communidad de Orgullo Gay
Box 5523
Puerta de Tierra 00906
(809) 722-4669

## RHODE ISLAND

PROVIDENCE

Gay Group of AA
(401) 231-5853

Dignity (Roman Catholic)
Box 2231
Pawtucket 02861
(401) 724-0171

Integrity (Episcopal)
Box 71 Annex Sta.
02801

Metropolitan Community Church
Box 1942
63 Chapin Ave.
02901
(401) 274-1693

## SOUTH CAROLINA

COLUMBIA

Metropolitan Community Church
Box 11181
29211
(803) 798-3916

## SOUTH DAKOTA

RAPID CITY

Black Hills Gay Coalition
Box 8034
57701

## TENNESSEE

MEMPHIS

Metropolitan Community Church
Box 3538 Fort St. Sta.
38103

Gay Switchboard
Box 3620
38103
(901) 726-4299

## TEXAS

AUSTIN

Integrity (Episcopal)
Box 14056
78761

Gay Community Services
University Y
2330 Guadeloupe St.
78705
(512) 477-6699

Austin Lesbian Organization
Box 3301
78764

Gay Political Committee
Box 1255
78767

Gay/Texas
Office of Student Activities
University of Texas
78712

DALLAS

Dignity (Roman Catholic)
Box 813
Arlington 76010
(817) 640-0482

Metropolitan Community Church
3834 Ross Ave.
75204
(214) 826-0291

Community Service Center
3834 Ross Ave.
75204
(214) 826-2192

Gayline of Dallas
Box 5944
75222
(214) 241-4118

FORT WORTH

Agape Metropolitan Community
Church
251 Vacek
76107
(817) 335-7355

Daughters of Bilitis
Box 1564
76101

GRAND PRAIRIE

Metropolitan Community Church
Box 718
75050
(214) 436-6865

HOUSTON

Dignity (Roman Catholic)
Box 66821
77066

Integrity (Episcopal)
Box 16041
77022
(713) 523-4609

Metropolitan Community Church
Box 13731
77019
(713) 526-8223

Gay Activists Alliance of Houston
Box 441, University Center
University of Houston
77004
(713) 749-3489

Gay Political Caucus
Box 16041
77022

Houston N.O.W. Sexuality &
Lesbian Task Force
% Women's Center
3602 Milam
77002
(713) 524-5743

Texas Gay Task Force
% Integrity
Box 16041
77022

LUBBOCK

Dignity (Roman Catholic)
Box 16065, Sunset Sta.
79490

Lubbock Gay Awareness
Box 4002
79490

SAN ANTONIO

Dignity (Roman Catholic)
Box 12260
78212

Gay Switchboard
1136 W. Woodlawn
78201
(512) 733-7300

UNIVERSAL CITY

Texas Gay Task Force
Box 2036
78148

UTAH

SALT LAKE CITY

Grace Christian Church
% Ron Linde
2510 Glenmare St.
84106

Metropolitan Community Church
Box 11607

870 West 4th South
84111
(801) 531-9434

Gay Community Center
Box 6077
84106

## VERMONT

BURLINGTON

Counseling for Gay Women & Men
% Vermont Women's Health Center
158 Bank St.
05401
(802) 863-1388

Gay in Vermont
Box 3216, North Burlington Sta.
05401

Gay Student Union
University of Vermont
Billings Center
05401
(802) 656-4173

MIDDLEBURY

Gay People at Middlebury
Middlebury College
05753

## VIRGINIA

CHARLOTTESVILLE

Gay Student Union
Peabody Hall
University of Virginia
22901

NORFOLK

Virginia Lesbian /Feminist Group
Box 11103
23517

RICHMOND

Gay Rap
10 W. Cary St.
23220

Gay Liberation Front
% Kenny Pederson
505 Brookside Blvd.
23327
(703) 266-2691

ROANOKE

Roanoke Valley Trouble Center
3515 Williamson Rd.
24012
(703) 563-0311

WILLIAMSBURG

Gay Liberation Group
College of William & Mary
Campus Center
23185

## WASHINGTON

BELLINGHAM

Gay People's Alliance
Viking Union, Rm. 212
Western State University
98225
(206) 676-3460

OLYMPIA

Evergreen College Gay Resources
    Center
Evergreen State College
98505
(206) 866-6544

PULLMAN

Gay Awareness
Washington State University
Compton Union
99163

SEATTLE

Commission on Ecumenical
    Ministry
St. Mark's Cathedral
1245 Tenth Ave. E.
98102
(206) 323-0300

Dignity (Roman Catholic)
Box 21494
98111
(206) 454-7700, 722-4722

Metropolitan Community Church
Box 12020
128 16th Ave. E.
98112
(206) 352-1872

Assault Hotline (Victims of rape &
  verbal abuse)
(206) 329-HELP

Seattle Counseling Service for
  Sexual Minorities
1720 16th Ave.
98122
(206) 329-8707, 325-5550

Gay Community Center
110 Boylston E.
98102
(206) 322-2000

Lesbian Resource Center
4224 University Way NE
98105
(206) 632-4747

Gay Community Social Services
Box 22228
98122

Gay Feminists Coalition
% Metropolitan Community Church
Box 12020
98112

Gay Students Association
Box 96 HUB (FK-10)
University of Washington
98190
(206) 543-6106

TACOMA

Tacoma Counseling Service
712 S. 14th
98405
(206) 272-3847

WISCONSIN

MENASHA

Fox Valley Gay Alliance
Box 332
54952
(414) 232-2948

MILWAUKEE

Gay Alcoholics Anonymous
Newman Center
2528 E. Linwood
53211
(414) 272-5273 (ask for Group 94)

Council for Religion and the
  Homosexual
% GPU
Box 92203
53202

Dignity (Roman Catholic)
Box 597
Newman Center
2528 E. Linwood
53211
(414) 276-5218

GPU Examination Center for VD
Farwell Center
1568 N. Farwell
53202

Gay People's Union
Box 92203
Farwell Center
1568 N. Farwell
53202
(414) 271-5273

Grapevine
% Women's Center
2211 E. Kenwood Blvd.
53211

Milwaukee Teens
% GPU
Box 92203
53202

University of Wisconsin-Milwaukee
  Gay Student Assn.
Box 10
Student Union
53211

## CANADA

## ALBERTA

CALGARY

Dignity (Roman Catholic)
Box 1491 Sta. T
T2H 2H7

Lesbian Drop-In
338 14 Ave. SE
(403) 266-2552

## BRITISH COLUMBIA

VANCOUVER

Gay Alliance Toward Equality
Box 1463, Sta. A
(604) 255-7820

Gay People of Simon Fraser
% Student Society
Simon Fraser University
(604) 876-4704

Gay People of UBC
Box 9
Student Union Bldg.
University of British Columbia
V6T 1W5

Lesbian Caucus of the BC
  Federation of Women
Box 4294

Search
Box 48903, Bentall Centre
V7X 1A8

Search Community Services
1367 Richards St., #301
(604) 689-1039, 689-1119

VICTORIA

Victoria Women's Centre
552 Pandora St.
(604) 385-3843

## MANITOBA

WINNIPEG

Dignity (Roman Catholic)
Box 27
Transcona PO
Transcona R2C 2Z5

Gays for Equality
Box 27
UMSU
University of Manitoba
R3T 2N2
(204) 474-8216

A Woman's Place
143 Walnut St.
R3G 1P2
(204) 786-4581

## NEWFOUNDLAND

CORNER BROOK

Community Homophile Association
Box 905
A2H 6J2

ST. JOHN'S

Canadian Homophile Association
Box 631, Sta. C
A1C 5K8

## NOVA SCOTIA

HALIFAX

Gay Alliance for Equality
Box 161, Armdale Sta.
B3L 4G9
(902) 429-6969

Halifax Women's Centre
5673 Brenton Place

Box 5052, Armdale Sta.
B3L 4G9
(902) 423-0643

## ONTARIO

### GUELPH

Guelph Gay Equality
University of Guelph, Rm. 221
N1E 4U5
(519) 824-4120, X-8575; 836-4550

### HAMILTON

McMaster Homophile Association
Box 44, Sta. B.
L8L 7T7
(416) 527-0336

### KINGSTON

Queen's University Homophile
  Association
Student Affairs Centre
51 Queen's Crescent
Queen's University
K7L 2S7
(613) 547-2836

### LONDON

Homophile Association of London
649 Colbourne St.
N6A 3Z2
(519) 433-3762

### MISSISSAUGA

Gay Equality Mississauga
Box 193, Sta. A
L5A 2Z7

### OTTAWA

Metropolitan Community Church
48 Bruyere, #1
K1N 5C5
(613) 233-6463

VD Clinic
250 Somerset E.

Gay People of Carleton
% CUSA
Carleton University
Colonel By Drive
K1S 5B6

Gays of Ottawa/Gais de L'Outaouais
Box 2919 Sta. D
K1P 5W9
(613) 238-1717

Ottawa's Women's Centre
821 Somerset St. W.
(613) 233-2560

### THUNDER BAY

Northern Women's Centre
Box 314, Sta. F
120 W. Amelia
P7C 4V9

### TORONTO

Dignity (Roman Catholic)
Box 249, Sta. E
M6H 4E2

Hamispacha (Jewish)
1179A Bloor St. W.
(416) 960-0053, 653-0498

Integrity (Anglican)
Box 463, Sta. J
M4J 4F2

Metropolitan Community Church
20 Trinity Square
M5G 1B1
(416) 364-9799, 364-9835

Toronto Area Gays
Box 6706, Sta. A
(416) 964-6600

Gay Academic Union
Box 396, Sta. K
M4P 2EO

Hassle-Free Clinic
201 Church St.
M5R 1Z1
(416) 363-6103

Community Homophile Association
199 Church St.
M5R 1Z1
(416) 862-1544

Gay Alliance at York
York University
4700 Keele St., Downsview
M3J 1P3
(416) 667-3509, 667-3632

Gay Alliance Toward Equality
193 Carlton St.
M5A 2K7
(416) 964-0148

WATERLOO

Waterloo Universities Gay
   Liberation Movement
Federation of Students
University of Waterloo
N2L 3G1
(519) 885-1211, X-2372

The Women's Place
42-B King South
(519) 886-1620

WINDSOR
Windsor Gay Unity
Box 7002, Sandwich Sta.
N9C 3Y6
(519) 252-0979

Women's Place
327 Ouellette Ave., #202
N9A 4J1
(519) 252-0244

QUEBEC

MONTREAL
Église Communautaire de Montréal
   (Interfaith)
(510) 845-4471, 489-7845, 288-1101

Naches (Jewish)
Box 298, Sta. H
(510) 738-9003, 488-0849

Central Homophile Urbain de
   Montréal

6581 St. Laurent
(510) 279-5381

Gay McGill
3480 McTavish, Suite 414
(510) 392-8037

Gay Teenage Group
4515 Ste. Catherine West
(510) 934-0721

Gayline
(510) 931-8668, 931-5330

Montréal Lesbian Organization
3591 St. Urbain St.
H2X 2N6
(510) 842-4781

QUEBEC
Centre Humanitaire d'Aide et de
   Libération
BP 596, Haute Ville
283 Rue des Franciscains
G1R 4R8
(418) 525-4997

SASKATCHEWAN

SASKATOON

Gay Community Centre of
   Saskatoon
Box 1662
310 20th St. East
S7K 3R8
(306) 652-0972

*EUROPE*

Direct initial inquiries to:

*Gay News*
1A Normand Gardens
Greyhound Rd.
London W14, England
(01) 381-2756

Gay Switchboard
London, England
(01) 837-7324

# Sources

The bulk of the material in this book derives from interviews with gay men and women, physicians, public health officials, and a variety of professionals who work with gay people. The following sources were useful in amplifying the interviews and helped resolve technical inconsistencies.

ANDREWS, VALERIE. "The Joy of Jogging." *New York.* December 27, 1976, 10:1, 60–63.

BLOOM, MARK. "Homosexual Doctors." *Medical World News.* 1974, 15:4, 41–51.

BOSTON WOMEN'S HEALTH BOOK COLLECTIVE. *Our Bodies, Ourselves.* New York: Simon & Schuster, 1976.

BRYAN, JOHN A., AND PATTISON, CHARLES P. "Viral Hepatitis—A Primer." *Postgraduate Medicine.* 1976, 59:1, 66–72.

DIETER, NEWT. "A Time to Die." *The Advocate.* June 16, 1976, 192, 27–29.

DRITZ, SELMA, ET AL. "Patterns of Sexually Transmitted Enteric Diseases in a City." *Lancet 2,* 1977, 2:8027, 3–4.

*Gay VD: Facts for Men and Women.* Los Angeles: Gay Community Services Center, 1975.

GITECK, LENNY. "The Doctor Is In . . . And Gay." *The Advocate*. July 27, 1977, 220, 16–17.

GREEN, FRANCES (ED). *Gayellow Pages*. New York: Renaissance House, 1977.

*Health and Venereal Disease Guide for Gay Men*. New York: Gay Men's Health Project, 1976.

"Homosexual Doctors." *Medical World News*. January 25, 1974.

*How Much Do You Know About the Gay Rights Issue?* New York: National Gay Task Force, 1977.

JONES, TONY (ED). "Healing—New Ways to Get Better." *Quest*. 1977, 1:2, 97–112.

KANTROWITZ, ARNIE. "Dirty Old Men." *The Advocate*. June 16, 1976, 192, 21, 29.

KRAMER, NORMAN D. "The Gay Man's Drug: Poppers." *The Advocate*. June 30, 1976, 193, 22–23.

LEE, PHILIP R. "Self-care Deserves Strengthening—and Physician Support." *Medical World News*. 1977, 18:20.

LEONARD, GEORGE. "The Rediscovery of the Body." *New York*. December 27, 1976, 10:1, 34–41.

LEONARD, GEORGE. "The Search for Health: From the Fountain of Youth to Today's Holistic Frontier. *New West*. January 3, 1977, 2:1, 14–15.

SHILTS, RANDY. "Alcoholism: A Look in Depth at How a National Menace Is Affecting the Gay Community." *The Advocate*. February 25, 1976, 184, 27ff.

SHILTS, RANDY. "The Decade's Best-Kept Medical Secret: Hepatitis Doesn't Come from Needles." *The Advocate*. January 12, 1977, 207, 23–26.

SHILTS, RANDY. "The Hazards Of Sex." *The Advocate*. December 15, 1976, 205, 27–30.

SHILTS, RANDY. "A New Plague on Our House: Gastro-intestinal Diseases." *The Advocate*. April 20, 1977, 214, 12–13.

SHILTS, RANDY. "Sexual Dysfunction: Its Ups and Downs." *The Advocate*. August 24, 1977, 222:32–34.

SHILTS, RANDY. "VD and Other Sexually Transmitted Diseases in the Gay Community." *The Advocate*. April 21, 1976, 188, 14–18.

THOMPSON, MARK. "Gay and Gray." *The Advocate*. June 16, 1976, 192, 30–31.

WEST, KAREN. "Drug Abuse." *The Advocate*. June 30, 1976, 193, 21–23.

WILLIAMS, BOB. "Downers, Uppers, and Hallucinogens." *The Advocate*. June 30, 1976, 193, 24–25.

YEAGER, ROBERT C. "The Self-Care Surge." *Medical World News*. October 3, 1977, 18:20, 43–54.

# Further Reading

The following bibliography, which emphasizes holistic medicine and self-care, is designed for those who wish to assume more personal responsibility for the management of their health.

"Alive and Well" *Health Right Newsletter* Winter 1975 (for women).

ALLISON, LINDA. *Blood and Guts: A Working Guide to Your Own Insides* (A Brown Paper School Book). Boston: Little, Brown & Co., 1976.

BARKER, THEODORE X. (ED.) *Advances in Altered States of Consciousness and Human Possibilities, Vol. I.* New York: Psychological Dimensions, 1976.

BARKER, THEODORE X. *Hypnosis: A Scientific Approach.* New York: Psychological Dimensions, 1969.

BARKER, THEODORE X. *LSD, Marihuana, Yoga, and Hypnosis.* Chicago: Aldine Publishing Co., 1970.

BARKER, THEODORE X. ET AL. *Hypnosis, Imagination, and Human Potentialities.* Elmsford, N.Y.: Pergamon Press, 1976.

BAKER, THEODORE X. (ED.): *Biofeedback and Self-Control 1970–1976; Aldine Annuals on the Regulation of Bodily Processes and Consciousness.* Chicago: Aldine-Atherton, 1970–76.

BENSON, HERBERT. *The Relaxation Response.* New York: Morrow, 1975.

BLUM, HENRIK L. *Expanding Health Care Horizons.* Oakland, Ca.: Third Party Associates, 1976.

BROWN, B. *New Mind, New Body.* New York: Harper and Row, 1974.

BORMAN, LEONARD D. (ED.) *Explorations in Self-Help and Mutual Aid: Workshop Proceedings.* Evanston, Ill.: Center for Urban Affairs, Northwestern University, 1975.

CANNON, WALTER B. *The Wisdom of the Body.* New York: W. W. Norton, 1939.

CAPLAN, GERALD, AND KILLILEA, MARIE (EDS.) *Support Systems and Mutual Help.* New York: Grune and Stratton, 1976 (13 papers).

CARLSON, RICK J. *The End of Medicine.* New York: John Wiley & Sons, 1975.

CASSELL, ERIC J. *The Healer's Art: A New Approach to the Doctor–Patient Relationship.* Philadelphia: J. B. Lippincott, 1976.

DAVIDSON, RICHARD J., AND SCHWARTZ, GARY E. "The Psychology of Relaxation and Related States: A Multi-Process Theory." In David Mostofsky, ed. *Behavior Control and Modification of Physiological Activity.* Englewood Cliffs, N.J.: Prentice-Hall, 1976.

DUBOS, RENÉ. *Beast or Angel? Choices That Make Us Human.* New York: Scribners, 1974.

DUBOS, RENÉ. *Mirage of Health.* New York: Anchor, 1959.

DUBOS, RENÉ. *Man, Medicine and Environment.* New York: Mentor, 1968.

DUBOS, RENÉ. *Man Adapting.* New Haven: Yale University Press, 1972.

EHRENREICH, BARBARA, AND ENGLISH, DEIRDRE. *Witches, Midwives and Nurses: A History of Women Healers.* Old Westbury, N.Y.: The Feminist Press, 1972.

ENGEL, G. L. "A Life-Style Conducive to Illness." *Bulletin, Menninger Clinic* 32: 355–65, 1968.

FABREGA, HORACIO, JR. *Disease and Social Behavior: An Interdisciplinary Perspective.* Cambridge: MIT Press, 1974.

FOX, RENEE C. "The Medicalization and Demedicalization of American Society." *Daedalus,* 106: 9–22, 1977.

FRANK, JEROME D. *Persuasion and Healing,* rev. ed. Baltimore: The Johns Hopkins University Press, 1973.

FUCHS, VICTOR R. *Who Shall Live? Health, Economics and Social Choice.* New York: Basic Books, 1974.

GARTNER, ALAN, AND RIESSMAN, FRANK. *Self-Help in Human Services.* San Francisco: Jossey-Bass, 1977.

GRAEDON, JOE. *The People's Pharmacy: A Guide to Prescription Drugs, Home Remedies and Over-the-Counter Medications.* New York: St. Martin's Press, 1976.

*Health Activation News* (quarterly newsletter). Center for Continuing Education, Georgetown University, S.S.C.E. Box 7268, Arlington, Va. 22207, $4 per year.

*Healthwise* (videotape self-care education program). Healthwise, Inc., 111 South Sixth, Boise, Id.83702.

HORNSTEIN, FRANCIE; DOWNER, CAROL; AND FARBER, SHELLY. *Gynecological Self-Help.* Los Angeles: Feminist Women's Health Center.

HUTSCHNECKER, A. A. *The Will to Live.* New York: Cornerstone Library Publications, 1951.

ILLICH, IVAN. *Medical Nemesis: The Expropriation of Health.* New York: Pantheon, 1976.

KATZ, ALFRED, AND BENDER, EUGENE I. *The Strengths in Us: Self-Help Groups in the Modern World.* New York: New Viewpoints, 1976.

KIEV, ARI (ED.) *Magic, Faith and Healing: Studies in Primitive Psychiatry Today.* New York: Free Press, 1969.

KLEINMAN, ARTHUR; KUNSTADER, PETER; ALEXANDER, RUSSEL; AND GALE, JAMES L. (EDS.) *Medicine in Chinese Cultures.* Washington, D.C.: Fogarty International Center, 1973.

KNOWLES, JOHN (ED.) *Doing Better and Feeling Worse: Health in the United States.* New York: Norton, 1977.

KRIEGER, DOLORES. "Therapeutic Touch: The Imprimatur of Nursing." *American Journal of Nursing* 75: 784–87, 1975.

KRIPPNER, STANLEY, AND VILLOLDO, ALBERTO. *The Realms of Healing.* Millbrae, Ca.: Celestial Arts, 1976.

LALONDE, MARC. *A New Perspective on the Health of Canadians.* Ottawa: Government of Canada, 1974.

LANDY, DAVID (ED.) *Culture, Disease and Healing.* New York: Macmillan, 1977.

LESLIE, CHARLES (ED.) *Asian Medical Systems.* Berkeley: University of California Press, 1976.

LEVIN, LOWELL S.; KATZ, ALFRED H.; AND HOLST, ERIK. *Self-Care: Lay Initiatives in Health.* New York: Prodist, 1976. (Includes 50-page bibliography.)

MCKEOWN, THOMAS. *The Role of Medicine: Dream, Mirage or Nemesis?* London: Nuffield Provincial Hospitals Trust, 1976.

MAHONEY, M. J., AND THORESEN, C. E. *Self-Control: Power to the Person.* Monterey, Ca.: Brooks-Cole, 1974.

MILLER, SIGMUND STEPHEN. *Symptoms: The Complete Home Medical Encyclopedia.* New York: Thomas Crowell, 1976.

*New Realities* (The Holistic Health and Human Potential Magazine). P. O. Box 26289, San Francisco, Ca. 94126.

ORNSTEIN, ROBERT E. *The Mind Field.* New York: Grossman/Viking, 1976.

ORNSTEIN, ROBERT E. *The Psychology of Consciousness.* San Francisco: W. H. Freeman, 1973.

PELLETIER, KENNETH. *Mind as Healer, Mind as Slayer.* New York: Dell, 1977.

PORKERT, MANFRED. *The Theoretical Foundations of Chinese Medicine.* Cambridge: MIT Press, 1974.

PORKERT, MANFRED. "Chinese Medicine—A Science in Its Own Right." *Eastern Horizons,* February, 1977.

POYNTER, F. N. L. (ED.) *Medicine and Culture.* London: Wellcome Institute of the History of Medicine, 1969.

*Preventive Medicine USA: Health Promotion and Consumer Health Education.* A Task Force Report sponsored by the John F. Fogarty International Center and the American College of Preventive Medicine. New York: Prodist, 1976.

RISSE, GUENTER; NUMBERS, RONALD L.; AND LEAVITT, JUDITH (EDS.) *Medicine Without Doctors: Home Health Care in American History*. New York: Neale Watson Academic Publishing, 1977.

SAMUELS, MIKE, AND BENNETT, HAL. *The Well Body Book*. New York: Random House/Bookworks, 1973.

SCHWARTZ, GARY E., AND BEATTY, JACKSON (EDS.) *Biofeedback: Theory and Research*. New York: Academic Press, 1977.

SEHNERT, KEITH W., AND EISEMBERG, HOWARD. *How to Be Your Own Doctor (Sometimes)*. New York: Grosset & Dunlap, 1975.

SELDIN, DONALD W. "The Medical Model: Biomedical Science as the Basis of Medicine." *Beyond Tomorrow: Trends and Prospects in Medical Science*. New York: Rockefeller University, 1977.

*Self-Help Reporter*. Bi-monthly newsletter of the National Self-Help Clearinghouse, 184 Fifth Avenue, New York, N.Y. 10010.

SELYE, HANS. *The Stress of Life. rev. ed.* New York: McGraw-Hill, 1976.

SCHMALE, A. H., AND IKER, P. "The Affect of Hopelessness and the Development of Cancer." *Psychosomatic Medicine* 28: 714–28,

SHELDON, ALAN. "Toward a General Theory of Disease and Medical Care." In Sheldon, Alan; Baker, Frank; and McLaughlin, Curtis P., eds. *Systems and Medical Care*. Cambridge: MIT Press, 1970.

SIDEL, VICTOR, AND SIDEL, RUTH. "Self-Reliance and the Collective Good: Medicine in China." In Veatch, Robert, and Branson, Roy, eds. *Ethnics and Health Policy*. Cambridge: Ballinger, 1976.

SIDEL, VICTOR, AND SIDEL, RUTH. *Serve the People: Observation on Medicine in the People's Republic of China*. Boston: Beacon, 1973.

SOBEL, DAVID STUART, AND HORNBACHER, FAITH LOUISE. *An Everyday Guide to Your Health*. New York: Grossman, 1973.

SOBEL, DAVID S. (ED.) *Health & Healing: Ancient and Modern*. New York: Harcourt Brace Jovanovich, 1978.

STOYVA, JOHANN. "Self-Regulation and the Stress-Related Disorders: A Perspective on Biofeedback." In Mostofsky, David, ed. *Behavior Control and Modification of Physiological Activity*. Englewood Cliffs, N.J.: Prentice-Hall, 1976.

TORREY, E. FULLER. *The Mind Game: Witchdoctors and Psychiatrists*. New York: Bantam, 1973.

VICKERY, DONALD M., AND FRIES, JAMES F. *Take Care of Yourself: A Consumer's Guide to Medical Care*. Reading, Ma.: Addison-Wesley, 1976.

WEED, LAWRENCE L. *Your Health Care and How to Manage It*. Burlington, Vt.: Promis Laboratory, University of Vermont, 1975.

"What Can One Woman Do?" *HealthRight* pamphlet, 175 Fifth Avenue, New York, N.Y. 10010.

WHITE, KERR L. (ED.) *Life and Death and Medicine*. San Francisco: W. W. Freeman, 1973.

# A Bibliography
# for Professionals

The following bibliography has been selected particularly for psychiatrists, clergy, social workers, counselors, attorneys, and other professionals who work with gay people.

## BOOKS

ABBOT, SIDNEY, AND LOVE, BARBARA. *Sappho Was a Right-On Woman: A Liberated View of Lesbianism*. New York: Stein & Day, 1972.

BAILEY, D. S. *Homosexuality and the Western Christian Tradition*. Garden City, N.Y.: Archon Books, 1975.

BOGGAN, E. C.; HAFT, M. G.; LISTER, C.; AND RUPP, J. P. *The Rights of Gay People*. New York: Sunrise Books, 1975.

CHURCHILL, W. *Homosexual Behavior Among Males: A Cross-Cultural and Cross-Species Investigation*. Englewood Cliffs, N.J.: Prentice-Hall, 1971.

FISHER, P. *The Gay Mystique: The Myth and Reality of Male Homosexuality*. New York: Stein & Day, 1972.

FREEDMAN, M. *Homosexuality and Psychological Functioning*. Belmont, Ca.: Brooks/Cole, 1971.

GAGNON, J. H., AND SIMON, W. *Sexual Conduct: The Social Sources of Human Sexuality*. Chicago: Aldine, 1973.

GEARHART, SALLY, AND JOHNSON, WILLIAM R. (EDS.) *Loving Women/Loving Men: Gay Liberation and the Church*. San Francisco: Glide, 1974.

HITE, SHERE. *The Hite Report*. New York: Macmillan, 1976.

JOHNSTON, JILL. *Lesbian Nation: The Feminist Solution*. New York: Simon & Schuster, 1973.

KATZ, JONATHAN. *Gay American History: Lesbians and Gay Men in the U.S.A.: A Documentary Account*. New York: Crowell, 1976.

KLAICH, DOLORES. *Woman Plus Woman: Attitudes Toward Lesbianism*. New York: Simon & Schuster, 1974.

MARTIN, DEL, AND LYON, PHYLLIS. *Lesbian/Woman*. New York: Bantam, 1972.

MCCAFFERY, J. A. *The Homosexual Dialectic*. Englewood Cliffs, N.J.: Prentice-Hall, 1972.

MCNEILL, J. J. *The Church and the Homosexual*. Mission, Kans. Sheed, Andrews, & McMell, 1976.

MILLER, M. *On Being Different: What It Means to Be a Homosexual*. New York: Random House, 1971.

PITTENGER, NORMAN. *Time For Consent: A Christian's Approach to Homosexuality*. London: SCM Press, 1976.

SAGHIR, M. T., AND ROBBINS, E. *Male and Female Homosexuality: A Comprehensive Investigation*. Baltimore: Williams & Wilkins, 1973.

SHERFEY, MARY JANE. *The Nature and Evolution of Female Sexuality*. New York: Vintage, 1973.

SIMPSON, RUTH. *From the Closet to the Courts: The Lesbian Transition*. New York: Viking, 1975.

TRIPP, C. A. *The Homosexual Matrix*. New York: McGraw-Hill, 1975.

VIDA, GINNY (ED.) *Our Right to Love: A Lesbian Sourcebook*. Englewood Cliffs, N.J.: Prentice-Hall, 1977.

WEINBERG, G. *Society and the Healthy Homosexual*. Garden City, N.Y.: Archon, 1973.

WEINBERG, M. S., AND COLIN, J. W. *Male Homosexuals: Their Problems and Adaptations*. New York: Oxford University Press, 1974.

WILLIAMS, C. J., AND WEINBERG, M. S. *Homosexuals and the Military: A Study of Less than Honorable Discharge*. New York: Harper & Row, 1971.

## ARTICLES

American Civil Liberties Union. "Policy Statement on Homosexuality." ACLU, April 13, 1975.

American Psychiatric Association. "Resolutions on Homosexuality." Press release and rationale paper, December 15, 1973.

"The Constitutionality of Laws Forbidding Private Homosexual Conduct." *Michigan Law Review* 72: 1613–37, 1974.

GEIS, G.; WRIGHT, R.; GARRETT, T.; AND WILSON, P. R. "Reported Consequences of Decriminalization of Consensual Adult Homosexuality in Seven American States." *Journal of Homosexuality* 1: 419–26, 1976.

HUNTER, NAN, AND POLIKOFF, NANCY. "Custody Rights of Lesbian Mothers: Legal Theory and Litigation Strategy." *Buffalo Law Review* 25 (3), 1976.

LAMORTE, MICHAEL W. "Legal Rights and Responsibilities of Homosexuals in Public Education." *Journal of Law and Education* 449–67, 1975.

LAWRENCE, JOHN C. "Homosexuals, Hospitalization and the Nurse." *Nursing Forum* 305–17, 1975.

LEE, J. A. "Forbidden Colors of Love: Patterns of Gay Love and Gay Liberation." *Journal of Homosexuality* 1: 401–18, 1976.

"The Legality of Homosexual Marriage." *Yale Law Review* 82: 573–89, 1973.

LESTER, ELENORE. "Gays in the Synagogue." *Present Tense: The Magazine of World Jewish Affairs* Autumn 1974.

LEVITT, E. E., AND KLASSEN, A. D. "Public Attitudes Toward Homosexuality: Part of the 1970 National Survey by the Institute for Sex Research." *Journal of Homosexuality* 1: 29–44, 1974.

LYON, PHYLLIS, AND MARTIN, DEL. "The Realities of Lesbianism." In Bunch, Charlotte, and Cooke, Joanne, eds. *The New Women: A Motive Anthology of Women's Liberation.* New York: Bobbs-Merrill, 1970.

MINNIGERODE, F. A. "Age-status Labeling in Homosexual Men." *Journal of Homosexuality* 1: 273–76, 1976.

RASHKE, RICHARD. "Homosexuality and the Church of Today." *National Catholic Reporter* March 26, April 2, 9, and 23, 1976.

"Sexuality Clearances for Homosexuals." *Stanford Law Review* 25: 403–29, 1973.

SILVERSTEIN, C. "Even Psychiatry Can Profit from Its Past Mistakes." *Journal of Homosexuality* 1: 153–58, 1974.

SILVERSTEIN, C. (ED.) "Symposium on Homosexuality and the Ethics of Behavior Intervention." *Journal of Homosexuality* 2: 1977.

## NEWSPAPERS, PERIODICALS, NEWSLETTERS, PAMPHLETS

*The Advocate.* One Peninsula Place, Bldg. 1730, Suite 225, San Mateo, Ca. 94402.

*American Psychiatric Association Gay Caucus Newsletter.* R. Pillard, M.D., 700 Harrison Ave., Boston, Ma. 02118.

*The Cellmate* (for gay prisoners). Board of Prison Ministry, Metropolitan Community Church, Box 36277, Los Angeles, Ca. 90036.

*Christopher Street.* 60 W. 13th St., New York, N.Y. 10011.

*Dignity* (for gay Roman Catholics). 755 Boylston, Rm. 514, Boston, Ma. 02116.

*Gay Health Reports* (newsletter of Gay Public Health Workers). 206 N. 35th, Philadelphia, Pa. 19104.

*Gay News* (Europe's largest-circulation gay newspaper). 1A Normand Gardens, Greyhound Rd., London W14 9SB, England.

*Gays on the Hill* (news of gay civil rights progress in the U.S. Congress). Suite 210, 110 Maryland Ave. N.E., Washington, D.C. 20002.

*Gay People and Mental Health.* Suite 3-B, 490 West End Ave., New York, N.Y. 10024.

*Integrity* (for gay Episcopalians). Box 2516, Chicago, Il. 60690.

*It's Time* (newsletter of the National Gay Task Force). 80 5th Ave., Rm. 506, New York, N.Y. 10011.

*Journal of Homosexuality*. Haworth Press, 174 5th Ave., New York, N.Y. 10010.

National Council of Churches, *A Resolution on Civil Rights Without Discrimination as to Affectional or Sexual Preference*, 1975. National Council of the Churches of Christ, 475 Riverside Drive, New York, N.Y. 10027.

*Newsletter of the Association of Gay Psychologists*. Box 29527, Atlanta, Ga. 30359.

*Sexual Law Reporter*. 3701 Wilshire Blvd., Suite 700, Los Angeles, Ca. 90010.

*Theological-Pastoral Resources*. Dignity National, 755 Boylston, Boston, Ma. 02116.

United States Civil Service Commission. *Press Release on New Guidelines for Federal Employment*. U.S. Civil Service Commission, Washington, D.C., July 3, 1975.


## BIBLIOGRAPHIES AND DIRECTORIES

BULLOUGH, VERN L., ET AL. *An Annotated Bibliography of Homosexuality*, 1976. Garland Publishing, 545 Madison Ave., New York, N.Y. 10022.

*Gayellow Pages*. Box 292, Village Station, New York, N.Y. 10014.

*Gay Professional Organizations and Caucuses (U.S.)*. National Gay Task Force, 80 5th Ave., Rm. 506, New York, N.Y. 10011.

*Gay Rights Protections in U.S. and Canada*. National Gay Task Force, 80 5th Ave., Rm. 506, New York, N.Y. 10011.

GITTINGS, BARBARA (ED.) *A Gay Bibliography*. Task Force on Gay Liberation, American Library Association, Box 2383, Philadelphia, Pa. 19103.

# Index

acne scars, 157
adenomyosis, 153
*Advocate, The*, 6, 19, 41, 43, 64, 66, 70, 76,
   98, 99, 102, 103, 109–111, 113, 115,
   118, 135, 167
aging, 136–161
  adaptations to physical changes in, 139
  causes of, 145–146
  disorders associated with, 146–155
  personal perspectives on, 141–145
  physical appearance in, 155–159
  physical effects of, 145–159
  in popular caricature vs. "composite
   man," 143
  psychological adaptations in, 139–140
  psychological problems in, 140
  sexual adaptations in, 140–141
  sexual response in, 154
  younger gays' views on, 142–143
Airola, Paavo O., 166, 172
Albolene cream, 79, 98
alcohol, 26, 29, 39, 53, 60, 66, 67, 79,
   107–120
  dangers of, 108, 110–112
  downers with, 120, 121, 122
  fermentation and distillation of, 110
  heroin vs., 110
  methyl, 111, 135
  physical effects of, 110–112, 113

  safe consumption of, 112–113
  sexual dysfunction and, 91, 112
  tolerance of, 113
alcoholic cardiomyopathy, 111
alcoholics:
  agencies for treatment of, 118–120
  co-alcoholics and, 114–117
  in gay community, 109–110, 113–115
  physical care of, 117
  psychological problems of, 111, 113
  self-image of, 117
  statistics on, 109
  treatment of, 117–120
"alcoholic thinking," 111
amebic dysentery, 40–43, 77
  causes of, 41
  diagnosis of, 42
  as "endemic," 40
  prevention of, 43
  statistics on males with, 40
  symptoms of, 41–42
  treatment of, 42
American Psychiatric Association, 10
amphetamines (speed), 108, 124–125, 126
ampicillin, 26–27
amyl nitrite (amyl), 67, 68, 69, 108,
   132–135
anal intercourse, 78–81
  cancer and, 80, 147

233

R. D. FENWICK is a free-lance writer specializing in holistic health and the human potential movement.

RICHARD C. PILLARD attended Antioch College and the University of Rochester Medical School. His psychiatry training was at Boston State and University Hospitals in Boston. He was an NIMH Research Scientist Development Grant awardee and has done research on psychotropic drugs and marijuana. Dr. Pillard is a co-founder and Medical Advisor to the Homophile Community Health Service, a pioneer clinic in the field of gay mental health. He has written more than thirty articles on psychopharmacology and on issues in mental health relating to gay people.

In 1976, Dr. Pillard and Dr. Harlan Lane went to Africa to examine a boy said to have been raised by monkeys. An account of this expedition, *The Wild Boy of Burundi* will be published in the fall of 1978. Dr. Pillard is currently Associate Professor of Psychiatry and Visiting Physician at the Boston University Medical School.